The Latecomers

ALSO BY HELEN KLEIN ROSS

What Was Mine
Making It: A Novel of Madison Avenue
The Traveler's Vade Mecum

The Latecomers

HELEN KLEIN ROSS

LITTLE, BROWN AND COMPANY

New York   Boston   London

Little, Brown and Company
Hachette Book Group
1290 Avenue of the Americas, New York, NY 10104
littlebrown.com

First Edition: November 2018

Little, Brown and Company is a division of Hachette Book Group, Inc. The Little, Brown name and logo are trademarks of Hachette Book Group, Inc.

The publisher is not responsible for websites (or their content) that are not owned by the publisher.

The Hachette Speakers Bureau provides a wide range of authors for speaking events. To find out more, go to hachettespeakersbureau.com or call (866) 376-6591.

ISBN 978-0-316-47686-7
LCCN 2018937250

10 9 8 7 6 5 4 3 2 1

LSC-C

Printed in the United States of America

*This novel is dedicated to my Irish-American
mother, Margaret Whelan Klein.
For Katherine and Margaret, too.
And, of course, for Donald.*

One tree is black.
One window is yellow as butter.

A woman leans down to catch a child
who has run into her arms
this moment.

Stars rise.
Moths flutter.
Apples sweeten in the dark.

—Eavan Boland, "This Moment"

Author's Note

Although many of the events that take place in this story are historical occurrences, this novel is a work of imagination. (As Muriel Spark observed, it is a blow to a novelist's pride of invention if readers think otherwise.) But as I live in a small town in Connecticut in a house similar to the one described, perhaps it is necessary to say that the characters and the town they occupy are works of fiction, not disguised biography. While the story isn't fact, I hope it rings true for readers who believe, as I do, that fiction is the conduit of our deepest truths.

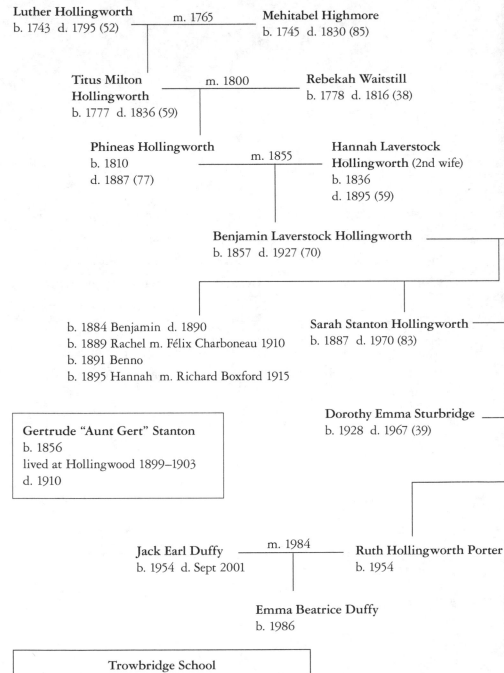

Luther Hollingworth
b. 1743 d. 1795 (52)

m. 1765

Mehitabel Highmore
b. 1745 d. 1830 (85)

Titus Milton Hollingworth
b. 1777 d. 1836 (59)

m. 1800

Rebekah Waitstill
b. 1778 d. 1816 (38)

Phineas Hollingworth
b. 1810
d. 1887 (77)

m. 1855

Hannah Laverstock Hollingworth (2nd wife)
b. 1836
d. 1895 (59)

Benjamin Laverstock Hollingworth
b. 1857 d. 1927 (70)

b. 1884 Benjamin d. 1890
b. 1889 Rachel m. Félix Charboneau 1910
b. 1891 Benno
b. 1895 Hannah m. Richard Boxford 1915

Sarah Stanton Hollingworth
b. 1887 d. 1970 (83)

Dorothy Emma Sturbridge
b. 1928 d. 1967 (39)

Gertrude "Aunt Gert" Stanton
b. 1856
lived at Hollingwood 1899–1903
d. 1910

Jack Earl Duffy
b. 1954 d. Sept 2001

m. 1984

Ruth Hollingworth Porter
b. 1954

Emma Beatrice Duffy
b. 1986

Trowbridge School
Castle built 1860 by tobacco baron for German wife
Inherited by daughter who turned it into a school
Benno 1905–1909
Vincent 1924–1928
Emma 2002–2005 centenary class

Hollingworth
Family Tree

Wellington, CT
founded 1741

Nettie Wallace b. 1883,
daughter of former slaves
who moved north and died in
Blizzard of 1888

m. 1885 ————— May Stanton Hollingworth
b. 1865 d. 1899 (34)

Alma Brigg Porter
b. 1867 d. 1955 (88)

m. 1910 ————— Edmund Fitch Porter
b. 1884 d. 1939 (54)

m. 1952 ————— Vincent Hollingworth Porter
b. 1909 d. 2005 (96)
adopted 12/24/1914

Hollingwood Help
Nettie 1888–1915
Bridey 1909–1928
Lilah 1926–1948
Locals 1948–1964
Bea 1964–1999
Arlette 1986–

Abigail Fitch Porter (Ruth's sister)
b. 1956

Norah and Hugh Molloy, m. 1891, Ireland

Brighid b. 1892 (Bridey) Molloy
emigrated US April 1908

Kathleen b. 1894
Jeremiah b. 1896 d. at birth
Quinn b. 1897
Dan b. 1899
Margaret b. 1901
Nell b. 1902
Patrick b. 1904 d. 1905
Deirdre (Daisy) b. 1906

Emma

Upper East Side, Manhattan

September 2001

Emma pushed through the door of the ladies' room by reception and turned on a tap and held her palms upward, letting cool water run over the veins in her wrists, the trick Arlette had taught her when she was in pre-K, to calm herself.

When Emma came out—there was her mother. Her mother was usually careful about looking her best when she came uptown to Thatcher, but now her mascara was running, her lipstick was gone, her face was wet with sweat and tears. Her mother hugged her and, for once, Emma hugged back, taking refuge in her arms as if she were a little kid instead of a freshman in high school. Her mother said she was there to take her home.

Suddenly, girls around them were talking, saying that Emma and her mother could come home with one of them, they all lived so close, only blocks away.

But Emma wanted, for once, the same thing her mother wanted, which was to go home. She hoped her father would be there. She knew her mother was hoping this too.

When they got to the street, they saw that many stores had already closed; hastily lettered signs were taped to accordion gates: CLOSED DUE TO TODAY'S CIRCUMSTANCES.

"We'll need money," her mother said, but the ATMs they passed were DOWN UNTIL FURTHER NOTICE. Long lines snaked from banks, and from pay phones.

Later, Emma found it ironic that the parents who had resisted giving their kids cell phones were finally persuaded to change their minds by the events of a day on which cell phones proved useless.

A huge crowd had gathered in front of the electronics store. What was on sale that so many people would take this moment to line up for? Then she saw—they were watching the TVs in the window. Emma and her mother stopped to watch too. News was coming so fast, it had to be reported in what looked like ticker tape running across the bottoms of screens. *South Tower Collapsed.*

They watched the tower come down again and again. Each time it fell, Emma was flooded with gratitude that her father worked in the other one. But then they showed footage of the North Tower and she felt a stinging at the back of her eyes. Windows in the towers were designed not to open, yet it looked like people were leaning out of them. Dark spots drifted down the sides of the building. Emma guessed it was debris from the fire, but then the cameras zoomed in and she saw—the dark spots were people. People were jumping. Some fell upright; some arched as they descended, doing backward Cs, like victory jumps, and Emma closed her eyes and did what she hadn't done since she was a child: she reached for her mother's hand. Her mother squeezed it and brought the back of Emma's hand to her lips.

Emma felt certain that her father wasn't one of the jumpers. He'd never have jumped, since it would have meant jumping away from them.

When they got to the subway at Eighty-Sixth, a sign at the entrance read NO MORE SERVICE TODAY.

They headed to Third, where going against traffic they saw—an army tank! Had a war started?

Her mother raised her arm to hail a cab. There were no cabs in sight. But after many changes of lights, a slightly battered car stopped in front of them. Car service. Emma's mother opened the back door and Emma slid across several rips in the vinyl, making room for her mother. But she didn't slide in.

"Take this to a Hundred and Twenty-Fifth Street," she said to Emma, fishing a twenty out of her wallet. "Take the train to your grandfather's. Wait at Hollingwood until I come up with Daddy."

At the sound of "Daddy," Emma's eyes filled.

"No!" Emma said, pushing the money away, sliding back across the seat toward her mother. "I'm staying with you. I want to go home!"

"They're not letting anyone south of Fourteenth now. Do this for me, Emma. I can't worry about you too." She shoved the bill into Emma's blazer pocket.

The car pulled away and Emma heard from speakers in the dashboard, "The National Guard on alert...fear of biological hazards."

Alone in the backseat, she started to cry. She imagined her parents breathing in poisoned air, catching some terrible fatal disease. And what about her cat?

She had an appointment with the orthodontist later, but how straight your teeth were didn't matter anymore.

Traffic was terrible. It took a long time for the car to get forty blocks north to the station. The driver and she didn't talk. They just listened to the news.

When Emma pulled the bill from her pocket and handed it across the front seat, the driver didn't take it.

"Keep it, peaches," he said. "I'm not car service. I just stopped at the light. But you take care, you do what your mama says."

"Thanks." She nodded, thinking his kindness would have seemed extraordinary on any day but this.

Were trains still running? Were her grandfather and Arlette safe?

Hollingwood had stood in Wellington, Connecticut, since her great-great-great-grandfather built it in 1853.

Would it still be there?

Part One

1

Bridey

Hollingwood

October 1927

That morning, hours after the cock crowed but before the town-hall bell chimed eight, Bridey mounted narrow steps leading up from the kitchen, holding tight to the fluted handles of a silver oval on which Mr. Hollingworth's breakfast quivered. Serving gloves weren't insisted upon at Hollingwood as they were in the big houses on Fifth Avenue, where a friend from home worked, but Bridey sometimes wore them anyway—it spared prints on the silver, which saved time in the long run; the trays and pouring pots needn't be polished so often.

Mr. Hollingworth's breakfast was meager fare compared to the morning feasts she and Nettie used to cook up: blood sausages and custards, fruited popovers and muffins, eggs poached and scrambled and over easy or hard, depending on how he and his four children preferred them that day. But that was years ago, when the children were children, and breakfasts were rollicking starts of days in the dining room instead of quiet meals for an invalid who spent most of the time in bed.

A poached egg on toast is what she was carrying now to Mr. Hollingworth, along with a pot of coffee and a pitcher of cream she'd skimmed from the top of a bottle left this morning by the Byfield boys who'd taken over their father's milk route. The bread was rack-toasted, despite the newly acquired electric toaster, which she hid in the pantry so it didn't rebuke her. Sarah, the eldest, had brought it back from a traveling exhibition of housewares in Hartford, but Bridey didn't trust the contraption, convinced that its complicated workings couldn't be depended upon to produce the shade of toast she was after and, even more important, couldn't be depended upon not to electrocute her. She'd racked toast on a fire for almost all of her thirty-four years. What would be the advantage of doing a task differently when it was one she had mastered and could do by hand without thinking? The electric cream separator, from the same exhibition, sat next to the toaster, both shrouded by covers that shielded them not only from dust but from Sarah's notice should she wander into the pantry, an unlikely occurrence.

Bridey appreciated electrification in moderation. The house had been electrified ten years ago, soon after she'd stepped off the boat from the west country of Ireland, where electric lights were unheard of and they got along fine without them, thanks very much. Now, she appreciated being able to sew or read at night, which was hard to do by the flickering light of a candle. She sang the praises of the electric icebox. But Americans believed that if a thing was good, much more of a good thing was even better. Electric irons, electric sewing machines, even electric lighters for men's cigars— Bridey couldn't see the need for any of these, though Mr. Tupper, the electrician, assured her that such laborsaving devices were already proving indispensable to housekeepers.

A bell sounded in the stair corridor. The rear kitchen door. Bother. Bridey stepped backward and, careful to keep the tray in balance, turned and descended the steps. She set the tray on the counter, covered it with the silver dome, removed her gloves, and crossed the kitchen to open the door.

There, on the gray-painted porch, stood Mr. Tupper. It was as if he'd heard her maligning his work in her head.

"Come in, come in." She swung the door wide to welcome him warmly, feeling a need to make up for the offense.

Mr. Tupper took off his cap as he stepped inside and set down his toolbox on the wide pine-board floor. "The Canfields were top of my list today, but they have guests stopping, so I'm here to replace your duals if it suits."

"That would be grand," said Bridey, pulling the door closed behind him. The sparrows were cheeping like chickens today. Yesterday, the door had been left ajar and one of them had flown in and it had taken her a mortal hour to shoo it out of the house.

When Mr. Tupper electrified Hollingwood, Mr. Hollingworth, like most home owners in Wellington, had prevailed upon him to convert existing gas fixtures to duals. Duals were lit by both electric lines and gas so that if electricity had turned out to be a passing fad, the lamps could be reverted to gas without the expense of calling Mr. Tupper again. Now it was clear that the invention had caught on and people were going all electric for safety reasons. Duals were proving to be temperamental. Last month, a leak of gas from a dual had caused a house just off Main Street to burst into flames. Mr. Tupper was so busy, it took months to get an appointment with him.

Today was far preferable to the December date marked on the wall calendar. It was still October. The holidays were a good ways away and whatever mess was about to be created would be certain not to interfere with holiday houseguests and entertaining. What's more, Sarah and Edmund were abroad now, which meant they'd be spared seeing the mess that inevitably resulted from a visit by Mr. Tupper. Sarah became nervous when things in the house had to be changed

Hollingwood had been built by Sarah's grandfather, a governor of Connecticut who had drawn the plans for the house himself, which accounted for why the house wasn't like any Bridey had seen. It was the biggest house in town, built with stones mined from local quarries that weren't around anymore. The house looked to Bridey like a house in a fairy tale. It rambled this way and that, with long hallways and bow windows and several porches and sunrooms and a four-story octagonal turret. The windows at the top of the turret were arched and color-stained like church windows and whenever Bridey went up there to sweep up dead flies or dust the old telescope that nobody used, she stopped a moment to gaze through the colored panes, taking in the holy beauty of the field and the lake and the evergreens bordering everything, like a backdrop.

Bridey offered Mr. Tupper tea and a scone still warm from the oven and he ate efficiently, standing up at the worktable, careful to keep crumbs from falling onto his beard. As he dunked the scone into the teacup, he apologized for having to cut a hole in the wall. His work would damage the wallpaper, he said, which would have to be replaced. The thought of that made Bridey wonder if she ought to put him off after all. Perhaps she ought to consult Sarah, but Sarah was in Italy with Edmund on an extended lecture tour of the lake towns to celebrate their wedding anniversary. Their sixteenth. They'd married the summer after Bridey came to Hollingwood, and had her coming here really been so many years ago?

Sarah was the only one of the children who lived at home now. She'd returned to Hollingwood with Edmund soon after they married, having discovered that two Mrs. Porters in a house was one too many. Sarah was educated in many things (politics, painting, gardening) but left on her own, Bridey guessed, Sarah wouldn't be able to boil an egg. Sarah was always seeking happiness afar, in every place but home, though that was where she was certain of finding it.

To Bridey's mind, Vincent had suffered mightily because of this.

Bridey, always alert to the boy, had spent years trying to relieve his suffering due to his mother's inattention to him and it saddened her to know that she could not relieve it altogether. But now—Vincent wasn't a boy anymore. He would be eighteen next birthday and how lucky for him, for all of them, that the Great War was over so the prospect of his being sacrificed for it needn't be contemplated.

If Bridey turned Mr. Tupper away, it would be weeks before he came back, then it would be Christmas, a season of parties and celebrations, and it wouldn't do for the front hall to be in a state. As Mr. Tupper finished his scone, Bridey went down to the basement and came back with old sheets from the rag bin. She'd learned the hard way about covering the furniture.

She led Mr. Tupper through the butler's pantry and, with an elbow (her arms were full of the sheets), pushed the glass plate on the door panel, swung through the door, and took him left past the linen closet so as not to lead his work boots across the good dining-room rug.

As she turned into the hallway, she saw the scrolled brass arms of the dual to be replaced. Bridey hated to think of harm to the wallpaper beneath it. But there was a good wallpaper man in town now, and the decorator from France who'd hung the paper originally had had the foresight to leave an extra roll in the attic.

Mr. Tupper helped Bridey draw sheets over chairs and tables in the hall, then Bridey returned to the kitchen, touched the silver pot to make sure it was still warm (Mr. Hollingworth didn't take hot coffee, due to sensitive teeth), slipped on the gloves, lifted the tray, and again mounted the stairs.

As she rounded the first landing, the hall shook with a great pounding and Bridey was visited by a terrible vision. Mr. Hollingworth's bedroom was just above the spot where Mr. Tupper was working, and Bridey imagined shifts in the old wall causing the ceiling above it to fall and then Mr. Hollingworth's floor crashing through and there would be Mr. Hollingworth, sliding down to the front door, still in his bed.

To steady herself, Bridey kept her hip against the wooden rails that ran along the top of the landing. It was a habit acquired long ago to keep from falling back down the narrow stairwell. The hallway was dim in the service quarters where only she lived now. When Nettie left to get married, Bridey hadn't taken her room, even though it was larger. She stayed in her little room at the top of the stairs with the low ceiling and a window that looked out on the lake. She liked it there. She liked the light.

Last year, Mr. Hollingworth lived in Nettie's old room, moving temporarily from his bedroom to Nettie's because hers was a north room and the darkest. At times, even the slightest light hurt his eyes. Bridey had run up drapes in the sewing room for him, heavy velvet curtains that Nettie, on a visit from Massachusetts, smiled to see—their formality so out of place in a servant's bedroom.

As Bridey crossed from the service hall to the bedroom wing, the pounding in the front hall became louder, and then came a crunch and the sound of falling plaster, by which she knew that the wall had been breached. Bridey was glad that Sarah—who felt any harm done to the house as a blow to herself—was spared this.

Bridey tapped with the toecap of her shoe, seeking the step up. She would tell Mr. Hollingworth that the egg was newly laid by Thisbe. Thisbe was the best layer in the henhouse, her eggs always firm and delicious. Was it an egg from Thisbe? Bridey couldn't recall. She'd gathered the eggs yesterday, not today. But old men, like small boys, needed reasons to believe what you wanted them to believe. Mr. Hollingworth's appetite—what was left of it—was best in the morning. He'd barely touched his dinner last night. He had to eat to keep up his strength. She wanted to make this meal as appealing as possible to him.

To that end, Bridey had prettied the tray. A picture postal from Sarah had come in the morning's mail, sent from a town with an unpronounceable name. The town was built on a mountain and looked made of toy blocks. She'd propped its painted portrait against the bud vase that held a purple anemone, the last flower the cutting garden gave up.

She hoped Sarah had remembered to send a postal card to Vincent at school.

It was Vincent who had named the hen, a few years ago, the summer before he went to school across the lake. How seriously he'd prepared himself for Trowbridge, lifting barbells and eschewing white bread, adhering to a new eating regimen to build himself up.

His incoming school assignment had been to translate the story of Pyramus and Thisbe from Latin to English, and Vincent, after poring over a book in the porch off the library, had regaled Bridey with the tale of two young lovers kept apart by their families. It was all she could do to hide her brimming eyes by training them on the needle she was using to letter one of his handkerchiefs; she had to bite her tongue to keep from telling him the story it reminded her of.

She sang out as she always did upon approaching Mr. Hollingworth's room.

"Your breakfast, Mr. H. Our Thisbe did her best for you this morning!"

The door was kept ajar and she pushed it gently with her elbow, already drawing in her mind the shape of the coming day. She would get Mr. Hollingworth properly propped on his pillows, taking care to keep his chest upright to avoid the danger of food falling into his windpipe, and while he was eating and reading papers magnified by a hand glass as big as his head, she'd go downstairs to the pantry to finish mixing beeswax and vinegar and then set to polishing the wood in the library. Friday was cleaning day. This schedule—Monday for wash, Tuesday for ironing, and so forth—was the same one she'd learned back in the class on practical housekeeping at St. Ursula's. More and more houses were shaking off this old system in favor of letting housekeepers decide for themselves what to do, but Bridey kept to the old schedule, finding that it allowed her to do the work most efficiently, especially important now that there was only one person left in the house to do it.

The sheets didn't stir. How could he have slept through the noise from below? As she neared the bed, she guessed that the extra sleep would be good for him. He slept little these days; he complained about the sleeplessness almost as much as the pain. Maybe Young Doc had given him a sleeping draft when he'd come to mix his dosages last night. The medicines were a new treatment he'd started giving Mr. Hollingworth after Old Doc died last year. It seemed to be working.

She settled the tray on the bedside table. His head was turned to the wall. Perhaps he'd taken sick in the night. Had he acquired a fever? She stepped forward to feel his forehead and when she touched his skin, she felt a coldness, a lack of charge, and when she bent over his face and saw his staring eyes, she apprehended—first in the hairs on her forearms, then in the hairs on the back of her neck—that Mr. Hollingworth wasn't sleeping. He was dead.

She drew back suddenly, knocking the tray off the table, sending the plate and pot and creamer and vase clattering to the floor.

"You all right, Miss Molloy?" Mr. Tupper called from downstairs.

Bridey didn't answer. She couldn't believe Mr. Hollingworth was gone. The fits of blindness had ceased. Mr. Hollingworth had regained some energy, enough to take a constitutional around the house with her every so often. He'd improved enough for Sarah and Edmund to go on their long-planned anniversary trip. But now—

Bridey sank to her knees, crossed herself, and prayed, gazing at the man he had been. Mr. Hollingworth had been kind to her. He had been a kind man. He had taught her to swim. He had saved her life and the life of her son.

She heard Mr. Tupper's tread on the stairs, then in the hallway. She turned to see him bowing his head. Mr. Tupper was a big man. His head reached almost to the top of the ceiling, but he wasn't bowing his head because of that.

"God rest his soul," he murmured.

Bridey went to the window and drew back the curtains. She lifted the sash, just in case it was true that an open window eased the flight of the soul.

She turned back to the bed and pulled the sheet over Mr. Hollingworth's face. The sheet was splattered with coffee, but that didn't matter. She gathered what had been dropped, returned what she could to the tray, and asked Mr. Tupper to help her make calls. She was afraid of the telephone.

Watching her step as she balanced the tray she carried, she led Mr. Tupper down to the telephone table, a little round pedestal under the stairs, and he lifted the receiver and asked the operator for Young Doc. Doc was at the hospital now, but his office girl would give him the message.

She then told Mr. Tupper to ask for Vincent's school. For Hannah's bridal home in Litchfield. For Benno, who would be at the factory.

Mr. Tupper spoke through perforations in the receiver to the operator, and after he did this, each time, he handed Bridey the receiver, which she held at a distance as she enunciated words carefully, speaking as if to someone almost deaf.

"He's gone!" she shouted. "Come home."

Rachel lived in France. Both she and Sarah would have to be cablegrammed. She asked Mr. Tupper could he go to the post office to send word to Sarah and Rachel. He could. She wrote down numbers for him, from a book.

Bridey had to work on keeping her thoughts together; they were running all over, like headless chickens.

After Mr. Tupper left, she heard Young Doc's Packard come up the drive. She was in the kitchen, at the sink, washing the breakfast things that hadn't broken. When she looked through the window and saw Young Doc getting out of his car, she left the kitchen, wiping her hands on the hem of her apron, but he was already coming through the door, without knocking, which was unusual for him. "When did it happen?" he asked her.

"I found him just now, this morning," she said.

She glanced at the clock on the hall table. It was near nine. Vincent was probably getting the news from the headmaster. He'd be home soon.

Something about the arrangement of Young Doc's features wasn't right. She'd expected compassion. Instead, he looked angry. As if she had done something wrong. Had she done something wrong? She couldn't imagine what it could be. She always followed exactly the routine he'd set out for her, administered the dosage of medicines kept in the fireplace cabinet, mixed fresh every night and left for her in a tiny glass tumbler.

After taking off his hat but not his coat, Young Doc bounded up the spiral stairs. What was his hurry? Perhaps he doubted Bridey's pronouncement. That Mr. Hollingworth might not be dead hadn't occurred to Bridey, but now she supposed she could have made a mistake. And wouldn't a mistake like that be a happiness to discover? But her heart remained heavy. She didn't think she'd made a mistake.

Young Doc had a boyish manner. Old Doc had been the family doctor for years but now Old Doc was gone and Young Doc had taken over. She guessed he'd be Young Doc for the rest of his life.

When she came into Mr. Hollingworth's room, Young Doc had opened the old man's nightshirt and was pressing a stethoscope to his chest. Bridey flinched, feeling the cold of that disk. But of course, Mr. Hollingworth couldn't feel it now.

Young Doc rose from the bed and turned toward the window, putting the stethoscope back in his bag. Bridey moved to rebutton Mr. Hollingworth's nightshirt. It was then that Mr. Tupper came into the room.

"There weren't enough numbers. Postmistress says there's a number missing."

Mr. Tupper's eyes went to Mr. Hollingworth and fixed on his right arm, which was flung over the sheet, his hand drooping over the side of the bed.

"If I didn't know better, I'd think the poor man had been poisoned," he said.

"What?" said Bridey, startled.

Mr. Tupper approached Mr. Hollingworth and took up his hand.

"White lines in the nail bed. They taught us in training to watch out for that. Arsenic exposure. Green paint and wallpaper are mixed with it, you know."

Bridey leaned closer. Faint white lines arced over the nail bed. Why hadn't she noticed those lines before?

"You're a doctor now, are you?" said Young Doc, turning.

Mr. Tupper flushed and looked away, toward the window.

Young Doc continued. "The technical term is *leukonychia striata*. Its appearance can indicate arsenic poisoning, yes, but also a multitude of other conditions...liver disease, malnourishment."

Young Doc looked at Bridey.

"Miss Molloy, have you been withholding nourishment here?"

"No, indeed!" Bridey said. But she recalled Mr. Hollingworth's lack of appetite lately, and perhaps she ought to have been more forceful in urging him to eat. Was her failure to insist that he eat more to blame for his death?

Mr. Tupper returned his gaze to the doctor. "The day Miss Molloy withholds food from a man is the day turtles sing," he said and chuckled, so as to make light of a serious thing. But—Bridey was shaken.

"Come, Mr. Tupper, let's find the right number." She was overcome with wanting to leave the room and felt free to do so now that Mr. Hollingworth was rebuttoned and decent.

She let Mr. Tupper go first out of the room and was made to wait just outside the door while he stopped to adjust the seat of a wall sconce he'd installed years before. Bridey, standing in the well of a hall turn, saw the doctor open the high cabinet by the fireplace. It was where the medicines he mixed were kept. He took the blue bottle and pushed the cork down tight into its neck. He jammed the bottle into a pocket of his coat. The medicine in the blue jar was as precious as gold. Another patient would need it.

Bridey turned from Mr. Tupper and went down the back stairs and through the kitchen to the telephone table; she opened its drawer and found the book. She met Mr. Tupper in the kitchen, gave him the number, and unlocked the front door for him. Getting to the post office was quicker by way of the front.

She heard the doctor come down the spiral stairs and started in that direction to see him out. As she approached the hall, she saw the doctor reflected in the glass door of the china press. Why was he lingering in the hallway, glancing around furtively? Perhaps he was looking for her to give further instructions. But no. Now he stepped off the runner and moved to the wall. There was a hole where the dual fixture had been. She was glad to see it was a neatly cut square. Mr. Tupper did meticulous work.

The doctor patted his coat pocket, took out the bottle, held it up to examine it, then, to Bridey's astonishment, dropped the bottle into the hole in the wall. She heard the glass tumble and hit the lathes before landing.

She stayed where she was, watching Young Doc's reflection in a pane of the press as he took up his tall hat from the bench, put it on, and moved toward the front door. He stood a moment, pulling away the lace curtain to look out a sidelight. Then he reached for the brass knob, swung the door open, and closed it behind him—and Bridey went cold from the small of her back to the top of her head.

2

Bridey

Liverpool

April 1908

No one without a ticket was allowed past a certain point and Bridey watched people standing inside tight circles of luggage, trying to stretch out the few moments they had with loved ones who were boarding the ship and whom they might not see again for years, or forever.

Women stroked the cheeks of boys; men patted the hair of young girls; babies in arms were squeezed between mothers and fathers when the mothers leaned in for a kiss. A white-haired woman in a flouncy cloth bonnet shrugged off her shawl and wrapped it around the thin shoulders of a girl who looked to be no more than nine. Apparently, no age limits applied to those who could book passage, now that steamer companies had relaxed rules, seeking to fill new, larger ships.

The woman ahead of Bridey in the line was a few years older than her, perhaps twenty. Her hair fell in dark waves on her velvet coat collar. The man she was kissing, his eyes became wet, and his tears must have displeased her because her gloved hand gently pushed at his shoulder. "Go on with ye, now. Go on, get on."

Bridey thought she saw the coat of her father and worried that he'd come after them. But the man in her father's mac wasn't her father, and Bridey was glad to be spared the sight of anyone she knew.

Thom was right for insisting she come with him, she saw that now. She'd resisted for months. They'd entertained other plans. For a time, it seemed to make sense for him to go over first and send for her later. But in the end, it was clear that if they were to be together, they'd have to leave together, and, though their escape hadn't worked out exactly as planned, they were together now, which both agreed was the most important thing.

She couldn't have stood being separated from him as some girls were separated from their sweethearts who'd left, who were gone sometimes for years and sometimes forever. She didn't want to be writing him letters; she needed Thom to be near her. Her desire for him was in her, inside her blood. She'd met him last year at a solidarity dance. As soon as he came into the hall, with his neat red hair and smart tweed coat, walking sure, which meant he was not on the drink, lots of lasses were on him, wanting him to ask them to dance. She'd thought him too handsome to dance with herself. But after he'd gone a set with each of the forward Flaherty twins and then a girl she didn't know, he had walked toward her while she was standing at the punch bowl with Liadan O'Callaghan. She'd thought he might be coming for Liadan, who was the prettier one, taller, and her hair was flaxen instead of dull broom straw. But another boy had in that moment intercepted Liadan and was leading her away, which made Bridey think the new boy might turn on his heel, but there he was before her, asking if she was free for a spin. She'd turned to the bowl to ask its permission—she didn't know what possessed her to do that—and he'd laughed with his eyes. She couldn't tell their color in the light, but his lashes were long. The teeth in his smile were straight and strong. The two of them danced that set and then another, and there'd not passed a day in a year when they'd not been

21

together at least for a few minutes and wouldn't her parents be surprised to know that.

In the cart from Kilconly to Tuam, the bus to Galway, the long train ride to Dublin, both of them sat alert on the hard wooden seats, taking turns keeping an eye on their luggage. Her black oilskin grip and his suitcase secured with a leather strap contained everything they needed to start their new lives. On the overnight ferry from Dublin to Liverpool, they'd tied their bags with twine to the shelf rails above them and again took turns keeping watch. They couldn't sleep anyway, so excited were they about their future. Her insides roiled with the prospect of what lay ahead, the thrill of doing what so many wanted to do but couldn't, which was go to America.

What gnawed at her, cutting into her happiness, was that the thing that most people *were* able to do, they had not been able to manage.

Father McGrory had not been in the rectory yesterday, though they'd knocked on his door before six in the morning. They'd wanted Father to marry them before they left. Their knocking had roused his cantankerous housekeeper, who had come to the door, blanket pulled around her, yawning under her sleeping cap. She'd told them that the priest wasn't there; he'd received a call in the night from a midwife. It hadn't occurred to them that the priest wouldn't be there. They'd not mentioned their coming to him, afraid if he knew beforehand, he might think himself duty-bound to betray them to her parents. She and Thom were old enough now; he couldn't refuse them. It was days after her sixteenth birthday. They no longer needed the consent of a parent. But Mrs. Taggart had closed the door against them.

Bridey dreaded going home, which she'd assumed they would do. How could they travel together unwed? But Thom put a hand on her back and said, "We've got to go, Bridey, the tickets will expire if we don't use them." His brother had sent tickets from a place called Poughkeepsie. Pink slips of paper so valuable, they seemed to glow in his pocket. They cost two months of what Thom earned working as an apprentice to Mr. Dollard the carpenter. But in twenty-four hours—if they turned back—the tickets would turn into worthless pieces of paper.

A strange weight settled in Bridey's chest, which she tried to ignore as she followed Thom down the stone steps of the rectory house. The mist was so thick it obscured the fields. It was spring, when the rains came. They could see the lane only a few paces ahead, but that was all right. They'd grown up on these lanes. They could walk them blind. They were headed to the calling place where Mr. McGallahey's cart brought people to the station in town. They were surprised to hear the three-minute bells. Thom was carrying both of their bags and he shifted hers sideways onto his head, balancing it with one hand, and seeing this made her laugh because he looked like drawings in books written by missionaries of heathen-born women toting water from wells. But with the weight shifted, he could walk faster. The bells rang again. They had to hurry. The cart was known to leave early if one of the passengers slipped McGalla-hey a coin. No one wanted to be late for work, not day-laboring men or women employed in houses as maids and cooks and laundresses. Ten minutes late, and an hour was docked from the pay.

I'll soon be one of them, Bridey thought with excitement. But she wouldn't be working in a house in Listowel, where household staff came and went with the day. She'd be working in the grand city of New York in one of the big houses on a street called Fifth Avenue.

A girl she knew from St. Ursula's already had a job there, in a house so important, they paid handsome wages for someone to do only ironing. Ironing was all Adelaide had to do, she'd said in a let-ter written on paper fine as tissue. Bridey had seen the letter because it had been passed around church during the Feast of St. Blaise. The lines had been long because of an outbreak of consumption in the next parish. They'd waited three-deep in the vestibule to get to the altar to have their throats blessed, which provided time for anyone interested to read Adelaide's letter.

Rich ladies in New York preferred Irish help, Adelaide had reported in the fine looping penmanship taught to girls by the nuns. In New York, the Irish weren't afraid to work and no work was beneath them. They were honest when sober and could not only read but were clever with household allowances, stretching a penny to the length of a pound. They didn't have pounds in America; Bridey knew it was dollars. She'd have to learn money as soon as she got there. She wasn't worried. She was good with money. She'd earned top marks in Sister Jerome's bookkeeping class.

When the ship docked in Liverpool, they disembarked and Bridey was glad that Thom's old school chum Gerald was as good as his word. There he was on the docks waiting to meet them. Gerald had left County Galway a few years before. He'd come to Liverpool on his way to America but as soon as he'd gotten here, he'd landed a job. He was a carter, taking tobacco off ships and hauling it to waiting warehouses. It was a good job, allowing him to marry a Liverpool girl, and now they had a baby. The baby had something wrong with it, something wrong with its legs, so he and his wife couldn't ever go to America. That America wouldn't take you if you weren't perfect was common knowledge, widely disseminated in travel pamphlets and advertisements for steamships. If you had something wrong with you, America would send you back to where you had come from. Everyone knew someone to whom this had happened. A few years before, the McGivneys of St. Carthage's had gone over with four children, two sets of twins. But one of each pair had been refused entry because of trachoma. Those two had to come back and live with an aunt in Listowel. The aunt was their mother now, raising Irish children who were mirror images of their American siblings growing up in New York.

Gerald took Bridey and Thom to a little café where his friend waited tables and, without their asking, the friend set tea trays before them.

"Make this your last scran for a while," Gerald warned, picking up his sandwich and biting into it with gusto. "Whatever you eat after this, you'll have to see again on the ship."

Bridey, sipping her tea, asked what he meant.

"As soon as the ship's on its way you'll be sick as a small hospital. It happens to everyone." Gerald reached into his coat pocket and pulled out something brown and small that he rolled across the table to them. Bridey gamely rolled it back and Gerald flicked open the blade of a pocket knife and brought it hard down on the shell. "Nutmeg," he said, splitting it in half. He pushed the halves across the wood table, one for each of them. "Put this under your tongue as soon as you sail," he said. "You might still get sick, but it won't last as long."

He began to talk of America, giving them advice. At first Bridey was skeptical, as Gerald himself hadn't been to America. But soon she understood that he knew what he knew because ships not only left Liverpool but returned with homecomers, and they shared things they'd had to find out the hard way.

"Once you get off the boat, don't cough," he warned. "They have plainclothes guards on the lookout for consumption and the typhus, and the least sign of a cough can get you sent back or tossed into infirmary."

And suddenly, Bridey needed to cough. The cough turned into a coughing fit, which was odd, as she hadn't even a cold, and she groped in her pockets for her handkerchief, the new one her sister

Kathleen had embroidered for her birthday. Seeing her initials in her sister's fine stitch tugged at something in her.

"Drink this," Thom said, pushing his pint toward her, but she picked up her teacup and swallowed down the black tea and the coughing stopped, making both Thom's and Gerald's faces relax, and she tucked the hankie inside the sleeve of her jumper so it would be easy to get at in case she needed it again.

"Better drink up—there's none of that where you're going," said Gerald, nodding to the tea she'd left in her cup.

"Do they not have tea in America?" Bridey was surprised. She'd supposed they had everything.

"The tea there tastes like dishwater, undrinkable without lots of milk and sugar." Luxuries they wouldn't be able to afford, not at first.

The prospect of tea-less afternoons made Bridey feel bereft. She looked around for what else she soon wouldn't have and saw, under glass, treats she'd had only on special occasions and now might not get the chance to try again—scones and porter cakes and pasties and black pudding and crubeens. She wondered if she would ever come back. Adelaide had been gone for two years and Bridey knew there'd not been mention of a return visit.

Of all she'd miss, her siblings came first. She imagined sending tickets to all of them, mailing prepaid passages as Thom's brother had done, drawing them one by one to America, weaning them from this hard, hardening country while they were still soft enough to be induced to leave it.

Her parents could not be moved, she knew that. They were as immovable as the great mossed-over stones that grew out of the cliffs. Her parents' immovability against Thom was the reason she was having to go in the first place.

It wasn't Mam so much—Bridey felt that in a place deep inside her, where she'd been a girl once, Mam understood and was silently on the side of her eldest daughter.

Mam wasn't, of course, free to say as much. Why? Because of Da! Da was dead set against the Flynns. He said they had the bad blood. Bridey knew from experience that once resistance took hold in Da, it was impossible to surmount, his objections intractable as the Rock of Cashel. He'd forbidden Bridey to marry a Flynn. Thom was Thom Flynn. Thom's grandfather on his father's side had taken the Molloy farm. The farm had belonged to Bridey's father's family for generations. Wilf Flynn had won the farm in a card game and—to the great dismay of her family—he had taken it. Poor Da had been twelve when his family dragged him away from the house he was born in, a white, rambling clapboard with porches added whenever the farm had had a good year.

They moved down the hill, reduced to a small house on a lane and a few chickens, so Da had had to go to work selling eggs from a cart at Roscommon market. He got laboring jobs in town—when he could.

It was irony that Thom was leaving because he didn't want to work a farm, and that was the reason his older brother had left too.

Her family had gathered as usual around the oilcloth table the night before. It was their last supper as a family, though no one knew this but Bridey. Usually when people left for America, a big sendoff was given them, an American wake, but if one had been given her, she wouldn't have been able to leave. She wouldn't have known how to say good-bye.

Mam served fried boxty. It was Lent, so every day was meatless, not just Fridays. The boxty was good. She forked into the fried pancakes, relishing them. Her brothers took turns keeping the fire a-roar in the stone hearth behind them. There were seven of them around the table; there would have been nine if two had not died, and for the first time Bridey was glad for their absence. It was less weight on her.

Quinn told of winning a geography bee and the room seemed to undulate with talk and laughter and smoke and the fragrance of onions browning in butter, and she was happy there were too many around the table for anyone to take notice of the tears stinging her eyes. She knew that she wouldn't see her mother's kitchen again for a long time.

Her father wasn't there. They never waited grace for him anymore. He'd told her mother to stop waiting, saying, "One less holy obligation on my unholy back," and so her mother no longer waited the blessing for him. She always set up his place at the head of the table, but sometimes whole meals would go by without him in the chair. Still, even when he wasn't there, he was present; it was as if his ghost were sitting there, judging them.

When the boxty was done, her brothers leaned back in their chairs for a smoke, and that's when their father came in, and they knew by the slow way he took off his boots that he was full of the drink.

Her mother jumped up to get a plate she'd kept hot for him by the stove, and Bridey was relieved to see Da weave his way to the table; sometimes he didn't want to eat at all, just went to the bedroom and stretched out in his coat on top of the quilt. But if he came to the table, it meant he wasn't so bad. Da's chair scraped the floorboards as he pulled it out and her mother set his plate on the table. Then he sat heavily and picked up his spoon and brought the steaming spoon to his lips, and Bridey pictured her mother's good food fighting the drink in him.

In America, she wouldn't have to see her father like this.

Her brothers' talk resumed and her sister Kathleen drew the dish of salt toward her and leaned over to salt their father's boxty for him—he'd stopped being able to taste things unless they were very salty or sweet.

Now Kathleen would have Bridey's chores to do as well as her own. This Bridey regretted, but what could be done?

The first ticket she'd send would be for Kathleen, but how could poor Mam manage without her? Kathleen was second oldest, right behind Bridey. Kathleen could sew and clean and cook and didn't mind doing those things, in fact liked to do them, unlike Bridey, who was always wanting to steal away with a book. Before all this happened, Bridey had imagined herself a shopgirl in town wearing smart shoes and hats.

3.

Bridey

The *Mauretania*

April 1908

The ship looked grand in its dock on the Mersey, huge and white and glistening. It had had its maiden run only a few months before, the man who examined their tickets said. The ship looked like a massive white swan next to the gray ugly ducklings docked beside it, boats made to carry mail and tobacco and other kinds of cargo. Bridey knew that not all of the passengers were leaving Ireland forever, as she and Thom were doing, but were traveling on holiday to see what they hadn't seen, to have interesting things to write about in diaries or on postal cards with colorful stamps that would wend their way back to friends and relatives, sometimes reaching them after they themselves had wended their way home.

But those people sailed saloon class; none of them would be with Thom and Bridey in third.

Bridey was shivering as she followed Thom up narrow steel steps to the door on deck E. It was the lowest passenger deck but far above the level of the dock. She was cold despite the coat and hat she was wearing. Her Easter outfit wasn't new. It had been sent by her aunt whose daughter—Bridey's cousin Agnes—had left to work as a stenographer in London, and clothes good enough for County Kerry weren't good enough there.

"You can always tell the Irish here, they look like cows in their dowdy browns," Agnes had said with a laugh when she'd come home for Christmas. She'd told her mother to send Bridey and her sisters a box of things she hadn't brought over. They'd been wearing her hand-me-downs for years. Bridey didn't mind. Agnes had always had style, though where she got it from, Bridey couldn't imagine. Agnes had grown up the same as she had, in a mean parish of heatless houses where things were always dusted with a layer of soot from smoke from the fire or the stove. Yet to see her at church, you'd think she'd just stepped off the streets of Paris.

Bridey had dressed for the ship in Agnes's gray walking coat with buttons covered in plaid that matched the cuffs, which Bridey thought made it look smart, though she guessed if the coat wasn't smart enough for London, it surely wasn't smart enough for New York. Still, Bridey knew that even the smartest clothes wouldn't disguise the fact that she was an Irish girl fresh from the west country. She was sorry that the coat was emigrating to America, which meant her sisters wouldn't be able to wear it as they usually did with clothes she got from Agnes.

She'd send them clothes as soon as she could from America, fancy high-heeled shoes and silk stockings and the kind of dresses they'd seen in the magazines. She followed Thom down narrow corridors, swaying, trying to find their berth. It must have taken a forest of timber to build such a long row of panels and doors.

The sound of the engine was deafening. They couldn't talk to each other or to anyone they passed; no voice could be heard above the roar of machinery.

Finally, the number they were looking for appeared on a narrow door: 2435A. Thom pushed it open and as soon as she followed, the door swung shut behind her. She saw it wouldn't stay open unless it was propped. With the door closed, the room was almost pitch-black. There were no windows or even portholes. Just a narrow bunk bed and a rack for the luggage and a small table and lamp bolted onto it. This would be their home for ten days. As Bridey moved to find something to prop open the door, Thom reached his arms around her from behind.

"C'mere, Mrs. Flynn," he said, untying her kerchief and kissing her as he'd so often done before, but now she was panicking. She saw, in his mind, there'd be no reason to stop—no Mam or Da to discover them, no constable lurking to give them the stick, no siblings to pop up from behind a tree and pretend to shoot them, as her brother Dan had once done.

The problem was, she wasn't Mrs. Flynn. But perhaps that could be rectified on the ship? Surely there was a priest somewhere on the manifest.

"Thom, we shouldn't—" she began, but he cut her off.

"I love you, Bridey," Thom murmured into her ear. His warm breath on her neck sent bright arrows through her. "This is the beginning of our life together."

It was true. They belonged to each other and always would. A piece of paper wasn't needed to convince her of that, was it?

She knew only vaguely what was expected of her. She didn't know the specifics. She had no older friend or big sister to shine light on exactly how to carry off the wedding night. But—it wasn't her wedding night. As things proceeded, this fact began to paralyze her. To have relations with a man you weren't married to was a mortal sin and if you died with a mortal sin blackening your soul, you'd be relegated instantly to eternal damnation. There was no ambivalence about this, the catechisms made clear. If you committed a mortal sin and died without the chance to confess it, God had no alternative but to send you to hell. And hell was the worst thing you could think of, the nuns had assured her. For some, it was fire; for others, ice—which it would be for her. She hated cold more than anything.

"I'm so cold," she said, shaking in his arms. She was shivering from fright, which she didn't want him to know.

"Let's get under the covers," he said, pulling back the blanket and the clean sheet. He moved to take off his shirt, but she turned away and pulled her Easter coat tighter around her. The thought of undressing in front of him mortified her. Seeing this, he rebuttoned his shirt.

She continued to sit next to him on the bottom bunk, fully clothed. They sat side by side on the mattress that was flat as a flounder. She didn't move away from him as she was tempted to do. Something in her resisted—she guessed that moving away from him would be rude. The ease between them had gone. It felt as if she'd been made to room with a stranger. That the love between them could burn itself out hadn't occurred to her before. The thought of losing him frightened her more than anything. She imagined the boat docking in America ten days from now. If he didn't love her then, they'd have to go separate ways. She began to cry. What would she do? She imagined a poorhouse. He bent toward her in the dim light and stroked her wet cheek.

"We don't have to do anything you don't want to do," he said gently. He curled his clothed body around her and they lay together until they both fell asleep, lulled by the creaking noises overhead and the rocking and the churning and clangs made by the ship.

She woke in the night nauseated and sweating and it took a moment to figure out where she was, and when she did, her next thought was that God was punishing her for sharing a bed with a man not her husband. Thom was sick too. They'd forgotten to suck on the nutmeg. Thom fell out of bed to his hands and knees and vomited onto the floor, and soon she joined him, heaving out the contents of her stomach in wave after wave until there was nothing left to come up. The heaving continued into the next day, which distracted her from worrying about anything else.

A few days later, they stopped being sick, and when a deckhand came with a mop to swab the tiles and prop the door open to let out the stink, they left the cabin and went to the third-class dining room. There they sat side by side, squeezed onto a bench at a long table where other diners already sat, talking of how hungry they were after days without eating. Bridey was glad that she and Thom had not been the only ones sick. A waiter gave them metal bowls and cups and utensils and said they were to be used for the entire trip, washed by themselves and carried back and forth to the dining room. Menus were passed and Bridey and Thom gave up their bowls to be filled. Thom chose salt porridge but Bridey wanted to try food she'd never had and selected names that looked lovely in beautifully penned script: grapefruits and French plums. She said they tasted like heaven and urged spoonfuls toward Thom, but he wanted only his porridge.

They gave up their cups to be filled with water, but it was a long time before the cups came back. Thom asked for a drink from a man next to him, and he offered a sip to Bridey too—by this time, she was burning with thirst—but Bridey waited until their own cups were returned.

After breakfast, they climbed up narrow rungs to the lowest deck (their pink tickets permitted them no higher), where they joined a crowd of people waiting a turn at the rail. Seeing Thom among other people always startled Bridey because when they were alone, she imagined him taller than most men, but seeing him in a crowd reminded her that he wasn't. When they reached the rail, she felt no bigger than the head of a pin, standing with others along its great expanse. They saw sky for the first time in days. They luxuriated in salty breezes and spray from the turquoise sea that seemed to stretch endlessly in their wake. It wasn't endless; it led back to Ireland, but nothing of that could be seen anymore. Bridey wondered aloud if they'd ever see it again. Thom said he guessed they would, when they showed their children where they had come from. This sent something warm through Bridey. After a few minutes, they were jostled by others wanting a look, and they joined a crowd of people waiting for the lift. They hadn't known there was a lift. It would take them down to their floor six flights below deck. But the lift wasn't running. The lift boy was sick. So they climbed back down the rungs.

Now there was no place to go but their room. The stench was gone. Thom let the door close. They sat on the bed—there was nowhere else to sit—and being sprayed with the sea at the rails must have stirred something primal in Thom, and in her. He leaned closer and kissed her, lifting his hand to cradle the back of her head, and she didn't mind. She discovered that she was helpless against this, helpless not against him, but against the desire for him. Seeming to sense this, he pulled her closer so that she felt the muscles of his arm and thighs move against her. Gently, he pulled her with him to lie back on the bed. She knew he was waiting for a cue from her and she gave it to him when she didn't resist him unbuttoning her blouse, pushing the bone buttons one by one through stitched slits, which made the blouse fall open, revealing her chemise, the only barrier between his hand and her bodice. She felt his fingers on the skin of her torso for the first time as he dipped his hand beneath the linen and settled it on her stomach. The bodice was a fortress of hooks and buttons and stays so daunting that undoing them sometimes foiled even herself. He must have felt daunted because his hand moved away and down to her skirt, which he didn't seek to unhook but lifted by its hem, and then he thrust his hand beneath layers, his fingers tracing the length of her legs in her dark cotton stockings; when he came to the skin of her thighs, he slowly, slowly rolled down the cotton until first one leg lay bare in her skirts, then another. Now he was fingering the lace of her drawers, rubbing the linen that covered her secret flesh. She felt tingles in every reach of her body. His hand hesitated. She opened her eyes and saw his were closed and this gave her courage to move her hands, which had lain limp on the bed. She reached up and undid the stays of her corset and when she had bared her breasts, she was gratified by the look on his face, which seemed a cross between hunger and astonishment. "What a beautiful lass you are," he said. He turned away from her and undid his belt and unbuttoned his trousers and then he turned back and she was alarmed by the size of what made him a man. How much bigger it was than the dangles of baby brothers, which could be covered by a cotton nappy kept handy so they wouldn't spray her when she changed them.

He rose on his knees above her and she squeezed her eyes shut. She tightened all over, bracing herself.

"Relax," he whispered close to her ear. But she couldn't relax. What they were engaged in was anything but relaxing. It was terrifying and thrilling and made you aware of places in you that you didn't know you had.

He tried to push into her, but it wouldn't go. Then it did, which hurt like the devil.

Her favorite part was lying in his arms after it was over, inhaling him and a strange perfume, the scent of what they had done together. She drifted to sleep in the crook of his elbow.

They discussed the possibility of finding a priest to marry them on the ship—but they didn't dare risk exposing the fact that they were occupying one berth in an unmarried state. Bridey was afraid of their being demoted to steerage, which wasn't private berths like the one that they had but an open room in the cellar where people slept on wooden bunks as if in a stable—men and women and children too. She was grateful to Thom's brother for spending extra for third.

The next morning, Thom woke with fever.

She hadn't worried at first. She brought down the fever with yarrow she'd packed with other herbs in a quilted roll-up bag tied with ribbon she'd sewn herself for the journey. She gave him tea—every so often, she'd spoon small sips into him, and then his cheeks were less flushed and his forehead cool instead of clammy.

The tea had worked, and then it had not. When the fever was accompanied by a burning thirst, she sought the ship's doctor—there was a doctor on board—but their tickets didn't afford access to him. There was a nurse, but the waiting list was days long. Bridey rapped on door after door along the third-class corridor, seeking someone who knew healing. Mrs. Ahearn, a few rooms down, was traveling with a small daughter she'd left in Ireland as an infant and had come back to get, and she advised her to get water reserved for cabin-class passengers, told her that third used steerage water from wooden casks so leaky, they let poisons in.

Mrs. Ahearn wouldn't come to their cabin for fear of catching something and passing it on to her daughter, but she lent Bridey a wooden crucifix to lay on Thom's chest. It had been blessed at Lourdes and had healing properties.

Getting water from cabin class proved impossible.

At night, Bridey slept curled around Thom under the small pile of material she'd assembled to try to warm him—the boiled-wool blanket stamped in big letters with the name of the ship, their two thin coats. She guarded the crucifix so it wouldn't slide off his chest. She prayed, murmuring incantations she'd memorized from *Key of Heaven*, the little prayer book her gram had given her for her confirmation. She said rosaries. Our Fathers. The special prayer to Saint Jude.

She used all the tricks she'd learned from Mam, who had

brought more than one baby back from the brink. She'd asked a waiter to boil an onion in milk and pepper, which he agreed to do in exchange for her penning a letter to his sweetheart in Limerick. He didn't want the sweetheart to know he couldn't read or write.

Thom lay on their narrow bed day and night, flushed and shivering; only occasionally did he drift off to sleep. He slept like an angel—no snoring or moving about, as still as a child with not a thing on his conscience. But when his form remained still for too long, she'd bend over him and put a finger under his nose, as her mother used to do to make sure a baby was still with them.

She drank beef tea herself to keep up her strength. If she got sick, she couldn't take care of him.

For hours, she'd watch him by the light of the bulb in the bolted-down lamp, the only light there was in the cabin. But soon, she had to attend to him in the dark, as any light pained him. There was a narrow vertical gap in the corner of the room where the wooden walls didn't quite meet, allowing light from the corridor to penetrate the dark berth. But soon even this sliver of light was too much for him to bear without crying out. Each time she had to leave the room, to empty his chamber pot or use the lavatory herself, she stepped carefully to block the light from the corridor so as to avoid inflicting pain on him when he was feeling so much of it already. She felt anger at light that stole through cracks between wall panels pulled apart by lunges and setbacks by which Bridey knew that the ship must be making progress but it sometimes felt as if they were being rammed and made to go backward.

She often wished she herself could go backward. She replayed the scene in front of the rectory again and again in her mind: She and Thom are at the door and Mrs. Taggart tells them Father McGrory isn't there. Instead of insisting the tickets must be used, Thom agrees that they should try for America some other day. It's still before dawn and Bridey has just enough time to run home and creep through the window of the room she shares with her sisters, and Kathleen wakes and looks quizzically at the old oilskin grip Bridey is pulling up through the window after herself—but her sister remains quiet when she sees Bridey put her finger to her lips. Kathleen pulls the blanket over her head, rolls to the wall, and goes back to sleep before Mam calls them to help her with the kitchen fires, the babies, the sweeping, the bread.

Upon waking before morning that day—she knew. Thom was gone. He lay perfectly still, his mouth no longer a mouth but an odd-shaped gap in his face, and when she touched him, there was a coldness she remembered from when she'd found her baby brother dead in the pram where he slept. It was her job in the morning to get Pat and change his night nappy. But he hadn't been awake, which was unusual, and she'd reached out and felt that his cheek had gone cold as a stone.

They bound Thom like a mummy, in sailcloth. The cloth, she realized, was weighted with links of chain in the hems. The priest, who was a minister so he wasn't really a priest, anointed first Thom's head, then his feet, with thumbs dipped in holy water, begging God to grant him the new life promised in the waters of baptism. His black robes flapped about him as he said those same prayers over the bodies next to Thom—another man and a baby who'd succumbed to ship fever too. She could barely see through the tears wetting her face, which was also wetted by drops of sea from waves overtaking the rails as if to seize what was being promised before it was given.

"As we commit these bodily vessels to the deep..."

Now Thom was slowly tipped over the rails, and part of her was going with him. Yesterday, she'd been tempted to send Mrs

39

Ahearn's crucifix with him, but when she woke up this morning, she'd decided not to. Not only because she was sure Mrs. Ahearn would want it back, but because it was the last thing that Thom's living body had touched; it gave her comfort to feel it against her own skin. She undid the handkerchief in which she had wrapped his half of the nutmeg, never used, and sent the small offering after him. The girl she had been with Thom was dead now, as dead as he was.

Would he go to heaven? She worried about this. He'd not had a chance to confess after what they did. What they'd done was a mortal sin—there was no way around that. But they'd proven their intention to marry, hadn't they? They'd tried to get married, they'd wanted to get married, but through no fault of their own, the priest had not been there when they called.

They shouldn't have taken off in the spring. It was April, and contagion was in the air, everyone knew. The priest not having been there to marry them was a sign that they should have postponed their trip. But they hadn't heeded the sign.

Thom had said it was normal that it hurt, her first time. Then he'd gotten sick, and now there would never be a next time. That was punishment enough, wasn't it, for Thom and for her. The God she imagined was the God the nuns described, a God who seemed less stern and more yielding than the God praised by priests—that God was too merciful to consign a man as good as Thom to suffer the permanent fires of hell. Wasn't He?

She herself would go to confession. She knew there was at least one Catholic church in New York. Adelaide had included with her letter a picture postcard of a church called St. Patrick's, named for the patron saint of their own country.

Bridey thought God would take into account that there had just been the once.

"...Grant them peace and tranquillity..."

The raging waters were anything but tranquil, the waves rising up, slapping the sides of the ship. Thom was slid feet first past the rails. She imagined him slipping down to the ocean's depths, the sheets about him unwinding, his gesturing fingers stroking braids of seaweed as he had once stroked the braids of her hair.

4

Vincent

Lower East Side, Manhattan

1909–1914

His mother was Irish, or so he'd been told. Whatever name she had given him had burned only briefly, extinguished when he was just three months old by the nun who received him at the St. Joseph's Home for the Friendless.

Each child at St. Joseph's was given a new name to protect the anonymity of the mother so she could reenter society, relieved of her crime. It was against the law for a woman to bear an illegitimate child. However, few were prosecuted. It was thought that the heart-breaking consequences of her transgression was punishment enough.

At four months old, he was taken in by foster parents who christened him Vincent McNulty. A few years later, they'd brought him back. Then, at the age of five, he became who he would be for the rest of his life: Vincent Hollingworth Porter. In later years, he speculated on what his birth name had been. Something Irish, certainly, Seamus or Paddy or Malachy. He was glad he'd ended up bearing a name that didn't label him a bogtrotter—though his fire bush left little doubt of his ancestry. Even the hair on his arms was red.

At St. Joseph's, he liked to play the game of Who Is My Mother. He—like the other children—imagined his mother to be beautiful and important and he nurtured the idea that she'd come back to get him. He pictured an elegant Irish lady with elbow-length gloves and hair in a sweep at the back of her head, as red as his own. He imagined her married to a man of great wealth, living in a big fancy house—this was before he learned that most Irish ladies who lived in big houses did so only because they cleaned them.

Sometimes children at St. Joseph's were retrieved. By their mothers, usually, but sometimes their fathers came back to get them and take them to be a family again. This had happened to other boys. One winter night, three brothers with whom he shared a bench at meals didn't show up for dinner. This was unheard of. Dinner was the high point of the day. Their bowls of stew had been divided among him and two others. The boys' father had come to get them; Sister St. Hilda, the kind one, had told him this. The boys' aunt had come from Ireland to help their father, who couldn't take care of three boys by himself. Their mother had died and it was against the law for a man to raise children in a house with no woman in it. And so their father had brought them to St. Joseph's while he searched for a proper replacement mother. It had taken a year, said Sister St. Hilda, and involved letters, telegrams, passage procured on a steamship. But the boys had been rescued, a thing Vincent never stopped wishing for while he was there.

His earliest memories were of the home of Mr. and Mrs. Mc-Nulty. They were the foster parents who'd taken him in as an infant. Their flat on Mott Street was poor but nicer than most flats in Five Points so it easily passed inspection by the observing committee of the Sisters of Charity.

Infants went to foster families if any could be found—in the year he was given to St. Joseph's, 1909, the home had become overcrowded, due largely to waves of immigrants. Immigrants were surging onto New York's shores in unprecedented numbers, a million a year. Most confronted a new world far different from the gilded life of ease they'd half expected. Sometimes, circumstances were too mean to allow for the upkeep of even one child. His mother, he'd been told, had wanted to give him a better life than the one that she could provide.

St. Joseph's sought to place out their infants to foster homes—the demands of babies far exceeded those of older children. Cribs were needed, and hands to diaper and feed and rock and dress. Research by social scientists revealed that a real home could give babies a start in life superior to what an institution could provide, even one run by the good Sisters of Mercy.

The McNultys were on a list of prospective parents who would take a child in and care for it in return for a monthly allowance. They had a two-room flat. They'd wanted to have their own child but this hadn't happened, though they'd been praying for it for years. Then, a year after they took in Vincent, Mrs. McNulty discovered herself in the family way. Once their baby was born, and born healthy—a girl—Mrs. McNulty told anyone who would listen that she was worn off her feet trying to take care of two babies.

The McNultys considered returning Vincent, but they didn't, and not only because they had grown fond of Vincent, who was a beautiful child with bright eyes and a ready laugh. Mrs. McNulty told a neighbor who remarked on it later that she suspected some strange causal connection between Vincent's arrival and their own child coming to them. If they gave their foster back before his fifth birthday, when their contract was up, would this shift some sequence in the natural order of things and result in the premature death of their real child? Mr. McNulty brought in a respectable wage as a cable layer for the city, but they had come to depend on the monthly allowance, which Mrs. McNulty was able to stretch to cover other household needs benefiting Vincent too.

Vincent's first memory was of sitting at a round oilcloth-covered table with the people he thought of as his mother and father in a small dining room. He must have been three. Lolo, the baby, was crying softly in the next room. His mother was asking why the doorbell was ringing, and when his father said that it was probably a rat gnawing at the basement wires, she wrinkled her nose. Then a strange man was sitting next to him at the table. His collar was black instead of white. He asked Vincent if he was well cared for, happy. Vincent didn't know. He'd never considered if he was happy. He looked up at the tin ceiling where metal stars twinkled, reflecting the gaslight, then down to his mother's face and his father's, both yellow-lit by the lamp. Their expressions were grave. "Yes," he said. He knew that this had been the right answer because it made the man and his parents smile. The man said, "Good," and added that he must come around now and then to make sure.

Vincent understood that he did not belong to his parents outright, as Lolo did. This was why they loved Lolo more, though before she was born, Vincent had felt himself cherished.

The memory of the man in the collar conflated with another memory of something that might or might not have happened the same night: the flare of his father's temper at dinner as he hurled a piece of meat across the table at his mother. It splattered against the wallpaper behind her, staining the pattern of teakettles.

5

Bridey

Ellis Island

April 1908

After Thom's burial, Mrs. Ahearn invited Bridey to stop in their cabin, but Bridey wanted to be alone. She navigated down several winding flights of iron stairs, back to her berth.

She had never been really alone before. She'd often wanted to be, before she met Thom—craved it, even. Every now and then she'd manage to escape the noise and clutter and neediness of a big family by wheeling out on a borrowed bicycle to a dune where she could while away an hour or two reading a book from the lending library—a novel by Elizabeth Gaskell or Lillian Spender or the latest by Mrs. Humphry Ward—but she soon had her fill of this kind of solitude. She was always glad to go home to laughter and talking and the smell of whatever Mam had going on the stove.

Bridey didn't herself know how to cook. Her mother said teaching her was more trouble than it was worth. She thought of her mother's kitchen and guessed they were sitting down to dinner just now, her sister Kathleen filling plates from pots bubbling on the wrought-iron black stove, fire jumping in the grate; her mother filling the cups with water from the old iron kettle, the one with her grandmother's thumbprint worn into the wood handle.

Now what would she do? She couldn't go back. Her missing Thom was physical, as if she had lost an arm or a leg. She imagined ascending to the rails and jumping in after him. She said a prayer for the ship to go down.

She was unable to eat for the rest of the journey. There were two days remaining and she spent them curled on the bed, her head in his peacoat. She inhaled the blue lining and tried to commit his scent to memory. She didn't want to forget him. She concentrated on imagining the way he was when he was alive: the feel of his red whiskers against her cheek, his dancing blue eyes, the way he held the back of her head when he kissed her.

She willed him to come to her in a dream so that she could see him again. They used to laugh at the Widow Crawley, who signed cards from herself and *ARC,* meaning Angel Ronald Crawley, who had passed away decades before. Now Bridey thought of her not with ridicule but with tenderness, understanding something she wished she didn't have to understand.

After a day, Mrs. Ahearn rapped on her door. Bridey assumed she was there for the crucifix, but Mrs. Ahearn said she didn't want it back. She'd come because dinner was oxtail soup, which would be strengthening, and Bridey needed her strength.

For whose sake? Bridey thought but didn't say. Who needed her now? Who did she have to keep herself strong for? She couldn't imagine being able to go to the dining room. The smell of food repulsed her, as did the prospect of the room rowdy with diners whose lives were the same as they'd been when the ship had set sail while hers had been turned upside down.

At Mrs. Ahearn's insistence, Bridey turned on the light and found her metal bowl, which she handed to Mrs. Ahearn to fill and bring back for her. When Bridey drank the soup, sitting on the bed, she felt as if she were betraying Thom in some way. It was the first meal she was having without him. The next day, as soon as the breakfast bugle played, Mrs. Ahearn knocked again, but Bridey didn't answer. She couldn't rouse herself from the bed. She didn't want to eat anything. Her body seemed to have slowed to a stop. All she could do, all she seemed to require, was sleep, that elixir, the one that held the only curative for her.

"Thom." She murmured his name as she drifted into dreams, willing him into them, but he didn't appear.

She knew she'd have to make herself presentable before she got off the ship. She knew if she didn't, they might send her back. She couldn't bear the thought of having to return. She guessed the journey might kill her.

She stood in line for the lavatory assigned to her deck. The line stayed long the entire twenty-four hours before landing, and when it was finally her turn, she didn't queue for the shower. Instead, she drew a wet cloth across herself in front of the washbowl. She didn't want to turn the tap that would set off a pour of ice-cold water from a spout in the wall. She'd used it just once, right after Thom and she did what they did. It was the first time she'd stood under a shower. The house she'd lived in had only a tub you had to fill with water heated up on the stove. It had taken her a long time to work the handle so that the water turned off and by the time she stepped out, she was a block of ice.

They announced the time of entering port—five fifty the next morning—and many, like her, were up before dawn, dressed to look their best upon meeting America. Even steerage passengers were permitted on the promenade deck as they sailed into the harbor. They were given little American flags and as they waved them, some people gasped, some cried, some put their hands over their hearts as the ship made its slow way through misty air, approaching the giant green lady wearing a crown of spikes, holding a torch aloft, aglow in the fog. The lady's giant back foot was lifted, the heel interrupting the drape of her robe, as if she were about to do an Irish dance step. The sight was breathtaking, and Bridey's eyes filled as she thought of Thom, who should have been seeing it with her, waving his hat with the other men at the rail.

The passengers were directed, with their luggage, onto a ferry, which carried them to an island crowded with so many buildings, she thought at first it was the city itself. She meant to stay with Mrs. Ahearn and her daughter but as they mounted the plank that led to the ferry, Bridey was told to step aside and the others were waved on. She'd thought the man who had stopped her meant to help with her luggage—she carried both her own grip and Thom's suitcase. But he offered no assistance as he led her to a room, where a doctor in a long white coat asked her to take off her coat, and she panicked as he poked at her bodice with shiny instruments. He examined her tongue, her ears, the whites of her eyes, her hair. What if she'd caught Thom's disease? Would they send her back? She was released, but by then Mrs. Ahearn was gone and so Bridey rode the ferry to America with hundreds of strangers.

They had to wear tags, as if they themselves were pieces of luggage. Once the ferry was docked, she followed other passengers to a cavernous room where arched windows reminded her of windows in church. She'd never seen so many shades of skin or heard the sound of so many languages.

The lines were long. At the beginning of the lines were pews where you could sit. While Bridey was sitting, a woman in an apron brought around a big basket filled with cuts of white bread. The bread was fluffy and sweet and tasted like cake. Bridey had never tasted bread so delicious. The bread she knew was heavy and brown, the doughy part almost as hard as the crust.

She sat in one line, then stood in another. They were lined up like cattle being brought to a fair, separated by iron rails. Finally, it was her turn to stand in front of an inspector with a shiny beak on his cap and a mustache that looked like an upside-down horseshoe. He looked down on her, gazing from a high seat behind a wooden table tilted against her.

"Name?"

"Brighid Molloy."

The man bent closer to the broad page with hundreds of names inked on it in small, spindly handwriting.

"Bridey," she said. Perhaps Bridey had been the name on the manifest.

"Bridey?" he repeated, still staring at the manifest. Could it be that he'd never heard the name before? "Age?"

"Sixteen."

"Are you married or single?"

Later, she realized she could have easily lied and should have done so, said she was married, a lie they'd not be able to disprove—but the grandness of the Great Hall, the impressiveness of the man's giant mustache, the fact that she wasn't in possession of a certificate that said so, the fear that a misstep might get her sent back—all these conspired to make Bridey say, "Single." And once she said it, she couldn't take it back, though she didn't realize the need for taking it back until later.

"So, you're Bridey, but you yourself never been a bride, eh?" He looked at her, and the ends of his mustache rose, and the grin that he gave her seemed lascivious. Did something show? Could the man somehow see that her maidenhood was missing?

His next question relieved her: Did she have any identifying marks? It meant he couldn't see what she didn't want seen.

"A strawberry mark. On my stomach." A birthmark. Thom had traced his finger around it, calling it Italy. He'd promised to take her there someday. She was relieved that the inspector didn't ask to see it.

He continued with questions he read from a list: Are you an anarchist? Have you been in prison? Have you been in an institution for care of the insane? Is someone forcing you to come to this country?

No and no and no and no, she said. Though the last no wasn't perfectly true. She'd been forced here, in a way, by her unyielding father. She guessed she would never see him again.

The inspector pointed her toward the money-change station, where she opened Thom's money belt at her waist and pried out a few bright Irish pounds that were transformed into dull gray dollar bills. The final stop was the customs interrogator, which took a lot of time because he checked the pockets not only of the clothes she had on, but of all the clothes in her luggage. She wondered why but didn't dare ask.

Then she realized that she was being released. Another boat would ferry her and the other newcomers to the shore of America. The people crowded around her were now happy, unlike in the Great Hall, where most were still fearful they might be sent back. The ferry approached, and people cheered as it docked, and even before ropes were fed out of portholes, the crowd streamed toward it, carrying her with them.

She stood on the open deck crushed against others. Whistles and horns and foghorns and talk filled the air, but no language she could understand, except for the universal cries of babies. She looked up at the American sky, where seagulls called and swooped. She was glad her bags weren't among those they marked with droppings. The boat docked again, throwing everyone forward, and then she was pushed off the boat and through the gates of the New World.

Beyond the gates, people fell into each other's arms. Some held up boards with names painted on them. She guessed others, like her, were there to meet relatives they'd never seen before. She didn't know what Thom's brother looked like. She'd never met Denis. She scanned the crowd for faces that resembled Thom's. She dreaded having to tell Thom's brother the news. Evening was falling and people were hurrying every which way; it was hard to find a quiet place to stand. She stood with her back to a stone wall, her luggage in front of her. She toed Thom's suitcase so it was ahead of her grip—perhaps his brother would recognize it. She scanned the crowd, alert for a face that echoed Thom's fair coloring or his red hair, but hours later, she was still standing there. Night was falling. It was beginning to rain. She worried about what she should do.

"Are ye Catholic?" she heard.

A gray-whiskered man in a bowler hat moved his umbrella so it covered her too.

"Yes."

"Alone are ye?" His eyes were kind.

She nodded. "Are you Thom's brother?"

"I've no brother Thom. Is it Thom's brother you're expecting?"

"Yes," she said. "Denis Flynn. He works in a factory. Do you know him?"

"Denis the factory man would describe half of what's living at the foot of this island, miss."

"His parish is Poughkeepsie."

"Poughkeepsie! That's as far away as the bloody North Pole. He might not get here until next week."

He asked where she'd come from and said he was from a county not far from Kilconly too. He could take her to a boardinghouse. He worked for several boardinghouses in the area, as a plucker.

"A plucker?" In her mind, Mam appeared, defeathering a chicken.

"Boardinghouses seek good girls that won't be no trouble. There's trouble enough for house matrons down here. I've got an eye for what's trouble and what's good girls like ye."

He produced a shiny flat box that he opened and offered out to her. Cigarettes. She declined.

"Another notch in yer favor." He struck a match and squinted an eye as smoke drifted into it. "I know a nice place."

It was raining harder now. The fabric of the umbrella drooped between stays. Rivulets streamed from its slope, just missing her face. The bags by her feet were getting drenched, and if she didn't go with him, she'd soon be drenched too, and what respectable place would have her, looking a fright? She guessed by now that Thom's brother wasn't coming. She hadn't spoken to Thom about the arrangements. If the place Denis lived was so far away, perhaps he'd sent someone for them. But that someone would be looking for a couple, not a girl by herself.

She decided to go with the man. What else could she do? But then Mam was in her head, calling her a gom, asking what had gotten into her to think of walking off into wide America with this stranger already bending to take up her bags? Bridey saw how easily the bags might be spirited away, and that would leave her with only Thom's money belt under her skirts.

"No, thank ye," she said. "I'll wait. He'll be here, I know."

Now the man straightened and peered at her through smoke from the cigarette at the side of his mouth. With two gloved fingers, he reached for the cigarette and waved it around for emphasis as he said, "It's night soon and a girl like you don't want to be at the mercy of men who occupy this place at night."

She imagined herself kidnapped. She fingered the corner of the prayer book in her pocket. Perhaps she should follow him.

Then she heard bells. There was a church nearby. She'd find refuge there.

Once she and Thom had run into a church to escape her father. He'd seen them together and had come after them. They'd slid into the front pew just as a Mass was beginning. She'd turned again and again to see her father filling the church doorway, but he couldn't come after them in a church. They'd stayed in the pew for another

Mass, and another. Finally, when she looked to the door, her father was gone.

The man tipped his hat and said he'd be back in an hour and he guessed she'd be grateful to go with a gentleman then. He tossed away the stub of his cigarette, rolled his umbrella into a walking stick, and, leaning on it, receded into the crowd.

She waited until the bells rang out again and followed the peals that sounded above the din of clopping hooves and whips cutting the air and screeches of trolleys and wheels clattering over stone. She weaved around corners and through narrow streets until she saw a steeple rising between flat-topped buildings. Who at home would believe there were buildings as high as a steeple?

She found the church set back from the street. Iron gates guarded its entrance. THE CHURCH OF THE HOLY ROSARY said a sign there. The gates were open, and as Bridey passed through them, a statue of Mary glowed in the dusk, gazing at her invitingly, with open arms. Bridey mounted shallow concrete steps leading to the front door. The door was of heavy brass-studded wood and it took a few tries at a metal pull to achieve an opening wide enough to push herself and her bags through. The church was dark. She stood, waiting for her eyes to adjust. Then she saw, as at home, a marble font of holy water breasted out of a wall. She dropped her bags, slipped off a glove, dipped the tips of two fingers in the water, and made the sign of the cross. The church smelled like home, its air fragrant with lingering incense and ashes and dust. The church was magnificent. Its center aisle was wide as a brook. The altar seemed a furlong away. Brass and gold glinted on white linens covering the altar. Behind the altar gleamed a crucifix as big as the wall.

She'd thought the church was empty but the squeak of a kneeler made her look up and see a figure silhouetted against a bank of flickering offertory candles.

Now came heels clicking from another direction. A priest. He turned and saw her and the hem of his cassock lifted and lowered as he approached the back of the church, where she stood.

The kneeler squeaked again. The figure rose and Bridey saw it was a woman great with child. The woman receded into the shadows. A side door moaned as it opened and closed.

"Welcome, daughter." The priest had been fingering beads, but he dropped the beads and reached out both hands. The beads didn't fall to the floor; they were attached to his robe. "Are you in need?"

A few minutes later, he was leading her through a courtyard and down a lane to the Mission of Our Lady of the Rosary for the Protection of Irish Immigrant Girls. He said that she needn't carry her bags, that they'd send a man from the mission to fetch them, and they did.

6

Bridey

The Battery, New York City

April 1908

For the first time in weeks she woke in a bed that wasn't in motion. She didn't move, not wanting to disturb the girl next to her. She was afraid of waking the other girls in the bed too. She hadn't met them yet. Mrs. Boyle said they turned in early because they got up early to get to work.

Bridey could tell by the gray light in the room that it was morning. She saw numbers painted on the black headboard, brushed on crudely in white: 1, 2, 3, 4. Her place was 3. She shifted her cheek on the mattress to avoid a straw poking through and saw that beneath the white numbers on the headboard were shadows of other numbers, gold-painted in elegant script. The gold numbers could still be seen, rising like ghosts beneath the black paint, 1, 2, 3. There was no 4, which meant that three used to share this bed instead of four. Bridey longed for the luxury of that earlier time until she realized that, as she was last to be taken in, there wouldn't have been a place for her then.

Above the headboard was a sign stating the rules for washing sheets.

The girl beside her gave out a soft fart. Bridey didn't mind. She was used to sharing a bed. She'd slept with her sisters. And Thom, of course. But she didn't have to try to avoid contact with him or her sisters as now she tried to avoid nudging the girls on either side of her. The girl beside her shifted and groaned, which set off groans from the other side of the bed.

"Ah, the biddy's been at it again, grabbing FOBs."

"What's this one's name?"

"Ay, sleepynog. Fresh-off-the-boat! We're talking to you!"

Bridey sat up, feeling it was undignified to introduce herself to strangers while reclining. Her nightcap had come off on the pillow. "My name is Brighid," she said as she put it back on. "Bridey, they call me."

"Ah, that was me best friend's name in little school," said the girl lying to her left with a sigh. "I'm Maura and that's Fran and that's—"

"I can tell her myself, thanks very much," said a girl, sitting up. She held out her hand to be shaken. "I'm Mary Ryan. And I've got first dibs on the loo." She laughed as she slid out of bed, then: "Oh, the floor's a blessed block of ice this morning!"

Breakfast was at six. Mrs. Boyle had informed Bridey the night before that if she wanted to eat breakfast, she had better come to table then, because once breakfast was cleared, the next meal served would be supper at seven. There was no midday dinner. Most girls were working girls who wouldn't be there for it and Mrs. Boyle ran a home, not a short-order establishment, thank you.

Bridey thought the breakfast was the most delicious one she'd ever had: white bread, the same fluffy kind as had come from the lady with the basket, three choices of marmalade, and tea or coffee with milk and sugar in cubes—something she'd never seen before.

Mrs. Boyle led the grace, then went around making conversation with girls at each of the tables, reminding them that there was only one cube per girl, saying she'd had to put a limit on cubes after certain girls took to pocketing them.

There were eight girls at Bridey's table and at six thirty, Mrs. Boyle rang a big brass bell, and all the girls stood and filed out of the room. Most were going to a factory, she learned, and within a week, Bridey was going with them. The factory made the new kind of blouses called shirtwaists—or at least, the style was new to Bridey. It was like a man's shirt with a long row of front buttons, tailored to be tucked in, as a man's was, at the waist. She learned from the other girls that it had been worn here for some time. In fact, some of the girls said shirtwaists were going out of fashion and they were already worrying about their jobs, thinking the factory might go out of business if the men who ran it didn't switch to whatever style women on Fifth Avenue would want to wear next.

The workday went from seven thirty to four thirty and Bridey was exhausted by the end of it. She felt herself to be one of the machines, putting her hands through the same motions hour after hour: push, pull, thread, repeat. But she earned six dollars a week, more than she'd imagined ever earning in her life, more than a month of Thom's wages. She was a stitcher assigned to one of the darkest tables—daylight fell on just the one row of machines that was near the window. Mary Ryan was at the light table, having ascended to senior stitcher in the three years she'd been there. Bridey worked her machine by the light of a gas lamp that lit the back of the room day and night. The factory never stopped; it worked by night too, though Bridey didn't work then and none of the mission girls did. Who would chaperone them back and forth from Washington Place late at night and in the wee hours of morning?

Bridey walked home with other girls and was usually first to put her hand on the brass knob in the shape of a cross centered on the heavy wooden door. When she turned it and entered the building, she always breathed in relief, coming home to where she felt safe. New York City was an exciting but dangerous place. The streets were crowded with carts and two-horse taxis and motorbuses and gigs and delivery trucks fancily lettered with the name of what they were delivering. Today, Celebrated Hats narrowly missed a knot of high-hatted men gathered in calm conversation as omnibuses swerved around them and trolleys whipped by on iron rails embedded in the cobblestones. A girl could get killed in New York by just standing still.

But she wouldn't write that in her first letter home. She meant to write her first letter on Sunday. Sitting at the machine had given her plenty of time to think what to say.

Before she and Thom left, she'd imagined writing home. She'd thought that she and Thom would go to a photographiste shop and take a wedding picture that could be enclosed with the letter. Her mother would be glad to see her beautiful in the borrowed dress; her father would be beside himself for a while, but after a tear in the pubs, he'd come around.

But Thom Flynn was dead. And Bridey was living in a place so far away from her family, it might as well be the moon.

She'd write about having a job and eating bread that tasted like cake. She'd enclose a gray-green dollar note they could exchange for a bright pound to take away some of the sting of her letter. She lifted at the prospect of her mother being able to sew new dresses for the girls to wear at Christmas this year.

7

Bridey

Downtown and Uptown, New York City

August 1908

Rise and shine!" Mary Ryan nudged Bridey awake at five thirty. The oppressive August heat that had kept them awake last night had lifted. Mrs. Boyle wouldn't let them sleep on the fire escapes as their neighbors did. The wet sheet they'd hung in front of the window to cut the heat was now dry and Mary pulled it down on her way out of the room to the hallway—the air now allowed through the window was sweet and resonant with coos of mourning doves.

"*Rise* is a word that Marys shouldn't take lightly today," said Bridey in a whisper so as not to wake others. It was the Feast of Our Lady, the day the Virgin Mary was assumed into heaven, body and all. This year, it fell on a Saturday, and that was especially lucky for Catholic girls as they got a half day of work on this holiday and Saturday was already a shortened day, which meant half of seven hours instead of nine. The bishop himself was said to have intervened with New York's bosses to make sure Catholic workers could fulfill holy days of obligation.

Bridey and Mary were going to the six a.m. Mass at the chapel downstairs so they wouldn't have to go to Mass later. But the Assumption wasn't all they were observing today. It was also Mary's birthday. To celebrate after work, Mary was spending money sent by an uncle and treating herself and Bridey to a trolley-car ride to a secret destination uptown.

As Bridey lay in bed, waiting for the lavatory, she said a prayer that today would bring on her turns. She was tempted to reach down and touch herself, to check, but what if Maura next to her on the bed wasn't sleeping but awake to see this under the cover? She knew Maura Callahan would report her lickety-split to Mrs. Boyle, and Mrs. Boyle would turn Bridey out, kicking her to the street for a display of immoral behavior. Bridey restrained herself until she was alone in the jacks and could pull down her knickers. The linen was unspotted, its whiteness a reproach. Bridey counted on her fingers, as she'd done many times. It would be four months soon. She hadn't needed rags since she was in Ireland. But—

She couldn't be expecting. Each morning, she put a hand to her stomach to feel for a pulse of something growing within. Each morning, she was reassured by the fact she felt nothing. And you couldn't conceive the first time you did it—this was a fact that everyone knew and that had been confirmed to her by Aideen Muldoon with whom she'd worked the white-elephant booth at the Christmas bazaar. Aideen had been to France and knew everything.

The waistbands of both of her dresses had become tighter, which dismayed her, but surely the explanation was that food was starchier here and more plentiful. She'd have to cut down.

Bridey hadn't shared her worries with anyone, not even Mary. But the girls had comforted her without knowing they did so. Soon after she arrived, Jewel Whelan remarked on how strange it was that girls who lived together came to be synchronized. Perhaps, Bridey thought, her body was slow to get in step, like a dull dance partner who takes forever to learn

Or—this was more likely—perhaps her body was like Mary's. Mary had reported that when she first came to America, it took months for "Miss Pinkerton" to catch up with her. She attributed this to the strain of so many new things to adapt to—different foods, water, weather, and what was hardest for a country girl to get used to, the constant presence of noise. Even Mary, who hailed from Limerick, complained of the noise. The clatter of horse hooves on uneven stone, claps of whips by impatient coach drivers, toots of bus horns, foghorns on the water (their windows faced the Battery), and often, they were wakened by the shouts of men in brawls that spilled out of taverns and into the street. Further conspiring against sleep was the fact that it was never completely dark in their room—gaslight from lampposts and carriage lamps flickered up from the streets. Here, torches weren't required to walk at night. Bridey had had to wean herself away from needing the dark to sleep—she hadn't realized that darkness broken only by moon or stars was a gift.

All these shifts could doubtless account for her body's reluctance to resume its old, reliable ways.

Rolling up her stockings, fastening her corset, Bridey thought of Thom, as she did many times each day. She wasn't a virgin but a secret widow! She nursed this flame burning in her, concealed from the rest of the world.

Surely Thom, looking down, wouldn't allow anything bad to happen to her.

Bridey and Mary pushed bobby pins through the lace of their chapel veils as they passed through the kitchen, nodding to Sister Bertram, who wore an apron over her habit and was pushing a wooden spoon back and forth in a big bubbling pot. It was porridge this morning. Bridey's stomach rumbled—but they couldn't eat a thing before going to Mass. Taking Communion required fasting from midnight. If you ate after midnight and received Communion, that was a mortal sin on your soul.

Six a.m. Mass at the mission chapel was only half filled. Most people were going to late-afternoon Mass at Holy Rosary, which Mary said would be standing room only because of the pageant. Each year, congregants gathered from as far away as Canarsie to take in the living tableau of the Virgin Mary ascending to heaven. A schoolgirl was chosen every year to be wrapped in blue and white linens, put into a basket, and pulleyed up into clouds constructed near the ceiling. Holy Rosary was the parish of carpenters from the 608—the Irish local, not the Italian one. Mary said that the life of a young girl could be trusted to the master craft of only the Irish.

The Mass felt endless. Why was it priests went on longer on holy days even though they knew people had to be off to work? By the time Bridey and Mary were crossing themselves to the words that released them—*In nomine Patris, et Filii, et Spiritus Sancti*— the church bells were ringing seven, which meant Mrs. Boyle had cleared breakfast and they had to run, hungry, to catch the omnibus.

The trip uptown to the factory was torturous—ten perspiring bodies pushed together on seats meant for five. Some riders hung off the roof, not having the fare but deciding it was too hot to walk. Every time the pulling horse stopped, the carriage lurched backward, threatening to throw them off the roof and thrusting Bridey and Mary into even closer contact with their seatmates.

When they reached Greene and Washington, Mary tugged the strap, which tugged the driver's ankle, and they finally alighted, lifting their skirts just high enough to clear the vehicle's running board, exhaling at release from the crush of the car.

The Asch Building had elevators, but Bridey and Mary rarely took them. They were usually out of service, but even when they were working, they were slow as molasses, and the girls couldn't wait for them without risking the forelady marking them tardy, which meant their pay would be docked. Every three minutes you were late cost you fifteen minutes of pay. Also, taking the stairs meant they could avoid Mr. Zito, the elevator operator, who spent slow trips leering at them.

Bridey almost fainted on the stairs to the ninth floor. She was not only hungry but hot, and the heat got worse as they climbed higher and higher. Just in time, Bridey thought, they mounted the last step, pushed open the door, and hurried down the dark corridor. The wide floorboards groaned and creaked beneath the *tap-tap-tap* of their heels, a sound Bridey always found terrifying, as if the floors were speaking some sort of a warning.

When they pulled open the heavy door of the cutting floor, the clatter of sewing machines was deafening. Bridey settled onto the stool in front of her machine, grateful for the chance to sit down. But something was wrong. She felt woozy and had to will herself not to faint. The heat was overwhelming. Blackness encroached from either side, distorting her vision. It was as if blinders were slowly enfolding her face. She knew from experience—she'd been a fainter since she was small—that lowering her head and dropping it between her knees would return her to feeling herself again. She pretended to look for something on the floor, a bobbin or a needle, and when she felt better—which took just a moment—she flung herself up to a normal seated position. She glanced around to make sure that no one had noticed. She didn't want to be attracting attention.

The machines were positioned so closely, the women behind them sat elbow to elbow. The woman beside her was an Italian lady who didn't speak English. What fortune it was, Bridey thought, to have immigrated to a country where her own language was known. The woman's name was Rosa. Or Rose. Or Rosita. A fragile child about seven stood by her side. She was there every day, wearing a scissors leashed to her apron, metal glinting about her small fingers as she helped her mother by snipping threads from seams.

Bridey saw that the woman's foot on the pedal had stopped. This startled Bridey. The woman's foot was never idle. Now she was digging in her apron's deep pocket and bringing out a piece of dark-crusted bread. The woman smiled at Bridey and offered it to her. The gesture caught the attention of the child, who, in Bridey's memory, had never spoken.

"Mama!" the child cried.

Bridey longed for the bread—her hunger had returned—but she nodded to the girl, and the mother shrugged and gave it to her. The child took it and forced the whole of it into her mouth, eyeing Bridey as she chewed as if she were afraid Bridey might come and pry it from her teeth.

Bridey's hunger sharpened, and she turned away. From the corner of her eye, she saw Rosa's hand dip again into her pocket, and out came another piece of bread. Bridey took it this time. She bit into it eagerly, and before she swallowed, the mere act of receiving the crust in her mouth had allayed pangs in her stomach. The bread was wonderful, and the pleasure of eating it was twofold: the sweetness of its yeasty taste in her mouth and the anticipation of the next bite of what remained in her hand.

As she swallowed the last of it, she nodded her thanks to Rosa, who alarmed her by pointing to the waist of Bridey's apron and smiling, then holding her arms as if cradling a baby.

The clatter of machines went silent; all Bridey could hear was a ringing in her ears. Her insides welled up and she stood and tried to get the forelady's attention to request permission to go to the lavatory. But the forelady was talking to the foreman and Bridey had no choice but to run from the room without her permission. She reached an empty stall just in time, flipped open the wood lid, knelt, and threw up into the box what had been threatening to come up on the floor. She was surprised to see how much had been in her, and after she was emptied, she pulled the chain and sat back on the dirty tiles. She couldn't be expecting. She had just gotten stout. That woman didn't know her; she had made a mistake.

Bridey heard the door to the loo creak open, and she fumbled in her skirt for a handkerchief and wiped her mouth before coming out of the stall. There was the forelady, standing with hands on her hips.

"Trying for a quarter of a day instead of a half?"

"My...time," Bridey said, willing it to be true, hoping the words said out loud might bring it on.

At noon, she and Mary left by the Washington Place door, which the door guard unlocked after checking their purses. Light felt sharp as knives in their eyes after a morning in the dim factory, and Bridey squinted against it and also against assaults of dust, which she knew to be horse dung.

They were almost run over by a passing fire engine clanging its bell as the captain stood at the helm, whipping the horses to go faster. Bridey crossed herself as she always did when fire engines went by. Mary made fun of her for this, but Bridey couldn't get used to them. Each siren made her imagine people engulfed by flames, and she prayed that the firemen would reach them in time.

Mary had saved up coppers to take them uptown by trolley. The El was closer but Mary wouldn't ride Els, warning Bridey of the dangers inherent in traveling "on stilts." The Els had killed people. A few years before, an El car had fallen off the tracks, dangling above Fifty-Third Street. Mary had shown her a clipping that described the gruesome scene of people falling out windows to their death below. She'd saved the article in her box of keepsakes because it had happened on the very day in 1905 she had come to America. *September 11, a Day of Infamy in New York!*

Bridey was glad to be riding in the earthbound trolley. Mary had pulled her into a seat up front, in the open air, where they were refreshed by a bit of breeze created by the car's movement. As the trolley moved north along iron tracks laid into the dirt, the streets grew more crowded. Pedestrians—men in top hats, women with parasols—walked willy-nilly in front of them, apparently unfazed by the oncoming trolley that Bridey feared was likely to hit them. The blue uniformed conductor used both gloved hands to maneuver the gearshifts and proved to be expert at slowing the car to avoid collisions, though it seemed to Bridey there were some near misses.

Mary gave a nod and soon they were stepping off the trolley's running board to a street that was paved. Bridey spotted a sign.

"Is this Fifth Avenue, then?" she asked. Limestone mansions lined the street. Adelaide was working in one of them, and Bridey felt far from the self she had left behind in Kilconly, the girl who had imagined walking down Fifth Avenue and stopping someone to ask which was the house Adelaide Conroy worked in. She'd written to her sister for Adelaide's address. She meant to come back and knock on a door.

The houses around them were grand and imposing. This area of the city was more dignified than the neighborhood where the mission was located, although now they were made to circumnavigate a very undignified advertisement on the sidewalk. A lady in a black dress was covered by footwear of all shapes and sizes. Slippers dangled off her bodice, metal tins of shoe polish hung over her shoulders, on her head she wore boots fashioned into a hat. SALE PROCEEDING AT HYMAN'S FOOTWEAR said a placard pinned to her blouse. She looked pained, and Bridey averted her eyes. Then the lady turned and glided away from them, and Bridey saw that she was on roller skates. A sign on her back listed the store's address. Gratitude surged in Bridey for the job that she had. She complained of it plenty—the hours, the heat, the boredom—but she was now reminded that working in a factory was better than many jobs she might have been given.

They ducked under a striped awning and Bridey realized the door they were approaching wasn't to a house but a store so big, it took up a street block.

"B. Altman's," Mary said. "It just moved here. It used to be on Ladies' Mile." One Sunday, she'd taken Bridey to Ladies' Mile, a shopping district on Broadway where you could buy anything from all over the world: dry goods and groceries, millinery and haberdashery, even live snakes and dogs and birds. Bridey had been surprised by the prices for creatures that in Kilconly could be gotten for free.

A gloved doorman in a gilt-braided uniform opened the door for them as if they were ladies who'd stepped off a carriage instead of a trolley. As soon as they entered, Bridey sighed in amazement. The store was as grand as the cathedral in Derry she'd once been to on a school retreat. A grand palazzo of pillared floors spiraled above, higher and higher, to a soaring painted dome. In Derry, one of the priests accompanying them had complained of money spent on cathedrals in such a poor country, but Bridey had felt glad of the opportunity to immerse herself in such beauty; it did something to her brain, opening it to grandness she had never imagined. In the rear of the store, a wall (a whole wall!) was covered by the drape of an American flag. It was the largest flag Bridey had ever seen.

They toured the store as if it were a museum, which in effect it was to Bridey, who was not able to afford a purchase. Their heels clacked on the marble as they wandered through departments, admiring counter after counter of posh goods: feathered hats, ostrich fans, gold watch fobs, silk shoes, flouncy dresses of fine tulle.

At a display of shirtwaist blouses, they fingered the embroidery at the necks and assessed the lay of the collars and cuffs, wondering if they'd touched these blouses before. Perhaps they had. The label bore the name of the factory in which they spent most of each day.

They stopped at a long glass counter under which summer

gloves were laid out, and Bridey, just for fun, asked to try on a pair. She pointed to a handsome pair of white cotton gloves with black polka dots and delicate buttons that closed at the wrist. But when the salesgirl pushed the gloves toward her, Bridey decided against trying them on. She didn't want to show the salesgirl her hands, which were red and raw—not the hands of a lady—and so she shook her head and said she had changed her mind.

In Cosmetics, a lady with painted nails dabbed puffballs of powder against their cheeks, their noses, their foreheads, even their necks and invited them to choose from a gallery of lipsticks.

In Coats, Bridey experienced something strange. She had stopped to finger the fur collar of a fine wool and lost sight of Mary, and as she walked down an aisle looking for her, there, coming toward her—Bridey couldn't believe it—was her mother! There was Norah Molloy, plain as day, walking toward her. She knew that her mother could not possibly be there, and yet—there she was. Bridey's skin had prickled all over as she tried to absorb what was happening, what could not be so and yet what her own eyes were seeing.

Then she understood—it was herself. It was her own reflection in a glass affixed to a grand fluted pillar. Bridey's scalp tingled as she saw the resemblance that others had mentioned and that she herself had not been able to see. Now she knew. She looked like her mother. Foreboding rose in her, which she didn't understand until later.

They took a gilded elevator to the fourth floor where a ladies' waiting room was furnished to look like a library in a grand home—overstuffed chairs, mahogany bookcases lined with leather-bound volumes. Bridey and Mary relaxed on a dais, indulging in biscuits dispensed from a silver cart by a woman in a pink apron and what looked like a chapel cap pinned to the back of her head. Bridey couldn't believe the cookies were free.

On the fifth floor, in the Evening Room, they chose fabric samples and were guided to dressing mirrors where they could hold the fabric against themselves under electrified lights that could be adjusted to simulate the light of supper parties, of club dances, of midnight galas and rooftop soirees.

Bridey mused out loud about what it would be like to work in such a grand emporium, imagining being a shopgirl here herself.

"No chance of that," Mary said. "It's NINA here."

"What's NINA?" Bridey asked.

"'No Irish need apply.' Nor any other foreigner either, no Swedes, no Germans, no one who wasn't born in America. They hire foreign only in Brooklyn," Mary said.

If only it were possible to keep her heritage from being on display, Bridey thought. Perhaps she could pretend she was mute. She wouldn't have to speak to dispense biscuits from a cart. But other things besides her tongue would give her away: her pale skin that freckled and reddened in the sun; the look on her face, her eyes downcast instead of alert and assessing, the same expression by which she recognized other immigrants. Even a gait was telling, she thought as she followed Mary's sturdy backside shifting under her skirts.

The top floor was the Wedding floor, and it was crowded with veils, gloves, flowers, and laces in all colors of pastels. Brides-to-be and their mothers were selecting fabrics for gowns at one counter, braids and lace at another, and, at another, a designer sat surrounded by tissue patterns in front of a sign: SPECIALLY SELECTED TO MOST FLATTER A BRIDE, CUSTOMIZED TO AGE AND THE SHAPE OF A FIGURE.

"Let's go down," Bridey said. "I don't feel well."

"Really?" Mary looked surprised. "Is it the top floor? Have you never been on a tenth before?"

"It's not that," Bridey said. Sweat beaded on her brow.

Mary took a handkerchief out of her pocket and pressed it against Bridey's forehead. "You poor thing," she said. "You'll ruin your powder."

Mary steered her to a gilded wall and pressed a button to call for the elevator. Bridey apologized for needing to go home, adding that Mary might stay, but both of them knew that this wasn't an option. Bridey had so little sense of direction, she'd likely walk north and spend the night in a field in the Harlem countryside.

They descended to G, then navigated through the departments, trying to thread their way out of the store. As she followed Mary through aisles gleaming with merchandise under glass, Bridey felt suddenly better. She stared at the girls behind counters. They did, indeed, look very American. It wasn't just the whiteness of their teeth or how they fixed their hair, it was the way they stood upright, unapologetic, free of the deference apparent in the postures of those who had lately come to this country.

A man shouldering a wide roll of carpet hurried in their direction, and Bridey stepped aside to let him pass. As he went by, Bridey lifted a protective hand to her waist and was seized by the meaning of this instinctive gesture, which she'd seen Mam do countless times to keep a baby inside her, safe.

Bridey had a baby inside her.

Her bones went cold as her heart confirmed what she already knew.

She was going to have a baby. She was going to have Thom's baby in America.

She heard Mary calling to her from across a distance.

She braced herself against a glassed-in display of shirt collars and tried to think of what she should do.

8

Sarah

Hollingwood

1908

Sarah turned a brass key on the table lamp and adjusted the shade fringed with pink tassels, redirecting the circle of light to fall on the pages of a new library book in her lap: *The Wonderful Wizard of Oz*.

It was after supper and Sarah had adjourned with her father, brother, and younger sister to the library. Her father was in his favorite chair, attending to his pipe, and Benno and Hannah were at dominoes on the bearskin in front of the fire. From the other side of the wall came distant sounds of Nettie washing dishes. The air was scented by curls from the pipe, smoke from the coals, and ribboned fir boughs decorating the mantel.

Sarah cleared her throat and began reading aloud, starting with a note from the author headed "To My Readers": "'I would much rather be your story-teller than to be the President.'"

Benno gave out a hoot.

Their father removed the pipe from his mouth. "L. Frank Baum would indeed be more fit for the Executive Mansion. He would at least fit!"

President Taft's exact weight was a subject of public conjecture. It was rumored to be over three hundred and fifty pounds.

"It's not called the Executive Mansion anymore," Benno reminded him. "Roosevelt named it the White House, remember?" Their father had hated Roosevelt and now he hated Taft, whom he never called President Taft but President Take Advice from Teddy.

To head off the political discussion started at supper, Sarah went on to the first chapter:

A little girl rose from her seat and walked to the door of the car, carrying a wicker suit-case in one hand and a round bird-cage—

"There's a bird in the story!" Hannah looked up from the tiles and smiled at Sarah as if she'd put a bird in the story herself. Hannah was a lover of all God's creatures great and small. Last week, she'd coaxed a wren into the house, afraid it would freeze, and wouldn't put it out until Nettie told her a bird in the house meant someone was going to die.

"Are you Dorothy Gale?"

"Yes," she—

Fiddlefrogs! The page wouldn't turn; it needed cutting. Sarah pulled open the drawer of the ebonized side table and lifted the paper knife from its bed of green felt. Apparently, this book had been received not by the librarian but by the assistant librarian, who was distracted now that she was finally engaged to be married. Sarah hoped she herself wouldn't have to wait for a proposal until she was an old maid of twenty-six.

The knife was polished bone and shaped like a sword, a souvenir from her parents' wedding trip. They'd toured castles in Scotland. Its hilt glittered with tiny stones; its blade was inscribed with the name of a castle, HAWTHORNDEN, that had all but rubbed away. Sarah positioned the knife at the top of the page and sliced. Touching the blade gave Sarah the same pang she always felt when she touched something her mother had used often. The house was full of such items: the sewing scissors in the shape of a bird, the cloisonné jewelry box, the silver-backed brush set on the vanity table Sarah shared with Rachel.

Only Rachel was missing from this family tableau, gone with friends to the Majestic to see *The Christmas Carol*. The film was just fifteen minutes long, but there would be caroling afterward, so it was too early for her father to be doing what he was doing, which was shifting the bit of his pipe back and forth in his mouth while inclining his head in the direction of the front door.

From where Sarah was sitting, she could see the front door and she glanced at her father to tell him no one was there. That was a quirk of this house; due to reflections in glass doors and curves in some walls, you could see around a few corners. Sarah's grandfather Phineas had been the house's designer, though he wasn't an architect but a politician. This was an old family story that seemed to suggest that being born a Hollingworth meant you could do anything, or at least whatever you set your mind to.

"You read that part already," said Hannah, and Sarah realized she hadn't turned the page. She found her place and resumed but the reading was interrupted again, this time by Rachel striding in from the front hall.

Rachel was two years younger than Sarah and was free to be a girl as Sarah was not, even when Sarah had been Rachel's age, nineteen. Sarah was the eldest and since their mother had died nine years ago in confinement, Sarah had shouldered the burden of motherhood.

"'God bless us, every one!'" Rachel cried out. Her face was flushed; the shoulders of her mink pelisse were white with snow. "You were right," she said, looking at Sarah. "That film was killing!"

She crossed the room and greeted their father with a peck on the cheek, by which Sarah knew she wanted something from him.

"Dear Father," Rachel said, shrugging off her cape and perching herself on the tapestried ottoman.

"Dear daughter," said their father, playing along.

Sarah was continually dismayed by how easily men—including her father—could be duped by feminine wiles. On the infrequent occasions when Sarah had used them, she'd been immediately seized by regret and embarrassment for both herself and the victim.

Rachel continued. "Dottie Canfield's mother is becoming the new head of Christian Benevolence."

Why would Rachel care about this? Rachel's enthusiasm for church activities revolved around socials, not charitable works.

"Oh?" Their father pushed his glasses farther up on his nose, a gesture he used when feeling in need of defense.

"She's organizing a new mission. She's taking a group by train to New York every Wednesday to work at a home for the poor."

Sarah closed the book, keeping her place with her finger, so as to focus on the information forthcoming about a possible opportunity for weekly excursions into New York.

Their father was silent as he removed his pipe from his mouth. He reached for the tamper, and his attention was suddenly consumed by the little silver stick stirring around and around what was left in the bowl.

"Can I go?" Rachel asked.

"*May* I go," Hannah corrected, moving a tile.

"You're too young," Rachel said to Hannah.

Their father, seemingly satisfied with the mixture, reinserted the pipe in his mouth. The reflection of the fire glinted in his rimless glasses as he looked at Rachel.

"You're too young too," he said. "Too young to subject yourself to the preying ways of scalawags down there."

If Sarah were in Rachel's shoes, she would have reminded her father that nineteen was not the age of a child, that he'd wooed their mother when she was nineteen and married her when she was twenty. Their father saw them as children long past the age when mothers of other girls started plotting bridal paths for them. That she had no mother to do this was a relief to Sarah but also a worry.

Rachel said nothing, either because she didn't think of what Sarah thought of or because the firmness in their father's voice convinced Rachel that pleading her case further was hopeless. She fled upstairs in tears.

But a seed was planted in Sarah: to combine Christian charity with sightseeing trips to New York.

9

Sarah

Hollingwood

1899–1903

Sarah's mother's death had come as a shock to even Doc Spencer, who had been the family's physician for years. Both he and the midwife thought her mother's confinement would be a success. Her mother was a Stanton, meaning she was of sturdy stock. She'd already had four healthy children. She'd taken the strengthening regime recommended to her during the last weeks of her gravidity: lying in bed in the west Yellow Room, looking out at the lake, taking in cold, health-promoting breezes through the door to the Juliet balcony, which even in winter was to be left open for an hour each day. The Yellow Room regimen had proven successful to past bearers of Hollingworth babies too.

Sarah had been twelve. Before leaving for school, she had kissed her mother on each cheek, one peck for her mother and one for the baby. There appeared to be nothing wrong with her; she sat propped up on pillows, looking fine in the pink quilted bed jacket on which Sarah, for a Christmas gift, had embroidered her mother's initials.

"Good-bye, my dear," her mother had said. Later, Sarah re-played these words again and again, gauging them for the weight of finality.

That afternoon, she'd walked home from her sixth-form class at Mrs. Flanders to find no one in the kitchen—not Cook, not Nettie; it was too soon for Benno and Hannah to be home from elementary. Sarah had hung up her coat and hat in the front hall and gone upstairs to see her mother. There was stillness in the house and this was unusual and should have warned Sarah that something was wrong. She didn't notice the stillness, so intent was she on greeting her mother and asking if she could go skating with Lil that evening. The lake was still frozen. There would be a full moon, and this might be the last chance of the year.

Her mother's door was closed, which usually meant that the midwife was there. Sarah's habit was to listen at the door before knocking. But before she reached the door, her father opened it and came out. Why was her father home in the afternoon?

Her father closed the door behind him and looked at her, but he said nothing, just reached into a pocket in his vest and pulled out a watch and clicked open its case. He tilted it so that he could read its face. It seemed to glow in the dim hallway, a tiny moon.

"Father?" she said.

He looked up and she saw what she'd never seen before or since.

Her father's eyes were red and wet. He had been crying.

He spoke with difficulty. "Your mother and the baby—have gone to rest."

His eyes moved to the watch, which he snapped shut abruptly, closing the gold fitting over its face, then he stuffed it, chain and all, into his waistcoat pocket, and to her dismay, he walked away, his slippers silent on the runner leading to the stairwell.

Sarah watched him slowly descend the spiral; first his feet disappeared, then his legs, his shoulders, and finally his head, and it wasn't until he was gone altogether that she apprehended the meaning of what he had told her. Her mother and the new baby weren't resting—they were dead.

Sarah's instinct was to run away from the door, but something pulled at her, drawing her to the portal that stood between her and her mother. Her hand hovered over the knob, then she put her fingers on the cut glass. If the doorknob turned from the other side, it would be a sign that she'd misunderstood her father, she should enter. Her fingers lay listening, as when she rested them on a Ouija planchette. But the knob remained dumb. Sarah bent forward, put her ear to the keyhole. She heard nothing.

Her hand, of its own volition, twisted the knob. It was dim in the room. The curtains were closed. She could barely make out the gray lump in the bed. The midwife, Mrs. Dunstable, was there, silhouetted by the window. Her back was to Sarah; she was busy with something.

Sarah moved toward her mother's bed. The air smelled of some sort of metal. She bent to kiss her mother's sleeping face, but when her lips touched her cheek, she pulled away, shocked by how cold it was, not like her mother's skin at all.

"Sarah, dear," said Mrs. Dunstable, walking toward her, her arms full of dirty sheets to be washed. "God has called your mother to Him. He's let her take the baby, so they wouldn't be parted. Do you want to kiss your little sister good-bye?"

Then Sarah saw that the bundle in Mrs. Dunstable's arms wasn't just sheets—the sheets were wrapped about a small, dark motionless form.

She turned and hurried out of the room, pulling the door so that it shut loudly behind her.

Close the door, don't slam it, her mother would say—but now what her mother would say didn't matter.

Sarah ran down the hall to her bedroom. She closed its door and threw herself on her quilt. She sobbed onto its silken blue stars, then slid down to the floor, knelt by the bed to pray, but reached under the bed skirting for the dress box she kept there. She took off its top and pulled back the tissue and there lay her once-beloved lady dolls. They had been birthday gifts from her mother. She hadn't played with them in a long time. She gathered them up, all three, and hugged their porcelain limbs and sawdust bodies, not caring about crushing their satin dresses or tiny silk hats, burying her wet face in their real hair, guessing she would never play with them again.

There came an outpouring of condolences from friends and relatives, neighbors, and men who worked at the factory. A wreath of white flowers tied with black ribbon, a gift from the church, was delivered and affixed to one of the front double doors. Cards and flowers and sympathy pies were delivered. The foods came in dishes wrapped in tea towels, brought by children of cooks who worked in other houses, to the back kitchen door. Their own cook, Mrs. Simpson, who lived in the gatehouse with Mr. Simpson, who chopped wood and mowed, accepted the dishes with gratitude. Good cook as she was, it would have been impossible for her to keep up with feeding the waves of guests, all of whom, it seemed, arrived hungry.

"Death makes the living ravenous," she said, putting together another tray of ham salad sandwiches. She spoke matter-of-factly, which stung Sarah, who was delivering an empty tray to the kitchen, though she knew that the loss of her mother was a blow to Mrs. Simpson too; she had been with them for years.

The west parlor was usually a jovial place where cards were played and parties given after the rugs had been rolled up and the furniture removed to the barn. On quiet family evenings, her mother had played their favorite songs on the piano as corn popped in the hearth or while they competed in charades, but now the room was steeped in eerie solemnity, lit by tapers aglow on brass sticks under the mirror draped in black crepe.

From seven in the morning until ten at night, visitors came to pay their respects, walking into the house without banging the brass lion, quietly pushing open the wreathed door, and, without waiting to be greeted, turning into the parlor. There was Sarah's mother in a black coffin, holding a prayer book, laid out on white satin that was puckered like the inside of a fancy candy box. The casket was in the same corner of the room where Sarah's older brother had lain years before in a much smaller box. Her mother's hands were a strange color, darker, as if they'd been carved out of laundry soap. Sarah averted her eyes from the hands and stared at her mother's face instead. The face was reminiscent of her mother's, but it was not her mother's, as a painted portrait recalls the image of the sitter but isn't the sitter. She pictured her real mother floating invisibly above, looking down on her, holding the baby.

Sarah didn't cry then, though she'd wanted to. She listened, nodding politely, as people spoke kindly of her mother. She felt it was important to stay dry-eyed so as to set an example. Rachel was ten and Benno was eight. Both, like Sarah, had been excused from school for the week. They spent whole days crying, their faces red and swollen, their new black-bordered handkerchiefs perpetually soggy. Nettie took the handkerchiefs from them every night and washed and ironed them before morning. She said it helped to be busy.

Poor Hannah, the youngest, just four years old, kept asking for Mother; why couldn't she come back? Hannah said she needed her for only a moment.

Sarah cried only in places where she couldn't be seen, taking refuge by the lake or in the room at the top of the turret or in the hiding place on the second floor between the wall and the spiral staircase that had been made when the stairs were moved from the front of the hall to the rear. Only alone was she able to cry. She felt her mother's loss was personal, as if a hand had come down and scooped out her insides.

Their aunt Gert came for the funeral and didn't leave. Instead of a wreath, Aunt Gert brought a sapling. It looked like a mummy wrapped in thick layers of gauze. Their father spent an afternoon in his shirtsleeves digging a hole for it in the front yard. He put it in the middle of the yard, he said, so that when it grew big, they'd see it from any front window and be reminded of her. The sapling was a stick no higher than Sarah's waist. She couldn't imagine it growing into a tree.

Aunt Gert moved into the room on the third floor that adjoined Hannah's bedroom. Sarah was relieved that the Yellow Room, where her mother had lain, hadn't been given to Aunt Gert, although she was surprised that Aunt Gert didn't request it, as it was the nicest sleeping room in the house.

Aunt Gert wasn't really their aunt; she was their mother's first cousin. Sarah had met her only once before, at a family wedding. Aunt Gert herself had never been married. Sarah and Rachel guessed that she never would be because she was not only old, but she was broad in places where a lady ought to be narrow and narrow in places where she ought to be broad.

When Sarah's mother died, Aunt Gert had been caring for an invalid uncle in Baltimore. A nurse had been hired for him so that Aunt Gert could come north and take care of Sarah and her siblings. This was a kindness on the part of not only Gert but the uncle.

It seemed a bad match at the start. Aunt Gert was of the Baltimore branch of the Stantons, and though the war had been won, many differences remained between those living below the Mason-Dixon and those living above.

Aunt Gert's speech was different—she pronounced *aunt* with a short *a,* as if she were an insect—but more than that, she brought notions that struck Sarah and her father and siblings as strange: that children should address their elders as *ma'am* or *sir,* that tea could be iced any time of year, not just summer. Her father had had to gently dissuade her from restarting the clocks and unveiling the mirrors weeks before mourning custom dictated.

Once things had settled enough to return to routine, Sarah had been at the breakfast table with Aunt Gert (like everyone else in the house, Sarah was expected to arrive on time at the table, though she still couldn't eat much) when she saw Aunt Gert lean back in her chair and peer under the tablecloth, and Sarah knew she was feeling with her shoe toe on the carpet for the buzzer under a bump in the floral design. Aunt Gert found the buzzer and pressed her heavy shoe against it, calling for the cook.

Sarah knew that Mrs. Simpson wouldn't like this. Sarah's mother had used the buzzer only when entertaining, and then only to call for Nettie or whoever was waiting table, never for the cook, whose meat pies and lemon tarts excited such talk that if she ever had reason to seek employment elsewhere, her mother said, Mrs. Simpson could write her own ticket.

Mrs. Simpson would know the buzzer wasn't meant for Nettie. It was laundry day and Nettie was in the basement preparing lye for the wash. So through the swinging door of the pantry Mrs. Simpson came, rolling her white sleeves down over her jowly arms, asking if the breakfast had been what was wanted. Aunt Gert said it was. The hotcakes had been hot and the bacon crisp and delicious. Then Aunt Gert presented her with a piece of paper on which she had penned, in neat hand, a list of menus for the week.

Mrs. Simpson's cap descended lower on her brow as she read the list, then, looking up, she straightened and spoke not to Aunt Gert but to the oil portrait of Sarah's mother hanging above the silver tea service. She regretted to inform the good lady of the South that most of the ingredients for the dishes could not be had until summer.

After that, Aunt Gert didn't bother Mrs. Simpson, who continued to cook what she had been cooking for years; after all, that was what the family wanted.

Another complication arose in Aunt Gert's treatment of Nettie. Nettie was part of the family, but this was something Aunt Gert couldn't abide.

"Where I come from, decent good manners requires knowing your place, and knowing your place is a comfort to everyone." In her opinion, help didn't mix with the helped, for the sake of them both.

But Nettie wasn't just help, they all explained—first her father, then Sarah, then Rachel and Benno. Each one described Nettie's unique situation, but Aunt Gert observed that they seemed to care less about who the girl was than they did about all the many things she was *not*.

Nettie had come to them before Sarah was born. She'd been the child of former slaves in Kentucky who, twenty years ago, had moved from Lexington to Wellington to work in the blast furnaces. Both of Nettie's parents had died in the blizzard of '88, so when Nettie was five, she'd become a ward of the town, and the town had looked for a family to take her. The Hollingworths had been approached, not only because they had space to accommodate her, but because they were known to possess the temperament to benefit from a "livey-in," which most of their neighbors, self-reliant New Englanders, staunch cherishers of privacy, couldn't abide.

And so Nettie came to them when the oldest Hollingworth child, the first little Benjamin, named after their father, had been four. They'd called him Benjie. Their mother appreciated the help Nettie provided by simply being a child, a playmate to Benjie. Nettie engaged him in ways nobody else could.

One day, without anyone noticing he'd left the yard, Benjie wandered down to the lake and drowned.

After that, Nettie didn't talk for a year.

Sarah had been too young to remember this, but she'd heard the story. After Benjie died, Nettie had just—stopped talking. Old Doc was called but he couldn't figure out what was wrong. Everything else about her was normal.

After her playmate died, Nettie stopped going to school. The teacher had sent her home, thinking her impudent for refusing to talk. Nettie never went back. She followed Sarah's mother around all day, helping with chores. Then one day, Sarah's mother was making a bed and stubbed her toe on the bedpost.

"Oh, I am stupid this morning," she said, to which Nettie replied, "No, you are not!"

Nettie continued to speak as if speaking were nothing unusual for her, as if she had never ceased doing it, and after that it seemed as if she couldn't stop speaking, as if to make use of all the words she'd stored up for a year.

Nettie didn't want to go back to school. She seemed content to stay at home, helping "Mama Worth," who didn't object, as there was no law saying she had to go to school. Nettie was good company and adept at chores, learning canning and gardening and washing and darning and sometimes doing these tasks faster and better than Sarah's mother, having come up with a way to do them more cleverly.

Nettie was seventeen when Aunt Gert arrived and by then she had carved out—or it had been carved out for her—a delicate position in the Hollingworth family. Part companion, part housekeeper, part maiden aunt, which meant she played nurse to any member of the family who needed her, even those who lived out of town. She was sent to Hartford to help out for a week when Hollingworths there were felled by the grippe.

At home, Nettie did the washing and the marketing and harvested crops from the garden, which Mrs. Simpson cooked and which Nettie enjoyed at the dining table with the family when guests weren't dining with them. When guests were in, Nettie waited table and ate in the kitchen with Mrs. Simpson.

Sitting at the table with Nettie was something that Aunt Gert couldn't get used to, though it had been thirty years since the Proclamation. The first few nights Aunt Gert was with them, she pointedly ignored Nettie at the table, and wouldn't accept dishes passed from her hands. One night, she resisted coming to the table altogether, complaining she was having one of her spells and would need to take dinner upstairs in her room. Sarah wondered if this would be the pattern, that they'd dine without their aunt except when company joined them and Nettie stayed in the kitchen.

But as soon as their father had led them in grace, he put down his napkin and went upstairs and knocked on her door and spoke to her, and when he returned, Nettie, who hadn't touched a thing, lifted her plate and said she didn't mind eating in the kitchen.

"Sit down!" her father boomed, sounding as if he were angry with her, which Sarah knew he was not, and it pained them all to see a tear fall from Nettie's bowed head onto her plate.

"I'm sorry," said her father. "I'm sorry for everything."

Sarah worried about Nettie's feelings, which must surely be hurt, but when she took Nettie aside to apologize for her aunt's ways, Nettie shushed her, perhaps worried that her aunt would overhear them. She said she didn't mind and that Sarah mustn't mind either.

Aunt Gert slowly changed her thinking about Nettie, and not because Nettie tried to win her over, but because she didn't. Nettie simply went about her work as she always had, treating Aunt Gert as a housekeeper would treat a piece of furniture too heavy to move, something that must be worked around. After a few weeks,

Aunt Gert began talking to Nettie, even at the table, asking her to pass the saltcellar or butter dish, just as she'd ask others in the family to do.

Their father praised Aunt Gert's change of heart, explaining to the children, out of the hearing of their aunt and of Nettie, how hard it was to abandon ways you've thought were the right ones for forty-three years.

One thing Aunt Gert didn't change, though Sarah's father wished her to change it, was her avid belief in the value of temperance. She drank pots of green tea, which she recommended for health, but none of the family could acquire the habit.

Soon after Aunt Gert appeared with the family at church, she was invited by someone in the next pew to join the Wellington chapter of the Female Christian Temperance Society. Soon, their aunt banished wine from their table, which wasn't a hardship for anyone but their father, and even for him, *hardship* would have been too strong a word, as he never drank more than a glass or two. But Sarah knew it was an annoyance he felt obliged to conceal. An exception to the rule was allowed when guests dined, in which case a glass was always offered to Aunt Gert, which she predictably refused, looking sorrowfully down at her plate.

Aunt Gert stayed with them for four years, and although she never replaced their mother, or tried to, she became part of their lives in ways that Sarah wouldn't appreciate for a decade.

The tenderest time Sarah recalled having spent with Aunt Gert occurred soon after she came to them. It was a day in spring and Sarah was walking home from school, having been dismissed early because of a stomachache. After crossing the bridge, she'd felt something strange on her thigh, and she ducked into the woods to pull up her skirts and see what was bothering her—she guessed it was some sort of flying insect. She was horrified to discover a trickle of blood on her leg. She grabbed leaves to wipe it away. She thought she was dying. She pictured her father losing first a son, then a wife and infant, and now his eldest daughter, on whom he doted. How would he manage? She limped the rest of the way home, not because her leg was impaired but because all her powers of perception were trained on the leg, alert to the possibility of a recurrence. Her skirts were white and she trembled to think of the spectacle that blood would make on the eyelet cotton. She walked home the back way and, passing the garden fence, saw Aunt Gert on the kitchen porch, bent over her mending bag.

As soon as she saw Sarah, she rose from the wicker table.

"What happened?" Her aunt looked alarmed and Sarah worried that her skirts had been ruined. She glanced down and was relieved to see this was not so. She couldn't speak. She didn't know what to say. She began to cry and Aunt Gert took her schoolbag from her and slid arms about her and drew her to the wicker sofa, where they sat together, Gert stroking her hair like her mother used to do, saying, "It can't be so bad," which made Sarah sob because she knew it was worse.

Finally, she said, "There was blood . . ." She didn't even have to finish the sentence.

"You poor child," Aunt Gert said, then she whispered a torrent of assuring words in her ear—"normal" and "healthy" and "becoming a woman"—and when Sarah felt calm (though confused), she composed herself enough to enter the house and greet Mrs. Simpson, who was peeling potatoes for supper, and then follow Aunt Gert up two flights of stairs to her bedroom, where she opened, with difficulty, an overstuffed bottom drawer and brought out a box of white knitted towels and safety pins.

Later that night, a painful case of sumac poisoning—those leaves!—broke out on her upper thigh, which was most embarrassing, but her aunt got up to nurse her with a plaster of ragweed and calamine lotion. Her case lasted days and Sarah was relieved that her aunt mentioned her ministrations to no one.

Aunt Gert stayed with them until Sarah turned sixteen, which was old enough for a girl to mother her siblings. One morning her father drove Aunt Gert to the train to New York, where she would meet a cousin's husband's sister who wanted a companion in Virginia. It was May and Sarah said good-bye to her aunt on the gravel drive as her father slid her trunk and valises into the rear of the carriage. As she waved good-bye to the carriage, Sarah felt a gust of relief. Turning back toward the house, she saw that the windows were open and the curtains were blowing out. It seemed to Sarah that the house, like her, was exhaling with the expanse of new freedom, and Sarah felt guilty for the gladness she felt in Gert's going. It took years before she realized the magnitude of the gift that Aunt Gert had given to her and her family.

10

Sarah

Wellington, Connecticut

December 1908

Sarah sometimes worried that she'd end up like Aunt Gert. She was twenty-one now and several of her friends had already married. Her father sometimes joked that he wished his daughters to remain bachelor maids. Fear rose in Sarah whenever he said this. As the eldest, she'd be responsible for him in his dotage and she worried that his message was coded for her.

Her sister Rachel, unburdened by this concern, entertained the modern notion that she might not marry at all. She pointed out that unlike most girls, they didn't *have* to marry, meaning that because their grandfather had started a brass-works factory that was the biggest employer in town, they were relieved of having to find husbands to support them.

Sarah needn't marry for money, but if she was to be happy, she certainly needed to marry for love!

Sarah had known Edmund since they were children. He wasn't a playmate, but Wellington was a small town, so you couldn't not know someone who had also grown up there. Their families had both picnicked at the town grove, paraded down Main Street on Decoration Day to the cemetery to put flags on soldiers' graves, attended church socials and lectures by speakers who traveled great distances to deliver enlightenments.

She'd always liked Edmund. He was a quiet boy who let his actions speak louder than his words. Once, as a teenager, he'd stayed out all night with search parties walking the woods to help find a little boy who had wandered away from a gypsy encampment. Edmund had been the one to find him shivering inside the hollow trunk of a tree.

"I'm no hero, I just have good eyesight" was the modest quote that appeared next to Edmund's photo on the front page of the *Wellington Record.* Sarah had cut out the picture and pressed it into her diary.

Edmund was a few years older than Sarah. He'd attended Yale, where he'd stayed not four years but seven in order to go to law school, and he'd graduated near the top of his class, according to not just hearsay but the *Wellington Record.*

She'd heard he was making the grand tour of Europe, so now she was surprised to see him seated in the row ahead of her at the foundlings' Christmas pageant in the church basement. She began speaking more loudly to her brother next to her in the hopes that her voice would carry and cause Edmund to turn. It did. And when he turned (how glad she was to be wearing the new yellow dress Mrs. Hauptmere had just finished), he insisted on exchanging seats with her so that her view of the stage would not be obstructed. Sarah took Edmund's place next to his cousin Millie, who wanted to chat, but Sarah resisted Millie's conversational advances, pretending to study the program so she could eavesdrop on the talk behind her. Edmund and her brother discussed schools—her brother would graduate from Trowbridge next year and, like most students in his class, was going to Yale.

Listening to them, Sarah entertained a possible future in which the two would be brothers-in-law, chatting over a breakfast table. She guessed that if she and Edmund married, she'd have to leave Hollingwood and move into the Porter House on Vine Street. Or would Edmund wish to build a house of their own? Edmund's father had died last year and Edmund was taking a position at Squire, Boggs, and Porter (his father had been the Porter), but she supposed he'd want a few years of practice under his belt before assuming the expense of building a house.

Throughout the changing tableaux of manger scenes, which children enacted each year to show gratitude for the congregation's largesse, Sarah could barely keep her attention on the stage, so conscious was she of Edmund's eyes on her upswept hair. She couldn't help putting her gloved hand to it to see that the combs were still in place. The combs were her best velvet-trimmed ones—she was glad of that too.

Usually after the children's speeches of gratitude, Sarah enjoyed sampling sweets and snacks set out on doilied tables by the refreshments committee, but this year, she refrained from indulging in even Mrs. Hazelden's cook's tea tassies, wanting to impress Edmund with her ladylike virtue of self-restraint.

She was thrilled that he seemed to want to talk only to her. He told her of seeing London Bridge in a fog and of catching a glimpse of King Edward in a carriage. They talked of the new penny with Abraham Lincoln on it instead of an Indian and she wondered if it would still work at penny arcades. She told him of finding a ten-dollar bill in a new pair of shoes she had bought. She'd taken it to the pharmacist, who'd examined it under his microscope and declared it to be genuine, and she was giving half of it to the orphans tonight.

When conversation flagged, he brought her a teacup of punch from the bowl, which she let him refill only once, demurely shaking her head at his offers of more.

"Will you be at the Redfields' ball?" he asked, and how glad she was to be able to say yes.

For the first time in Sarah's twenty-one years, her father would allow her to attend the annual masquerade. Guests were invited from out of town, including foreigners about whom little was known but their country of origin, and despite this they were encouraged to conceal their identities with masks, which posed too many dangers to Wellington's younger female set, according to her old-fashioned father.

But now—she was of age!

"What are you going as?" Edmund asked. He thought he'd be Dracula. Sarah had heard this was the most popular men's costume, as it required no more effort than to turn up one's collar.

She had been planning on going as an Apache maiden, but now she decided to go as something more fetching—perhaps Cleopatra. She could get something up from her grandmother's trunk.

And so, a week later, in a New England parlor transformed into a magnificent ballroom by silken wall coverings and strung lanterns, a red-lipped Cleopatra in turban and beaded dress, emboldened by a golden mask that half concealed her face, announced to Dracula her plans to spend 1909 engaged in Christian benevolence, working for the betterment of impoverished souls in New York.

11

Bridey

The Battery, New York City

Autumn 1908

Luckily, her body's burgeoning coincided with the onset of the cold weather, which came earlier here than it did in Kilconly. Bridey wrapped herself in woolens and coats, both hers and Thom's. She didn't care if it made her look daft. She needed to hide her condition—her delicate condition, though she didn't feel delicate—if she was to remain employed.

She was almost six months along. Only Mary knew. Bridey kept herself covered in front of their bedmates. She was grateful to her nightdress for billowing conspiratorially about her whenever she slid out of bed, wakened each night now by what felt like a hand pressing down on her bladder.

Mary had given her place number 4, farthest from the wall, so Bridey didn't have to climb over anyone when she had to go to the hall at night.

"Too much tea," she lied when Maura complained of being woken by the nightly creaks of Bridey's feet on the floorboards. Bridey made note of which floorboards creaked and devised a path that led around them. Her bedmates didn't suspect, but Bridey worried, knowing her condition would eventually be obvious even to maidens. She'd soon be unable to tie the strings of her apron.

Mary had helped her try to get rid of it. They had pooled their money to buy cures for female complaints from a cart of remedies next to the fishmonger's at the Pearl Street market. Week after week, they'd tried herbs recommended in pamphlets, first pennyroyal, then parsley root, ginger, and chamomile. None of them worked and Bridey took this to be a sign from God that the child of Thom and herself should be born. Mary pressed on further, making her a cup of turpentine tea, which was said to succeed in most cases.

But Bridey refused it, pushed away the steaming cup that Mary had sneaked up to her in the closet under the stairs on the top floor leading up to the roof, the place where they usually conversed in private. The smell of the drink was so rancid that one inhale propelled Bridey up the stairs to the roof, where she was sick on the tar. Afterward, while putting her handkerchief to her mouth, she stood with Mary looking over the brick wall, gazing down at the town where her child would be born.

She knew that having a baby would bring much difficulty, so much that she couldn't envision it all now. But—a bright side came to her—her baby would be an American baby, entitled to all that the New World had to offer.

She prayed to the Holy Mother for strength. She prayed that God's plan for her and her child would be merciful.

One morning after Mrs. Boyle led grace at breakfast, she made her way to Bridey and said that Sister Superior wanted to see her. Bridey swallowed twice to force the buttered bread in her mouth past the rise in her throat.

Sister Superior was the nun in charge of the mission, someone Bridey had seen only at a distance, a dark silhouette at the other end of a hallway or a black form in a row of black forms in the front pews of the chapel, obstructing her view of the priest.

Obediently, Bridey folded her napkin and rose from her place on the bench, but Mrs. Boyle stayed her with a hand on her shoulder.

"Not now, dear. Before supper," she said.

Bridey's innards roiled all day, adding to the disturbance to which she'd become accustomed.

"Maybe she wants you to help decorate for Rosary Day," Mary said hopefully as they lingered outside the elevator at the factory. Bridey could no longer take the stairs. The last time she'd walked the nine flights, she'd had to use the banister to haul herself up the last steps while stabs of pain shot like arrows into her core. She was grateful to Mary for not taking the stairs either.

The upcoming Feast of Our Lady of the Rosary was a celebration day at the mission, but Bridey guessed from Mrs. Boyle's tone that Sister Superior's intention wasn't that.

The cage's motor screeched as Mr. Zito approached. He maneuvered the bottom of the cage up and down until it was level with the floorboards so they could step in without having to jump. They went to the back of the car, to distance themselves from him. They didn't talk about Sister Superior again, not in front of Mr. Zito, who puffed his cigar and, as the cage rose, swiveled in his stool and stared at their chests until they crossed their arms so he couldn't stare anymore, nor at the break when they met at the window to eat sugar cubes from their handkerchiefs, nor on the bus coming home, which was so crowded that they were forced, as usual, to share a seat meant for one.

They both guessed why Sister Superior wanted to see her. Bridey wore the larger of her two dresses with a smock she'd borrowed from Mary tied loosely over it. Before the dinner bell rang, Bridey walked carefully down thinly carpeted stairs, and instead of turning right toward the dining room as she usually did, she turned left and made her way down the hallway to forbidding carved-oak doors left slightly ajar. She tapped lightly and heard "Come in." Far away, Sister sat bent over papers on her desk illuminated by a paraffin lamp. Bridey walked slowly, as if meekly approaching a stage. When she finally reached the desk, Sister Superior looked up, and her rimless glasses slipped farther down the slope of her nose.

"Miss Molloy," she said, fixing her gaze on Bridey's torso, which made Bridey instantly start crying so hard that she could not follow what Sister was saying; she caught only a few phrases, like "grievous sin" and "a moral example for the other girls." It wasn't until there was a noise at the door and Sister's forefinger wagged and the porter entered with Thom's suitcase and her grip—they'd been packed already—that Bridey realized that she was being expelled immediately from her room and, she guessed, from her job, which had been contingent on her having a place there.

"The Sisters of Mercy have a place for you," Sister said, handing Bridey a card: *St. Margaret's Home for Fallen and Friendless Girls.* "Mr. Hopper will deliver you there."

Mr. Hopper was holding out her two coats, but before she took them, she untied her smock. "This is Mary Ryan's," she said, taking it off and revealing her size, for what was the point of concealing it now?

She reddened as if she were stepping from underthings. She folded the smock neatly and set it on the chair in front of Sister Superior's desk and then, suddenly, turned and took off her scapular—two woolen squares embroidered with an image of Our Lady of Mount Carmel that she wore on a brown string around her neck. Mary had admired it. Bridey fumbled for the pocket in the folds of the smock and slipped the scapular into it.

Now she took the coats from Mr. Hopper and put them both on, then followed him out. He held a bag on either side of himself, like ballast. She was crying so hard, she could barely see. They left by a side door and he settled her into the carriage, but before he shut the doors, he surprised her.

"Do you have in mind another place to go?" he asked. "A relative, perhaps? A good-hearted friend? The Sisters of Mercy ain't none too merciful, if you know what I mean."

Her sister had sent Adelaide's address and written, *She's happy to help if you have any need.* The address had been blazing in Bridey's mind ever since: 907 Fifth Avenue. She'd meant to visit before this.

"It's a far ride," Bridey warned Mr. Hopper.

"Nonsense," he said, buttoning the rubber apron over his legs. "Let a man do a good turn for a pretty lady." He shook the reins and they began to move.

Bridey wondered how much longer she'd be pretty. Soon, her waist would expand unignorably.

What would she do when she got to Adelaide's? She had no idea. She invented scenarios, all of which were unlikely, the least likely being that Adelaide would volunteer to take Bridey's baby back to Ireland, saying it was hers. Then Bridey would return to Ireland too and pretend to fall in love with the baby and selflessly raise it, ostensibly so that Adelaide could return to America.

The carriage stopped short, making Bridey hit her knees on the driver's seat, when an omnibus swung out in front of it, even though Fifth Avenue was far wider than streets downtown. To her right was green, which reminded her of home. Just like at home, a low stone wall bordered a meadow where flocks of sheep grazed.

"The Central Park," Mr. Hopper called back to her. "My cousin is one of the shepherds there. The sheep keep grass down and keep it green, too, what with the natural course of things."

She'd never been to the Central Park. She'd read newspaper accounts of castles and a pond and a carousel where children rode fantastic carved beasts that went around on a turntable rotated by draft mules straining at their harnesses. Did Adelaide live near? Perhaps she could go there.

What a difference it was to alight from the carriage onto a walk made of pavement instead of dirt. No oyster shells crunching under her feet or horse patties to look out for. The walk was wide and quiet, not teeming with pedestrians, clear of carts and street hawkers, no drunks sprawled on the curb. It was as if Mr. Hopper had transported her to another world.

She thought to knock at a back door, but Mr. Hopper took her bags, brought them right up the front steps, and dropped them at the bright red door. She guessed things were differently done in America, that a servant might receive callers at the front door. As she lifted the heavy brass knocker, she heard the whip crack behind her and the clack of hooves on the pavement.

The heavy door opened. A tall white-haired man in a black cutaway looked down at her.

"Is Adelaide home?" asked Bridey.

Home. She anticipated the joy of seeing someone from home. She didn't know what Adelaide could do for her except make her feel less alone. She couldn't think beyond a day or two now without growing upset.

"Whom do you wish?" said the man, and Bridey worried that Adelaide had already been dismissed from her job or that she'd committed the wrong address to memory.

"Adelaide Conroy," said Bridey. "From Kilconly. In Ireland. She works here?"

The man took a step back, tugging each of the gloves at the wrist, as if the gloves were for boxing and he was readying for a match.

"The servants' entrance is at rear," he declared, England in his voice. He pushed the door closed.

Both cases were too heavy for her to manage, so she walked

them one at a time back down the steps, around the walk, through a gap in the iron railing, and down a brick path that led to a narrow door.

A woman in a puffy white cap answered, brushing floured hands on an apron.

"You're just in time," she said, wiping perspiration from her cheek with the unfloured back of her hand. "Dinner's almost on and I'm at wit's end. Take off your coat and get a move on to the kitchen."

Bridey slipped off her top coat and, not seeing any place to hang it, left it draped over the bags that stood side by side at the door, like sentries.

"Is Adelaide Conroy here?" Bridey asked, speaking now to the back of the woman's apron. It didn't tie around her; it buttoned, which was an elegant style that Bridey had never seen.

Either the woman didn't hear Bridey's words or she was ignoring them. She remained silent as they neared a doorway from which came a clatter of pots and dishes and the most heavenly scent Bridey had ever inhaled—a rich, meaty smell.

"The new girl at last," said the button-aproned woman as they entered the kitchen. A man who wore a tall white hat that was stiff at the sides and like a muffin on top was stirring a big pot with a long wooden spoon. Two girls Bridey's age wearing hairnets and high-bibbed aprons bent over a table chopping fruit.

The man in the hat looked up from the pot and raised a dark eyebrow.

"I see," he said, training his gaze on Bridey's midriff. "Two for the price of one?"

The button-aproned woman turned around and faced Bridey, seeing her for the first time. Her eyebrows came together. "Is Mrs. Bocholt at the agency gone blind now?" She picked up a knife and it seemed to Bridey she was tilting it threateningly in her direction.

"I'm not from an agency," Bridey explained. "I'm here to see Adelaide."

"The under-laundress," said a girl at the table.

"I'm a friend from home," said Bridey. She could feel her face growing as red as the apples the girl was chopping. How she longed to swipe one of them. By now, she was starving. Fresh fruit had been a rare treat these past months. Her hometown had been poor, but its abundance of freshly picked things to eat now made it seem like a town of great wealth.

"Why didn't you announce yourself at the start?" said the woman, annoyed. "Adelaide will be down for the service dinner shortly." She waved the knife at the door to the kitchen. "You wait out there."

Bridey settled herself on the plain pine bench on the other side of the wall, in sight of her luggage. She wondered if she'd know Adelaide. It'd been years since she'd seen her. But when a small parade started down the hallway toward her, men in brass-buttoned jackets, women in caps and white aprons, she had no trouble seeing Kilconly in the slight red-haired girl walking fast on flat slippers, unpinning a cap and shaking out her hair as she walked.

"Adelaide?" she asked, and the girl looked sharply at her.

"I'm Bridey, from Kilconly. Bridey Molloy," she said.

"Oh, gah!" Adelaide put a hand to her mouth to cover a cry of pleasure and then threw her arms around Bridey.

Bridey stayed sitting to conceal her secret for as long as she could, but when she pushed herself up from the bench and stood, Adelaide's eyes grew round. Bridey looked down in shame and shook her head slightly. "A sad case, I am," she said. "I'll tell ye later." And then she said a word in Irish, a word with no equivalent in English or any other language, a word that expressed lamentation for misfortune and a person who regrets the misfortune but also embraces it. When Adelaide heard *ochón,* her eyes filled, and she took Bridey in her arms again, and how good it felt to Bridey to be embraced. She could almost smell gorse in the hair brushing her cheeks.

"You'll stay with me while the parlor maid is away," Adelaide said. "And then we will figure out what to do with ye." What a comfort were not only her words, but her voice with the kiss of Kilconly in it.

Adelaide's room was at the top of the house. It was the smallest bedroom, Adelaide said, and the one nobody wanted because of five flights of steps that got narrower and narrower the higher you went. But it suited Adelaide to be so near the roof, which was where much of the work of a laundress took place. She'd started out as an under-laundress but now, after almost no time at all, she was a laundress, with better pay. That was America.

Adelaide's promotion had apparently not been noticed in the kitchen, Bridey thought. She had to pause at a few landing turns to catch her breath, her hand gripping a carved iron rail. Adelaide waited patiently without stopping her chatter meant to prepare Bridey for the meanness of the room she shared with Mary Julia. But once Adelaide pushed open the door, the room seemed to Bridey not mean, but magnificent. It boasted not one but two windows, and Bridey moved to take in the view. The windows were set into a deep casement that jutted out past the roofline, and looking through them gave Bridey the same sensation she'd gotten when peering into periscopes at a fair. The upper part of the city was spread out below her. Red brazen sun turned the sky crimson and purple and pink behind a dark hodgepodge of buildings silhouetted in the distance. The sun was sinking behind the far boundary of the great park. The park divided east from west like a Red Sea of trees turned scarlet and orange and every color in between.

"Tá sí an-álainn!" Bridey exclaimed, setting her bags down. It was

good to be with someone who knew that Irish had the best words for what you were feeling, especially in the presence of beauty.

"I guess," said Adelaide. "I never look out. This one's Mary Julia's," she added, laying Thom's grip on a thin woolen blue blanket pulled tight over a sheet. Its weight on the bed set beads of a ruby-colored rosary swinging against the iron rails of the headboard.

"If you want a view, you can join me tomorrow upstairs on the roof, beating carpets," Adelaide said. And then she hurried them back downstairs for dinner.

Mrs. Tubbs had been none too pleased when Adelaide asked if Bridey could join them, but she agreed and soon Bridey was feasting on a meal more sumptuous than she'd ever had: peas and lamb stew and potatoes and pickled beets. For dessert, a kind of fruit she'd never seen before: banana. It was cut up into slices and added like coins to the top of vanilla pudding. The fruit was slippery and sweet and like none she had tasted. If this was the supper served to the servants, Bridey couldn't imagine what exotic fare would be set out in the dining room above.

None, it turned out. The family, the Hathaways, were off to their country estate in Long Island, having taken the parlor maid with them.

How long will they be gone? Bridey was tempted to ask, but she felt that doing so would be impertinent. She guessed by the rosary left behind on the headboard that they'd return before Sunday, when the parlor maid presumably would need the rosary for Mass. Tomorrow was Wednesday. That gave Bridey a few days of refuge before she must go to the sisters. She felt for their calling card in her pocket. A sharp corner dug into the pad of a finger.

That night, in bed, Bridey spoke to Adelaide, her voice low, modulated to reach just across the narrow gap between their beds.

Speaking to Adelaide's listening ears in the dark, Bridey felt relieved of a great weight, almost as if she were in a confessional booth. But she could never confess to a priest all she was confiding to Adelaide, who murmured no judgment, only encouragement: "Go on, go on." They both knew girls this had happened to, but only at home. Edith Fitzgerald and Brenda McGrath had had babies taken in by their mothers, who raised the babies as their own children. The town pretended to believe the babies were the girls' siblings, though everyone knew the truth, and the girls knew that everyone knew it. But the town could be trusted to keep the secret for the babies' sake and for the sake of the families.

Bridey wouldn't want her mother to take in her baby, couldn't imagine imposing this shame on her mother, on her family—but what did she want for her baby? She didn't know.

Bridey told Adelaide of Thom's burial and was saddened to think of him now, alone in dark waters, his linens unraveled, his pale body being made to swim among colorful fish. He'd never learned to swim—none of them had—but perhaps in death he'd been granted that knowledge.

The next morning, on their way to breakfast, Adelaide said, "It's too bad you're in the state you're in. We're in need of a tweeny. The last one ran off with the window washer. But you're too racked, for sure, to be going up and down cleaning boots."

It was nice of Adelaide to suggest that she might be employed, but Bridey knew she was not employable. At least, not in a good house like this one. It was not only a mortal sin to do what she did—she guessed she could never receive Communion again—but as long as the child was with her, before or after its birth, her moral condition disqualified her from work in a home with a good family. How grateful she was to Adelaide for the compassion she showed her, the dignity she accorded Bridey despite her transgression, the evidence of which she could see clear as day.

Bridey rarely slept through the night anymore. She was thankful for the moonlight streaming through the windows in Adelaide's room that helped her find the chamber pot under her bed. It was not easy to maintain balance over it, given her new center of gravity, but she eased herself quietly, as she learned to do as a girl, and when she was finished, she slid the pot in its wooden box back into place and returned to her bed, glad that Adelaide's gentle snores continued uninterrupted.

It was grand to have a mattress all to herself, but the mattress was narrow, not much wider than she was, she who was wider now and becoming ever more stout. She'd have to let out her waists soon.

She turned, trying to find a more comfortable position. Her tossing set the rosary beads in motion, clinking against the metal rails of the headboard. She stopped moving on the mattress until she was reassured by Adelaide's steady breathing that she was still asleep, then shifted again, maneuvering carefully so as not to set the beads moving.

As she turned, she was shocked by a stab of pain. A cramping. It felt like something was jabbing at some organ deep inside her. What was wrong? Was something wrong? She turned onto her back, causing a clattering at the rail, but no matter the beads now. She put a staying hand on her belly to steady whatever was happening in there. What was happening? Was she losing the baby? She hoped it wasn't that. True, she'd tried pennyroyal and parsley root tea, but that was in early days when the baby was a mere seed; it hadn't yet grown. Now she could feel it, a whole baby, and she would no more do away with it than murder Adelaide in the bed beside her.

She talked to the baby. (She was convinced it was a girl.) *What's wrong, little wee one?* she asked silently, her blood going cold. If something happened on these white sheets that were not hers, what would she do? Adelaide couldn't help her. Adelaide knew even less about babies than Bridey did, being the last born in her family. But even being eldest didn't help Bridey now. She knew everything about how to take care of a baby but nothing about what to do for it before it was born.

She longed for her mother, longed to ask her things she'd never thought to ask before. Her mother was an expert at having children. She'd done it nine times, and now Bridey wondered that she'd made it look easy.

The pain went away. She tried to go back to sleep.

She'd not received a letter from Mam yet, though she'd written her. She'd written to everyone in the family except Da, whom she'd included in the letter addressed to her mother. This is what she'd told them: She'd come to America to find her fortune. It was an old story. The Irish left Ireland and would send for their kin or forget them. Thom Flynn was on the boat too, she had written, and died of ship fever. She didn't say more. What could she say?

Sometimes, like now, she felt Thom's absence to be almost as strong as his presence had been when she'd looked into his eyes and her heart would race. Now that he was gone, she felt as a patient must feel after a limb has been amputated. An uncle had lost an arm in the Fenian Rising, and when she was a child, he would confuse her by asking her please to scratch "me phantom *lámh*." He told her he woke up every day surprised that it didn't show up in the sleeve of his nightshirt.

She'd even written to Daisy, the youngest, who was only two. She'd folded a page in half and slipped the pressed head of a daisy into the fold. She'd found the daisy on the bus to work one day— it had fallen onto her skirt from a gentleman's lapel—and seeing it made her long for her baby sister, whom she guessed she'd never get to know. *An American daisy for a beautiful Irish one,* she'd written on the page before folding it. On the outside of the fold, she'd written Daisy's real name, Deirdre, in big block letters, hoping they'd help her learn to read.

The only letters to Bridey had been from her sister Kathleen. Kathleen said that Mam was too busy to write, and perhaps this was true. When Bridey left them, Kathleen said, she'd taken her helping hands to America, which had left Mam (and Kathleen) with much more to do. Bridey believed that Mam was still angry with her. How much angrier she would be if she knew Bridey's condition, which Mam would blame on what she erroneously believed to be Bridey's impetuous ways.

Bridey could never impose another baby on Mam. Mam was a mother, though, and because of this, Bridey trusted that she wouldn't be able to hold a grudge against her forever. (Would she?) Bridey pictured herself going home sometime in the future, hand in hand with a beautiful American child. Mam, seeing how lovely her grandchild was, would forgive Bridey.

Mam appeared to Bridey sometimes in dreams. In these dreams, Mam has come to America, turned up to surprise Bridey. "Don't tell your da," she'd always say, putting a finger to her lips before drifting, ghostlike, into the ether.

Unlike other mothers in the parish who had achieved the same number of children as Mam by bearing twins or, in the case of the Kerrigans, triplets, her mother had had only one child at a time, and perhaps due in part to her body concentrating single-mindedly on the task, she had lost only one child along the way. The Kerrigans' last triplet had been born dead. (Died of impatience, the midwife had said.)

Mam had lost one child during childbirth. Jeremiah had been a big baby, almost ten pounds. He'd strangled himself being born while Bridey was at school. He'd choked on the cord wrapped not only around his neck but around his waist and ankle. The midwife had never seen a cord that long. She'd said—it always hurt Bridey to hear it repeated—that Bridey's brother had hung himself in the womb.

They'd lost Patrick well along after his birth, at six months. The priest had consoled them by saying again and again it was nobody's fault; it was God's will.

Once, when Mam had been pregnant with Pat, she'd stood at the stove, stirring a pot with a long wooden spoon, and suddenly grimaced, then she smiled and, with her free hand, took Bridey's hand and put it to the waist of her apron. "Can you feel it?" she'd asked, pressing Bridey's hand to her belly. "Can you feel the kick?" As soon as she touched it, Bridey had pulled her hand away, repulsed not only by the movement of something unseen but by the hardness of her mother's belly, which she hadn't expected.

And now Bridey realized that what she'd felt was a kick. Only a kick! Her baby was kicking, making herself known, reminding Bridey of her presence. As if Bridey could forget. She was flooded with relief and gratitude to a benevolent God and pulled the pillow over her head to block out the night and its terrors about what was to come—would childbirth kill her, and if both she and the child survived, what was to become of it, and of her?

If her poor baby died at six months, like Pat did? She wouldn't think of that.

She prayed to Our Lady to bestow on her sleep, the only relief available to her.

She was woken in dimness by a cacophony of bells hauling her out of a dream in which she was giddy with relief to discover that Thom wasn't gone after all; he'd been hiding all this time in the hollow of the elder tree on his father's farm, the one her grandfather had planted when the farm had been his.

A groan, a slam, and the bells fell silent.

"Bollocks!" she heard from the other bed. "I forgot to pull out the alarm. I can sleep in another half hour today. Mr. H. is away—I don't have to iron his bloody papers."

So now they made clocks that crowed like a rooster. In a city, it made sense, Bridey thought as she replaced the pillow over her head. At the mission, girls were wakened by a rap on the door and a stern "Time to rise, girls" from Mrs. Boyle. Bridey hadn't considered how Mrs. Boyle herself was wakened, but if she'd had to guess, she'd have assumed it was by a street knocker-upper paid to tap his long sticks at windows.

When Adelaide left to attend to her duties, Bridey opened her eyes. There was a small stack of hardbounds on a bedside table. Bridey turned the stack so she could read their spines: a small leather-bound Bible, a red Catholic missal, a romance by Arnold Bennett she'd already read, and *How to Keep House,* by Mrs. C. S. Peel.

Bridey took up Mrs. Peel's literary offering and, upon opening it, was intrigued by chapter 1, titled "How to Keep House":

Year by year, the domestic problem becomes more difficult to solve.

Bridey hadn't known there was a domestic problem. She was interested to learn of it. Turning the pages, she became as engrossed as if she were reading a novel.

It is the duty of the presiding mistress to ascertain that her servants are well-fed and well-housed.

Bridey learned that going into service provided advantages besides salary and a clean and luxurious place to work. She wondered if a housekeeper with her own sitting room might be permitted to keep a baby there. She imagined it: A plump and perfect baby girl, so adorable she becomes the darling of the family for whom the housekeeper works...

But then she came to this:

The moral tone of the household is dependent on her.

And she remembered her own irremediably immoral state.

Still, she took in "Rules for Waiting at Table" and "The Incompetence of Mistresses" before accompanying Adelaide down to breakfast.

A bounty of eggs scrambled with rashers and leftover peas and thick slices of toasted, buttered bread and homemade pear jam! The jam was to be eaten, said Mrs. Tubbs, because the Hollingworths had given jars of it for Christmas and now it was October and Sarah Hollingworth was coming to visit this weekend and had been known to wander devil-may-care into pantries (but was forgiven for it, being from the country), and the jam had to be eaten so as not to give offense to the family who gave it to them. The jam was delicious. Bridey spread it with a pastry knife thick on her bread and wished she could send it home to her family. The jam they knew was made only from berries.

Throughout her stay in the Hathaways' attic, Bridey retired to Adelaide's room as often as she could to take in the words of Mrs. Peel, acquiring insights into a profession she'd thought she'd known but realized that she knew little about, although the nuns had taught some of it: how to set a tea table, how to clean wallpaper, how to fold napkins and polish the inside of a sterling teapot.

She asked Adelaide if she could please find her pencil and paper, and in the next days, she copied out much of the book. While taking air in the park or helping Adelaide on the roof or lying on the borrowed bed in her room, Bridey took down the instructions regarding dismissal and engagement of servants, how to stock a larder, how to rid a kitchen of flies.

When she ran out of paper, she was told to fetch more herself from the refuse box near the fireplace in the kitchen.

And that was how Bridey came upon a pamphlet for the Lucretia Bell Mission for Fallen Women and Wayward Girls, an organization that offered sanctuary and guidance and help in rehabilitating lives.

12

Sarah

Five Points, Manhattan

March 1909

The Wellington station was easily within walking distance of Hollingwood, but it had snowed again the night before the new charitable chapter of Christian Benevolence was performing its first mission, so Mr. Canfield picked up Sarah, along with the few other girls, in a sledge to bring them to the station, where Mrs. Canfield and other ladies were already waiting. They were taking the 8:13 to New York.

Upon climbing into the sledge and taking the seat next to Lil, Sarah wished she had brought a fur muff. Both Clara and Dottie were warming their hands in their muffs. Sarah had left hers home, on Nettie's advice not to trust it to the dangers of coal soot or light-fingered city folk. The muff had belonged to her mother. But Clara and Dottie didn't have to worry about soot blackening theirs, which were sable, not rabbit, as her mother's was. The style had changed since her mother had acquired it, but that didn't matter to Sarah and Rachel. Rachel would never forgive Sarah if she'd come home without it—Sarah would never forgive herself.

She got down from the sledge and followed the others into the unheated station. Her hands felt frozen in spite of her wearing two pairs of kid gloves and she again wished she could warm them in the silk lining that once had warmed the hands of her mother. Perhaps her hands were cold partly because she was nervous. She hadn't been to the city in over a year and she had never been to the part of town they were going, which was the vice district.

On the train with the girls and Mrs. Prebscott, a chaperone, she played cards: bezique and five hundred and red and black. They talked of what they would do and see in New York—on another trip. This one would be taken up wholly by charity. The trip had gotten the girls out of their town for a day, and they'd be able to repeat this adventure once a week. Soon, they'd be familiar enough with traveling to the city, they hoped, to be trusted to take the train unescorted by matrons. Clara talked of seeing the new Beaux Arts renovation of the Metropolitan Museum; Dottie described a walk down Fifth Avenue to see the dairy in Central Park; Sarah yearned to see a real play on Broadway and impress Edmund with her fine observations about it.

And then Dottie was collecting the cards and slipping them back into the hard leather case because they were pulling into the Grand Central Terminal.

Stepping down from the train into the glorious light of the great glass train shed at Grand Central, Sarah was suffused with awe of human invention and industry. It was as if she were entering a tunnel made of metal and sun. How much the age she was living in made possible, she thought, trying to keep up with Mrs. Canfield as she weaved through crowds in the covered part of the station.

The station was still decorated for the centenary of Lincoln's birth, which had been celebrated the week before. A wall as wide as a field was entirely draped by an American flag. Suddenly the memory of Wellington's town-hall decorations glowed in Sarah—her sewing circle had stitched the bunting that had festooned the podium. But now those decorations seemed gimcrack compared to those she was passing—red, white, and blue ruched swags spilling from ceiling to floor, pinwheels the size of wagon wheels spinning, which relieved the heat in the station.

Mrs. Phelps from the Church of Land and Sea met them under a gold clock near the timetable boards. When Mrs. Canfield remarked on the decorations, she flapped her gloved hands.

"Oh, if you think this is something, you should have been here last week!" Mrs. Phelps was a big woman, heavily powdered and wrapped in furs. "They set up stadium seating here and the Metropolitan Chorus came and sang dressed in red, white, and blue, so when they stood in special arrangement, they looked like Old Glory!"

New York was a living "stupendifier," Sarah thought. The last time the circus had come to Wellington, a clown had pulled into the ring a wagon on which lay a huge red cone labeled THE STU-PENDIFIER. The clown had jumped out of the ring to collect small objects from the audience, then returned and fed the objects, one by one, into the small end of the cone. After a drumroll and clashes of cymbals, the objects blasted out the other end of the cone, and they appeared transformed, vastly enlarged. A handkerchief had become a bedsheet. A coin, a gold brick. Her father's boutonniere had come out of the cone as a huge, flowering tree.

Sarah loved to go to New York, but she also loved to come home to where days passed at less of a fever pitch. If she had to live in New York every day, she guessed she might die of chronic over-excitement.

"We'll take the subway, all right?" asked Mrs. Phelps, already leading them there. "It's the most reliable mode in this weather. There's not a hansom large enough for us all, and trolleys are so unreliable. If there's even the smallest amount of snow on the tracks, the driver has to get out and shovel."

Sarah settled her skirts on the wicker seat of the subway so as not to snag them on a stray spring poking up through the braid— her father had once torn his trousers this way. The shriek of wheels made it impossible to talk to Clara or Dottie on either side of her, so she sat quietly observing the other riders. At this time of day, most of the passengers were ladies. Coats were slimmer this year, more tailored, with shoulders not as wide. And hats! The shapes were different and trimmed with not only ribbon, but feathers. Sitting across from her was a woman in a wool derby pinned with a spray of bright feathers. The campaign that Mrs. Roosevelt was waging for Audubon to keep feathers on birds apparently hadn't convinced fashionable ladies in New York.

Above the hats gleamed advertising placards listing the superior qualities of brands of laundry starch, health tonics, whiskey, stove polish. The man pictured in an ad for Owl Cigars looked remarkably like Edmund.

She'd seen Edmund several times in the weeks since the Redfields' ball. She'd been thrilled that soon after the ball, he'd visited Hollingwood on the pretext of consulting her father on town matters. Sarah saw, by the way Edmund's eyes lingered on hers, the real purpose of his visit and guessed her father had seen it too. Her father had retreated to his study, saying he needed to find something, and had stayed away much longer than the time needed to retrieve it, leaving Sarah and Edmund in the parlor alone, except when Nettie discreetly delivered the tea tray.

One of the aspects that Sarah most appreciated about Edmund was his forthrightness. He didn't flirt or boast or flatter. He said what he thought, no matter to whom he was talking. Perhaps this directness had to do with his being schooled as a lawyer.

But she worried that their talk was relegated to a plane so high and dry that romance wouldn't ever be able to take root.

For example, in the time her father was gone from the room, Edmund tabulated the number of inches of snow fallen that year and elaborated on his mother's remedy for grippe (horseradish tea with old honey), and as he spoke, Sarah felt despair that their talk was a frigate going in the wrong direction and that she would prove unequal to shifting its course.

She knew there were womanly arts by which to steer conversations, but Sarah was not acquainted with these. Catharine Beecher's seminary had educated her only in the academic subjects she would need for the early intellectual and moral training of her future children. She despaired of her lack of motherly guidance in matters she knew other girls to be tutored in. Though some (like Rachel) did not appear to need tutoring. At a luncheon social last week, Sarah had been astonished to find her sister surrounded by gentlemen who were kept rapt by her describing to them a recipe for a bar of fruit bran.

Did Edmund think her provincial? He had been to Europe. The farthest she had dared fling herself was to Catharine Beecher's in Hartford, a short train ride away.

She was glad that charity work would be taking her into New York once a week so she'd have more topics to discuss that would be of interest to Edmund.

They got off at Spring Street and mounted the stairs to the exit. They navigated around mounds of snow on sidewalks crowded with other pedestrians and horses tied to concrete troughs. (The troughs were either empty or full of ice. The poor horses! Where did they quench their thirst here in winter?). They had to dodge peddlers hawking eggs and spices and live chickens and ducks.

At the corner of Mott Street, Mrs. Canfield asked a policeman to escort them farther. As soon as they crossed Canal Street, sidewalks fell away; the streets were unpaved. Oyster shells, shards of bottle glass and crockery, and horse dung were embedded in the dirt. Sarah saw there was a saloon on every corner. The ladies discreetly lifted their skirts to keep their boot braids from grazing the filth. Nettie would have a job cleaning Sarah's boots tonight.

"Tenant houses are now called tenements," said Mrs. Phelps as they passed a long row of flat-faced buildings. In many windows gaped holes stuffed with old newspapers, and Sarah ached for the children whose faces gazed out. It was early March and unseasonably cold.

The policeman stopped suddenly and pointed to a window above a Chinese restaurant.

"That's where poor Elsie Sigel met her slayer," he said.

"Who?" asked Mrs. Prebscott. She was hard of hearing and apparently hadn't wanted to go to New York wearing the little trumpet she usually tucked behind her ear.

"Elsie Sigel, the missionary stuffed in a trunk by two heathens she was helping," said Mrs. Phelps, and Sarah walked more quickly to be nearer the policeman.

When they turned a corner, a sign painted on brick proclaimed THE LUCRETIA BELL MISSION FOR FALLEN WOMEN AND WAYWARD GIRLS.

"I'll leave you now, good ladies," the policeman said with a touch to the shiny beak of his cap. Mrs. Phelps pressed a coin into his other gloved palm; he acknowledged it with a nod, turned, and whistled as he walked away.

Sarah was a tall girl, but mounting the steps, she felt inconsequential behind the imposing figure of Mrs. Phelps. She braced herself for what she would see. She imagined the home would be dark and untidy, foul with odors and loud with the crying of emaciated babies. She guessed the women would be slovenly.

But here was a woman in a crisp, pink-striped uniform and a

jaunty pink cap welcoming them into a clean, polished vestibule, inviting them to give their wraps to a maid who asked if they wanted tea. No? The uniformed woman volunteered to take them straight to the nursery and led them down a polished corridor, and as they proceeded, a group of young women advanced toward them.

Here came the wayward girls, huge at the waist, some big as tubs, and as they drew near, Sarah was stunned to see just how young they were, some not much older than Hannah.

She felt her face redden; she was unable to keep from imagining, or trying to imagine, these girls engaged in the adult act that landed them here. Their faces weren't hardened, as she had expected; they looked as innocent and girlish as those of her classmates at Catharine Beecher's. As Sarah and the other benefactresses passed, one of the wayward girls whispered to another behind a cupped hand and they both laughed, and Sarah marveled at the pluck it must take for a girl in such dire straits to find anything funny.

They were led up three flights, and as they mounted the stairs, they began to hear them—the babies. The cries came through the wood of the floors, irrepressible sounds of humans too small to talk. High-pitched and frantic cries that Sarah remembered from when her own siblings were infants, railing against what they seemed to feel was incarceration in bodies too small to impose their own will. Sarah had been surprised that a person so tiny could make itself heard in every corner of a house as sprawling as Hollingwood.

They came to double doors with frosted panes on which letters were stenciled, DAY on one and ROOM on the other. The woman in the cap pushed open both doors and there were the babies. Such beautiful babies, lying or sitting behind iron rails. Some were old enough to reach through the bars, but most were infants, lying three to a crib.

Here was a crib in which all three infants were sleeping. How could they sleep in a room loud with wails? Sarah knelt by the bars and reached a finger through, and, to her surprise, the baby nearest her took it, seizing it in his sleep, and gripped it with a ferocity that didn't show on his face. He was a boy, she decided. Unlike his bedmates, who were bald, he had hair aplenty. His hair was red—not screaming red, but dark red, almost brown like brick. He remained sleeping, his cheeks pink, his lips pursed as if for a kiss. He was the most beautiful baby she'd ever seen.

If Edmund and she married, Sarah would waste no time acquiring babies herself. She wanted four. Two boys, two girls, in that order, so that the girls would have older brothers, like she'd had Benjie.

"That's our Thomas," said a nurse from the other side of the crib. "Isn't he dear?"

"He's divine," Sarah murmured over the sleeping child.

"Ah, here's his mother now," said the nurse.

And Sarah turned to see a girl far younger than she was who was wise to all that was still mystery to Sarah: love between a man and a woman, carrying a child, and the brutal, life-threatening process of giving birth.

Of course, childbirth for Sarah would be less of an ordeal than it must have been for this poor girl. Women of Sarah's set now had certified doctors to deliver their babies with scientific precision.

"This is Lulabelle," said the nurse.

The girl kept her eyes down, but Sarah caught an upward turn in her lips, and what was signified by this change in expression? A smile? A smirk?

Sarah stood. The girl was short, and in the company of diminutive girls, Sarah sometimes felt like a giantess.

"I'm Sarah," she offered, lowering her head, extending her hand.

But the girl didn't take her hand. Nor did she look up. She kept her eyes to the floor as she brushed past Sarah, lifted the baby, then turned her back and walked away, her shoes clacking on polished wood as she swung through the doors.

13.

Bridey

Lucretia Bell Mission for Fallen Women and Wayward Girls

January 1909

Bridey had been certain the baby would be a girl. The others had noticed she was carrying high, and this coupled with the fact Bridey had been sick in the mornings in the early days had convinced them of the baby's sex.

One of her roommates had done the ring test, which clinched it. One night, as they were readying for bed, the girl they called Liza had asked Bridey to lie on her cot. Liza had slipped the wedding ring off her finger and tied it with thread and held it over Bridey's enormous stomach. Others had gathered, shivering, as they were in various stages of undress—so many different belly sizes and shapes!—to watch the ring swing on its axis above Bridey, to see what kind of pattern it made. Liza held the ring low so that it almost touched the flannel of Bridey's gown and as she watched the ring move in a circle, Bridey was mesmerized by it, this plain pewter band that was shiny with power because the girl it belonged to was a girl who had known marriage. Liza's husband had died in a work accident at his job on the docks. But Liza was still a Mrs. and would be a Mrs. for the rest of her life, even if she never married again.

"A circle," said Liza and she declared Bridey's baby would be a girl.

No true surnames were used here. No true Christian names either. Friendships at Lucretia Bell were meant to be temporary. In this way, a girl could be granted a new life, one in which she could start over, freed of the shame of her past. A motto was engraved prominently in many places: *Go forth and sin no more*. The founder of the home was a man who had lost his daughter to scarlet fever.

The Lucretia Bell Mission was a Protestant organization. The Protestants were kinder than the Catholics to women who had babies on the wrong side of the blanket, as Adelaide put it. Adelaide heard this was so from the gardener's wife's sister who had worked as an in-between at the home for unweds where Sister Superior had meant Bridey to go. There, the sisters required daily penances that included waking in the wee hours to sweep the floors and polish pews or washing your hands until they were red and raw. As payment for having been cared for, you gave them your baby to be placed in a good home that you, the mother, couldn't provide.

The Lucretia Bell Mission's literature mentioned no penances. It was run by the Protestants, and Bridey knew that the Prods didn't do penances. Also, if you wanted, there was a lying-in period of six weeks with your baby during which you could decide whether to keep it or give it away.

Bridey guessed she would have to give her baby away—what else could she do? She'd lost her place at Our Lady of the Rosary and with it her job, and how would she and a baby live?

Sometimes, she imagined sailing back across the Atlantic, surprising her family with herself and an infant and a story about a husband in America who had died, like Liza's. But even if she could have afforded a return ticket, she couldn't imagine making the trip with a newborn, a trip so harsh she didn't think a baby could survive it. She wouldn't be able to bear another burial at sea.

She'd stayed with Adelaide for a few days, then Adelaide had accompanied her to the mission on her day off. They'd taken an omnibus downtown to Bleecker Street, which had been a long ride, made longer by the fact that they occupied the front seat and so were subjected to not only the twists and turns of the carriage but the stench of the horse's relieving himself—Bridey had made the whole trip with a handkerchief pressed to her mouth and nose, shielding herself against the nauseating effects.

It was the first time she'd entered a Protestant institution. Adelaide had been the one with the courage to knock on the door, and the door was opened by a kind-faced woman in a white uniform who took Bridey's luggage and set it in a corner, then ushered them down a long polished hall, past a chapel. Bridey peered through the windows in the chapel doors, which were closed. There were pews and an altar and a cross above; she was surprised to see how much it resembled where Catholics prayed. Going into a Protestant church was a sin, but that sin was so dwarfed by the one that had brought her here, she guessed it was impossible for her soul to be blackened further.

They were ushered to an office and into seats in front of a grand desk presided over by a stern-faced woman who looked her over, adjusting her lorgnette now and then as she peered across the vast mahogany plain.

Adelaide giggled, by which Bridey knew she was nervous. Bridey herself was terrified. If the Protestants didn't take her, she'd have to go to the nuns, who would not only not forgive her but make her suffer for her sins—that's how some of them were. Bridey worried that the woman would turn her away. The description in the pamphlet promised shelter and new hope to any soul in need.

Bridey put a hand on her protruding stomach as if to remind the woman that an innocent baby was seeking mercy too.

The woman asked a few questions about where Bridey had come from. Then she smiled and asked what name Bridey would like to take while she lived there, and Bridey suppressed a cry of relief. Girls here didn't divulge their real names, the woman said, so they could start out fresh after leaving.

"What about Mary," Bridey said, to keep alive the name of her friend.

But there was already a Mary.

"Lulabelle!" Adelaide blurted out, making Bridey smile. Lulabelle was a cow in the town they'd grown up in, always breaking past the fence and wandering down lanes, poking her head through open windows.

Bridey nodded and the woman dipped her pen in the ink to record this. The name didn't matter. It would last only months.

She was assigned to a cot in a row of cots in the dormitory. Everyone was given a job. Bridey (Lulabelle) helped in the kitchen, rising before dawn to dress and descend three flights of stone stairs to the basement, where she learned to cut, chop, peel, and mince under the instruction of Sister Martha (who wasn't a sister), a huge woman in an apron who did everything twice as fast as Bridey could manage even though her fingers were so plump they looked like white pudding sausages.

After two months, when a girl assisting at the laundry had to move up, Bridey was asked to take her place in the steamy basement, where she was glad to go because winter had come and it was a delight to be warm. Bridey learned secrets from the head laundress: how to lift sodden clothes with wooden tongs, how to steer them through a mangle, how to knead soap dough to make bars of it, and other tricks Mrs. C. S. Peel had not mentioned.

*　　*　　*

Bridey felt as enormous and heavy as if she'd swallowed a mountain. Everything swelled. Not only her midriff but her cheeks pushed out, and her chest had to be wrapped so her blouses fit. Even her ankles, which she'd always been proud of, lost their definition so that her legs were planks above the tops of her shoes.

"Going up?" asked the elevator operator, a pock-faced girl.

"No," said Bridey, shaking her head.

"Going up" meant you were having your baby. She wasn't having her baby yet. It wouldn't come out. Which was why she had an appointment with a nurse.

The girls at Lucretia Bell weren't permitted to ride the elevator unless they were going to the top floor—the birthing floor. The elevator at Lucretia Bell took its time, which was fine with Bridey. She didn't like doctors. She harbored a fear of anyone medical. A doctor had killed her uncle Mart by measuring out the wrong dose of medicine. Another had made her aunt Polly blind in one eye.

The elevator seemed to be attesting to her enormousness by the protests of its narrow cage, which drew slowly up, chains clanging, gears screeching, ascending to the nurse's office. The cab jerked to a stop, then started again, like a climber gathering strength to complete his ascent. The walls of the elevator were painted with colorful birds. The birds gazed placidly from behind bars, each in a bamboo cage. The cages were the same, but the birds were different: peacocks and parrots and bluebirds and finches. The painter was a Lucretia Bell girl who had signed her name in a corner in a flourishing hand: Thomasine. Thomasine! A perfect name for Bridey's own baby, a name in which Thomasine's father could live. But surely Thomasine hadn't been her name, no more than Bridey was Lulabelle. She wondered where "Thomasine" was now and whether or not she had kept her baby.

The nurse's crisp white cap and white apron made Bridey fearful, but soon she relaxed, feeling herself in caring, gentle hands. After examining her, the nurse suggested that Bridey discontinue the raspberry tea that she drank every day as a tonic, as all the girls did, to strengthen the muscles that kept babies in.

"Now we need to encourage Baby out," said the nurse, making Bridey's throat tighten, as this brought to mind her fear of the baby making its exit, which Bridey knew would bring pain. Worse than the physical pain would be the mental agony of having to make a decision.

Part of Bridey wished things would go on forever as they were, her baby safe within as she followed rules, never having to decide things for herself. The next decision she made would determine the course of her life—and of another life too.

The Lucretia Bell midwife would deliver her baby. Rich ladies had doctors to bring their children into the world, but from what Bridey had heard from the girls, midwives were better. Doctors were men and couldn't be trusted to know things about childbirth, things a person couldn't know unless she'd been through it herself. The home didn't call doctors except in emergencies and often, the girls said, the doctor made things worse.

Mary Catherine, for instance, was a case famous among them. She'd been in labor, and then her pains had stopped. The midwife told her what she already knew. Her baby had died before it was born. They'd called the doctor to deliver the baby that was dead inside her. The doctor arrived drunk. It was a Saturday. He'd promptly fallen onto an empty cot and slept himself sober before applying his instruments to Mary Catherine. He had taken the child with so little care, it was like butchering, the midwife said. The doctor left, warning that Mary Catherine had a slim chance of survival. The Lucretia Bell nurses had washed her daily with carbolic water and she had recovered her health, but not her cheerful disposition. She would cry for no reason, explaining she didn't know why she was crying because her precious daughter was well kept in her heavenly home. Eventually, Mary Catherine had gone back to where she had come from in Holland. Bridey (Lulabelle) slept in her bed.

Whenever she remembered this story, Bridey felt newly terrorized by it and wondered if this terror was preventing the baby from coming out.

The best way to make a baby come out, Bridey knew from her mother and aunts, was to walk. If she'd been at home, she'd have been able to walk the hills as they had, up one lane and down another, inhaling whiffs of salted air, coats hugged tightly about them, flapping at their legs.

Bridey had to make do with turns around the dormitory-floor corridors, following black tiles set like checkerboard squares in a border between the white tiles and painted skirt boards. The home was four stories and she daily circumnavigated all but the top, which was the delivery floor, where she was not permitted to visit and that she did not wish to see.

She couldn't walk outside, of course. Not only because another snowstorm raged, beating wildly against windows, but because here, no self-respecting woman so far into confinement would dare to show herself on the streets. (She was self-respecting. She respected herself. This was another reason to give up the baby for adoption. The adoption would make her child legitimate.)

Here, going out in her condition in public would have been unseemly even if she'd been carrying a legitimate child, if Thom had lived to be her husband and shared with her a fine flat rented by earnings from his work as a carpenter, the work he'd learned under old Mr. Dollard. Thom had apprenticed with him since he was ten. He'd stop at his shop on his walk home from school. Mr. Dollard's own sons hadn't been interested in the trade. Mr. Dollard was the best in Kilconly. He not only trimmed doors and planed walls but whittled cradles and carved beautiful furniture and helped Thom make a bowl for his mother out of one piece of wood. She wondered if Mr. Dollard had received the news of Thom's passing. She imagined Mr. Dollard's face, disappointment in his jowls, when he realized all that he'd imparted to Thom over the years, skills he'd imagined would go to America and be part of the new country that was still getting built, had been for naught.

She imagined herself rocking a painted cradle Thom had made for their baby.

That night, it was her turn for the bathtub, and she sank happily into water still warm, though she was the third to use it. Her breasts, which had been small, seemed enormous. Her stomach rose like a white mountain, grand and imposing. Tiny blue tributaries traversed it and her breasts. Her little pink nipples had enlarged, dark and forbidding. There was a line on her belly from her navel all the way down, and it tightened sometimes as if to cut her in half.

She rested both hands on her roundness, hoping the baby could feel the embrace. Maybe it could. She thought of her baby as a person whom only she knew. Sometimes a miniature hand or foot outlined itself on her flesh, pressing against the world from inside her. Her stomach was now a hard thing, almost as hard as a door on which she could tap. "Knock, knock," she said, trying to make contact.

Did she pray? She prayed as she stepped from the tub (a tap had come at the door; her time was up). She prayed that the birth would be something she'd live through. She prayed the baby would not be deformed, would not come out a Mongoloid idiot. Her mother's cousin had had a child like that, and she had lived with her mother for forty-two years before passing away. "Happy years!" claimed the cousin. "I am blessed to have had her." Bridey's baby didn't have that option. If Bridey's baby wasn't perfect, adoption would be impossible. She'd have to decide whether to keep her daughter or place her for life in a grim institution.

As Bridey slipped a heavy white nightgown over her head, *Lucretia Bell Mission* embroidered in blue at the breast, she heard emanate from herself what sounded like gurgles and felt a fizziness, as if she'd turned into a glass bottle of carbonated water.

Soon, she would meet her baby. What would her baby think of her? She wished she were ready to welcome her with a home and a hearth and the carved rocking cradle that Thom would have spent these months preparing.

"I'm sorry," she said to her baby, gently moving the towel over the mound of her middle. She was sorry to be ushering her into the world in January, the coldest month of the year.

One of the girls had worked for a hairdresser and had brought with her an expensive bottle of Harlene. For three cents a head, she shampooed all the girls' hair with it once they neared their time so their hair would look fine when their babies came. She'd shampooed Bridey's hair that morning and now Bridey was standing by a sitting-room window, lifting her hair to dry it in the morning sun. Thom had loved her hair, called it a pour of honey. It was waist length, so drying it would take a long time, but putting her hands through it, she could almost feel how shiny it was. She would meet her baby looking her best.

She wandered to a reading table and glanced at the *Herald*, which had been left unfolded. She became engrossed in the story of a strange appearance. A winged creature had landed on the roof of a home in New Jersey, a never-before-seen species with the face of a collie dog and the head of a horse! As Bridey stared at the sketch, she felt something drop through her, pressing at her lower regions—causing something inside her to burst.

A whiteness went through her.

She was afraid of what she would see, looking down. The floor was a puddle that steamed in the cold.

No baby, though. She was glad of that. She didn't know what to do. What was she to do?

She couldn't think clearly. She twisted her wet hair, tucked it into her collar, and bent and reached for old newspapers in the tin below the table. She began sopping up water. She felt a dull pain at the small of her back. She got down on all fours. As she pressed the papers, letting the water soak in, she thought how good she suddenly felt. The pressure at the small of her back was relieved. She wished to stay on the floor in that position, not caring that she resembled a hoofed animal.

"Lulabelle?" One of the girls passing called to her, then, seeing her and not needing an answer, she said she would run downstairs and tell them to ring for the midwife.

Bridey stayed on her hands and knees, luxuriating in the relief she felt arching her back, as if she could throw off the pain like a wild horse tossing a saddle.

As she waited for help, she spoke to her child. *Oh, wee one,* she said silently in the voice she'd used for months. *Oh, wee Thomasine.* She wanted to prepare her baby for what was to come. But what was to come? Bridey had no idea.

She'd not seen a birth, though her mother had birthed eight children after her. She should have been there for Daisy's birth three years ago—her mother had asked her to be there without asking it outright, but Bridey had refused, without saying so.

"Go for Mrs. McGinn," Mother had said. She'd been standing at the stove, and she turned off the fire and clutched her belly and went to her bed. Bridey had taken the bike the midwife had left them and wheeled through town and found Mrs. McGinn hanging clothes on a line. As soon as she saw Bridey, she threw down her basket, disappeared into the house, then came out with her carpet-bag. She invited Bridey to ride on the seat behind her but Bridey said she'd go faster without a passenger. Bridey had walked home, taking the long way. When she got there, she was glad to find that Daisy had already arrived.

Bridey was finally "going up." The midwife, Mrs. Garelli, and her daughter Tess were helping Bridey into the elevator cage. There wasn't enough room for three of them, so Tess took the stairs, her quick steps echoing in the stair column beside them. Bridey distracted herself from the pain in her back by counting the girl's steps, which were so fast, she was already on the floor waiting for them when the cage stopped. Tess and her mother guided Bridey across the hall to the birthing room and then helped her out of her skirts and stockings and into a clean white frock that ended above her shins.

The room, which Bridey had resisted seeing before now, was plain. Just a cot, a table, a coal stove, and a window. It was midafternoon. The winter light was weak. The room was cold. Bridey was glad when Tess got the stove going.

The first thing the midwife did was tie up Bridey's wet hair (Bridey didn't care about her hair now) and anoint the area behind Bridey's right ear with a dab of lavender oil. She said it would lessen the pain. Tess helped Bridey onto the bed. She was a small girl of about fourteen, but her slender arms were remarkably strong. The bed was a thin mattress covered with a rubber pad secured to the sheet with safety pins.

There was a big pot on the stove, and the midwife heated it. Soon her daughter was putting a cup of pennyroyal tea to Bridey's lips. By this time, Bridey was moaning. She felt ready to rupture. The midwife helped her, gently, to stand, then walk, then she had her squat on the floorboards, hanging on to the rails at the foot of the bed. Bridey clutched the rails, which seemed to her to be the bars of a prison. The daughter did what her mother instructed, which was to press her fist into the small of Bridey's back.

"Harder," said the midwife.

"Harder," said Bridey. The girl could not press hard enough there. It felt as if the weight of the world were boring into the base of her spine, and the only relief from it was the fist of the girl pressing against it to obliterate what was happening there.

Then the pressing didn't work anymore.

The pain came and went and came again. Bridey took her hand from the rail and the midwife put a comb into her palm.

"Squeeze," said the midwife. "Direct your pain into its soft teeth."

Bridey squeezed the comb in her hand, focusing on the lesser pain of slender ivory teeth biting into the pad of her thumb.

Soon, she was swallowed into delirium. She imagined that what was inside her trying to get out was the winged creature she had been reading about; it was scrabbling against her innards, destroying her in its attempt to escape.

She begged the midwife to cut off her legs, to let out the baby. Bridey had not known there was so much pain in the world. She felt aged by the knowledge and terrified of not being able to survive it.

She prayed to Saint Gerard, patron of motherhood. She cried Hail Marys to Saint Jude, the patron of desperate cases. She prayed to Thom to take her to him. She felt desperate to leave all this and be with him.

Tess didn't seem frightened as Bridey would have been as a girl. She was glad of that. The girl prayed with her sometimes. She was glad of that too, grateful to be among those of her faith. Tess crossed herself, then crossed Bridey's forehead with her thumb, which suddenly worried her—was it some sort of anointing that meant she was dying? She begged for laudanum, which she knew was reserved only for cases over which doctors presided. But surely her case now required a doctor?

The midwife guided her back into the bed.

"Push," she said. "Push."

Bridey mentally gathered what strength she felt was left in her body and bore down on her center, and then—the midwife was lifting a wet, wriggling lump from between Bridey's legs.

"A boy," said the midwife.

"Are you sure?" Bridey said.

"A boy," confirmed the midwife's daughter.

Not Thomasine. Mikeen. It was Thom's middle name. Bridey's heart beat in her throat as she watched the midwife turn her son upside down. Her fingers were red with Bridey's blood. She held his ankles with one hand, as if he were a plucked chicken to be made into soup. He was no bigger than a roaster and Bridey wondered that something so small could have survived the ordeal.

"Is he sound?"

The midwife didn't answer, just swatted his back as if chastising the poor child for the unlucky choice of being born to Bridey. After the slap came a sound that seemed both a human cry and a lamb's bleat, more a plea than a scream. He was covered with what looked like smears of soft cheese.

"A fine boy," said the midwife. She wiped him and rubbed him with olive oil, then set him on Bridey's chest. She felt a jolt as his bare skin touched hers. The baby was red and wrinkled and as young as a human could possibly be—and yet he looked like an ancient creature.

The midwife now took two pieces of string from the table. She tied the string around the cord, a thick blue pulsing rope that connected her to her baby as if he were meant to be towed. The midwife tied the string in two places, close to the baby and then close to Bridey. It looked as if she were tying a sausage. Then she dipped scissors into the pot on the stove and came at the cord. Bridey closed her eyes. She thought it might hurt. She shielded her baby's eyes, which made the midwife laugh. "He can't see anything yet," she said. The Harlene was a waste.

After the cord was cut, when her son was no longer part of her body, the midwife fluttered a square of muslin over him. His smell filled her with gratitude and something she'd never felt before. She pulled the cloth tighter to bring their bodies closer together, to keep him warm. She was so happy, she felt almost drunk.

"Mikeen," she said. "My wee little Magee." How she wished Thom were with her. But he was with her in their baby's fair skin, his dimpled chin, the swirl of red on the back of his head.

The tiny eyes were closed, but the lips were moving, groping. She lifted her breast toward him. His lips sought, found the nipple, latched on. There came a sharp pain when he began to suck. She felt a shifting inside her, and something slid into place.

She—was somebody's mother.

She'd watched mothers suckle their young countless times—dogs and sheep and cows in the field—so she imagined that nature's method of supplying nourishment would come to her naturally. She'd often seen her own mother nurse a baby, usually while doing other things too—stirring a pot or wetting the tea—so Bridey was surprised that the next time the little face was put to her breast, it turned away. The boy's face crumpled, as if he knew he ought not to attach himself to her.

It took Mrs. Garelli a good while to guide him back to her, and after some hours, when his lips finally relented and latched onto her dripping nipple, Bridey cried out in pleasure, so grateful was she for the pain of this reunion.

She spent weeks in the lying-in room, where new mothers were encouraged to stay with their babies to endow them with the strengthening gift of their milk, to advance the health of infants to the optimal level needed to fortify them against the trauma of separation. She spent hours singing lullabies her mother and grand-mother had sung to her, those she'd hummed to her siblings to put them to sleep: "Balleamon Cradle Song," "Fairy Lullaby," "Shoheen Sho Lo." She'd never closely attended the words before, but now they struck her:

> *Hush-a-by baby, babe not mine,*
> *Shoheen sho, ulolo,*
> *Shoheen sho, strange baby O!*
> *You're not my own sweet baby O!*

"'You're not my baby,'" she sang as she rocked him gently in her arms, watching his eyelids descend as she held him, steeling herself against what the song said. She imagined being able to keep him. But how could she keep him? She had no place to live. She had no job and no prospects for one with an illegitimate baby in tow.

Adelaide came to visit. They thought of ways that Bridey might keep her baby or, failing that, keep a know on where he was. They thought of swaddling him, putting him in a basket, and leaving him on the doorstep of the Fifth Avenue house where Adelaide worked. But Adelaide said Mrs. Hathaway wouldn't raise him, she'd give him away. She had three children already—and Adelaide said she wasn't the motherly type.

> *You're not my own sweet baby O!*

It was Sarah who convinced Bridey to give up the child. Sarah's en-treaties had begun almost as soon as she met Bridey at the mission.

"Which are you?" Sarah asked. "A fallen woman or a wayward girl?"

Bridey had been startled. But later, she saw that Sarah had only been trying to lighten a bleak situation. Bridey appreciated the lack of judgment in Sarah. Righteousness had been apparent in the faces of the other women who had accompanied Sarah that first day.

Later, Sarah decided it was better to be *wayward* than *fallen*. "Less of a climb back up," she'd said, smiling.

"Think of his future," Sarah urged Bridey in serious discussions, and though Bridey had resisted her entreaties for weeks, she knew in her heart she couldn't keep him. How could she keep him? Still— she prayed. She prayed to Saint Brigid, her patron saint, the protectress of newborns.

The mission didn't press her to give up her baby. It said in the literature they'd accommodate mothers and babies for as long as was needed. But Bridey knew there was an end to the charity even good Protestants were capable of.

On Good Friday, she walked to service at a Catholic church a few blocks from the mission, the Church of St. Mary in the Fields. It was in the middle of a dark, greenless part of town, and what better example, thought Bridey, of people in one place wishing to be in another.

The church was crowded with people praying the stations as the priest walked the incense around, swinging the smoky brass chimney on its chain. As the air filled with the scent of holiness and bells rang and the priest murmured Latin she knew from her parish, Bridey knew with calm certainty what she should do.

She would give up her son. That's what was best for him. She would give up her son, as the Father gave up His only Son too.

When she got back to the mission, she went to the nursery and took Mikeen from the crib. He was two and a half months old already, too big to share a crib with more than one other. She brought

him back to her bed, where she lay him down gently and explained to him what she needed to do. As she spoke, she gently took off his dress and ran her hands over him, following the sweet curve of his cheeks, his doughy tummy, his pillowy thighs. He had Thom written all over him—in the red of his hair, in his cobalt-blue eyes, in the dimple in his chin.

He didn't seem to take after her in any way. Suddenly, she felt desperate to mark him, to leave him with some sign of herself. But a baby could be marked only by things that would hurt him, and by this design, it was obvious that God had never been a mother Himself.

The next day was Holy Saturday, and she stood in line with many others for confession. When it came her turn, she'd gone through the velvet curtain and knelt in the dark, airless confessional box, waiting for the little door to be pushed aside, the one that closed over the screen between her face and the priest's. When the door slid open, Bridey murmured her sins and was told to repent and say a whole rosary. She'd said the first decade at the altar, kneeling on a velvet hassock; the next four she said fingering her beads on the walk back to the mission.

When Sarah came the next Wednesday, Bridey told her of her decision and asked her to find a foundlings' home for Mikeen, one that was Catholic. She wanted to make sure that her baby would be baptized. If he wasn't baptized by a priest, no matter how good was the life that he led, he wouldn't achieve heaven.

The next week Sarah said that she had located a Catholic foundlings' home. Bridey asked if she herself could bring Mikeen there, but they wouldn't allow it. So Bridey let down her arms, and a nurse took her baby. The last of him she saw was his red screaming face, a dark moon rising and falling over a white shoulder.

14

Sarah

Wellington, Connecticut

April 1909

Engraved invitations to a party in honor of *Edmund Fitch Porter's Achievement of One-Quarter of a Century in Age* were delivered by hand and *Miss Sarah Stanton Hollingworth* was pleased to receive one.

On the Saturday after Easter, a party was held at the Porter house on Vine Street, and Sarah was delighted when, soon after she arrived, Edmund pried her from a conversational knot and whisked her to a passageway where they were alone.

"I want to read you something," he said, turning to the glass doors of a bookcase that rose to the ceiling. The shelves sagged, laden with leather-bound volumes. Edmund slid the glass doors apart and pulled down a slim book.

"I just received this. From a bookseller in Paris. They finally brought it out in English. After a hundred and fifty years!"

He began to read from *The Rubáiyát of Omar Khayyám.*

Awake! For Morning in the Bowl of Night
Has flung the Stone that puts the Stars to Flight

Stars! At last Edmund was speaking to her of stars!

How handsome he looked, his dark hair falling over his brow, intent on reading to her, leaning on the polished banister, one boot propped on the first step of the stairs. She hoped—she dared hope!—he would mark the occasion by giving her his Yale ring, the precursor to rings of more enduring significance.

But now here was her brother appearing in the passage to distract him.

"Didja hear? Peary made it to the North Pole. It's ours! Our flag's there!"

And now Edmund's attention turned to her brother as he explained the impossibility of territorial jurisdiction in the high seas, and as Edmund held forth, citing international law, Sarah saw for herself a bleak future as an old aunt to her brother's children, waiting on a dock with them as they waved good-bye to Benno and his wife, such a happy couple boarding a steamer bound for capital cities in Europe that Sarah herself would never be able to visit because she'd be an old maid like Aunt Gert!

When Edmund began talking of nautical miles, Sarah seized the conversation and asked him to tell them about Paris, hoping that Benno would drift away.

"Paris!" Edmund said. "City of Love!" Then he brightened and launched into descriptions of fountains and arrondissements and an exhibition of modern locomotions, not only autos but flying machines and now Sarah saw that Benno wouldn't walk away and how foolish she was to hope tonight for a ring. How long and winding was the road to engagement, belying the straight paths of courtship laid out in lady columns.

Sarah was pulled into conversation with several ladies from Christian Benevolence who were discussing whether or not poverty was a choice. Mrs. Prebscott believed that if people were counseled correctly, fewer would make the ill-advised decision to be poor.

"But no one chooses to be born without advantages," Sarah was saying when Rachel tapped her shoulder. Their father's carriage was waiting for them.

Edmund appeared suddenly and offered to get Sarah's coat. His face was shining as he made his way back to her, steering her mother's fur cloak through the crowd. As he laid it over her shoulders and she slipped her arms into it, he advised her to search for her gloves and make sure that both were still there. She reached into the pocket and pulled out one white kid glove, then the other; she tucked one glove under her arm and slipped a hand into the other, fitting her fingers in, one, two, three, four—

"What's this?" Sarah said. She pulled off the glove, shook it, and there in her palm lay—an engagement ring.

There were fifty people in the room, but for Sarah there was only Edmund, who was glowing with pride in her and—she knew—in himself for navigating what was, unhelpfully, not set down in law books.

15

Bridey

Wellington, Connecticut

May 1909

When Sarah told Bridey that she'd persuaded her father to hire her at their big house in Connecticut, Bridey was glad for the chance.

On the train, Sarah said, "Just—don't divulge you're a girl from the mission. Let him think you were staff there, not a charity case."

"What about the other ladies who saw me?" Bridey asked, recalling powdered faces and fine hats.

"Oh, they won't remember. They move to a different mission each week. It's only me who asked to stay behind."

Sarah urged Bridey to take a room on the second floor next to Nettie's, but Bridey chose the room at the top of the service stairs. Sarah had warned there was no stove in it, but Bridey was used to a room with no stove. The room was small and spare but, ah, how it suited her. She had a whole bed to herself! It was a small bed, but the sheets were clean (she herself washed them) and so was the quilt.

(They gave her a quilt! A star pattern in shades of blue, her favorite color.) Beside the bed stood a pine stand, a trunk for a closet; a colorful rag rug brightened the wide-board floor. Above her bed she'd hung a crucifix, the one from Lourdes, the one Mrs. Ahearn had given her and didn't want back. Every morning when Bridey woke, she touched two fingers to the wood of the cross, which was the last thing of this earth that had touched Thom when he was living, then kissed the fingers that had touched it, knelt on the rug, and said her prayers. Then she stood and turned in a circle, facing first the bed, then the window, then the trunk, then the tear-a-page calendar on the wall, knowing that once while she was going around, she'd faced her son for a moment too.

Bridey took her dress off the hook and buttoned its front. Her milk had finally stopped. But she'd be bursting with love for her baby for the rest of her life. It was a kind of love she'd known only after becoming a mother. Taking care of other people's children didn't count, even if those children were your own siblings. She loved her siblings with all her heart—but it wasn't a mother's love. Yet she wasn't a mother. This was an agony she hadn't foreseen.

She tore a page from the calendar. Sunday, May 9. She had been here almost three weeks. Her baby was almost four months old. What did he look like? What did he see? She imagined him growing out of new clothes, surrounded by shiny toys, good food being pushed through his lips with a silver pusher.

The plaster ceiling was so low in places that even Bridey had to duck her head. She liked the fact that the room was low-ceilinged and not fit for anyone else but her. The Hollingworths were tall and thin in their Protestant way. They were nothing but kind to her, but she drew strength from being able to retire to her solitude. The only person who visited was Nettie, who was taller than Bridey but not by so much that she had to crouch here.

Nettie was kind to Bridey, something Bridey hadn't expected.

She knew from Adelaide that longtime staff weren't always accepting of newly hired help. But Nettie's work for the Hollingworths was mixed up with her gratitude for the family's charity, and this Bridey had in common with Nettie. When Bridey asked Nettie if she imagined moving on, Nettie said she'd promised Mrs. Hollingworth that if anything happened to her, she'd stay until Hannah, the youngest, was married. Nettie said she was happy enough here and then shrugged and added, "Where else would I go?"

Where else would either of them go? thought Bridey. She saw herself an old lady, slowly climbing the stairs to her room on ancient legs. But she was just seventeen; it would be years before she had to think about being old.

"Mornin', Nettie," Bridey said in the kitchen. Nettie was taking a tray of sugared biscuits out of the oven and Bridey longed for one but couldn't break her fast until after Communion. Nettie went to the Baptists, who didn't meet until late.

Bridey pulled on white gloves, slipped out the back kitchen door, and set off for Mother of Sorrows. She loved walking to Mass, smelling fresh wood and straw and clover warmed by the sun as she wended her way on paths so like those of her childhood. Haycocks and oat shocks stood in the middle of stone-walled fields. She heard the calls of bobolinks and the melancholy bleating of sheep. She followed the dirt path circling the lake and nodded hello to a boy carrying a pail of brown spotted fish. Then, through woods, past a grove of flowering pear trees, along the fence of the dairy, up a hill, across the lawn of the gray convent, and there was the church, its red doors thrown open, its white clapboards glowing, its bell tower standing sentinel over the triangle of park made by the meeting of two roads.

She was welcomed by the deacon and she dipped her fingertips into the font, then crossed herself and took a seat in a pew near the front, but not the front pew. She liked to be early, liked having a few moments to herself in silence, taking in the brightly colored glass in the pointed windows, the carved statues beautifully painted, some clothed in robes. Seeing Saint Joseph with his hammer in hand always made her miss Thom. How much more cheerful was Mother of Sorrows than the church at home where she and Thom might have married. There, the windows were dull glass and the statues unpainted, colorful only during Lent when they were shrouded in purple.

Bridey said silent prayers for herself and her son. She said a prayer for Thom, who might be in purgatory. She prayed for each of her family back home, including the two who were gone, Jeremiah and Patrick. She pictured them as baby angels nestled in clouds. She marveled that she'd been gone from home for more than a year now.

Her family felt distant, the string that had once been taut between them frayed and grown slack, consisting now only of intermittent correspondence with her sister Kathleen. Kathleen was the only one who wrote back, although Bridey had written them all (except Da), even remembering their birthdays. Her siblings' birth dates were emblazoned on the inside of her skull. As oldest, she remembered, because each birth had meant the loveliness of a new baby, yes, but also another mouth to quiet, to feed.

Bridey regretted that her letters were lies. Not outright lies, but lies of omission, which the nuns at St. Ursula's had warned were worse.

I've been hired to work at a big house in the country, she wrote a few weeks ago. *A beautiful mansion. The family is fine and give me board and good pay.*

She didn't mention that she sometimes suffered from their mam's "dark demons." On the worst days, her mother had lain in bed, turning her back to them. Bridey hadn't guessed that her mother's pain had been physical. She'd thought the pain was all in her head. But now she wondered how her mother got up at all, weighted by the awful anvil of sadness that Bridey came to know for the first time after Thom's death.

Bridey's aunt was the only one who could make her mother feel herself again, bringing over teas and a foul-smelling plaster of something. What was the plaster? Bridey wished she could run over to her aunt's house and ask. Last week, Bridey had cut her hand on a nail sticking out of the bench wringer and hadn't noticed until she saw in the clean barrel that there was blood on the sheets. She'd bound her hand and rewashed the sheets. If it became known that Bridey sometimes suffered from melancholy, she could end up in an asylum. There was one up the road, Laverstock Farm for Lunatics, named for its benefactress, Sarah's grandmother. They warded the paupers along with the mad, and so Bridey did her best whenever melancholy descended to conceal it. But today (thank the Lord) was a good day!

At sermon, Father Callaghan talked about mothers, praising them as the unsung heroes of the faith. He said that today was an important day, as it marked the first Mother's Day, a day to honor mothers that would be set aside each year from now on.

Mother's Day! Another ingenious invention of the Americans, who were always thinking of ways to improve things, unlike her people, who preferred to leave things as they had been since the Druids. Baskets of white carnations came down the pews, and each mother was invited to take one. When the basket came to Bridey, her hand hesitated over the fragrant froth of white ruffles—

"Mothers have secrets that men never learn," boomed the priest from the pulpit, and Bridey was unable to let go of the basket until the man sitting next to her gently took it and passed it to the nun beside him, who passed it on.

Bridey recognized him! He was Oskar Engel, the German coachman at Hollingwood. What was he doing here? She hadn't known he was Catholic. When Mass was over, he offered to take her home in the car, but Bridey declined, feeling intruded upon.

Bridey

Wellington, Connecticut

June 1909

Bridey arrived in the kitchen one morning just as Nettie was spatula-ing fried cakes from a pan onto a silver platter. Bridey trayed the platter, added a maple syrup pitcher and four little glasses of juice (two orange, two plum), picked up the tray, navigated the narrow passage through the pantry, and swung through the door that led to the dining room. Most of the family were already assembled—Sarah and Benno and Hannah and Mr. Hollingworth. Rachel rarely came down for breakfast, preferring to ring the call bell around noon, at which point Bridey carried her breakfast up to her.

Benno was talking excitedly about something in one of the morning papers. His voice seemed to have deepened in the six weeks since Bridey had come. Benno was the same age that Thom would have been—eighteen—but he had the gleam and gloss of a much older man. Perhaps this was partly due to his wearing a three-piece executive suit. During school holidays and summer vacations from school, Benno worked at the Hollingworth factory, training for the day he'd assume its management.

"But why can't we get a Nevo, Father?" Benno was saying. "It's 1909! Why must we live as if it's the 1800s?"

What is a Nevo? Bridey wondered, wishing she could swipe at the trickle of sweat meandering down her back. It was the hottest June in Connecticut on record.

"*Oven* spelled backward!" said Benno, pointing to the ad. "It's fueled by ice instead of coal!"

"The Canfields already have one," put in Sarah.

But their father didn't look up from the stocks page. "A contraption like that is a needless extravagance," he said. "Mr. Hayden tells me it requires hundreds of pounds of ice cut from the icehouse."

He turned to Bridey as she took up the tray. "Are you feeling up to that swim lesson soon, Miss Molloy?"

Everyone else at Hollingwood called her Bridey, but Mr. Hollingworth insisted on Miss Molloy. She didn't mind. He spoke with the formality of people born in the last century. Of course, Bridey herself had been born in the last century, but in the 1890s, which didn't count because that was when changes were already in progress. The decade she was born into felt to her less the end of a century than the beginning of one, like a musical prelude leading up to a score.

"To be sure," said Bridey, though she was terrified of the water. Even the word *swim* set her heart pounding. But Mr. Hollingworth insisted that everyone on the property know how to swim.

"It's because of my brother who drowned," Sarah had told her.

That Bridey didn't know how to swim had surprised Mr. Hollingworth and everyone else she'd been serving at a luncheon party soon after she'd arrived.

Wasn't the place where she grew up by the sea? they inquired.

And so Bridey came to learn the American view of the Irish: they all lived by the sea. She didn't take up their time to explain that

145

Kilconly was a half a day's ride from Galway Bay—but only if the cart horses were going—and the only other place to learn to swim was the lake given over to fishermen who didn't abide splashers disturbing the source of their livelihood. She'd never forget the terror of falling out of a boat at age three, of the darkness as she sank, breathing in water—then the strength of her father's hands, squeezing her ribs as he drew her to him. She'd breathed in blue sky and his whiskey breath, grateful for both.

Nettie showed her a photo of the brother who had drowned. They were in the library and Nettie was demonstrating how to clean the glass dome over the wax flowers displayed on the mantel. Nettie opened a small brass frame set next to it. The frame folded. On one side, under a glass bubble, was a lock of dark hair. On the other, a portrait of a little boy and girl holding hands.

"That's Sarah." Nettie pointed and Bridey could just make out Sarah's face in the tiny girl dressed in scallops and frills. She was holding the hand of a boy in a white suit. She was standing, but he was sitting, dwarfed by the dark chair. Something was odd about the way he was perched on the cushion.

"He's dead," Nettie told her. "That photographer came round to take this after he went. His mother, she wouldn't put him in the ground without having something to remember him with."

Bridey's horror was momentary, displaced by a sudden longing for a photo of Thom. Even one taken on his deathbed would comfort her now. It had been a year and she couldn't believe she'd already forgotten the exact shape of his eyes.

Bridey wished she had someone with whom she could talk, really talk, about Thom and the baby. Nettie would be sympathetic, she thought. Nettie had a big heart. She was ten years older and though she had never married or been a mother, Bridey knew she knew things. But—Nettie was a talker. Bridey worried that telling her secret to Nettie would be like blowing on the feathery seeds of a dandelion, sending them adrift to the milkman, the iceman, the fruit-and-vegetable man (now toting a box through the screened door of the kitchen), and from them to the town where people would think ill of the Hollingworths for taking in a girl who was not only Irish but a slattern. (She knew from Nettie that some in town were suspicious of the Irish.)

She shuddered to think of Mr. Hollingworth—who needn't have given in to Sarah's request for another livey-in—discovering what Bridey was by hearing it in town.

Bridey couldn't talk, really talk, to Sarah. Even though Sarah was five years older than Bridey and had graduated from Catharine Beecher's seminary, she seemed unconversant with the hard truths of the world.

When Sarah and Bridey first met, Sarah's greatest fear had been that her younger sister Rachel would marry before she did. Now that Sarah's wedding to Edmund was set for next June, Sarah worried that Halley's comet, which was predicted to come in May, would destroy the world, and all her wedding plans would be for nothing.

One night, Bridey sat with Sarah, helping her ready her trousseau. They were both engrossed in working needles on lace when one of Sarah's needles fell to the floor. She looked up, and Bridey saw that her cheeks were aflame.

"But if we're consumed by comet gas, what will be the use of antimacassars?" Sarah cried.

Bridey consoled her with soothing words while thinking that if she herself went with the comet, it might be a blessing, as long as her baby was spared. She said a silent prayer that his parents had bought the pills being advertised everywhere, protection against the effects of the gas.

17.

Bridey

Hollingwood

June 1910

If Bridey had known about the appalling American practice of displaying wedding gifts as if arranging them in a shop window, if she'd had any inkling that an entire bedroom would be cleared for their display—bed and bureaus and bookcases removed to the barn; tables brought up, draped in linens, and decorated with flowers chosen to set off the gifts—if she'd known that the giver of each would be identified by a little undeniable card penned in the florid hand of the stationer's wife famous in town for being good with the quill, Bridey would have waited until *after* the wedding to give Sarah her gift.

Sarah had told Bridey that she disdained as vulgar the old-fashioned practice of displaying gifts publicly in a downstairs parlor. But how could Sarah think herself discreet in relocating her gifts when everyone who set foot in the house was brought up to see them?

Emptying the room had taken all of a morning. Bridey had filled boxes with books from the bookcases that Oskar and the hired man then took to the barn. The men had had to make many trips to wrestle heavy wood pieces through doorways and down the narrow stairwell, shifting the weight of them back and forth to avoid nicking the plaster.

When they'd made the last trip, Bridey had stood in the emptied room, letting herself expand in it, filling its emptiness, imagining herself its mistress, before dusting and sweeping it.

"Take Duxie upstairs for a quick viewing, will you, Bridey?" Sarah had asked. Most girls were already seated in the parlor for the bridesmaids' luncheon, but Sarah's friend Duxie had been late. She was a slim, fair young woman whose movements were birdlike and quick, as if she were given less time to do things than others were, which was often true, though the fault was Duxie's own. She was known to be a latecomer, tardy to almost every event to which she was invited. Hostesses who had been burned by this failing deliberately advanced times on invitation cards to her. This Sarah had done too, which was why Duxie's appearance came as early as soup. But she begged to see the gifts before sitting down, presumably so she'd be able to join in the talk at the table about them.

Duxie was already handing her hat and parasol to Bridey, who deposited them with those of others on the front-hall bench, then led Duxie upstairs. As she mounted the spiral to the hallway and the viewing room, she could feel Duxie's impatience as Bridey's steps slowed.

Bridey dreaded turning into the room. The gleam from the display seemed to reach into the dark hallway, illuminating it.

The room had looked bigger without anything in it. Now it was filled with fine china, polished wood, gilt-framed etchings, fine Smyrna carpets unrolled just enough to reveal bright silk threads and gold braids. And so much silverware! She'd had no idea so many implements existed: croquette servers and oyster forks, tongs for asparagus and muddlers for chocolate, tiny spoons for bouillon and long-handled ones with holes in their bowls to drain liquor from olives. Duxie had given Sarah a set of silver berry forks.

And then there was Bridey's gift for all to see, an ugly duckling in a line of swans. The gift Bridey had worked on night after night, by the light of the little paraffin lamp on her bedside table. *Miss Brighid Molloy* accused the card beside it. The *M*s and *B* seemed to be shouting. She hoped that Duxie wouldn't notice it. But: "How cunning the work is," Duxie said, her gloved fingers reaching. Then, to Bridey's mortification, Duxie lifted her gift—a humble lace doily.

The doily was crochet lace, not point lace, which Bridey regretted. She would have liked to spend time creating thousands of tiny stitches, releasing a pattern of intricate swirls, as she'd learned to do in Sister Hortense's class. But she hadn't linen thread here, only cotton. The doily was done with nothing so fine as a needle, only a steel crochet hook.

She'd wanted to give Sarah something to express what she couldn't in words, gratitude that she hoped showed itself in the careful stitching that had taken up many hours.

"Wherever did you find it?" Duxie asked, looking at Bridey through the latticed design.

And when Duxie heard that Bridey had made it, she squealed, *"Yourself?"* in what seemed to Bridey misplaced admiration, and later, when Bridey served luncheon, trying not to make a clatter while removing a tray of two-handled cups and then serving creamed oysters and molded lobster, passing plates of stacked triangles of olive sandwiches, she was, to her surprise, complimented on the gift by several girls at the table.

In the years following, the skill Bridey had learned from the nuns, who'd said that it was a womanly art every girl ought to acquire, became a source of pin money, as word got around that Bridey could provide for a song what was impossibly dear in New York on Ladies' Mile.

18.

Sarah

Wellington Congregational Church, Connecticut

June 1910

At the first strains of *Lohengrin*'s wedding march from the organ newly installed in the balcony, members of the procession left the vestibule, and Sarah watched them proceed up the aisle—first, the ushers in twos (how handsome Benno looked in his cutaway frock coat), then eight bridesmaids, each pair dressed in a shade of pink lighter than the preceding two, then Rachel, the maid of honor, in palest pink, then Edmund's little niece in white tulle. And, finally, Sarah, who in a surge of modest embarrassment looked down and, through tears, saw her own white satin slippers embark on the most important walk of her life.

How glad she was for her father's steadying arm. As she proceeded up the aisle, she was surprised at the shakiness that came over her. Every part of her trembled. Even the brooch she was wearing, Edmund's wedding gift to her, pearls and diamonds in the shape of a comet, was in motion. Her nosegay, she feared, was bobbing like a drink toy

151

She calmed when she saw Edmund waiting for her at the end of the aisle, standing just inside the chancel. How handsome he looked in his dark frock coat, a curl of white ribbon on his lapel.

Then—"Slowly, daughter," her father murmured, making Sarah see that she'd hurried her step, and guilt came over her. This day was a euphoric beginning for her but signified for him an ending of sorts. As eldest, Sarah remembered her mother as the younger children could not. She was said to share myriad qualities with her, so Sarah's taking leave of the house meant that her father was, in a way, losing her mother all over again. She was glad her father would be going on a tour of the Continent with Benno, a gift for his graduation from Trowbridge.

She gave her father's arm three little squeezes, which was a code they'd shared since she was a child, each squeeze a silent word in *I love you,* and he answered with reassuring movements of the muscles in his upper arm that she could feel through his morning coat.

As they approached the front section of pews, she was gratified to see that the ribbons had been tied in little festoons at the pew ends, not fastened as barriers as they usually were. She silently thanked Mrs. Canfield, who knew all the niceties, a godsend to a bride who didn't have a mother to lead her.

They passed Edmund's mother in the front row, but even her loud sobbing in her black mourning cape and mantilla couldn't diminish the happiness burning in Sarah this day.

They reached Edmund, and her father guided her right hand into his left. She took the arm of her soon-to-be husband (*husband!*) and they faced Reverend Bierwirth in his swallowtail coat. Sarah's hand trembled as she clung to Edmund's forearm, and he rubbed her fingers with his own during the blessing, as if to impart to her some of his strength.

"...woman given to man to be a helpmeet to him and to bear his children..."

152

They turned to each other to say their vows. She had to avert her eyes from Edmund's face for a moment. Gazing at it felt to her like looking into the sun. He didn't repeat after the reverend, as she herself would do, but recited the phrases without prompting, having insisted beforehand on memorizing the words that would unite them for life.

How she longed for her mother's eyes on her now. Her mother should be here. And poor Aunt Gert, who had done her best for them in the wake of their mother's death—how sad they had been to receive news in the spring that Gert had perished in the upset of a cruise on the Chesapeake. The maple she'd brought as a sapling to remember Sarah's mother by had grown into a beautifully shaped tree in the front yard, and now looking at it made them remember Gert too.

Through tears, Sarah saw the glitter of the ring moving toward her. Unlike in her mother's day, when a bride delayed the ceremony while she struggled to remove a glove to take on a ring, Sarah simply pulled back a silk finger of her glove. (The left hand of the wedding glove had been bought already slit for this purpose, and thus, another old-fashioned custom had been improved upon by the same ingenuity that accounted for so many modern advancements.) Edmund slid the ring on. She was married.

The next time Sarah would be permitted inside the chancel, she'd be holding a baby. She pictured the infant almost obscured by the long drape of the lacy dress in which Hollingworths had been baptized for generations.

Sarah

Niagara Falls

June 1910

White rice and satin slippers hailed down on the leather roof of the carriage, thrown by exuberant well-wishers gathered on Hollingwood's entrance steps. Sarah glanced back for a last look as the wheels of the coach crunched over gravel. Everyone she loved was gathered behind her and for a moment, she wondered why she was leaving them.

Next time she passed through these stone gateposts, she'd be a matron making her home on Vine Street with Edmund and Edmund's mother in the big rambling house in which Porters had lived for over a century. She thought of the empty rooms darkened by velvet hangings on windows and tried to imagine her place in the rooms; she couldn't. But she didn't need to worry about that until she came back from the falls.

The carriage passed the little gatehouse, and she expected Edmund to take her in his arms and smother her with kisses as he'd promised to do many times in his letters.

Her heart started going faster when he turned to her and took

one of her gloved hands in both of his own. How passionate he was
in his letters, hundreds and hundreds of ivory pages flooded by seas
of blue-inked declarations of love and urgent unburdenings sent to
her sometimes twice a day: *I never before felt the perfect thrilling of love
I have for you . . .*

"I'm glad all that fuss is over, darling, aren't you?" he said.

That fuss? Was that all their wedding was to him—the culmi-
nation of more than a year's work on her part, hours, weeks, months
spent attending to the invitation cards, the trousseau, the teas and
cakes and gifts for the bridesmaids, their dresses and hers, the veils,
the flowers, the seating at tables at the reception, the menus, the
music, the color of ribbons to tie up little takeaway boxes of wedding cake? Decisions, decisions, decisions until sometimes at night,
she was awakened by nightmares in which she'd neglected a critical
detail or shown up at the church at the wrong time, having forgotten entirely the appointed hour.

"Didn't you like it?" she asked. "I suppose your mother would
have been happier if we'd gotten married at the town hall."

His hand slipped from hers and he brushed something invisible
from the gray bowler on his lap.

"Yes, I suppose she would have. She's in mourning, you know."

His mother had worn black in spite of the modern-day custom
that allowed even recent widows to set aside black for a wedding in
favor of gray. She'd not only flouted this rule but sobbed throughout the ceremony, indulging in wails so loud, they'd drowned out
even some of Reverend Bierwirth's words meant to mark the happi-
est day of Sarah's life.

"But your father's been gone for over two years now! You stopped
wearing your armband last year!"

"Oh, let's not talk about my mother," he said, taking up her
hand again. "Not on our wedding day! I don't want you to get in
a bad mood before . . . before we get to my uncle's." Edmund's uncle

had offered his house as a stopping place before they took the train to Niagara tomorrow.

It was shocking to her, the difference between the exuberant Edmund whose passions he'd expressed daily in letters and this quiet, halting man sitting stiffly beside her.

"Let's think of only happy things, dear heart," he said, suddenly animated. He rubbed his thumb and forefinger vigorously against her gloved hand as if to erase a mark on its whiteness. "Like—gee, what a lot of dandy presents we got!"

Had his mother complained that she hadn't written thank-you notes yet? Many brides did them before the wedding. But those brides weren't planning their weddings all on their own.

"Yes, the latest count was over five hundred," she said dully.

"You poor girl," he continued. "Having to respond to them all. I do pity you. But I guess you don't mind it as much as I would."

He continued to talk—about the trees they were passing, the likelihood of bad weather, the views they would see at Niagara, not only the falls but sites that held no interest for her, forts and Civil War monuments and a modern factory that used hydropower to make a new kind of cereal. As she watched his mustache moving up and down, she thought about all it concealed—not only his face, but the thoughts and dreams in his skull, passions that he had expressed beautifully to her on paper but that, she realized, he couldn't or wouldn't say to her in person.

Now that marriage had removed the need for him to write letters, would she ever again catch sight of the man she'd fallen in love with?

When they arrived at his uncle's house in Boston Corners, she was glad to see it wasn't the saltbox she'd been led to expect but a romantic stone cottage. "Shall I carry you over the threshold?" Edmund asked and though she said no, she was disappointed when he didn't insist, just put the great key in the door and held the heavy wood arch open for her, and so she stepped, without ceremony, over the doorsill and into the house where she would be separated from her maidenhood.

His uncle had sent a girl from the village to leave them a cold supper to eat by the fire. But the evening was too warm for a fire. And Sarah couldn't eat. Edmund, however, was ravenous. She sipped tea as she watched him down sandwiches of cold minced ham and take long pulls from a tall glass of beer. A bit of ham got caught in his mustache, and she wished, for the first time, that he was clean-shaven.

He urged her to join him in eating, but she declined.

After supper, she took a long time in the Quincy. It was indoors and conveniently just outside the bedroom. She brushed her hair with her mother's silver-backed brush and rubbed soap powder over her teeth, tasting that his uncle used the old-fashioned kind, with gunpowder in it. She took off her shirtwaist and skirts and corset and fluttered a new nightgown over her head. Bridey had embroidered on it the letters *SHP.*

Silk negligees and pretty underwear will go a long way to making a husband happy—this had been in a manual sent by Aunt Gert last year, after Sarah had written of her engagement to Edmund. The manual had come to Sarah by postal, hidden in a box of saltwater taffy, a concealment made necessary by the Comstock laws, which made it a crime to mail such instructives. Sarah had been grateful for her aunt's kindness but disappointed to discover that *What the Marrying Maiden Needs to Know* was devoid of any mention of parts of the body or suggestions more specific than *following a husband's guidance usually meets with a good outcome.*

She dared not ask married friends what to expect; they would think her unmaidenly. Wedding-night details were impossible to acquire from anyone but a mother, though one evening she'd braved the topic with Mrs. Canfield while they were folding tissue flowers to decorate baskets for the reception.

"I was wondering," she began, "about the night we get married..."

Mrs. Canfield looked up from the rosette she was wiring, smiled indulgently, and assured her that Edmund was a man of the world, and kind, and would tell her everything she needed to know—when the time came that she needed to know it.

When Sarah came back to the bedroom, Edmund rose from the table, where he'd been penning a note, then kissed her lightly on the top of her head and left the room in turn. When he was gone, she moved to the table to read the note. She'd hoped that it was something for her, but it was a letter to the uncle, thanking him for his generosity. *A better honeymoon hideaway couldn't be found and has contributed to a most successful start of our marriage.*

How did he know their marriage would be a success? So many people got married every day, all hoping, no doubt, their union would succeed. But sometimes it didn't. Sometimes one of them died, as had happened to both of their parents. Or one of them left, as had happened last year to a wife whose husband ran off with a fortune-teller who had come to town with a traveling circus. (She was glad Edmund didn't like circuses.)

Sarah crawled into bed and waited for Edmund under the heavy white sheets and old quilt. She clasped her hands across her lace bosom. Though it was June, her feet were so cold, she wished for a hot-water bottle to warm them. The rest of her felt damp and clammy. She worried that perspiration would ruin the beautiful silk of her nightdress.

Edmund returned to the room wearing a long dark gown. He bent to extinguish the candle on the bedside table and she heard him take off his glasses and rest them on a book. The ropes strained on their chains under the horsehair mattress as he climbed in beside her, and for the first time they lay together, side by side, in a bed. She was afraid to move. She was afraid that one of her limbs might touch one of his, which would make her seem forward. She was afraid of what was about to happen. Whatever happened, she guessed it would hurt. But she wanted a baby—they wanted a baby. And this, by God's design, was the way that you got one.

Edmund turned toward her and ran his hand over her silken landscape. She smelled that he'd cleaned his teeth with the soap powder too—this made her glad. He caressed her and she was surprised to feel that his touch sent tingles to parts of her he was not even touching.

"My darling," he said. "My love, my wife, my dear little Mrs. Porter..."

She was alarmed to hear the name of his mother. But, of course, now it was her name too.

Then he was covering her mouth with his and his fingers glided over her waist, her arms, her breasts, her neck, and breathing quickened in both of them and she whispered her love for him and embraced him tightly, her husband, the man whom she loved, now certain that their union *would* be a success—but then his caresses stopped. He gripped the small of her back with one hand and with the other pulled at the hem of her gown. Up, up, up he drew the silk until it reached, obscenely, the top of her legs. Then he knelt above her and, in the moonlight, she saw he wore an expression she'd never seen before, a grin or a grimace, she was not sure which, and it contorted his features so that he appeared to be untender, and now there was something stiff and hard ramming against her secret place and he moved above her faster and faster, oblivious to the violation she felt, driving the bed against the wall, so hard she feared its headboard would put a hole in the plaster. She cried out in pain—and then it was over.

"Are you all right, dear one?" he asked and as soon as she said, re flexively, "Yes," his breathing grew regular. But she could not sleep. Her eyes welled with tears. When she closed them, the tears trickled down to her ears. She made no sound. She didn't want Edmund to realize she was crying. But of course, he didn't realize it. She felt isolated, shut out by him in the act most essential to binding two people together. It seemed that he had forgotten even who she was, had forgotten anyone except himself. Beneath him, she hadn't been Sarah—she might have been anyone.

She stayed awake a long time, counting the swings of the uncle's pendulum clock. She calculated on her fingers—three hundred and sixty-five times a year multiplied by twenty-five years of marriage meant that their silver anniversary would signify over nine thousand consummations.

The next day, when Sarah came back to the bedroom after her toilette, she saw Edmund pulling a square of quilted cotton batting from between the sheets. There was a stain in the square.

"My mother gave this to me," he explained. "So that my uncle's bed fittings wouldn't...be the worse for our stay."

She burned with humiliation as he tossed it into the fire.

How glad she was to be leaving this cottage behind. She meant never to visit the house of his uncle again—of course, now he was her uncle too.

At the appointed hour, a carriage appeared to take them to the train. The train trip lasted all day. She shifted on the hard seat, trying to find a position that was comfortable. Every now and then a sharpness stabbed at her, reminding her of the previous night. She was glad that no one guessed they were newlyweds, save perhaps for the couple who shared their car for a while. The wife asked Sarah where they were traveling, and when she told her their destination, Sarah felt stung by the glances the couple exchanged.

Now she and Edmund were alone in the berth, sitting opposite each other, holding books. She was reading the latest Arnold Bennett novel, he, a history of the Peloponnesian War. Now he was looking up from the pages and talking to her about the speed of the train, reporting calculations of velocity made possible by some newly invented engine and piston. She found herself wishing she'd brought along some of his letters. She needed to keep alive in her mind the man whose heart she knew from words on a page. *I long and dream that our first night will be one such night where the light that comes into your eyes sometimes is more intense than ever.*

"Dash it," he said. "One of my pages hasn't been cut. Did you bring your paper knife?"

She flipped to the back cover and slipped from its wrapper the souvenir her mother had acquired on her own wedding trip. What had her newlywed mother been reading? Sarah had never thought to ask.

Her father, a businessman in command of his schedule, had been able to take his bride away for two months, not the two-week pittance that Edmund's law firm allowed. But now she was glad that their trip would be short.

She handed Edmund the knife and was dismayed to see that he handled it with none of the reverence she felt for an object imbued with the touch of her mother. He slid the blade over the fold at the top of a page, and the pages that were bound instantly fell apart.

When they arrived at the Cataract House, their carriage was welcomed by smartly uniformed attendants who took their suitcases and ushered them into the entrance rotunda. It was already dark, but they could hear the falls. It was touted to be only a stone's throw away. Their trunk, said the clerk, had already come. It was in the room. A white-gloved boy in brass buttons and epaulets led them through reception rooms and writing rooms and parlors furnished

161

with dainty chairs and tables and up two flights of plush-carpeted stairs. The plaque on the door read THE LINCOLN SUITE. The boy told them the former president and the First Lady had stayed there. The bed was enormous, the largest one Sarah had ever seen. Something trembled in her.

They'd arrived too late for supper. A makeshift meal was prepared, brought to their room, and set on a polished piecrust table before the fire: boiled eggs and cold potatoes and banana custard. That night, Sarah ate.

Things occurred in much the same way as they had the night before. Sarah was relieved that the WC nearest their bedroom was private. She changed in it, alone. Then he took his turn. He came back to the room, bolted the door softly behind himself, crossed the floor to her, blew out the flame, took off his glasses, and got into bed. Seconds later, it seemed, he was shifting to a position above her, balancing himself on his elbows, moving in violation of all the cautions and decencies in the world.

The second time didn't hurt so much. After he rolled back to his side of the bed (they had slept together only twice, but she now saw that already there was a "his" side and a "hers"), he fell asleep almost instantly.

If they'd made a baby already, it would come by next Easter. She guessed that a baby on the way would put a stop to this for a while.

They spent the next few days taking in sights that mildly interested Sarah but fascinated Edmund—battlefields and monuments, armories and caves, and the most hygienic food factory in the world, which manufactured the new shredded-wheat cereal.

She was relieved that, for a few nights, his roving hands stopped roving.

"My shy bride," he said and stroked her cheek, and they went to sleep holding hands, which made Sarah feel safely back in innocent girlhood and caused her, inexplicably, to well with the love for her husband that she ought to feel during the matrimonial act. What was wrong with her?

On the day appointed for them to take in the falls, they assembled with others in the hotel lobby, where they were outfitted with oilskin coats to protect them on the boat journey. Edmund seemed particularly relaxed and happy. In the boat, he amused other passengers by reciting into the wind a ditty he'd memorized from a guidebook. He gazed at Sarah as he recited, as if the song were a gift to her. It was about young Indian lovers. Sarah was mortified! She feared others in the boat would know they were newlyweds and would entertain themselves with mental images of what newlyweds did.

As the boat drifted toward the falls, the passengers, including Edmund, fell silent at the majesty of the seething cauldron. It was dazzling in its show of force. The boat pulled closer to the water falling in an obliterating sheet, surely a wonder of the world, not named so yet only because it belonged to a country too new to have earned accreditation.

The boat penetrated farther, beneath surging waters sending up mist, and Sarah was grateful to be wearing the coat over her cashmere traveling dress.

And then the boat passed *under* the falls, and it was as if they were passing through hell. Waters roiled about them, tossing and leaping and licking at them. It smelled like hell, too, or how Sarah imagined it would—sulfury and rank. She took Edmund's hand and he put a protective arm around her.

Then something inexplicable happened to Sarah. She felt beset by a sudden desire to plunge into the waters, join the frenzied whirl below, become one with the violence, give herself up to annihilating pleasure.

She had to fight down the urge to jump over the rail.

How appalled Edmund would be to know the thoughts tran-spiring under the hood of her slicker. She herself was appalled. She leaned into him and his arm restrained her and she braced in his hold until the boat was far away from the falls.

Later, on the dock, when Edmund shrugged off his coat and turned to hand it back to a crewman, Sarah took note of her hus-band's body—not just *him* but his *body*. She was moved, for the first time, by the shift of muscles at the back of his neck.

That night was scheduled a visitors' ball. Edmund had ventured the suggestion that they needn't attend every festivity they were in-vited to, especially a ball at which they'd know no one, but Sarah had been adamant in her wish to take part, pointing out that a bride had but a year to show herself off in her wedding gown before she had to send it to a dressmaker to have it remade.

After dinner in the dining room, as Edmund led them upstairs to change into their fancy attire, Sarah's mind grew transfixed by the sight of the back of his thighs pressing against the cloth of his trousers. When he reached the landing, he turned, waiting for her to catch up with him. After taking the last step, she surprised him by leaning into him—in a public hallway—for a kiss. Then, to his as-tonishment, she whispered into his ear that she guessed they didn't have to go to a ball that evening after all.

They stayed in the room that night and all the nights left to them there and grew to understand why Niagara Falls was the most renowned destination in the country for newlyweds.

20

Sarah

Porter House on Vine Street

Winter 1911

Six months after her wedding, Sarah began to fear that Rachel might have a baby before she did.

Rachel had married in the fall after a whirlwind romance with a Frenchman named Félix whom their father and Benno had met last summer while visiting relatives in Olargues. Félix's family owned a vineyard, and business brought him to New York, so one weekend he took the train up to Hollingwood.

Rachel almost instantly fell in love with him—not only because of his dark wavy hair and Continental good looks, but also because of his assertive manner and passionate nature, which were uncharacteristic of New England suitors. Félix had ideas and felt no compunction about expressing them. This sometimes made for excitement around the dining-room table.

"Vinegar!" he'd pronounce a glass of burgundy Bridey had poured, a wine that had been brought by one of the dinner guests.

It boded well for family relations, thought Sarah, that Félix and Rachel had married without fanfare (none of his family had been able to come) and left the country to live on his vineyard in Languedoc.

Sarah worried that Félix's passionate nature might result in Rachel bearing the first heir of this generation of Hollingworths. Their great-grandfather Titus, seeking to prevent squabbling among his six children, had instituted the Hollingworth custom of bequeathment. The bulk of the estate was entrusted to the eldest of a generation to hold and apportion to others as he saw fit given the circumstances of the day.

Edmund told Sarah not to fret about this. There was no use worrying about the future, and besides, Hollingworth Brassworks would probably not go on forever. Patents were coming across Edmund's desk that suggested tooling machines could make hand-forged brass obsolete

But how could that be? Sarah wondered. There'd always be a need for brass buttons—jackets and uniforms!—and brass bells and inkwells and doorknobs and bed rails and chimney tongs and ash-trays in every room of a house.

When she pressed her father gently about this, he assured her that the factory couldn't be more up-to-date. "We're starting brass rods for the new window treatments!" he said.

Still, Sarah wondered.

In late January, when the second month had passed without Sarah being "unwell," she visited Doc Spencer at his office, and, after asking her a few questions, he confirmed her suspicion, and Edmund and Sarah and the other Mrs. Porter celebrated with a bottle of champagne at dinner.

Suddenly Sarah noticed babies where she hadn't before: in woven baskets left on the wood counter in the general store as mothers browsed shelves, in high-wheeled wicker prams left outside the butcher's, in the arms of a nurse discreetly bringing an infant to be kissed before a hostess at a party sat down to the table.

Sarah also began to notice, advertised in magazines, special garments called maternity clothes. They were cleverly cut and draped to conceal a woman's condition, maternity dresses and even nursing shirtwaists, which had lacy frills that parted, allowing a mother to put an infant to her breast without even having to take off her blouse.

In the last generation of mothers, women never went out of the house if they were showing. Her mother had worn stiff corsets to conceal her condition for as long as she could before confining herself.

But Doc Spencer advised against corsets, even the new ones that you could sit down in. He showed Sarah a wax model labeled "Crimes of the Corset" that provided a vivid demonstration of how a woman seeking to achieve an hourglass shape deformed everything inside her, including a baby.

Sarah was horrified. Was that what had caused her own mother's death?

No, he said. Her mother had died of placenta previa. "A condition that medical science has come a long way in illuminating, which will help me prevent it from happening to you."

"How far along are you?" Edmund's mother asked Sarah every day for more than a week.

"Three months," said Sarah again and again, and each time she said it, his mother's reply was the same: "Three months! Oh, dear. That was when I lost my baby before Edmund. Be careful, dear, won't you?" She added that women who couldn't keep babies—of whom there were more than anyone guessed—usually lost babies at the three-month mark.

"Nonsense!" said Doc when Sarah consulted him, shaken.

Still, Sarah breathed easier when February was over, which meant the first three months had passed. (But had they? She worried. Perhaps her calculations were off. She should have thought to keep records of dates in notebooks, which was what her friend Lil did. Alas, Lil had shared this information with Sarah too late for it to be of use to her.)

If the baby was a boy, she wanted to name him Edmund, overriding Edmund's objection that three Edmund Porters were enough for the world. If it was a girl, she wanted May, after her mother, or Agathon, the name of a tragic heroine in a new novel. Edmund objected to Agathon, pointing out that the name would be shortened to Aggie. They resolved to choose a name that wasn't only beautiful but also couldn't be contracted.

21

Sarah

Hollingwood

July 1911

The migraines that Sarah used to get as a young girl recurred, and her feet and hands swelled, and Doc Spencer recommended she move back to Hollingwood. Her condition required that she not be upset or stressed or excited, which Doc knew was impossible in a house with two Mrs. Porters in it.

The bed in the Yellow Room was the only one big enough to accommodate childbirth, but Sarah did not want to stay in the bed where her mother had died. She moved back to the Rose Room that she'd shared with Rachel, a room that faced west and had a view of the lake and windows that could be lifted to let in cleansing breezes.

Edmund stayed on Vine Street with his mother. Alma Brigg Porter couldn't get by without her son because she was a widow who ran the house without help. Overhearing that the house had no help would sometimes startle one of the many people in Mrs. Porter's employ. But what she meant was that her cook, her laundress, her housekeeper, her hired man, her gardener went home at night; they didn't live in.

"I can't wait until you come home to us, dear," Edmund said to Sarah every day when he visited Hollingwood on his way home from the office. "Mother misses you too," he usually added, which Sarah knew wasn't true, but it was something Edmund wished were true and he hoped to bring it closer to truth by saying it.

Sarah wondered how it would feel to return to his mother's house with a baby.

The house on Vine would always be his mother's house in Sarah's mind. It was a house where nothing was done according to Sarah's wishes. When she'd wanted to rearrange the furniture in their bedroom, his mother said of course such a decision was up to Sarah. But then his mother had observed, with a pitiful look, what a shame it would be to move a wardrobe that had been made by Edmund's great-grandfather for that very corner.

Even choices of household products were not up to Sarah. After she and Edmund were engaged, Sarah had made a gift to his mother of bars of Bridey's soap, scented with mint from Nettie's garden. Those cakes still sat, every one of them, in the box Sarah had wrapped and ribboned a year ago. Mrs. Olsen, the Swedish woman who came in to do laundry, said she'd been told by Mrs. Porter not to use the soap as she believed it was too harsh to use on Porter linens.

Sarah's girlhood home still felt like *home* to her in a way she couldn't imagine the Porter house feeling as long as Edmund's mother was in it. But Alma Brigg Porter was only forty-four years old and came from a line of long-lived Briggs. She'd hosted a party last year for Edmund's grandparents' fiftieth wedding anniversary, to which his grandfather had worn his old Union uniform. Sarah tried to picture herself and Edmund celebrating fifty years together. That year was so far away, it was almost unimaginable—1959.

Sarah longed for her own mother constantly now. She had so

many things she wished she could ask her. She'd kept a bottle of her lilac perfume and every now and then she twisted off the cap and dabbed herself with a scent that brought back her mother—and imbued her with some of her mother's courage, she hoped. She imagined childbirth to be a physical feat as remarkable as scaling a mountain—something only men did, and now Sarah wondered if this was because childbirth was a feat unavailable to them.

Every day, Sarah grew more exhausted. Noon felt like midnight. Even the smallest chore—peeling an apple—felt as if it were a gargantuan task. Walking upstairs became overwhelming.

But one Sunday, she dragged herself to church services, wanting not only to get out of the house but to show off the new maternity dress she'd ordered! There, in the pew in front of hers, sat a couple new to town, the man dandling their baby. The baby was deformed. Something was wrong with its face. The parents seemed not to notice, treating it lovingly, absently patting its back as if it were normal, rocking it whenever it cried. If Edmund and she had that kind of baby, she was certain Edmund would insist on putting it in an asylum. Would she want to do that?

Please, God, don't let that happen to us! she prayed. She tried not to look at the baby for the rest of the service, remembering the old wives' tale (surely a myth?) that if expectant mothers gazed upon ugly babies, the babies inside them would turn out the same.

In the mornings, Bridey brought Sarah coffee and breakfast on a tray and read aloud to her from the newspapers.

"'For the first time in history, more than ten people flew in an aeroplane at the same time,'" Bridey read one day. "'Thirteen passengers were taken aloft from Mouzon, France, for a ten-minute drive in pure air'—"

"I wonder how close Mouzon is to Languedoc," Sarah mused,

stirring a bowl of hot oatmeal to cool it. "Maybe Rachel and Félix were among them."

"I should think they'd have more sense than to risk their lives in a man's untried flying machine!" Bridey said, adding, "Mother of Mercy!" before going on.

Then Sarah heard a sound she'd never heard from Bridey or from anyone, the cry of a wounded animal.

"What!" Sarah said. "What happened?"

"Oh no," Bridey said, burying her face in her hands. "Oh no, no, no..."

Sarah pushed the tray aside and got out of bed and lifted the page from Bridey's lap.

One headline spanned three columns:

Deadly Disaster at Shirtwaist Triangle Factory...146 Garment Workers Killed in a Fire, Most Victims Recent Immigrant Women Aged 16 to 23...

"They locked the doors," Bridey said, looking up. "They locked the doors to the stairwells to keep us from taking breaks."

"You worked there?" Sarah asked, horrified; what a despicable place of employment.

Sometimes, Sarah worried that she'd done Bridey a disservice by taking her out of the city, with all its prospects and opportunities for newcomers to this country to advance themselves. Now every doubt she'd had was removed.

22.

Bridey

Hollingwood

March 1911

It was too early for names of the dead to be printed, but Bridey knew Mary Ryan was among them. She felt the truth of this ring in her bones.

She covered her face with her hands and saw, as clearly as if it were happening before her, Mary smelling the smoke, shouting to others, leading them to the door, pounding and pounding on the metal, which soon became too hot to touch. She heard the chorus of screams from women as the dim room grew darker, then prayers as they apprehended the gravity of their plight.

She saw Mary pulling at the scapular Bridey had given her, tearing it out from under her collar, rubbing her fingers against the soft bit of wool said to spare anyone who dies wearing it from the Eternal Fire.

23.

Sarah

Hollingwood

1911

When the doctor came for the six-month visit, it wasn't Doc Spencer but Doc Spencer's son. Perk Spencer was just a few years older than Sarah and looked to her too young to be a doctor, but Doc had boasted his son was the best in his medical class at the academy in Pittsfield. He was taking him into his practice as an apprentice.

Doc had been called away by a case at the hospital, and Perk had been charged with taking her vital signs.

Sarah had to shake off a feeling of impropriety at being in a bedroom with a man who was not her husband. She sat stiffly in the Martha Washington chair by the window as she opened her mouth, obliging the tongue depressor and then the glass thermometer.

After he proclaimed her to be in the pink of health, he asked if she'd like to know the sex of her baby.

"Is that possible?" she asked, knowing that it must be. What a velocity of advances had been brought by this century.

"The heartbeats are foretelling," said Perk as he popped open the brass latches of his black leather bag. (The closures were almost certainly made in the Hollingworth factory, Sarah thought—and what a strange thought to have at that moment, just when she was about to learn their baby's gender. No doubt the strange thoughts were an effect of her condition.)

She watched Perk's hand graze the tools fitted in depressions in blue velvet lining: a red rubber-nosed hammer, an ophthalmoscope, cork-stoppered bottles of all sizes. He pulled the stethoscope out by its metal arms and inserted the rubberized ends of them into his ears.

"If the pulsations exceed one hundred and thirty," Perk said, "the child will be a girl; if under that number, you're carrying a boy." He asked her to take the disk of the stethoscope and press it against the mound of her waist. He turned discreetly as she unbuttoned her blouse, pulled aside her silk slip and her chemise, then buttoned herself up again over the chilly metal disk so that it appeared there was a snake coming out of her navel.

He listened while staring at the face of a watch that was strapped to his wrist. Young Doc was always touting something new. Sarah had heard that bracelet watches would replace pocket watches someday.

"A girl!" he proclaimed, retrieving the ends of the stethoscope from his ears.

"Are you sure?" she asked.

"Are you questioning medical science?" He smiled.

A girl! And she realized she'd been convinced it was (and had hoped for?) a boy.

Sarah wouldn't give birth at home as her grandmother and mother had done. Sarah would have her baby in the new lying-in hospital, a monument to the generosity of the town's leading citizens and to the forthrightness of the Ladies' Auxiliary chairwomen who made their appeals during unheralded visits.

Lying-in hospitals were springing up all over the country, offering the latest in hygienic care; according to circulars printed for fund-raisers, they would help bring forth babies of the better class. Doctors were trained to deliver babies, so mothers no longer needed to be dependent on the care of ignorant midwives. At the lying-in hospital, anesthesia was available, because painless birth had been discovered to be necessary for mothers of means. According to one pamphlet:

> The sedentary lifestyles, diets of rich foods, and steam-heated houses have weakened female physiology so that childbirth can cause complete nervous exhaustion in middle- and upper-class women. Lower-class women aren't faced with this problem, as their bodies are accustomed to manual labor.

How glad Sarah was to have been born into this modern era in which inventions were devised to make her life easier.

Some women went there to lie in as early as the third month of pregnancy, but Sarah wanted to stay in the comfort of home for as long as she could. Bridey and Nettie could be trusted to follow Doc Spencer's orders to serve a diet devoid of fats and sweets and with less meat than usual and to refrain from acquiescing to Sarah's morbid longings for items that weren't on Doc's list. Sarah had frequent cravings for rice pudding and sugared watermelon, and these, along with other dietary desires brought on by her condition, had usually—but not always—been denied her.

"I craved licorice," said Bridey. "I woke up wanting it and sucked it every day with my tea. It didn't hurt myself or the baby a bit." This was on the night she snuck a bowl of watermelon up to Sarah's bedroom.

Nettie and Bridey seemed wiser than Sarah was about almost everything, including childbirth, despite the fact that Nettie had never had a child; Sarah felt safe in their company.

But when July brought to Wellington the hottest summer on record, when her father closed the factory due to the heat and the men gathered around the thermograph near the town hall placing bets as it went to 110 degrees, when Main Street filled at night with exhausted mothers wheeling sleepless babies in prams, when mail delivery was suspended, when joyriders piled into cars and sped through town to catch a breeze, when Sarah was forced to move to the Yellow Room so she could seek relief in lake drafts, which could always be counted on to waft in from the balcony, but found the air in the Yellow Room as still and stifling as in the rest of the house— her father asked Oskar to get out the car, and he and Edmund delivered Sarah to the lying-in hospital.

24

Bridey

Laverstock Lying-In Hospital

July 1911

The Laverstock Lying-In Hospital was a mansion, even grander than the house depicted in the circular that Bridey knew Sarah hadn't meant her to see, as she'd hidden it in a drawer of her handkerchiefs; it contained observations such as "a danger for our nation is that birth is so painful for sensitive women of the upper classes that they have fewer babies, so propagation of life is confined to lower and immigrant types who are not capable of suffering." The words were offensive to Bridey, but Bridey was used to offense. It was not meant personally, she reminded herself every time she read criticisms (of which there were quite a number) of those of her nationality or religion or station. In cartoons meant to be funny, her people and Nettie's were sometimes drawn to resemble apes. It always surprised her to discover that citizens of the New World were sometimes as ignorant as the people she'd left behind in the Old.

She mounted the stone steps and swung through the arched wooden door. She was carrying a box for Sarah from home—books and *McClure's* and booties that Sarah had been stitching, such tiny booties!

Bridey was told to take the elevator to two. She was delighted to discover that the building was air-cooled! She'd never experienced air-cooling before. The lying-in hospital must be equipped with a Nevo. Waiting for the elevator, Bridey closed her eyes, luxuriating in the miracle of relief from the heat. She hadn't spent a night in her bed for a week. She and Hannah and Benno and Nettie had been sleeping in the icehouse atop stacks of hay. Bridey had nightmares in which she fell off the hay and concussed herself on the ice, although that would be impossible, as the straw lay on the ice as thick as a mattress.

Bridey found Sarah sitting up in a chair in a private room looking out on a box garden. Sarah was wearing a white linen gown, whiter than any garment Bridey had seen, and she wondered what kind of soap they used to get it that way.

Sarah was drinking a mug of hot vegetable tonic and reading a newspaper. The drink was concocted to strengthen the walls of the womb, she told Bridey, and made of a compound that controlled spasmodic contractions.

"It's surprisingly delicious. Would you like a taste?" asked Sarah, but Bridey declined.

Bridey set the box on a table by the foot of the bed, opened it, and showed Sarah all the things she'd brought.

"The booties!" Sarah said. "I'm so glad you remembered them."

They talked of the weather, the heat predicted not to let up, tar bubbling in New York streets like hot syrup.

"Seventy babies died in New York this week, this article says," Sarah told Bridey. "From the heat!"

"Poor babies," Bridey murmured.

"Yes, babies of the poor," said Sarah. "Who live in tenements without sunshine or air."

See? her eyes said. *Giving up your baby is what saved him.*

But only if a rich family took him, Bridey thought.

Thinking of her baby being poor made her sad and she blew her nose into the hankie with her initials: *BMM.* The hankie was a gift from her sister Kathleen; she'd embroidered it last Christmas. She and Kathleen always exchanged something small. Blowing her nose made her feel guilty—she owed Kathleen a letter.

After visiting with Sarah, Bridey left the room empty-handed. She passed the nursery and stopped to put her head against the glass. Every infant had a bed to itself atop a metal cart with wheels. The newborns were wrapped in blankets and positioned in the center of softly lined boxes like jewels. Two babies were sleeping, but one was awake, punching into the air with mitted fists as if it were a boxer.

Bridey's eyes filled and she hurried down the hall. Not wanting to wait for the elevator, she took the stairs, and the next day she offered to let Nettie visit Sarah instead, which Nettie was happy to do because of the Nevo.

Bridey kept to herself the real reason she didn't want to go back, which was that she couldn't bear the sight of newborns waiting to go home with their mothers.

25

Bridey

Hollingwood

July 1911

The great wave of heat that stifled the Northeast in July, killing thousands and sending some to the brink of madness, caused re-arrangements at Hollingwood not only because it removed Sarah to the lying-in hospital, but because it brought a Frenchwoman to live in the Yellow Room.

Benno was home from Yale for the summer and working on an article for the school magazine. He went down to New York to look up something in the new library on Forty-Second Street, and walking from Grand Central to the great marble edifice built where the pyramid used to be, he saw among throngs of heat-withered strangers a familiar face in the circle of a lime-colored parasol. It was Madame Brassard.

Mr. Hollingworth and Benno had met Madame Brassard in France. She made frequent visits to New York for her *métier,* which was stated on her card in elegant scroll; she was a *couturière pour la maison.* She'd been hired by Hollingworth relatives in Olargues to redecorate their twelfth-century villa

(Protestants stayed in touch with their relatives. Bridey admired it. With her people, when relations moved to another parish, the next time you saw them was at the wake.)

"If I'd had warning I was sailing into the hottest summer on record, I'd have put off my buying until autumn," Madame had said, according to Benno.

The *Farmers' Almanac* had predicted it, but Benno hadn't wanted to sound like a bumpkin.

The Victoria, she said, was a fine hotel, but even there they were setting up beds on the roof for guests to sleep in like gypsies!

That evening, Madame Brassard accompanied Benno on the train back to Wellington.

Now Bridey stood at the kitchen table, cutting circles in biscuit dough with a tin cutter. The bell register rang, startling her. The register was a little wooden box affixed to a wall in the kitchen, and the first time Bridey saw it, she'd mistaken it for a reliquary. Since Rachel had gone, she'd not been used to hearing it ring.

Bridey wiped her hands on the cotton loop draped over the hanging dowel. Nettie was in the summer kitchen in the basement, jamming strawberries, so there was no question of which of them would answer the bell. She walked through the butler's pantry (illogically named, Bridey thought, as the house had never employed a butler), pressed the glass push plate on the door, swung through, passed the linen closet (the ivory damask still needed ironing), and there were Mr. Hollingworth and Madame Brassard in the library, standing in front of the fireplace and gazing into its mouth.

Why had they rung? What could be wanted? Surely not a fire, in this heat. More water? No, the sweat-beaded glass pitcher still stood full on the side table. Perhaps the ashtrays needed emptying.

"My dear," said Madame Brassard, pointing to the brass fender. Though she was in her forties, she'd remained slim, and her hair was still honey-colored, twisted into intricate designs at the back or on the top of her head. How did she manage it? Bridey imagined clever maneuvering with hand mirrors.

"How long does it take you to polish that?" asked the Frenchwoman.

"No time," said Bridey. Did the fender need polishing? No; it gleamed.

"Would you like me to fetch a rag?" Bridey tried to recall when she'd polished it last.

"Non, non," said Madame Brassard. "We only wish to know how much of your time is taken up in the useless task of polishing fireplace articles."

"I... really can't say, ma'am," said Bridey.

"Hazard a guess. An hour? Two?"

Were they meaning to fire her? Now Madame was elaborating on the travails of American servants forced to keep shiny articles that should be made of a substance that did not need daily cleaning—like iron.

Daily cleaning? thought Bridey. Since when was she required to polish brass every day? But now Madame was talking of fireboards.

At this, Mr. Hollingworth put up his palm.

"My dear madame," he said. "I don't wish to outfit our library as if we lived in a boardinghouse!"

"Ah, Benjamin." (She pronounced his name with softened consonants, so that it sounded like contented lambs in a field: "Ben-shah-meh.") "I do not mean to suggest ugly parlor board covered with paper matching that of walls. I mean boards of the old style, beautifully painted. In my country, the finest painters don't think it beneath them to paint boards."

*   *   *

For meals, there were four in the dining room again: Mr. Holling-worth at the head of the table, Hannah and Benno at his sides, and Madame Brassard appropriating the foot, as if she were mistress of the house instead of a guest. Bridey marveled at the ease with which Madame Brassard violated customs, wielding fork and knife in the European way, her knife in her right hand, her fork in her left, a habit that Bridey had made herself unlearn, following Adelaide's advice.

Madame had a style. The glass through which she read morning papers wasn't a lorgnette on a chain that flapped against her breast but a glass circle affixed to a silver band on her forefinger. She wore daring fashions that Bridey had seen only in magazines, and when she wore common fashions, they were made less common by some alteration. Her white gloves weren't plain white, they were adorned with narrow black stripes or with tiny black buttons going up a side. She had straw hats that weren't the color of straw! One was rose and another peach, decorated with not only ribbon but netting. Her turbans were feathered! Her hobble skirts didn't make her mince as they did other women who wore them, and Bridey wondered how this was possible until she did laundry and saw that Madame's hob-ble involved hidden pleats allowing for ease of movement.

Madame Brassard engaged in a new form of calisthenics called yoga. This Bridey discovered without meaning to.

Ever since Mr. Hollingworth had taught Bridey to swim, when-ever her summer duties allowed, she rose from bed upon hearing the Angelus bells ring from Mother of Sorrows and walked down the grassy path to the lake. Bridey loved the beauty of still mornings and misty dawns and reveled in the cool waters, enjoying not only the relief from heat but also the solitude it afforded. At that hour, not even the fishing boats were out yet.

She'd often take a basket so on her walk back she could gather berries to serve with the breakfast or for Nettie's jam.

One morning, when she was about halfway down to the lake, she heard her name. She looked around, startled. Usually her early-morning walks had no witness but rabbits or deer or the blue heron that perched itself on the stone wall.

"Bridey" came again, and there, beyond the brambles, in a clearing she hadn't noticed before, was Madame Brassard. She stood on a towel wearing nothing but an odd-looking union suit, tight and black and cut off at the shoulders and above the knees. A wide band of silk was wrapped around her head. She wore colorful slippers that fit like socks. Light fell in columns through branches, illuminating her skin. Bridey felt as awkward as if she'd come upon Madame in her bath.

"I'm doing my contortions," Madame said.

Bridey looked around to make sure no one else was there to take in the disturbing sight.

"Yoga calisthenics! I learned them in India. Designed to keep possession of youth! I'm told they also provide a kind of enlightenment." She smiled. "But of that I'm less sure. Would you care to join me?"

And then Madame Brassard bent at the waist, arms outstretched, as if she imagined herself to be an aeroplane.

Bridey pulled her wrapper tightly about herself.

"No, thank you," she said and hurried back to the house. She refrained from morning swims after that, not wanting to be confronted with foreign calisthenics.

Another thing Madame Brassard did that was foreign: She sent postal cards to Paris written to—her dog! Her dog was named Pablo and how sorry Madame was to have to leave him behind with minders when she traveled. She referred to Pablo as *mon fils adoré*. She gave Bridey cards addressed to Pablo to take to the post office and Bridey practiced her French by reading them on the way, something about which she felt no compunction, as Madame had chosen not to conceal her words with an envelope, and besides which the messages were meant for only a dog! Perhaps Madame imagined that Bridey would not be able to read it, but this Bridey could do, thanks to Sister Joséphine. She'd had a strange way of teaching French at the convent, not from books but simply by speaking as she circled the classroom—*"J'entre dans la classe, je trouve le livre"*—until what she was saying transformed from gibberish into words, at which point Sister Joséphine allowed them the textbooks.

Madame sent Pablo pictures of sites of local interest—the lake, Trowbridge School, Main Street with its picturesque stores and old homes—but what touched Bridey was that Madame's beautiful handwriting flourished with passionate descriptions of what might interest a dog: trees and terrain and chaseable creatures such as groundhogs and woodchucks and rabbits and gophers.

Bridey realized that she herself might find comfort in doing something similar. She could write postals to Thom and the baby, and though the cards would never be sent, writing them would make her feel, for a moment, as if her separation was—only temporary. But, in the pharmacy, fingering painted cards, she discovered that she couldn't bring herself to part with even a penny for such a frivolous purchase.

The only person in the house who didn't take to Madame was Nettie. One thing that set Nettie against her was the way that she ate. Nettie said she hated how Madame "ate around things," never finishing either what Nettie gave her or the small portions Madame served herself. She never took seconds, even of Nettie's specialties like scalloped oysters and yam puddings, which elicited compliments and second helpings from everyone else at the table.

After Madame Brassard had been with them for two weeks, the heat was broken by a violent thunderstorm. Branches of the tulip tree scratched menacingly against windows on three floors of the house; winds took whatever wasn't battened down and even made off with a piece of the barn.

The heat wave was over, but still—Madame Brassard stayed. Her services, it seemed, were suddenly needed at the house. Hollingwood was to receive another visitor that summer, a personage even more exotic than herself.

The president of the United States would be coming to Wellington! President Taft was leaving his family vacation home in Beverly, Massachusetts, to make a tour of the country. The local Republican committee, on which Mr. Hollingworth served, held a special meeting to decide who in the town ought to host him. Many on the committee, and some who were its ancillary advisers—Alma Porter, Edmund's mother, was the most vocal of these—offered up their own houses, each making the case for his or her home's historical significance; it had sheltered a colonel in Ethan Allen's brigade, or it was shaded by elms planted by a Revolutionary regiment, or it had been built on the site of a significant battle—even if that battle had been ignored in history books. For a while, the Black Hart on Main Street was considered, as it was the oldest inn in the country and well appointed for the comfort of eminent guests, but the fact that its most noted guest had been Benedict Arnold might have been interpreted as an affront to Taft, whose patriotism was often questioned by Democrats.

In spite of Benjamin Hollingworth's reticence to offer up his own home—or perhaps because of it—Hollingwood was voted the most suitable choice to host a president. Not only had it been built by a man who'd served as Republican governor of Connecticut, but there was the school connection. Three generations of Hollingworths were Yale men. Taft was one, too, the first to be elected to the presidency—though Benno knew that his own pride in this would be scorned by fellow Trowbridgers at Harvard, which was already the alma mater of twenty-seven presidents.

And so Madame Brassard's profession became not just a matter of interest but one of fortuitousness. She was called upon to prepare Hollingwood to receive its most distinguished guest yet. She sent for her trunk from the Victoria, and soon the house was being transformed. The first point of attention was the Yellow Room, where the president would stay. It had the biggest bed in the house, not a small consideration, as Taft was the stoutest president on record. Bridey had seen pictures of him in illustrated magazines. He could fill the giant trousers that were displayed in Carrington's General Store and stretched from one wall of the store to another. Bridey wondered if Mr. Carrington would remove them out of respect.

"The blinds must be curtained," Madame Brassard said. "To eliminate affront of light first thing in the morning." The Yellow Room had been hers since she'd come to stay weeks before. Once, making up the bed, Bridey had seen a silken black mask on her bed stand. Now she realized what it was for.

A seamstress was hired to run up curtains from a fabric from Madame Brassard's trunk. Bridey offered to do this, but Madame said a professional was needed to work with the fabric, a special tapestry woven in a remote castle in Spain. Madame Brassard requested curtains be made, too, for the windows in the library, giving specifications for many festoons and pleats, and she introduced to Hollingwood the lambrequin, which Bridey thought a clever invention. It concealed the tops of window coverings, hiding clumsy folds formed by the curtain being drawn; Madame had gotten the idea from sleeping in beds in medieval castles.

Bridey and Nettie were thrown into a dither, trying to guess what should constitute the presidential breakfast. He would be staying with them for only a night; his supper and dinner would be provided elsewhere, which made Nettie feel both relieved and slighted.

But one morning, Hannah burst into the kitchen and told them the president wasn't coming after all.

"He's going to Stockbridge instead, to the Red Lion Inn!" Hannah had begun to wear her hair in complicated braided piles similar to Madame's, a style Bridey thought too sophisticated for a girl of sixteen.

"Why?" Bridey asked, but Hannah didn't know.

Later, Bridey heard Mr. Hollingworth explain at breakfast. "The uncle of a senator owns it. They've promised to do a fund-raising gala for him."

And Bridey saw that her own father had been right in a long-ago conversation by a fire—politics in the democracy of America wasn't so different from how wheels turned in parishes at home.

But still Madame Brassard didn't go. She continued the task of re-fitting the house, draping furniture with fabrics from her trunk, taking up carpets in one room and putting them down in another to cover parquetry designs she deemed "too aggressive."

Bridey wondered at Mr. Hollingworth's blithe acceptance of her changing what his family had lived with for years. But one night, she understood.

Gazing out the window of her little room in the attic, watching the moon rise over the lake, she saw Mr. Hollingworth and Madame Brassard in silhouette by the gazebo. He was standing, looking out at the lake. She rose from the bench and took his hands and they stood in embrace, gazing at the dark, shimmering water below.

Then one day, upon bringing ironed sheets to the Yellow Room to which Madame Brassard had returned after the presidential fiasco, Bridey noticed that her bed hadn't been slept in, although the sheets had been mussed to make it appear as if it had been. Bridey had changed enough beds to know whether or not sheets had been used. Later, when she went across the hall to Mr. Hollingworth's room, she found pale hairs on his pillowcases.

To Bridey's surprise, this discovery elicited in her only happiness, not condemnation. Mr. Hollingworth was Protestant, after all—mortal sin was beyond his capacity. Madame Brassard was a fallen Catholic. Her soul, presumably, could be blackened no further.

Bridey didn't blame Mr. Hollingworth and Madame Brassard for what they were doing because Bridey herself had done what they did. She'd crossed a Rubicon when she'd left Ireland with Thom, although she hadn't fully comprehended this until they were aboard the ship.

Bridey wondered if she herself would want that kind of happiness again. It had been three years since Thom had died. She still lived parallel to a life with him in it. In her mind, she was always living two lives, one without Thom and one in which he'd survived. Sometimes, she imagined them living in Oskar's gatehouse. Thom might have Oskar's job, driving a motor, and she'd decorate the pretty room at the top of the stairs, not the ugly room at the rear that Oskar had taken. She'd seen it once when she'd been asked to scrub his floors while he was on holiday.

Oskar. He insisted on accompanying her to and from church every Sunday, walking beside her after she refused rides in the motor. She wanted the exercise, she'd said. But really, she didn't want to be alone with a man in a car.

Oskar was German, not Irish, but in some ways, he reminded her, heartbreakingly, of Thom. He had the same broad shoulders, and eyes that spoke. Oskar, too, had been an altar boy. He, too, liked to build things. He had the same fascination Thom had had with clocks, but unlike Thom, he could take them apart and put them together. She hadn't had a clock in her room until Oskar found one in the basement and fixed it for her. When she'd thanked him, he kissed her cheek lightly, and this had caused something in her to stir. She began to see that Oskar was handsome; his thick blond hair curled, and the cut of his cheekbones was put into relief whenever he turned to talk to passengers in the backseat.

Sometimes, when thinking of Thom, she realized she was recalling something Oskar had said or done, and this unintended betrayal made her afraid she would be unable to keep the promise she'd made to Thom with her body, a pledge that made her feel as if they had married and that she ought to remain true to him no matter what happened.

26

Sarah

Laverstock Lying-In Hospital

August 1911

Edmund visited her every day, bringing flowers. But he was not there when Sarah's time came. She knew it was time when she woke in the night and felt that the bedclothes beneath her were soaked. Though she'd been told to expect this, she heated with shame. She rang the bell attached to a wooden rail at the side of the bed, which brought a nurse running.

"The regular doctor isn't on duty this time of night," said the nurse. "But the assistant doctor is here." The assistant was always there; he lived in a room in the basement. As soon as the nurse left to find him, Sarah was overtaken by pain so intense she wondered if she and her baby were dying.

She moaned as two men wheeled her bed out of the room and into a corridor.

"Don't worry," said one. "They'll give you something."

Someone screamed and then the screams filled the corridor and Sarah realized they were her own.

"Now, now," said a nurse, her head bobbing beneath a hat that looked like a folded luncheon napkin.

They were wheeling her into the birthing theater, which she recognized from a tour.

The doctor who must have been the assistant was there, holding his hands in the air. The nurse held a wash pan of water under his chin into which he dipped his beard—she guessed the water held some sort of disinfectant.

"What are you going to do?" Sarah asked.

"We're going to give you a beautiful baby," said the doctor, his hands still in the air, looking as if he were about to perform a magic trick.

"You'll meet your baby when you wake up," said the nurse.

"But I'm not tired!" said Sarah. Should she refuse anesthesia? She wanted to meet her baby as quickly as possible. But then the pain set off another earthquake inside her.

"You'll be tired soon," promised the nurse. "Start counting backward from one hundred."

Metal instruments gleamed in the white, white room. But what were the instruments for? Sarah didn't want to think about that.

She began to count: "One hundred...ninety-nine..."

A dark cup descended, covering Sarah's nose and her mouth.

"Breathe normally," the nurse said, but Sarah had to stop breathing. A foul odor was filling her nose, the foulest smell she'd ever inhaled. It reminded her of a smell from her childhood, when a banana had fallen behind the pie press and stayed there for weeks, creating a stench that leached up to the bedrooms.

She tried not to breathe it in but couldn't avoid that. The smell took on physicality, became fingers poking into her nostrils, reaching high into her sinuses, jabbing at the softness of her brain.

And suddenly, she was sitting on the gray-painted floor of the side porch, her back against the grooved column of one of the pillars. Her mother was there, tipping back and forth in the old wicker rocker. Her dead grandmother was smiling, and Edmund and her father and sisters and brother and a porch full of friends were there too—they were having a party, dining on egg sandwiches, pickles, and peaches and cream. A man appeared playing a hand organ and when he started to play "Emeline," everyone on the porch rose and (how did they fit?) began to dance, but Sarah couldn't get up to join them, though Edmund was reaching down for her hand; her back seemed to have become part of the pillar.

When she woke, she lay in a room bright with daylight. Her wrists were tied to the rails of the bed with rubber cords. A girl wearing a pink apron was sweeping a corner.

"Where is my baby?" Sarah asked, startling her.

The girl turned to face Sarah. "We didn't think ye'd be awake yet!"

"Where is my baby?" Sarah asked again. Her spine was cold. Something squeezed in her chest.

The girl hurried away and came back with a nurse Sarah had never seen.

"Where is my baby?" Sarah asked for the third time.

"We must be strong, Mrs. Porter," the nurse said, undoing Sarah's restraints.

Then there was Edmund, dropping into the wooden straight-backed chair by her bed.

How tired he looked.

He leaned and kissed her forehead, then took her hands in his. A chill went through her. The nurse walked wordlessly out of the room.

Sarah filled with realization: She must not speak of their baby. As long as she didn't speak of their baby, their baby would be fine.

"You look tired," she said, rubbing the back of his hand.

"Sarah," he began. His eyes were wet.

Her whole body ached. Her back hurt; her abdomen was sore; she felt as if she had fallen off a horse.

"What's it like outside?" she asked. "Has the heat broken yet?"

Soft columns of light formed golden squares on the polished floor. The window was shut, to keep the cooling inside.

Outside the window, leaves on the maple remained perfectly still. When the nurse came back, she'd ask her to open it.

"They did everything possible," he said.

Sarah pulled her hands away. "No, no, no." She sank her face into her palms and Edmund stood and cradled his wife in his arms, leaning over the protective rails.

"We're young," Edmund said. "We can try again."

"No," Sarah sobbed, pushing her face against the starched wings of his shirt, and when the fabric went limp with her tears, she looked up.

"Was it a boy or a girl?"

"I...didn't ask."

Then the doctor appeared—not the assistant who'd attended her, but the senior doctor himself. He told her how sorry he was for the outcome, which had been unavoidable.

"We did everything we could," said the doctor who hadn't been there.

Perhaps it was Sarah's fault. Why had she chosen to pursue painless birth? Coming to the lying-in now seemed to her a cowardly refusal of what had been proven necessary for centuries: the expulsion of a baby had to be the result of propulsion pains. In avoiding the pains, had she prevented the normal course of things from occurring?

Edmund inquired about the baby's gender.

"A girl," said the doctor.

"Rose!" Sarah cried, and Edmund's arms tightened about her.

A girl baby was to be named for Sarah's lost sister, the one who'd died with their mother. Perhaps if they'd planned to name her something else. Or...Sarah recalled her disappointment upon learning the baby's gender from Young Doc. It had been only momentary, but perhaps a moment was enough to poison a baby's will.

"Where is she now?" Sarah wanted to know.

"Who?" asked the doctor, unhooking a clipboard affixed to the footboard rails.

"Our baby!" Sarah said. "Can I see her?"

The doctor looked up from the clipboard, not at Sarah but at Edmund, who responded by stroking Sarah's hair.

"Shhh," he said. "Shhh." But his shushing elicited the opposite of the calming effect he'd intended.

Sarah threw off his arms.

"I want to see my baby!" she said, more loudly this time.

The men exchanged glances.

"You shouldn't think of it as a real baby," said the doctor. "The birth won't be recorded."

But Sarah recalled an undeniable baby. She had felt it kick and careen just below her belly's surface. She'd talked to it for months. The baby had been as alive as she was.

"Where is she?" Sarah said, turning to Edmund. "What did they do with our dear little Rose?"

Edmund's expression was helpless. He shifted his gaze to the doctor's shoes, and the doctor called for the nurse and the nurse reappeared and he asked her for something and then he was putting a needle into Sarah's arm, saying the fastest route to recovery was sleep.

"Time to change your wrap," said a voice brightly, as if Sarah were trying on coats to be worn to a party. Here came Mabel, her least favorite nurse. Sarah sat up in bed so her bed blouse could be lifted, and, with gloved hands, Nurse Mabel removed the damp gauze at her nipples and unpinned the muslin strips binding her breasts, unraveling Sarah like a spool of thread.

"When something like this happens," she said, repeating what Sarah had heard often in the past weeks, "it happens for a reason."

As the nurse pressed chilled tea towels against her, Sarah remembered looking at the deformed baby at church—perhaps there was something to the old wives' tale.

"Your milk will stop in a few days," the nurse promised, wrapping her tightly back up again.

But her milk didn't stop. It kept coming for weeks and all the tricks in the books wouldn't stop it, not cups and cups of sage tea, not cabbage leaves squashed to her breasts, not tinctures of jasmine and peppermint applied nightly. It was as if her body, like her spirit, was in despair, reluctant to give up this last evidence that she'd been with child.

Sarah felt she had lost more than a baby; she'd lost the child it would have grown up to be, the little girl playing with Sarah's lady dolls, the red-cheeked girl gliding beside her on ice, the bride who would walk down the aisle wearing the family veil.

At night, through open windows, Sarah heard, floating to her, a sound she'd heard all her life, one that had never before bothered her but now cut her so deeply, she couldn't sleep. It came from just over the hill, from the nearby dairy: the bellows of the milk cow separated from her calf and the answering cries of the calf calling out for its mother.

It had been explained to her as a child that a calf had to be taken from its mother for the sake of human children who needed milk for strong bones and teeth. But now Sarah wondered what harm it would do to let the calf stay with its mother.

And lying in her postpartum bed, bathed in moonlight illuminating her perpetually stained bodice, Sarah thought of Bridey being made to part with her son.

One thing Sarah knew: She could not return to the house on Vine Street, where a room stood ready to receive the baby she was not bringing home. The third-floor nursery, which had been Edmund's, had been outfitted for months, and not only with refurbished family furniture (the glossy walnut cradle had been carved by his great-grandfather) but with a modern layette of finely stitched flannels and all the assorted whatnots advised for babies these days: a tin box of talcum powder, a soft sea sponge, a jar of sweet oil, and a bottle of whiskey for teething. There was also a yellow-painted wooden baby rattle that bore teeth marks from Sarah and her siblings when they were young, and whenever Sarah thought of it, she felt like crying again.

27

Bridey

Laverstock Lying-In Hospital

September 1911

On the thirtieth day, when Sarah's course of isolation had lifted, Bridey made herself go to the lying-in hospital carrying an armful of hydrangeas from Nettie's garden. She found Sarah on the roof in one of the beds set up there, taking in the prescribed two hours of fresh air.

Sarah was dozing, so Bridey placed the fragrant boughs on the sheets. This woke Sarah, and Bridey took her hands and Sarah pulled Bridey into her arms and they hugged for the first time, and in that moment, they weren't lady and maid but two women crying, each for a lost child.

"I'm so sorry," Bridey said through her tears. "I am so very sorry."

Later, when they were alone in the room, Sarah talked of her ordeal, not only the physical pain of what happened but the pain of being asked to forget what her body would always remember.

"Whenever I do what the doctor says, I feel guilty that I'm forgetting her!" Sarah cried.

"You'll never forget her," Bridey said, wiping her own eyes.

"Once you're with child, that child stays in your heart." A midwife might have been able to save the baby, but what would be the point of telling Sarah that?

"I want to go home," Sarah said to a nurse. But they wouldn't send her home without a nurse to take care of her. Sarah insisted that Bridey knew nursing, and thinking quickly, Bridey declared that she had been a practical nurse back in Ireland.

A nun from the order of nursing nuns in the convent was called to instruct Bridey on the importance of ventilation and sitz baths and regular bedtimes preceded by the ingestion of liver pills, and Sarah was permitted to go home to the Rose Room, the name of which now had a tragic connotation.

28

Bridey

Hollingwood

September 1911

When Sarah came home, the first thing she noticed was that the massive brass knocker on the front door was gone.

"Where's the lion?" she asked and someone in the group gathered at the front door to receive her told her that it was in the basement. The Hollingworths never threw anything away.

Mr. Hollingworth stepped forward to take Sarah in his arms and as they embraced, Bridey saw Sarah looking behind him, at the Frenchwoman in a lawn dress the color of peaches.

How much did Sarah know about Madame Brassard?

Of course, she knew something.

"Nothing happens in this town that everyone in it doesn't know about," Nettie had said when Madame Brassard's visit had been reported in the *Wellington Record*. Bridey had been relieved that there was nothing untoward hinted at, as was sometimes done in the social column.

*　　*　　*

Bridey had refrained from talking about Madame Brassard during her visits with Sarah, although she'd wanted to talk about her. She'd wanted to prepare Sarah for the changes she would find at home, but something in Bridey cautioned her about doing this. Sarah was grappling with so much pain and change and sadness already. Bridey didn't know—nor did she feel it her place to know—how much about Madame Brassard she ought to share with Sarah.

"Sarah, this is Madame Brassard. You might recall that Benno and I spoke of her last summer..."

Mr. Hollingworth stepped back from Sarah and waved his arm to present the woman behind him.

Sarah straightened and Madame Brassard approached her. Sarah held out her hand to be shaken, but Madame Brassard leaned forward and kissed her, first on one cheek and then on the other.

"*Ma chérie,*" she said and Sarah's eyes hardened.

"Welcome to our home, Madame Brassard," Sarah said, stepping back to embrace the others waiting for her: Hannah and Benno and Bridey and Nettie.

Then Sarah took a sharp intake of breath. "The wallpaper is different!"

"*Oui,* stripes, *ma chou.* Instead of gloomy old flocks!"

Sarah didn't comment, looking the other way now, into the parlor. "What's happened to the silvers table?"

Mr. Hollingworth spoke softly. "Madame has done us the favor of modernizing our home—"

Hannah interjected excitedly, "It's not modern to have tables just to show off things that need to be polished! Nobody looked at those old things anyway!"

Bridey could see Sarah thinking, *When did Hannah start talking like that?*

"Perhaps when you're comfortably rested, you'll let Madame give you a tour," tried Mr. Hollingworth.

"I'll look forward to that," said Sarah, her voice thick with contempt.

A tour! Of her own home! Men sometimes had no idea the weapons their words were, thought Bridey.

No one mentioned the baby. The doctors had instructed the family to refrain from reminding Sarah of what it was best for her to forget.

Sarah's eyes filled and she said how tired she was; all she wanted was to go upstairs to bed.

Bridey helped her up the spiral stairs. Helping her was necessary now that the polished wood stairs had no carpet. Madame had declared that the zigzag pattern made by carpeted spirals was fatiguing to the eye.

"Is her idea to kill us?" Sarah murmured, gripping the banister.

Bridey hovered behind Sarah as she slowly mounted the stairs, the first stairs that Sarah had been allowed up in a month.

Bridey decided she ought not tell Sarah the extent of what had transpired between her father and Madame. Bridey guessed that no one but herself and Nettie knew that the pair's common interests went beyond home decoration.

Sarah reached the top of the stairs, and as soon as she turned into her room, she moaned.

"My vanity table moved? And why is the bed kitty-corner to the room?"

"Madame Brassard is a decorator," Bridey said. "She had some ideas." She didn't add that Madame Brassard herself had, for a time, occupied Sarah's room.

Sarah settled onto the vanity chair, Bridey remained standing, and in these postures resided the return of their roles. They were again served and servant. Standing by the bed, gripping the pincapple on the post, Bridey felt as if she had imagined the intimacy between them at the lying-in.

In Ireland, girls spoke of how much better it was to work for Americans than for the English because Americans were said to be friendlier to servants. Unlike the Brits, they didn't ignore you when you brushed elbows with them in hallways, didn't treat you as if you were a piece of furniture. But now it occurred to Bridey that the English way was better. In England, a servant knew what to expect. In America, the line between employed and employer always seemed to be shifting, but how it shifted and when was subject to the whim of just one of them.

"You should have told me," Sarah said, her eyes cold. "What's going on here?"

"I think she appreciates your father and this house," said Bridey.

"Appreciates? Or connives to own?"

"How could she own it?" Bridey said.

"By marrying my father, of course!" said Sarah, flushing, and Bridey saw that Sarah had already taken in all that had transpired, not only the changes made to the house, but the changes produced in her father.

Sarah didn't want things to change. Sarah wanted the house to remain as it was, a shrine to her mother, a sort of a tomb where all her mother's things and arrangements would be preserved just as they'd been when Sarah was little. But was that fair to Mr. Hollingworth? Mr. Hollingworth wasn't dead like her mother was. He was alive and a man, with a man's needs.

If Madame Brassard's influence had been limited to easily remedied changes, like rearrangements of furnishings, Sarah's resentment of her might have dissipated. But when one evening Sarah discovered Hannah engrossed in a copy of *Madame Bovary,* which Madame had lent to Hannah to practice her French, Sarah told her father their visitor must be asked to go, not only for the sake of the house, which had no more use for her services, but for the moral good of his sixteen-year-old daughter, who was too young to be exposed to the amorous desires as described by the French language.

Soon after that, Madame regretted to inform them that clients had called her away. Before she left, she came into the kitchen and pressed a banknote into Bridey's hand in a denomination so large, Bridey flushed and refused to take it. But later, Nettie told her that visitors from cities expected to tip, and, as it wasn't kind to disappoint them, Nettie had accepted what had been offered to her. Bridey regretted her ignorance in turning down what would have enriched her, proof she was Irish and not an American. But later, she was happy to discover the bill in one of her apron pockets, where Madame must have slipped it in spite of Bridey's protest.

Early one morning, Madame Brassard bade them good-bye in the front hallway, where the aggressive parquet was visible again, and set off for the station in the car driven by Oskar. Her trunk was enormous and wouldn't fit on the seat, so it had to follow in the family's old-fashioned carriage, which Mr. Hollingworth drove using a borrowed horse. He looked back now and then, making sure it didn't shift off the leather, keeping watch as carefully as if it were a coffin and the carriage a hearse.

After that, Mr. Hollingworth seemed quieter than usual, but by Thanksgiving, he had returned to his usual good cheer.

29

Edmund

Grand Central Station

Autumn 1911

Soon after Sarah moved back to Hollingwood, Edmund left his mother's house and took up residence with Sarah in her old girlhood bedroom. She needed him. Sarah had begun to see peril everywhere.

Hannah, who had the room above Sarah's, reported that Sarah often got up in the night. She knew because Sarah sometimes woke her, making some sort of banging. The first night he spent there, Edmund saw Sarah get out of the other bed and tiptoe from one rug to another as if they were stepping-stones, checking and rechecking the screen on the fire. By day, she circled the outside of the house, looking for potential causes of injury. She asked the hired man to roll up runners in the hallways, afraid that people might trip. She turned off the leads to gas lamps that Bridey had to ask Edmund to restart so she could do close work at night. They had a devil of a time talking her out of cutting down the old tulip tree; Sarah suddenly feared it would fall on the house.

Old Doc prescribed gardening, a treatment that Sarah dismissed at first, but one morning she went out wearing a straw hat and chamois gloves too big for her, and soon she was working the hard earth daily. Edmund stopped off at Vine Street and brought back, from the volumes he'd purchased in London, books by popular horticulturist writers. Sarah began to study landscape and gardening and how to winter flower bulbs and how to raise circular mounds for beds. She became taken by the newly popular picturesque-landscape movement, which sought to develop beauty in nature.

By fall, Sarah seemed herself again and she was finally declared fit to return to the busy life of a young matron.

Then Edmund encountered, to his surprise, a taste of the affliction that had beset his wife.

It descended on him without warning. He was on the train to New York for a business meeting in the company of one of his partners, Phillip Boggs. (Phillip, like Edmund, had been named for his father to ensure seamless succession in the eponymous law firm.)

As the train pulled into the darkness of the newly enclosed terminal at Grand Central, Edmund and Phillip were discussing a patent case. The case was for an adjustable-spring baby carriage. As Phillip described unique points of its design to protect the safety of infants, Edmund, to his horror, felt tears in his throat. To his own bewilderment—and that of Phillip Boggs, Esq.—Edmund's eyes filled, and to hide this condition, he drew a large handkerchief out of his trousers and blew his nose. Phillip fell silent, and, noting the vibration in the double gold chain draped across Edmund's vest, he turned his attention to gathering up papers and returning them neatly to his brass-trimmed leather case.

With a scream of the brakes, the train jerked to a stop.

"You go on," said Edmund gruffly. He dabbed at his eyes with his handkerchief as if the train weren't propelled by modern electricity but by old-fashioned steam filled with flying cinders. "I'll meet you under the clock at the Biltmore."

Once inside the terminal, Edmund sought refuge from the

bright electrification in the shadow of a supporting column. He leaned against the fluted marble and wept uncontrollably into his sleeve as travelers, ignoring him, milled about.

A felt-hatted man approached him, a stranger, and Edmund turned his back, hoping the man would go away. Finally, having regained his composure, Edmund looked up and was annoyed to see the stranger still there, keeping a respectful distance, but now stepping closer so that his words might be heard above the din of the crowds.

"I'm sorry for whatever ails you, sir, but I've got ails too. Can you spare a coin?"

Edmund raised his eyes to the ceiling, studded with thousands of man-made stars, then fished a copper from the pocket of his vest and gave it to the man, who nodded and then withdrew into the heedless crowd.

That night, as he and Sarah were going to bed, something about the curve of her bare, slender arm made Edmund decide to share with her the strangeness in himself he'd encountered that day. He waited under the quilt while she fussed with jars on the vanity, and finally they lay side by side in the dark.

"Good night," she said, nestling against him, and the clarity of his wife's voice made him, too, say, "Good night." He decided not to tell her what he'd intended to tell her. He guessed that calling up a memory of what she'd finally succeeded in putting behind her would set her back, and he was loath to do that.

30

Sarah

Wellington, Connecticut

1912–1914

One morning the Western Union boy rang the bell and delivered a cablegram from Languedoc. It was from Félix announcing the birth of a baby girl, Rosé Hollingworth Charbonneau. Rosé had an accent, as if she were wine.

The news, received joyfully by the rest of the family, made Sarah feel jealousy and despair.

Sarah herself would never be a mother. Doc Spencer had confirmed this—there was no hope of a child. The ordeal Sarah had undergone in the lying-in hospital had resulted in congestion of the womb and a displacement that could not be made right again. Sarah's dreams of jollying an infant on her knee, or holding the hands of a toddler learning to walk, or stroking the back of a child drifting to sleep were dashed. Whenever she recalled the nursery at the mission, cribs full of unwanted babies, she hated herself for failing to accomplish what others did without trying.

*　　*　　*

Then, one Sunday at church service, Reverend Bierwirth invited a guest speaker to the pulpit. The speaker was a social worker from the Children's Aid Society who talked passionately about the need to provide homes for children—thousands of them were neglected on streets or abandoned to orphanages in New York City.

The advocate was a hatless woman whose fuchsia gloves fluttered in the air like bright birds as she beseeched the congregation to help relieve a social ill caused by a crushing conflation of the two *i*'s, immigration and industrialization. As her hands flitted, the church sexton walked a basket of pamphlets from pew to pew, inviting interested congregants to take them.

"Who would take in someone else's problems," murmured Edmund's mother, passing the basket without dipping her hand into it, but Sarah, sitting next to her, took a pamphlet and glanced at it throughout the service, reading it behind the pages of her prayer book. It included a gallery of photogravure portraits of needy children, each captioned by a Christian name.

*All children are of **special promise** in intelligence and health and are in age from two years to twelve years and are sent **free** to those receiving them on ninety days' trial. Homes are wanted for the following children.*

Their faces were different, but their eyes were the same: huge and imploring.

We have so much, thought Sarah. Her white-gloved hand grazed Edmund's silk sleeve, dislodging an ostrich feather that had fallen from her hat. *All we're missing is a child to share it with.*

When Sarah got home, she showed the pamphlet to Bridey.

As Bridey read it, she started to shake.

"We need the hand glass," she said, and from a drawer in the breakfast room she retrieved a magnifier.

Peering through the circle, she pointed to an image of a child's face.

"This could be him," Bridey said, and Sarah looked closely. The portrait wasn't of a baby but of a small child.

"But his name isn't Mikeen, it's Vincent," Sarah observed.

"They rename the babies. He'd be the same age. Five years old." Bridey took the pamphlet from Sarah and brought the glass closer. "The same birth date! And the red hair!" Her eyes filled.

Until now, the faces had seemed to Sarah like those of angels fallen from anonymous clouds. She hadn't thought of their parentage. But now it occurred to her to wonder where the children came from.

"His face is the spitting image of Thom. But why isn't he with a family already? Do you think some harm has come to him?" She began to cry.

Sarah took Bridey in her arms and stroked her hair. "They probably haven't found a family good enough for him yet." This might be true. The advocate had implied that the best, brightest orphans were steered out of the city to be raised in pure air by families of means.

After a moment, Bridey stepped back and wiped her eyes quickly with a corner of her apron and Sarah gazed at Bridey, taking renewed stock of her. Bridey's skin was clear and her eyes were bright. She was fine-boned and handsome, with no physical deformities. She'd described Thom as handsome too. Both were Irish, yes, but this wasn't stated in the pamphlet. And being born of Irish parents didn't make a child Irish.

New theories hold that character is less a matter of birth than of environs, the pamphlet said.

Any child that she and Edmund took in would inherit not just the Porter name but the nationality of the parents who raised him.

Any son of hers would be more American than Rachel's daughter being raised in France, a girl who would learn to speak like a little foreigner, ornamenting plain words with guttural trills.

And now an idea took hold in Sarah. Why hadn't she thought of it before? By adopting Bridey's baby, if it was Bridey's baby, by adopting the infant she'd fallen in love with at the mission, she'd be giving Bridey the gift that would dispel her melancholy forever, but not only that, Sarah's child would be the eldest of the next generation. She guessed—Edmund later confirmed it—that according to the language of the bequeathment, he would be the first heir.

But Edmund didn't want to adopt a child. If they couldn't have their own children, he'd rather remain childless, he said, and this decision was backed by his mother, who told stories of terrible ends met by do-gooders who took in strangers' children in the name of benevolence. A distant Porter cousin had taken in a city boy to help work the farm; he'd smoked in the barn and burned it right down.

But as weeks went by, and Sarah's entreaties continued, Edmund fell silent in the face of them, by which Sarah knew he was rearranging obstacles in his mind, clearing a path to allow him to give her what she desired.

Part Two

31

Vincent

Lower East Side, Manhattan

1967

He was now fifty-eight but the memory of what had happened when he was four remained vivid to him, evoked by sounds or smells or sights as common as the strike of a match by someone sitting next to him on the subway.

It had happened before the Great War.

A morning. He and Lolo had been hungry for breakfast, standing at the window, watching their mother hang clothes in the yard. The yard was a narrow strip of weeds that separated the back of their building from the building facing the street behind them. He liked to play there.

He wished he were out there instead of inside with his sister. He wished he were down there collecting pieces of wood and stones and rubbish to build a fort. His forts were always torn down by bigger boys, but he didn't care. They were bigger than he was; they could do what they wanted. He liked making things they felt worthy of notice.

On the table behind them lay a box of matches. Lolo tried to grab the box, but he pushed her hand away. He was the grown-up when their parents weren't there. His father was at his job and his mother was below, reaching into the basket, unraveling a wet sheet, taking a fat wooden clothespin from her mouth, pinning the sheet to the line that drooped with the weight of the wash of their neighbors.

His parents had warned him against playing with matches, but now he wondered what it would feel like to strike one. Also, he wanted to show off for Lolo. She was two years younger. He'd named her Lolo. Her nickname for him had been Toddy, which he hadn't remembered until she reminded him of it years later—and when he heard that name again, as a man in his forties sitting across from her at a diner, it brought back to him the fragrance of her dimpled arms, the softness of her bright curls. She'd tracked him down from a note found in her mother's things. He'd been surprised to learn that her real name was Alice.

Slowly, he slid back the top of the matchbox. His heart pumped in his ears as his thumb obscured the woodcut face of the Indian in a feathered headdress. When the box was open enough for him to fit his thumb and forefinger inside, he drew out a wooden match. Lolo, watching him, leaned closer. He pulled back from her, holding the match, and carefully drew the red tip across the side of the open box, dragging it against the dark strip. A hiss and a satisfying surge of sulfur hit the air. The match came to life. Lolo gasped. They were mesmerized by the dance of flame near Vincent's fingers, yellow, then blue, then yellow again. The flame grew, then shrank, then turned into threads of smoke curling up to the ceiling.

Vincent eyed the yard to make sure their mother was still busy. Good. Now she was pinning his father's white collars to the line, an ordeal he knew would take her some time. He reached into the box for another match and scraped the tip against the side of the box. Lolo drew closer as fire bloomed on the match. It almost singed her hair. "Keep back," he told her, pushing at her. He struck another match; the flame flared and burned out. The air was smoky now, dense with the stink of sulfur that he could taste at the back of his tongue. He liked the taste. He struck another match. A breeze moved the curtains. Suddenly it was as if the lace wanted to play; it reached for the flame, caught it, and gave it to the lace panel beside it, and now fire was eating the wallpaper and he dropped the box of matches and shouted through the open window for his mother, who turned and looked up and threw a collar to the dirt and picked up her skirts and took the wooden steps two at a time.

Vincent grabbed Lolo's hand and pulled her away from the window, which was now framed by fire lapping the wallpaper; it was as if flames were bringing to boil the water inside the kettles dancing on the patterned wallpaper. The air was so thick and black with smoke, it was hard to breathe. He had to lead his sister out of the parlor, but which way was that? "Don't cry," he said, as much to himself as to her. He needed Lolo to stop screaming so he could think. With his free hand, he felt his way out of the room—here was the table, now here was the chair, now here was the sofa, the sideboard, the press, now the radiator, here was the hat rack, and the front door was swinging open and there, he saw with relief, was their mother. Her face was altered; he had never seen it like that before. Her eyes bulged, her cheeks were wet, her mouth was set in a strange way. She bent down and scooped Lolo into her arms and took him firmly by the hand. He was relieved not to be the grown-up anymore.

They hurried down the stairs so fast he was afraid he would fall. His mother pulled at him as she yelled "Fire!" to closed doors they passed and as they turned on the landing—"Fire! Fire!"—and now others too were hurrying down the steps, holding children and goods, all of them streaming through the building's small vestibule and into the street, shouting for someone to ring up the fire department.

The next thing he remembered was seeing his flat from the fire escape of the building across the street. Firemen maneuvered a huge white hose from the steam-engine pump at the back of a truck. The truck's team of horses were faced away from the fire, shielded from the sight of it by the blinders they wore. The hose spewed a stream of water through the window, filling up the apartment with water as if it were a goldfish bowl.

Neighbors took his family in for the night. It was the first time he ate a strange bread called challah that you cut by pulling it apart with your hands instead of taking a knife to it. They changed their clothes to go to sleep! They gave him a special shirt and pants they called pajamas. The pants were too big and the cord in the waistband kept untying itself, so when he walked out of the apartment to the water closet in the hallway, he had to bunch up the waist of the pants in his hand to keep them from falling.

The next day, his mother took him across the street to see what was left. They didn't need a key for the front door anymore. It was already open. The first thing he noticed was the terrible smell. It smelled like cooked broccoli. The rooms and everything in them were wet and blackened. His mother was crying again. He cried too. His father had beat him with a belt when he'd confessed what he'd done. He hadn't meant to tell him, but the words came out without his wanting them to. "I played with the matches," he heard himself say after his father asked what had happened. They'd lost everything.

Now his mother crouched on the blackened floor of the parlor, sobbing. He stepped carefully over the new landscape: charred books and pots and shards of dishes and glass. He made his way to the bedroom he'd shared with Lolo. His teddy was still there, on the bed where he left it—the blankets and pillow were ash, the bear blackened and soaked, but Teddy was there, a survivor. Vincent reached for him, but his mother shouted, "Leave that alone!" He wasn't accustomed to hearing her shout. She didn't shout when she got angry; she went quiet instead. Her shouting rattled him. When he looked at her, she turned away and told him they were leaving, there was nothing to save.

Before following her, he bent to the floor. There was something shiny glittering in blackness. He saw what it was. A marble. He picked it up and pocketed it and with a last look at Teddy, which made his heart squeeze, he turned and followed his mother, choosing his steps carefully, navigating peaks and valleys in the rubbish. Their home had become a foreign country.

Soon after that, the McNultys returned him to St. Joseph's. He didn't know he was going. Nobody said anything him. One day, his mother told him to dress in his good clothes, the tweed knickers and white shirt and black cap, the best of the clothes the Society of St. Vincent de Paul had given them. The clothes made him feel older. He liked feeling older. He put his marble in the pocket of the knickers. They left Lolo with a neighbor in the room next to the one where they now lived at the society and then Vincent and his mother walked to the corner and boarded a streetcar. It seemed a long ride. It took them through parts of the city he hadn't seen—they passed a park where he'd like to come back to play. He tried to memorize landmarks so he could find it again—black wrought-iron gates, a fountain of a fish spitting water—but he knew it was hopeless.

When they got off the car, they walked for a while, then mounted the steps of a forbidding brick building. At the top of the steps, he was alarmed to see a statue of a man with his heart coming out of his chest. His mother pulled back the iron knocker and beat it against the door. The door was opened by a tall woman in long blue dress and white collar and the strangest white hat he had ever seen. It stuck out at the sides, blocking her vision, like blinders for horses. The strange-hatted woman led them to a dimly lit room, sparsely furnished. The room was cold, though it wasn't cold outside. The woman gestured for them to sit on a bench before a huge wooden desk. Then her hands disappeared under her cape. She walked around the desk and took the seat behind it, and then she was looking down on them as if from a throne. Another woman came in, dressed like the first woman with even the same hat. How did they keep from bumping into things? he wondered. This woman took a chair beside the desk and the two women and his mother began saying things he couldn't understand, though he knew the words were about him. They frequently glanced in his direction. Then the woman behind the desk pushed a piece of paper toward them and his mother rose from the bench and stood over the desk, reading it. A pen stood in a brass stand next to an inkwell. His mother took the pen and dipped it in ink and signed the paper. She didn't sit back down next to him but bent and kissed his cheek, then she kissed the top of his head, which she usually did only when he was going to bed. "Be a good boy," she said, by which he knew— she was leaving him! Now he'd be all alone. He hadn't had the chance to say good-bye to his sister. He began to cry.

"Oh, they all cry at first," said one of the women in blinders, and this made his mother go out of the room.

The woman behind the desk got up and came toward him. "You're a clever boy, big enough to start school," she said. "You'll be going to school with other children, won't that be fun?" He asked if he'd be able to go home that night. "No," she said, saying nothing more, just taking him by the hand and leading him to a large room where boys and girls of all ages were playing. This calmed him, for a while. The children were welcoming and he learned a new game: wheelbarrow. One child picked up the legs of another, who walked on his hands to a finish line. There were wheelbarrow races and soon he was chosen to be a wheelbarrow himself and he discovered it was a game he was good at; he almost beat the wheelbarrow beside him. The race exhilarated him; he liked the feel of his feet in the hands of an older girl as he pushed himself forward faster and faster to please her.

At bedtime, he was put into a crib like a baby. He cried against the injustice of this, banging his head against iron bars painted white. He missed his sister and mother and father too. He thought of Teddy burned and abandoned on his old bed and longed for the comfort of Teddy's soft body. The only thing he'd brought from home was his marble. He sat up to retrieve it from the pocket of his knickers, which were hanging over the headboard. He held it tight in his fist until he fell asleep. He awoke in the night, soaked. He'd wet the bed, something he hadn't done since he was a baby. He didn't know what to do. He lay on the mattress, wet and miserable. He turned onto his back, stared up at a patch of moonlight on the ceiling, and rolled the marble between his palms, wishing it were a magic ball that could bring him back to the past.

When morning came, he was scolded and bathed and dressed in the same gray-and-white-striped rompers that everyone else wore. Breakfast was oatmeal. He couldn't eat it. His stomach was as hard as his marble, which he felt for in his pocket every few minutes to make sure it was still there.

When breakfast was over, they went out to play. The playground was a concrete yard separated from the sidewalk by a fence of wrought-iron bars that twisted into sharp points at the top, to prevent the children from climbing over them, he guessed. Other children tried to console him, but he didn't want their sympathy. Nor did he want to play, though a few boys tagged him, trying to get him to join their games. He stood by the bars, looking out to the sidewalk. Each time he heard the click of heels on concrete, he hoped it was his mother coming back for him.

He spent his days like that until school began and he grew consumed with what he was learning, or what he was expected to learn: handwriting and catechism and arithmetic and reading, which was his favorite because sometimes the class was no more than a story the sister would read to them from a book, stopping now and then to turn the book around to show them the pictures.

As Christmas approached, he hoped the McNultys would come to see him. Children said that on Christmas, a lot of the fosters came to see the children they used to have.

It was Christmas Eve. There was a large tree in the dining room decorated with candles, and the ceiling was strung with colorful lanterns that would all be lit after Mass the next day. The fosters came in, but his weren't among them. He ached most to see Lolo. He wondered if she missed him and what she had been told. During the carol singing, one of the nuns took him by the hand. "Vincent, there's someone here to see you." His heart turned in his chest. "Silent Night" became distant as the nun led him down a long corridor. He guessed they had finally come. He couldn't wait to see Lolo. They entered the room where he'd last seen his mother. There were two women there, but he didn't know either of them.

One was fair and one was dark-haired, and the dark-haired one stood up and walked over and bent down to kiss him. She had a nice smell, like some kind of flower.

"My name is Sarah," she said. "I'm your new mother."

She pulled back to look at him, and he looked at her too. His mind seemed to stop; he didn't know what to think.

There was a strange sound from the fair woman behind her and he realized she was crying.

The dark-haired woman turned to her.

"And Vincent," she said, "this will be your Nurse Bridey."

And then, for the first time, he was getting into a motorcar, black and shiny as the shell of a beetle.

32

Vincent

Upper Bloomingdale Roadway

December 1914

He sat between the ladies, breathing in their perfumes.

In the front seat ahead of him, a man in white gloves spun a steering wheel as they bumped over hills of snow on the road.

Every now and then, one or the other of the ladies—he couldn't remember their names—would bend down to kiss him or smooth the woolly rug that lay across all of their laps. Under the rug, he felt around in his pocket. Good. The marble was still there.

"Are you hungry for Christmas dinner?" asked the lady in the fur coat. Her hands were hidden in a muff that changed shape when her hands moved around, as if they were small animals trapped inside it.

"Yes," he said, though he wasn't hungry. He was used to being hungry, to wishing for more of whatever he'd just eaten, another bowl of soup or slice of bread, but every child at St. Joseph's was given the same amount of food, which was fair. If you didn't like what was served—beets, say, or broccoli—you could give it to somebody else who did like it, and then that child would owe you.

He'd gotten paid back in syrupped figs by a bigger boy last week. He'd liked the figs, which he'd never tasted before, and had eaten them gladly but became sorry later.

"We'll have so many delicious things to eat," said the other lady. Nurse, she was called. But she didn't look like a nurse. She didn't wear white. She wore a brown coat and a red knit scarf, which she took off and wrapped under his chin. This made him happy. It was cold in the car. Wind blew in through gaps in the rubbery windows that flapped wherever they weren't buttoned down.

"Roast beef and creamed potatoes and puddings and sweet cakes," the lady in fur continued, "and sausages and custards and oysters..."

He didn't like oysters, but knew it would not be polite to say so.

The driver called over his shoulder. "The next hill is steep. I'll have to put her in reverse and take her up backward."

"And nut loaf and molasses taffy..."

When the car jolted backward, Vincent tasted the porridge he'd eaten for breakfast. The porridge rose up and then fell back as the car went over bumps. Soon it would rise and it wouldn't fall back. But where could he upchuck? He didn't dare risk ruining the shiny car seat. They might bring him back, as the McNultys had done.

The car jerked forward and Vincent grabbed for the hands of the nurse. He vomited into them. To his surprise, the nurse didn't mind. It was the other lady who shouted.

"Oskar! Pull over! The boy is sick!"

He'd never seen snow on the ground so white. The nurse cleaned her gloves by pushing her hands into it.

When they got back into the car, the lady in fur sat nearer the door. He guessed she was afraid of the same thing he was afraid of— that he would be sick again.

They had to wait for the driver to start up the car. They felt the car sink when he jumped onto the running board. Vincent twisted in the seat and knelt so he could look out the back window. The celluloid was cloudy, but he could see the driver making winding motions, causing the car to rock back and forth until the car's music started up again, *clack-ha-ha, clack-ha-ha.* Then the driver ran around to the front and threw himself into the seat.

"Next time, you can sit up here beside me," he said over his shoulder as he steered the car back onto the road. "I'll teach you how to wind up a tin lizzie."

Was the driver talking to him? It seemed too good to be true. Vincent closed his eyes and imagined driving a motorcar. He was in the driver's seat and Lolo was sitting beside him, singing "Row, Row, Row Your Boat." Suddenly the car was tilting, front wheels up, and the car was lifting from the road and rising like a bird, headed for the clouds.

"Where are we going?" Lolo asked him, her voice surprisingly calm. She said his name again and again until he was awakened by the sound of it.

"Vincent, Vincent, we're home."

He lifted his head from the nurse's shoulder. There was a stain on her coat where his mouth had been.

Through the car's front window, he saw a building almost as big as St. Joseph's and worried they'd brought him to another orphanage.

The car door opened and a man reached for the fur lady's arm and then he was reaching for him.

"Welcome home, chap. I'm Uncle Benno. I'll carry you on my shoulders, like Saint Nick with his sack."

Strong arms pulled him across the seat and then he was sitting way up on the man's shoulders and he discovered the pleasure of viewing the world through the higher-up eyes of a grown-up.

The house was grand. Too grand for a place where orphans lived. A tower stood at one end. The walls were brown as chocolate.

The front doors opened and people called to them to come out of the cold. Vincent held tight to the man's hair to keep from falling as the man mounted steps and then ducked, bringing them through the doorway.

"Ow!" said the man, adding, "Kid's got a grip," which pleased Vincent—he was a boy strong enough to impress a grown man with his grip.

Once he was indoors, the air became warm and full of good smells.

The man swung him down from his shoulders onto a carpet. The carpet was floral and Vincent felt like some kind of flower himself as faces came toward him, peering down for a look.

"I'm your aunt Hannah," said a lady with beautiful golden hair. She wore slippers embroidered with colorful birds.

"I'm your aunt Rachel," said a lady in a collar made of white feathers that tickled his face when she bent down to kiss him. She held a little blond girl in her arms, who smiled at him, reminding him of Lolo. "And this is Rosé, your...your..."

"Cousin," said the fur lady behind him.

Hands removed his cap and took off his coat, and for the first time in winter, he was warm enough not to have to wear them indoors.

"And I am your father." This man didn't bend down. His eyes were hidden by smoke from his cigar. He held out a hand. It was big and covered with curly dark hair. Vincent brought out his own hand and shook the other, as he'd been taught to do.

"Come meet your grandfather, Vincent." The lady in fur wasn't wearing fur anymore but a dress made of pearls. She led him down a hall where lights cast shadows on wallpaper with stripes.

They passed a sofa with feet carved like lion's paws.

There was a man rocking in a chair by the fire; he was smoking a pipe and reading a magazine.

"Father, here is our Christmas present," she said.

Was he a Christmas present? Whose present was he?

The old man pulled the pipe away from his mouth and leaned closer to Vincent, who stared at the doily where his head had lain. Mrs. McNulty made doilies like that.

"They give you the runt?" the man said. This was a mean thing to say but the man's smile was kind. "How old are you, son?"

Vincent brought up his right hand and splayed his fingers as wide as he could to show the span he was capable of.

"Five! My. That's almost two hands."

"Yes." Vincent nodded, glad that his point had been made.

"And do you like your new mother?"

"Where is she?" Vincent said, looking around.

The man smiled again. "Not much of an impression you've made on him, Sarah."

The lady took Vincent's hand and bent down so that their eyes were level.

"I'm your new mother, darling," she said and he saw that she could put on a smile and take it off as easily as she put on and took off her furs. But her words were soft and they entered him. He had a mother! He had a mother who called him darling, the same as mothers in books called their boys! He would do nothing that would make her want to return him.

Then the nurse led him away. They went upstairs to his room. His room! He was to have not just a bed to himself, but a whole room!

"This room used to be Benno's," the nurse said, lighting the lamp on its wall. "It's the smallest bedroom, but it's the only one with windows on three sides, so you can see the sunrise and sunset both."

In the room were many things that he'd like to play with: a red rocking horse with glass eyes, a set of tin soldiers, wooden bricks, and a toy steam engine. He wondered if not only the room but the toys would be his. Perhaps they meant to give the toys away. A bag of toys once came to the orphans. The toys had been put on shelves in the playroom for everyone to play with. That would be the best use of old toys, better than leaving them for only one boy to play with, but he nurtured the hope that the toys would remain.

The nurse guided him to each of the windows, pulling on the loop of a paper shade, lifting it so that he could take in the scene. In the fading light, he saw a vast stretch of white leading to water that twinkled in the pink sun.

"Those branches that look like big bent arms? That's the tulip tree," she said. "In spring, it grows blossoms like yellow tulips. You'll see. And there is the lake, where you must promise never to go on your own, at least not before you learn how to swim. And that is the carriage house where the coachman who drove us today lives. His name is Mr. Engel." She blushed when she said this; he didn't know why. "But now we must dress and go down for dinner!"

He thought: *I'm already dressed.* He was wearing his best shirt and knickers from the Society of St. Vincent de Paul.

"Benno's old things have been washed and pressed," she said, pointing to clothes laid out on the bed. Dark knee pants and stockings and a white shirt with a stiff collar that closed with a bow. The clothes lay on the quilt in the shape of a person, as if being worn by an invisible doll.

The suit was all right, but he didn't like the shirt. It was fussy, like a girl's. He was glad there was a jacket that would hide most of it.

Before dressing him, she showed him how to use the lavatory in the hall. He asked her to leave him alone there and he stayed for as long as he dared, running his hand over smooth porcelain, twisting levers to make water rise in the sink. But what most dazzled him was what she called the throne. It was a white bowl so shiny, it glowed. You pulled on a chain and the water roared in and whatever was in the bowl went rushing away. For a moment, he worried that he'd dropped his marble in it by mistake. But the marble was still in his pocket. His hand tightened around it.

In the dining room, he was glad to be sat next to the nurse.

"You can call me Biddy," she said.

She placed a big book on the seat so he could reach the table. The table was laden with good food, but he was too excited to eat. He was told there'd be gifts to open after dinner!

The girl was too little to come to the table and conversation went on and on about things that didn't interest him—who might be getting a bronchial cold, the rising cost of postal stamps, the weather in the faraway place where the baby lived. A lady called Nettie came and went many times from the kitchen, bringing in silver platters and taking them away.

Finally, Aunt Hannah suggested they go into the parlor. He slid off the big book but knew enough not to run from the table. All eyes were on him.

The parlor doors were closed. The old man insisted that they all had to arrange themselves outside the arches before he would open them. The baby was brought downstairs wearing a beautiful dress. When the doors were pushed open, Vincent heard himself gasp. He'd never seen such a sight. In the center of the room stood a tree so tall, its top scraped the ceiling. The tree gleamed with silver roping and colorful cards reflecting the flames of candles burning in silver holders clipped to branches. Beneath the tree were stacks of boxes wrapped in brown paper and tied with red string.

He hadn't expected to get more than one present. But: "These are for you!" his new mother said with a smile, dropping one, two, three wrapped boxes into his lap.

He took up the smallest one and worked the string for such a long time that someone reached over, and in an instant, the brown paper fell away. The gift was something round, the size of his hand, metal and shiny.

"An autoharp!" someone said, and seeing that he didn't know what that was, his mother took it from him and placed it against her lips and out came a mournful and beautiful sound. He wanted to make the sound too, but when he blew on the same place she had, no sound came out.

He didn't want to open another present yet. He wanted to play with the present he had. But: "Open the others!" they urged and he had no choice.

He loosed from brown paper a silver pocketknife and then a real BB gun, but before he had a chance to examine them, they urged him to open his stocking. He reached for a sock on his leg, thinking they meant he should roll it down. This made them laugh. Someone flung a long red-striped sock far too big for him into his lap. He felt inside it. It held real oranges and a packet of gum and a roll of something. When he peeled back the paper at the top of the roll, he saw a stack of white circles with holes in the middle.

"Life Savers," said Benno. "To sweeten your breath before kissing girls."

Vincent put one in his mouth and a sharp sweetness made his eyes water. He wished he could share the candy with Lolo.

The baby's gifts were opened for her: gloves and shoes and ribbons and dolls. Vincent was glad she'd received nothing he wanted.

After the gift opening, the grown-ups recited a poem. Everyone recited a different part of the poem that ended with Old Saint Nick springing to his sleigh, giving a whistle, and flying away like the down of a thistle.

What is the down of the thistle? he wanted to ask, but he was afraid he'd be laughed at again.

* * *

Soon after Christmas, he kissed the baby good-bye. She and her mother were going back to the faraway place.

Then a doctor came to examine him so he could go to a school called kindergarten.

The doctor came with his son. He was a doctor too. Old Doc and Young Doc they were called.

The exam took place in the kitchen, where they thought he'd be warmest, standing by the coal stove. Biddy and his mother helped him strip to his skivvies. He even had to unbutton his union suit, which embarrassed him. He'd never been so closely examined. Nettie tried to put him at ease by saying, "Don't fret, you got nothing old Nettie hasn't seen before."

Old Doc declared him to be in fine fettle except for his posture. His posture had to be corrected.

"Curvature of the spine!" cried his mother, drawing a hand to her mouth, by which he knew the condition must be something bad indeed.

His mother looked at Biddy, and Biddy looked at him.

"Scoliosis," said Young Doc. "There's a liniment for it now."

Old Doc glanced at Young Doc, furrowing his brow. "Exercise is the thing," he said. "The only reliable cure. Without it, the child will be needing a back brace."

A regimen of strengthening exercises was prescribed—touching his toes, doing somersaults, and performing headstands against the wall, which Bridey helped him do each morning before breakfast, spotting him, which meant keeping him from falling.

33

Bridey

Hollingwood

January 1915

It was January, so Bridey lit the lamps by seven p.m., first the two-armed brass sconce in the vestibule, then the smaller sconces on opposite walls, then the brass Camphines lighting the spiral staircase.

She called to Vincent that it was time for bed—he had come to know that his bedtime was when lamps were lit.

She followed him up the spiral stairs, cautioning him to put his hand on the banister.

As they passed the first landing, the flame in the sconce flickered, then went out, and they had to mount the last steps in darkness.

"I've not brought a candle," said Bridey. "Can you lead the way in the dark to your room?"

The touch of his hand in hers sent a brightness through her.

"They have electric lamps at the home," he said as he led her across the dark hallway. "Why doesn't a grand house like this have them?"

Whenever he spoke of the home, Bridey felt a blow at her center.

"The home was in the city, Vincent," she said, feeling in the pocket of her apron for the matchbox. She lit the sconce on the wall by his door. "New ideas take longer to come to the country. Look how long it took ye to come to us! Five years!"

"Almost six," he said, a serious child. His birthday was at the end of the month.

She led him to the bathroom and closed the door and turned on the tap. Usually, she bathed him earlier, just after his dinner, and brushed his curls and dressed him in an ironed shirt and creased trousers, but Edmund and Sarah were not home tonight.

In the weeks since he'd been here, Bridey had pressed him about his time before coming: what he did, how he was treated, what he was fed—but his answers had been guarded.

"Mother told me not to talk about that," he said.

"Mother" always let loose a coursing in her: *I am your mother! Look at me! Do you not remember my voice, my smell?* But they'd been separated for five years. For him, it was a lifetime.

"Were they good to you there?" she asked, unbuttoning the waist of his knickers.

She knew he didn't like her asking him about the home, but she couldn't help it.

"Yes," he said.

"What was your favorite thing?"

He was silent as she unbuttoned his flannels and helped him into the tub. "There was a red-painted spring horse in the yard," he said finally. "I liked to bounce it." He splashed the water as if he were bouncing. "But you always had to wait your turn."

"What was the thing you didn't like most?" She tensed, hoping not to hear something bad.

"The stripes," he said.

"The what?" Her voice rose. She'd heard "strikes."

"Gray-striped playsuits. We had to put them on every day. They itched."

"Well, you'll never have to wear itchy stripes again," she promised, drawing the cloth over his neck, ears, the slope of his back. His immaculate skin. She kissed his hair, breathing in the smell of it.

He smiled. His cheeks had filled out since he'd come to them.

After the bath, she wrapped him in a white Turkish sheet and patted him until he was dry, then slipped the nightshirt over his head and brushed his thick curls and kissed the dimple in his chin, the same as his father's.

34

Vincent

Wellington, Connecticut

1915

Say *these*."

"These."

"Say *girl*."

"Girl."

His classmates laughed and imitated him: *dese, goil.*

Hearing his words in the mouths of others filled him with confusion and shame.

Their teacher, Miss Nelson, had a big lace bow where her neck should be. She wore the bow every day, and he guessed it was part of her uniform. The schoolhouse was cold. The kindergarten was on street level; older students were taught upstairs. When it was very cold, the students were allowed to slide off their benches and go to the stack of wood in the corner and choose logs, one for each of them, and carry them to the black stove at the center of the room and sit on them as if they were stools. The stools formed a circle around the stove. The stove sent out waves of heat, like invisible hands to warm them. When they sat on the stools, Miss Nelson told them stories instead of giving them lessons, as if they were cowboys around a campfire.

Some of the stories she read from books. His favorites were from a series called My Little Cousins, which told about children in different parts of the world. The children in *My Little Cousins in Holland* wore brightly colored costumes with shoes made out of wood. The ones in *My Little Cousins in Germany* called their grandfather Opa, just like he did.

One day Miss Nelson read from *My Little Cousins in Ireland.* In this story, children wore rags and ate potatoes straight from the ground. A girl raised her hand and volunteered that when Irish went to church, they ate flesh and drank blood. When he got home, he asked Biddy about this. She tried to explain using words he didn't understand, but she confirmed the eating and drinking. This made him glad his family was Protestant. No wonder the church she went to had the word *Sorrows* in its name. He'd never go there, although he'd promised her that someday he would.

Each morning, Nettie packed his pail with a sandwich of dried meat on thick slices of bread and a molasses cookie and when Miss Nelson declared it was time for lunch, he took out his pail and the room filled with the sound of paper being unwrapped. But he was the only one who didn't eat. He gave whatever he'd brought to his desk mate, glad to get rid of it. The boy he shared his desk with was Marion. He'd thought Marion was a girl's name, but apparently it was not. Marion nodded silent thanks each day, slipping the sandwich and cookie that Vincent gave him into his bag to hide it from the all-seeing eyes of Miss Nelson. Miss Nelson sometimes stopped by their desk and, observing that Vincent's lunch pail was already empty, said, "My! You are the fastest eater this class has ever seen!" Vincent's chest warmed in this lather of praise and he hoped she would pass him before rumblings in his stomach gave his secret away.

Vincent was determined not to eat or drink at school. If nothing went into him, nothing would need to come out.

He didn't want to have to go to the privy. He had gone the first day, holding hands with an older girl who had been directed by the teacher to show him where it was. The privy was behind the schoolhouse, a tall, narrow cabin near the woods. Their boots crunched on the snow as they approached it. A stench grew stronger as they got near.

"Girls on this side, boys on the other," the girl said, dropping his hand. She disappeared into the darkness on the girls' side. He ventured closer to the dark doorless doorway. The smell was overpowering. There had been an outhouse in the yard of the McNultys' apartment house but he'd never had to use it. There'd been a water closet in their hallway with a wooden box with a lid that flipped up and a brass chain you pulled to call up a trickle that coaxed down the evidence that you had been there.

He stepped into the dark place. He tried not to breathe. On the wall, a catalog hung from a hook. He knew from experience, you picked the pages glossy with pictures. They were the softest.

He'd thought he'd needed to come here, but the need went away when he stood next to the hole, staring into a dark, glistening abyss. Something moved down there and he jumped.

"C'mon," said the girl's voice from outside, and he turned and flung himself in the direction of it, almost tripping as he passed from darkness to light so bright it cut into his eyes.

After lunch, children formed a line for the drink bucket in which snow had been melting since morning. One by one, they pushed the shiny handle of the dipper into the water and balanced the scoop carefully as they raised it to their mouths. But Vincent only pretended.

Every day when he came home after school, he burst through the back door and raced to use Nettie's john (she called it her john), then he handed over his empty pail and asked her for something to eat, a request she was always glad to oblige. She marveled at his ability to "fit a man's worth of vittles into that bitty body." He ate this belated dinner sitting at the round table, warming himself by the kitchen stove, and was joined by Biddy, who came to him, interrupting whatever she had been doing, pulled up a cane-seated chair, and watched him eat, making appreciative sounds as he swallowed, cautioning him not to put too much in his mouth.

His mother and father he wouldn't see until supper when he was bathed and redressed and ready for the dining room.

In the first days of school, Oskar drove him there and picked him up in the sleigh. They called it a cutter. He loved sitting in it, loved snuggling next to Biddy under a furry lap robe in the open air, watching trees and houses go by. They let him hold the bell strap and shake it at horses and people coming in the other direction. There weren't any motorcars now. There was too much snow. Their car and that of anyone else who had one had been put up on blocks in a barn until spring.

But in the spring, Oskar didn't drive him to school in the car, as Vincent had expected. Some arrangement was made whereby he would walk to school with older schoolmates, twin girls who were ten. Fanny and Flo dressed alike and wore their dark hair in thick braids tied with big bows. It was said that nobody could tell the Glover twins apart, but Vincent could. The scatterings of freckles across their noses were different.

"Doc says that walking is good for your back," reminded Biddy as she readied him for school, tying up his high boots and buttoning the chin strap to the side of his cap. "If somebody offers you a ride in their car, don't get in." He knew she was thinking of the auto wreck last week. Everyone in town had gone out to see it. A car had turned turtle coming around a corner. But no one had been hurt. Biddy worried too much about everything.

He met the girls each morning at Dead Bird Rock in the woods just beyond the gate of his backyard and the most exciting part of the walk to school was crossing tracks of the train. Sometimes they had to wait for the train to pull through. When this happened, the twins dropped their book bags and squeezed their eyes and put their palms over their ears, but Vincent kept his eyes open, wanting to block out nothing of the smoking monster as it screamed by.

At the bridge, the girls sometimes stopped to drink from the stream by making cups of their hands. They helped him learn to read by stopping with him in the cemetery and tracing the letters on tombstones with their gloved fingers. By the fence near the road was a stone for a boy who had been born on the same day he'd been: January 23, 1909. After Fanny pointed out this coincidence, he steered clear of that stone.

Sometimes, they took their time going home, lingering by an old broken-down sleigh in the woods. They'd sit on it and pretend it was a covered wagon and they were heading west to pan for gold. They'd pan in the dirt with their fingers. The twins knew about gold. Their uncle had gone to Montana and brought back a gold nugget their father used as a paperweight. He'd brought the twins a gift too. They showed him a fancy pencil—half the pencil was made of glass and when you tilted it one way, a mule ascended a mountain of gold; when you tilted it the other way, the mule came down again.

The twins' father was a dentist. They lived in a big white house with a wraparound porch and a front parlor with a bay window through which—if you walked past it when the blinds were up—you could see their father at work. Once, as they went by the house walking Vincent home, they invited him in to meet their father. They didn't have a mother. She'd already died. They'd shown him her stone in the graveyard

When they came into the parlor, which was also their father's office, he was sitting at a desk, dipping his pen in an inkwell. A cigar sat in the brass hold of an ashtray, and a curl of smoke came up from it, as if it were smoking itself. Fanny said Vincent's name and her father looked up. He smiled, adjusting the wire frames of his glasses.

"So, you're the foundling," he said, which made Vincent feel as if the man had aimed a stone at his chest. A foundling was what he had been at St. Joseph's. But he wasn't that anymore. Now he was a Hollingworth. Vincent Hollingworth Porter. He lived at Hollingwood. He was a son now, a nephew, a cousin.

Mr. Glover smiled. "You look healthy enough," he said. "No obvious contagions." Then: "Open your mouth. I can tell by your teeth."

Reflexively, Vincent stepped forward, parting his lips, but—"Father!" Fanny and Flo said in unison.

Flo took Vincent's hand and led him to a tapestry-covered reclining chair on the other side of the room. In the wall next to the chair, she peeled back a flap, revealing the mouth of a copper chute.

"Want to see where it goes?"

He said that he did. They led him down rickety steps to the basement and across a dirt floor. The chute dropped into a tall barrel, taller than Vincent. He felt himself being lifted under the arms until he could see over the side. A briny smell filled his nostrils, then he saw—the barrel was half full of old teeth. Those tiny dead slabs pulled from mouths of the living gave him nightmares for weeks.

When he first came to Hollingwood, he'd not been able to sleep. It was too dark outside. Bridey would put him to bed and draw the blinds and an hour later, he'd call her back and she'd come. It became clear she ought to keep up the blinds, to let in whatever light came from the moon and the stars. He couldn't go to sleep in the dark. He needed noise, too, but about that she could do little. She told him to strain his ears for the sound of milk cows coming over the hills.

"*Nyaahhhhhhh,*" mimicked Bridey, "*nyaahhhhhhh, nyaahhhhhhh,*" which made him laugh. She sounded just like a cow in need of her calf.

Before turning down the paraffin lamp by his bed, she read him stories. During the day, she urged him to open the sliding glass doors of the grand bookcase in the library and search the lower shelves, which held children's books. He could choose whatever he wanted her to read to him that night. He could read by now, but he loved to be read to—he would love to be read to for the rest of his life. Many of the gold-stamped titles were too difficult for him to make out, so he chose books by the appeal of their painted-board covers: *Aladdin and the Magic Lamp, King Arthur, Ali Baba and the Forty Thieves.*

Some nights, his mother read to him instead—from the King James Bible. She helped him memorize short passages to recite to his father at dinner. The stories in the Bible described a world more gruesome than that portrayed in fairy tales. God was regularly drowning the earth, burning cities and everyone in them to death, asking a man to sacrifice his own son and then changing His mind at the last minute, leaving the man feeling guilty for the rest of his life.

But when they went to church on Sunday, which was a long day because there was not only a sermon in the morning but a talk in the afternoon, Reverend Bierwirth told stories about a God who wasn't the monster he was in his mother's Bible. The reverend's God was the same one he learned about from the nuns at St. Joseph's: a kindly old shepherd, benign like his sheep.

*   *   *

Vincent was only six, but he was often asked what kind of work he would do. He liked to work.

He'd liked it when Mrs. McNulty, after leaning out the window to bargain with a fruit seller, gave him money to go downstairs and buy the fruit. He liked when Nettie sent him to the henhouse with a basket, trusting him to return with unbroken eggs. He liked helping the hired man fix fences and helping Oskar polish the car and oil the sleigh.

The kind of work he didn't like to do was the kind of work that Bridey and Nettie did: cooking and cleaning and making the beds, the kind of work that nobody noticed but that still had to be done again and again. There was one exception—he liked to help Biddy in the basement on laundry days in winter. The basement was warmed by water boiling in large pots on the stove. He liked watching the steam rise as Bridey poured the water into a deep tin laundry tub with a copper bottom. He liked watching her feed soiled items one by one into the tub with a pole. Biddy's sleeves were always rolled up for this and he watched muscles move in her arms as she sank the long plunger pole into the tub again and again to move the laundry around in the soapy water. She told him stories as she stirred, about Spanish boars and leprechauns and fairy finders and lost ships, tales that continued as she lifted cleaned items out of the tub with the pole and shifted them into another tub. He loved her stories. Then, once the first tub was emptied, she invited him to use his arms to stir up the cooled water to retrieve any items the pole had missed. He sometimes brought up a handkerchief or shirt collar, and when he did, he felt as triumphant as if he'd caught a fish with his bare hands. He also liked helping Biddy make soap. The basement windows clouded as she spooned out globs of fat saved in cans and plopped them into boiling water to which she added carefully measured spoons of lye. He loved feeling the room grow heated and redolent with the clean smell of soap as she ladled the bubbling mixture into shallow, square cake pans. Once the soap cooled, she'd guide his hand on the knife handle and help him slice the mixture into oblong bars. (But a few years later, seeing advertisements for Fels-Naptha made him disdain her practice of making soap as old-fashioned.)

His mother didn't work, except in the garden, but she always seemed busy, putting on a hat to go to meetings or parties or teas. When he smelled her perfume, he knew she was going out.

His father went to work before he got up. His father was an important lawyer in town. Aunt Rachel's husband made wine. Uncle Benno worked in the brass-ware factory that his grandfather (Vincent's great-grandfather) had started. His grandfather was the boss there. He called his grandfather Opa after hearing Oskar call him that (but before realizing that Oskar never called him that in his grandfather's presence). The factory made candleholders and doorknobs and ashtrays and fenders, but "buttons are our bread and butter," Benno had told him, then—seeing Vincent's confusion—he explained what he'd meant.

"You'll join us at the works someday," his grandfather promised. When Vincent turned seven, they let him work on the line. Early one Saturday, he walked to work with Opa. Vincent would fill in for a boy who'd fallen sick with the quinsy. He spent a few hours assisting the boy's father, sweeping brass shavings into a pot. He received a nickel for his trouble and hurried home to hide the nickel in the box under his bed with his marble. He'd stopped carrying the marble around with him, afraid he would lose it, which would be like losing a part of himself.

When summer came, Vincent delighted in freedom not only from school but from the prospect of being cold. He hated to be cold more than anything.

After supper in the dining room, which was a pickled meal if the day had been too hot for Nettie to cook, he'd go for an evening walk down to the lake with Opa, who was teaching him to swim. Vincent wore swim woolens that Benno had worn as a boy. They were too big until Bridey pulled the belt tight. Opa wore an old-fashioned striped suit that scratched Vincent's arms as he held him in the water, but Vincent didn't mind. Opa taught him special ways to stroke the water to keep his body afloat. He taught him to move his arms and legs so they pushed him forward like an engine, as if his body were a car on the road. The first time Opa stood on the rock on the bank and urged Vincent to swim in the lake alone, Vincent braved himself in the direction of the lake's dark center, a place that terrified him because the lake was the deepest lake in Connecticut. It was so deep that it had swallowed a motorcar. A driver had parked it on a slope but had kept it running, braked on a rock that had given way. Vincent always kept his eyes open underwater, scanning for glints of metal.

When Opa and he returned, wet, from the lake, Bridey would wrap Vincent in a bath sheet and dry him and pull on his nightshirt and put him into bed between crisp sheets. She'd sit beside him on the bed or in a spindly rocker, reading stories or singing lullabies her grandmother had sung to her. Her voice was a boat that carried him off to sleep and he would try to postpone the first minute of slumber, floating along on the lilt of her melody, the sensuousness of the heat, the feel of his growing body dampened with sweat. It always seemed to him just a moment later that sunlight was cutting across his face. He kept his eyes closed for as long as he could, preferring to spend the first moments of each day watching shapes dance on the inside of his lids and feeling cool breezes cross from open windows surrounding him on three sides.

Summer days were for expeditions in which he was both leader and follower. If it was a fine day, he was allowed to leave after breakfast, after half an hour's practice on the piano, and return for dinner if he wished—if not, for supper. He knew it was suppertime by the town-hall tower clock that chimed every hour and every quarter-hour played bells.

The town held marvelous sights: Bright's Pharmacy with towers of candies in glass jars, sold by the piece, the black licorice sticks (his favorite) erect as soldiers in the tallest jars behind jars of sour drops and peanut brittle and butterscotch balls and bright-colored squares of sugared jellies. A popcorn wagon parked in front of the movie house all day, gently rocking from side to side, and he loved watching the explosions of kernels inside a glass globe. Sometimes, near the wagon, a man cranked a box organ held on a leather strap around his neck. The organ made tinny music that a monkey dressed in coat and tails danced to. Sometimes, Vincent brought out his autoharp and accompanied the organ, which made both the man and the monkey laugh.

One day that summer, a day so hot that Nettie said carrots were cooking themselves in the ground, Vincent wandered around town looking for something to do. He heard the *clop-clop* of a wagon. It was an ice wagon. His heart leaped at the prospect of cooling off with a sliver of ice in his mouth. The driver was occupied in the front seat peeling an apple, allowing the horse a slow enough pace for Vincent to hop onto the low step, then hoist himself into the wagon bed and search for shards of ice to suck. The wagon was almost empty of anything but straw and the sharp two-pronged pick, which Vincent was careful to avoid as he searched. Suddenly, he heard the crack of a whip and "G'up," and the wagon jerked forward and Vincent found himself in a wagon taking off at a bracing clip. From his perch in the wagon box, he saw they were leaving town. Now the wagon was hurtling at a pace far too fast for him to jump off it. He went cold in his head. The wagon was taking him deep into the country. What should he do? What if he saw Indians or bears? He began to cry. When the wagon finally stopped, he was surrounded by cornfields. Staring up at him from the ground was a boy his own age.

"Whatcher bawlin' for?" said the boy.

"I'm lost," said Vincent, drying his tears with the back of his hands. "I live in town."

"Oh, town," said the boy, as if it were the name of a person he hadn't seen in a while. He stared down at the dirt, tracing a circle in it with his big toe. "I guess you'll have to wait till Pa goes back there next week."

Vincent nodded, blinking to hold back tears.

And that was how he met Osworth Hayden.

Osworth helped him down from the wagon and brought him into the kitchen, which was the first room in the house. Mrs. Hayden was taking rolls out of the oven and Vincent ate a lively supper with Osworth and his parents and his two boisterous brothers around a table covered with a black-checked oilcloth.

Osworth's father drove him back to town, not in his wagon but in a buggy. Vincent and Osworth sat in the seat next to him, bouncing over hill after hill that separated them from town. It was almost sunset. The sky pinkened fields of corn on both sides. Soon after dirt roads turned into macadamized ones, they passed between the stone gateposts of Hollingwood. The buggy clopped around the circular drive and stopped by the high limestone step. Before Vincent's shoe touched the stone, he heard his name called. Bridey rushed out the front door.

"We were looking all over," she said, throwing her arms about him, but he drew away, embarrassed.

The front door was open and his mother hurried toward them, dressed in white, which made her look like a ghost in the dark hallway.

Nothing would do but that Mr. Hayden and his son have a second supper with them. As they ate, Vincent saw the house through the eyes of the iceman's son. As Osworth forked up cold chicken and carrot gelatin salad, Vincent saw him glance around furtively, taking in the high moldings, the gold clock on the mantel, the heavy glassed portraits weighing on the walls, and he realized that this house, which had seemed so grand and imposing at first, was now home to him, a place he hardly noticed at all.

He didn't see Osworth again for eight years. By then Vincent was at Trowbridge and on the first night he was there, Osworth was the scholarship boy waiting their table. Vincent recognized him at once.

But that night was many years in the future, and much would take place before then: Hannah and then Nettie married and moved away; Vincent broke his leg falling from the maple tree in the front yard; Prohibition made taking his first drink an adventure; and America finally dipped its toe into the war, prompting Oskar to sign up for the navy in spite of Bridey's pleading with him not to go.

Oskar wanted to enlist so he could pick his own branch of service. Before leaving, he gave them a map that had been advertised in the newspaper. They pinned it up on the kitchen wall, a Rand McNally designed to make it easy for them to locate "Brother, Relative, Friend when reading the letter from Over There."

35

Sarah

Wellington, Connecticut

1916

Sarah wanted to be a good mother. She'd read books and manuals recommended by experts.

"What experts?" Edmund had asked, and Sarah explained that she'd meant trustees of the Modern Mothers Club, whose members were mothers of children older than Vincent, children she hoped that Vincent would emulate.

Upon their advice, she'd read *The Care and Feeding of Children* and *Moral Instruction of Young Citizens.* She was on the library's waiting list for *Childhood Faults and Their Remedies.*

The club acquired most of its members when they were mothers of infants. Never before had it accepted a newly minted mother of a boy already six. But Sarah Hollingworth Porter was a desirable addition to any club in Wellington, being not only from the oldest of the old families but also congenial, versed in the ways of clubwomen, and in possession of a grand parlor in which meetings might be hosted.

Members knew the boy had been taken in, of course, but not even

Lil, who had been one of Sarah's bridesmaids, dared to inquire directly about his origins. Sarah found a way to address the question that hadn't been posed during tea intermission at the first meeting. She spoke of having relatives in the South, and this, Sarah knew by the looks exchanged, was all they felt they needed to know. In songs and novelettes and lady columns, women below the Mason-Dixon were always dying dramatically, sending children north to be cared for by relatives.

It was vexing to Sarah that no matter how many books she read or pamphlets she studied (texts that Bridey inquired about but never asked to borrow), she felt that she would never acquire the ease and naturalness that Bridey displayed in her relations with Vincent.

Sarah guessed that Bridey's facility with the boy was due partly to the primacy of a mother's bond with her child, a bond that was visible only to Sarah and Bridey and that Vincent must feel, of course, but that would never be explained to him.

Edmund tried to reassure Sarah she was doing well at the job.

"How lucky the boy is to have such a good mother, one who dotes on him but isn't doting in the extreme," Edmund remarked one morning at the dining table, looking up from his paper as they waited for Bridey to bring Vincent downstairs, dressed for school.

But Edmund's praise did not satisfy her. She wanted acknowledgment of her efforts from Bridey and Vincent.

Bridey knew how to play, really play, with a child. She got down on all fours without seeming to think about mussing her skirts. In playing with Vincent, she became a child herself—in this, Bridey's diminutive stature worked in her favor.

Sarah would come home from bridge club or civic league or a women's roundtable discussion to find Bridey and Vincent sitting on the floor engaged in a war of tin soldiers or building a city of wooden blocks on his carpet.

Though she never said so, Sarah worried that his seeing his nurse lowering herself to his level might later make Vincent less of a gentleman, that he might expect other women to step down from the pedestals to which honor and chivalry had elevated them. But she didn't know how to convey this to Bridey.

Sarah's duty to her son—and this was confirmed by the manuals— was to be his instructress, not his playmate. Still, every now and then she made an attempt to have the fun with him that Bridey did.

"Shall we play?" she'd ask Vincent, but whenever she did, he puffed out his lower lip and hiked up his thin shoulders, then let them fall back into place.

"I don't care," he'd say.

Whatever game he chose—jacks or float the feather or shoe the horse or bottle race—he grew quickly impatient with her inability to speak the language of it. He often accused her of breaking the rules. But where were these rules? No rules were ever stated or written down.

Once, playing hide-and-seek, Sarah searched for him throughout the house but could not find him in any of the usual places: not under the skirt of the telephone table, not in the dark stairwell on the second-floor landing, not under the bed in his room (she had to squat to see, which wasn't easy in a corset, even in a new boneless one), not in the tower room on the fourth floor for which the steps were steep and the treads so narrow that Sarah had to walk sideways to mount them. As she descended from the tower, her heart began to race—what if he had fallen out a window and was injured? Or lying hurt somewhere in the house, unable to speak? As she swung through the door to the kitchen, her face must have betrayed how stricken she felt because Bridey looked up from the dough she was pounding and said, her eyes twinkling, "Try the wash basket."

When Sarah looked blank, Bridey put forefinger to her lips and led her down steeply pitched stairs to the basement. At the foot of the stairs, Sarah came unexpectedly face to face with her mother's handwriting, carefully penned loops on labels glued onto jars of preserves still neatly lined up on wooden shelves. Seeing the labels made Sarah's eyes sting.

The basement was dank and dim, lit only by two narrow windows high on the wall. Sarah followed Bridey through the cellar, past apple barrels and potato bins, to the laundry room, a place that Sarah hadn't visited in years.

There was the green woven basket her mother had put Hannah in as a baby when she'd let her nap in the shade of the tulip tree. Now it was piled with dirty linens. Sarah squatted by the basket and thrust her arms into the pile and was thrilled to feel the warmth of Vincent's skin.

He rose like Lazarus, partly shrouded in sheets.

"I knew you wouldn't find me," he cried, triumphant. "Biddy had to tell you, didn't she?"

And Sarah felt betrayed by her own inadequacy, so obvious that even a child could see it.

Sarah's mother hadn't played hide-and-seek with Sarah or her siblings. Her mother hadn't had time to play children's games. She'd been kept busy with grown-up activities that Sarah, as a child, had been eager to learn: how to arrange flowers, embroider cushions, darn socks, and run ribbons through waistbands with a hairpin. These things her mother had taught her to do. That was a mother's job—to teach her child, to inculcate learning and discipline. But Vincent was a boy. What had her mother taught Benno, Sarah's brother, when he was small? Sarah recalled her mother only holding him in her lap, singing to him or reading to him from a tall book of tales still on a bookshelf in Vincent's room. It was her father who had taught him how to use a knife, handle a gun, catch a fish and clean it—things Sarah had never learned to do. She would speak to Edmund, remind him of his fatherly duties.

Sarah's favorite time of day with Vincent was after Bridey put him to bed. Sarah often read him stories from the big family Bible. Usually, before she finished reading, Vincent had surrendered to sleep and as soon as she saw that his breathing was regular, she moved from the chair to the edge of his mattress and stroked his cheeks and the tips of his ears, inhaling the smell of him, which was like apples, reveling in the feeling of possession of him, which came to her only then.

Sarah heard Bridey telling Vincent stories during the day, long involved tales that he sometimes begged to hear from Sarah, tales of wee people and kings and peasants imprisoned by cave dragons, and Sarah marveled at Bridey's ability to spin imaginative worlds. How did she remember so many stories? She guessed that Bridey's mind was freer than hers. Bridey's daily duties were domestic, requiring little of the concentration Sarah needed to take in lectures and symposiums and talks (this week: "Home Preparedness" and "The Liberty Loan") and attend meetings of clubs (not only Modern Mothers, but book club and bridge club and the Aftermath Club, the last formed to benefit local victims of tragedy) and remember changing locations and names of new members and also their social hierarchies both in the clubs and in circles beyond.

Still, Sarah was impressed with Bridey's imagination. Sometimes she listened at doors to her stories, interrupting only when a tale turned too mawkish or encouraged superstitions.

Catholicism was full of superstition. It was a primitive religion from which her own had advanced, and at times this primitiveness was made apparent, as when Reverend Bierwirth had had to gently persuade the pastor of Bridey's parish to remove from the church lawn an offering carved by a congregant: an enormous statue of Jesus bleeding from His wounds.

Some things about Bridey, Sarah didn't admire. The way she talked, for instance. Her brogue seemed to be getting more pronounced, not less. How could that be? The day Vincent dropped a toy on his foot and cried, "Mother of Mercy!" Sarah made him wash his mouth with soap and signed up Bridey for elocution lessons given by a member of the Expression Club. She also impressed upon Bridey the importance of resuming Vincent's exercise regime to strengthen his back, reminding her that daily practice was necessary to prevent a curvature in his spine. What she didn't say was that it was also important to ensure his good posture and carriage, marks of membership in a social set to which Bridey could never aspire.

Vincent was small for his age and one day when Sarah was coming up the back path toward home she saw, from under her parasol, Bridey coming down it with Vincent. He was on her back! Instead of having him walk upright beside her, Bridey was carrying him, his limbs wrapped around her shoulders and waist. She looked like a heathen carrying a heathen baby! What would people think?

"You'll make him a cripple" is what she said once she was near enough to be heard, and Bridey's face colored, though it was already red from carrying him. Bridey dropped her arms and Vincent slid off her back.

Raising a child with someone else was rather like having another marriage, Sarah saw. But in this marriage, Sarah played the man's role. Meaning she controlled the strings of the purse, so that if preferences differed, the ones that took precedence were her own.

Sarah had a dream that recurred several times in the months after Vincent came to them. In the dream, she held Vincent's hand. They were sitting on the wicker seat of a New York subway carriage, in the ladies' car, where he was allowed, being only six. There was some sort of commotion. The train stopped, the doors flew open, and passengers stood and pushed through the doors. She pulled Vincent's hand, and they were carried out of the car by the crowd. Once on the platform, she looked down and realized the hand she held wasn't Vincent's. It was the hand of her dead brother, the one who'd drowned years ago. She turned to the train, and her heart pounded as the train sped out of the station. Vincent was on it and she knew she'd never see him again. In her dream, she screamed, and in her bed, too, she screamed, which always woke her. Sometimes, it also woke Edmund, who'd turn to her and stroke her hair and tell her to go back to sleep, it was only a dream.

She wouldn't tell him what the dream was. She wouldn't tell anyone. It didn't seem like a dream that a mother should have, especially not just once but over and over. The dream added to a growing unease within her. She was not a real mother. She was an impostor.

Like most women she knew, Sarah wasn't a suffragist, nor was she sympathetic to the cause. In her experience, men acted honorably in voting for what was in the best interest of wives and mothers and sisters and daughters. To insist on having the vote yourself meant that you didn't trust the men around you. Men, understandably, found women wanting the vote upsetting. Women taking part in parades and protests and pickets thought they were striving to make their lives better, but what they were actually doing was shooting themselves in the foot by disturbing the peace within their own homes.

"I heard there were twenty-five thousand on Fifth Avenue last week," said Sarah's friend Letsie at a meeting of the Twentieth-Century Club. The meeting was in Letsie's parlor and she was doling out rags to sew into bandages for war relief. Most of the clubs had formed Red Cross units. President Wilson had so far succeeded in keeping America out of the war. But talk was that getting into it was inevitable.

"There were some of them marching right here in town," said Lil, frowning at the scrap she'd been dealt. Only yesterday, she and Lil were students in sewing circle, stitching at silks to add to their hope chests.

"I saw in the *Record* they were blocking town hall, wanting the selectmen to sign their petition!"

"I can't understand why they're so strident when getting the vote means the conscription," said Duxie.

"You mean they'd send ladies to war?" Sarah hadn't heard this.

"That's what my father said," said Lil.

"Mr. Canfield said the same thing," Mrs. Canfield confirmed. "What's sauce for the goose is sauce for the gander."

Sarah couldn't imagine herself shouldering a rifle. How could she shoot someone, even a Hun?

And if women went to war, they'd be shot themselves, and what would happen to all the children left motherless?

"I read that a bunch of them have been standing for weeks outside the White House. They hold up rude signs and shout insults at President Wilson as soon as he comes out of the gates." This was from Duxie, who was just coming into the parlor, late as usual.

"Where are their manners?" Mrs. Canfield shook her head and hunched over her needle, leading them, by example, to return to the work at hand.

Several weeks later, a great suffrage hearing took place in Hartford and the train to the capital took in female riders at every station. Sarah and other civic-minded women of Wellington were glad to find seats when they got on. They all wore red roses pinned to their coats to distinguish themselves from suffragettes, who wore yellow ones. The train pulled into Hartford and Sarah and the others alighted and hailed carriages to take them to Capitol Hall. When they arrived, they were dismayed to discover that all of the seats on the Anti side of the hall had been taken. This meant they were forced to enter on the Suffrage side, which made Sarah feel peculiar. As they strode through the door to the Suffrage side, she touched the red rose on her lapel and fingered its petals, hoping to make her stance on the issue apparent to onlookers.

As Sarah and the others filed into the august wood-paneled room, a famous suffragette from London, Mrs. Pankhurst, was already speaking. They lifted the tips of their parasols from the floor so as not to sound taps on the polished wood as they moved down the broad aisle and slipped into seats in a half-empty row.

"Women do not ask to be placed on a throne as goddess or queen," Mrs. Pankhurst was saying. "Women are content to be equal."

Sarah settled her parasol beneath the seat of the chair, its battered arms and straight back carved with initials.

"But at present, they are only half-citizens."

Sarah found herself leaning forward to listen.

Mrs. Canfield next to her did the same.

"I find those English accents hard to understand too," she said.

But that's not why Sarah was leaning forward. She was leaning forward because what Mrs. Pankhurst was saying was, surprisingly, of interest to her.

In other countries, women already had the vote. Australian women, with the exception of Aboriginal women, had been voting for years. So had women in Denmark and Finland and Norway.

"Nowhere," Mrs. Pankhurst said, emphasizing the word with a dip of her head, which set the feathers of her hat in motion, *"nowhere in the world has the right to vote resulted in institution of female conscription."*

A few seated on Sarah's side of the room clapped politely.

Mrs. Pankhurst continued, "The real reason women in America are kept from voting is the money being paid lobbyists by makers of liquor. Liquor manufacturers are terrified—*terrified!*—that if women get the right to vote, they'll use it to prohibit the sale of liquor!"

A roar of guffaws and jeers erupted on the other side of the hall, and Sarah wondered if this unlikely prospect could be true.

But that night at dinner, Edmund affirmed it was. He added, to Sarah's surprise, that he himself didn't see harm in suffrage.

"Now that Negroes are permitted to vote, women ought to be accorded the right, don't you think?" he asked.

She was stunned to hear her father, sitting at the other end of the table—her old-fashioned father!—agree.

"What do you think, Vincent?" her father asked, turning to the boy, who was spooning up the last of his soup. Sarah was gratified to see that he was doing it the way she'd taught him, dipping the spoon by pushing it away instead of drawing it forward.

"I agree with whatever Mother thinks," he said, looking at Sarah.

"You're a canny boy," observed Edmund.

"He'll be running for office soon," her father put in.

"And so handsome, all the women will vote for him," said Benno, who had stopped in for dinner.

What a changing world he was growing up in, Sarah thought. She had never imagined herself filling out ballots. But it was true that women were only half-citizens until they were permitted to vote.

She recalled Mrs. Pankhurst's parting words: "If what I have said here has pierced any heart, please know that we need your energy, your time, your devotion."

That night, while drawing the shades before bed, Sarah gazed at the full moon.

So much world existed beyond Hollingwood. How much good she could do by stepping out of her home. The truth was that with Nettie doing the cooking and Bridey looking after her son, Sarah sometimes felt her own presence at Hollingwood to be superfluous.

A few weeks later, when a suffragette knocked at the door seeking donations, Sarah gave her name to be added to the local volunteer chapter.

36

Bridey

Hollingwood

May 1915

Hannah's young man had finally proposed and when a date was set for another wedding at Hollingwood, the electrician Mr. Tupper was called to come and finally "wire the house up."

The wiring took many days of work—holes had to be made in walls in various inconvenient places, and the family contended with dust everywhere, even in Nettie's pudding.

Bridey showed Vincent how to read drawings in pamphlets laid out on the dining-room table and study the drawings to help Sarah choose fixtures. There were two style choices, sconces or pendants. Mr. Tupper said sconces gave you more for your money because their sockets could be used for not only electric bulbs but appliances. You could unscrew a bulb and screw an electric machine into a socket. Mr. Tupper predicted that electric conveniences would soon prove indispensable: electric coffeepots and chafing dishes, record players and flatirons, electrified vacuum cleaners and sewing machines you didn't have to pedal.

Bridey couldn't imagine sewing without pumping her foot. She was certain that without her foot to set a machine going, her thought process would be disrupted and she wouldn't be able to make a straight seam.

She saw the advantage of a coal-free electric iron, however.

It took over a week for the house to be wired. The elaborate two-armed sconce in the vestibule wasn't replaced, it was refitted as a dual, which meant one arm went modern electric, but another remained conventional gas.

Finally Mr. Tupper finished all the work, installing lamps in the rooms that needed electrification, fitting them with pull chains, and putting in a socket in each room that needed one, meaning each room in which was installed a lamp. As he was replacing tools in his large metal box, he mentioned that the meterman was so busy he wouldn't be able to come out for days. This meant an advantage for the Hollingworths, Mr. Tupper observed, because until a meterman came, the family couldn't be charged for electricity, no matter how many lamps they lit.

This inspired Hannah to concoct a plan of entertainment with Vincent. They announced it at supper at the dining-room table—which was now so brightly lit by an electrified chandelier that Mr. Hollingworth joked that they might all get sunstroke.

"The Hollingwood Lights Show!" Hannah declared. Vincent drew up paper tickets that he sold for a penny. Even Oskar in the gatehouse bought one.

The show would take place at eight, as soon as dusk fell. Vincent would be allowed to stay up for it. Nettie and Bridey could postpone the dishes.

That night, after the table was cleared, all were invited onto the front lawn, where Oskar had helped Hannah and Vincent drag chairs and benches from the barn and arrange them theater-style on the grass, under the maple.

It was an unseasonably warm evening. Wood frogs quacked

in the vernal pond that stretched from the maple tree to the field.

Mr. Hollingworth was first to take a seat. He settled himself, took his pipe from his jacket pocket, held a match to its bowl, and tilted back on his chair to look west as geese honked, flying into the red sunset.

Sarah came out and laid two handkerchiefs on a bench, whereupon she and Edmund sat down. Benno leaped to a chair, straddled it, and rested his chin in his hands, waiting. Bridey and Nettie were last to arrive, hurrying out of the front kitchen door, wiping their hands on tea towels, taking the last seats.

The air had darkened, acquiring a blueness.

The front door opened, and in its frame, Vincent appeared, dressed in turban and cape and wielding a wooden yardstick, his wand.

"I am Vincent the Magician, and you're about to see a magic light show!" He bowed, then closed the door.

They waited.

One by one, windows turned from black to gold.

First the sidelights on the front doors. Then windows in the parlor and the first-floor turret room. The dining room. The kitchen. The breakfast room.

Then Vincent pulled up the sash of a window upstairs.

"Now the second floor, ladies and gentlemen!"

One by one, windows lit on the second floor too. Mr. Hollingworth's room. Sarah and Edmund's. The Yellow Room and its tower dressing room. The sewing room.

Again a sash lifted and Vincent announced that the magic was moving up to the third floor.

Hannah's room lit up. The anteroom to the turret, and then the double arched windows in the turret where the glass wasn't clear but colored; reds, blues, greens, yellows shone brightly, as beautiful as the stained glass of a church lit at night.

"It looks like a grand ship in a harbor," said Oskar, who had taken the chair next to Bridey's.

She was reminded that he'd come over too.

"So it does," she murmured, thinking of the ship in its dock on the Mersey. Thom and she might have been a family here.

Now the front doors opened and Vincent reappeared.

"Ta-da!" he said, waving the yardstick. He burst onto the lawn and ran in circles, to great applause.

The sight was glorious. Thirty-five windows, Edmund counted. Then he rose from his place beside Sarah, and, seeing this, Vincent declared that the show wasn't over.

"Oh, yes, it is, my little man," said his father, smiling. "I'm afraid of wearing out our new bulbs."

Sarah rose from her seat beside Edmund and caught Vincent in her arms, and Bridey watched as she led him by the hand into the house.

Most of the others stood and followed them inside.

Bridey didn't move. Neither did Oskar. They stayed in their seats in companionable silence as, one by one, the windows went dark.

Then Bridey rose.

"Don't go in yet," Oskar said. He bent and plucked a violet from a patch of them in the grass and then presented it to her. She was glad darkness was falling so he couldn't see she was blushing as he pushed the stem through a buttonhole on her blouse.

She sat back down and they talked for a while, until the blue air blackened and she could barely see his face next to hers.

They talked of their hopes—he wanted to get into radios, there was a radio course he was saving to take. She imagined herself with a small shop in town where her lacework might go for a pretty penny. She talked of her family, saying how much she missed them and how she regretted not writing more often, although she'd arranged for money to be sent them each month. She didn't mention Thom and she wondered if he was refraining from talking of a sweetheart too. He spoke of the small town in Germany his family had come from. Bridey asked what food he missed most and he told her *dampfnudel,* a steamed bread, and she said she would try to make it for him. He had the recipe—it was in the things of his mother. Both of his parents were already gone. He confessed his worries about being a German these days. He worried that Americans would rise up against Germans. Everyone hated Germans because of the war. He'd heard that a few towns over, a library had removed all books by Germans. Bridey assured him that that wouldn't happen in Wellington. But Oskar was skeptical.

He also worried about going to war.

"They're saying the war will be over before America has to get into it," Bridey said.

But Oskar shook his head. "Germans don't give up so easily," he said.

When they stood, she could feel him leaning toward her, and his nearness sent a warmth through her. Her mind galloped suddenly with thoughts of marrying him—but how could she marry him? Have a child with him? She knew herself. She wouldn't be able to keep her secret from Oskar. She'd let it out, surely ruining Vincent's life, not to mention her own. Also, she realized, she couldn't bear to love anyone else, because she couldn't bear the possibility of losing another person she loved.

They walked in silence, crossing the dark lawn. At the porch, he bade her good night and she lingered at the doorstep, watching his silhouette on the gravel path until he receded into shadows.

37.

Vincent

Lantern Theater, Wellington,
Connecticut

1915

He learned to read not only from books but from movies. As different as moving pictures were, they always started the same, with words to songs played by the pianist, Mrs. Plunkitt, who sometimes came to the house to teach him piano.

The audience was invited to sing along.

Opa didn't care for the sing-alongs before movies, but Bridey did. Sometimes she took him to movies when Opa couldn't. Unlike Opa, who sat quietly while words to songs appeared on the screen, Biddy swayed and sang boisterously along with the crowd.

Vincent often played a game with himself during the sing-along when words and pictures illustrating the words were obscured by the shadows of people coming into the room. He tried to see if he could identify latecomers without turning around, to guess who they were by only their silhouettes on the screen. He was almost always right. The twins were easy to identify because of how their necks were distorted by the shadows of big bows; a hat that erupted in a fountain of feathers usually belonged to Mrs. Canfield.

Seeing a movie was like dropping through a hole to exciting places he couldn't actually visit: cowboy camps, wagon-train convoys, African jungles, the moon. The flickering grays and blacks and whites on the screen took him away to a different world, making him feel as if he were trying on some other life.

He knew that movies did this to others too. When Biddy brought him to see *The Immigrant,* which took place on a rolling boat, it felt as if the screen was rocking back and forth like the boat. When Charlie Chaplin was sick over the railing, Bridey excused herself, saying she'd wait for Vincent outside. When later he emerged, it took a moment before his eyes adjusted to sunlight, and he saw her rise from the bench by the stone watering trough.

His parents hadn't wanted Opa to take him to see *Birth of a Nation.* They'd heard it was frightening for children and might give him bad dreams.

"Nonsense," said Opa. "It's American history. The boy has to learn history."

Vincent himself very much wanted to go. He reminded his parents that he'd seen *Frankenstein* and had been able to sleep that night without trouble. He was thrilled at the prospect of accompanying his grandfather to a movie that would last over an hour, the longest movie ever made. It was so important, it had first been shown at the White House.

The doors to the theater were decorated with red, white, and blue bunting. The ticket window was covered by an American flag. The sing-along songs were all patriotic ones and Vincent learned the words to "She's a Grand Old Flag" and "Anchors Aweigh." Even his grandfather took part, humming along. The last song they played was the national anthem, which he'd never heard played in a movie house. The audience members rose from wooden chairs. Some faced the flag in the corner, some faced the flag on the screen, but all sang the words Miss Nelson had taught him, accompanying the words with the salute that was how you respected the flag men had died for: right arm stretched out, palm downward, fingers pointing to the stars.

The movie terrified him. His only comfort while watching it was that the story took place far away, in the South. Negro men seized white babies from the arms of their mothers. They shot little white boys as they slept in their beds. A whole town of unarmed white people trembled in fear of the Negroes until men rode in on horseback to save them. The men wore white masks—their horses did too. Vincent sounded out the name of the heroic troop in the title: *The Great Ku Klux Klan.*

The movie had three intermissions, and by the end of it, Vincent was so shaken he couldn't keep up with his grandfather on the walk home. He seemed in a hurry to get home for supper. When they got to where the road turned toward their house, he was glad that his grandfather suggested they sit on a rock for a rest.

"Did you like the movie?" his grandfather asked, hitching up his sock garters.

"Yes," Vincent said, not wanting to seem ungrateful to his grandfather for taking him to it.

"Do you have any questions about it?" Now his grandfather was taking a cigar out of his pocket and lighting it. Apparently, he'd decided that supper could wait.

Questions were tangled up in Vincent like a ball of saved strings, but he wasn't able to pick out just one.

"That picture was made by a man who needs to see himself as better than others," his grandfather said. "It's a picture made for men who need to see themselves that way too. I hope you're never that way yourself, son."

A warmth flooded his chest. His grandfather had called him "son."

They resumed their walk, Vincent staying a few steps behind his grandfather, both of them keeping well to the side of the road to avoid being hit by fast buggies and roadsters.

All the way home, the movie replayed in his mind, terrifying him all over again. When he followed his grandfather up the steps of the back porch and into the kitchen, Nettie was there, her dark arm wielding a shiny cleaver. He let out a cry and drew back.

It was weeks before he wanted to go to the movies again.

38

Hollingwood

Wellington, Connecticut

1915

Hannah married and left the house (her going-away outfit was a flapper dress that exposed a lot more than her ankles, and she wore extra-long ropes of pearls, long enough to fascinate Vincent, who made them spin like aeroplane propellers).

Soon after, Nettie got married too. She wore the Hollingworth family veil and a lace dress that Bridey had sewn. She wed Mr. Treadwell in a small ceremony at the Wellington Baptist Church. Her new husband was a blacksmith in a nearby town in Massachusetts. His parents had come north with hers from Kentucky. She'd been keeping company with him on Sundays and on her days off for years. The Hollingworths hosted a reception for them in the gazebo garden, which Sarah had designed and replanted based on drawings she'd found rolled up in the attic. Bridey made the luncheon, following a few of Nettie's favorite recipes.

With Nettie and Hannah gone, the house felt hollow, and Bridey was glad to be kept busy with Nettie's work in the kitchen until a day cook could be found. With only four family members left in the house, they didn't need a cook to live in.

At first, Nettie's care of the vegetable garden fell to Bridey too. But Bridey had grown up in a house in town on a patch of dirt too scant for a garden. She had neither training nor interest in the tricks of coaxing green from the ground, and so a girl had been hired to do the planting and weeding and watering.

The girl had been recommended, but her work was desultory, and when Sarah saw from a window that the girl was yet again leaning against a fence post blowing fluffed seeds of dandelion into the wind, she grew incensed enough to take a few coins from an envelope in her drawer, gather up her skirts, go downstairs, and walk outside to dismiss her.

The garden had lain fallow for the rest of that year, but the next spring the hired man was called in to do what Oskar might have done if he'd not left for war, which was clean out the brush and turn the soil in preparation for a victory garden.

The war, which had been going on in the rest of the world for some years, had finally done what everyone in Wellington had worried it would, which was come to America.

Printing presses everywhere were operating day and night, rolling out pamphlets to urge citizens to take part in war efforts. One of the ways suggested was for people to plant gardens to grow what they'd usually buy in stores so that store supplies might be sent to boys at the front.

Sarah's efforts on behalf of women's suffrage—organizing teas and luncheons and talks, not only in Wellington, but in towns leading from it to Hartford—diminished, as the stress of the country rose to a fever pitch, and men were whisked away from the workforce into soldiers' uniforms and sent for training in distant towns.

39

Vincent

Wellington, Connecticut

1917

Vincent knew why Oskar had enlisted. He went to prove that although he was German, he wasn't a Hun. The Huns were the reason Belgian orphans were starving—"Offer it up for starving orphans in Belgium," Biddy would say if he didn't want to eat his beets or broccoli. The Huns had blown up a ship called *Lusitania,* killing American tourists. The Huns had started a war with the whole world.

Being against Huns was expected if you were American. It's why they didn't sing "Tannenbaum" at carols or have German plum soup at Christmas anymore. It's why the sign on the vat of sauerkraut at the butcher's now said VICTORY CABBAGE. It's why Mr. Glover, the dentist, didn't have his assistant with the long braid down her back anymore, because she was from Düsseldorf, and a letter to the newspaper had been signed by patients threatening to take their teeth out of town.

Oskar told Vincent that for the first time, he was glad his parents were gone, otherwise they would have had to register their names and their bank accounts with the government and even allowed themselves to be fingerprinted, as if they were criminals. Oskar changed the spelling of his name from *Oskar* to *Oscar*, which made sense to Vincent. Now he had a *car* in his name! But the family ignored this new spelling in the letters they wrote him. Vincent saw this when he was invited to pencil a message to him at the bottom of a letter from Bridey that was then slipped into an envelope addressed to the Red Cross.

Vincent's mother's church club gave out pamphlets advising people how to grow their own fruits and vegetables so that food in stores could go to the boys at the front as well as to starving families abroad. His mother enlisted him as a Soldier of the Soil to help her plant peas and beans and carrots and tomatoes that Bridey could seal in a jar and store in the basement.

School had let out for the summer and now sometimes, after breakfast in the dining room with Opa and Benno, who left for the factory soon after Bridey cleaned away the plates, Vincent would accompany his mother down to the garden. He'd let her pull special rubbers over his shoes and strap the knees of his dungarees with pads, but after they reached the garden and he got down in the dirt, he usually forgot to do what his mother had asked him to do—press seeds around little hills of soil or in a line as straight as he could make it and then cover the seeds with pushes of earth—and instead found himself pulling worms from their holes or studying how ants built hills so much taller than themselves.

One morning at breakfast, after his mother had announced that she and Vincent would go down to the garden and weed, he excused himself and slipped out the back door, not the kitchen door, where his escape might be noticed, but the little-used door on the other side of the house that was the door to a mudroom. Vincent turned the brass knob and pulled open the door and stepped down and

271

opened another door and ran down the steps and out to the Hair Tree.

The Hair Tree was a willow with branches so long they fell to the grass, forming a curtain. You could part the curtain by pulling apart the strands, and when you had entered it, you found a world that had nothing to do with the world outside. The light was different—not sharp, but soft. If light was yellow in the world, here it was green. Noise fell away. Behind the curtain, it was quiet. Everything stilled. No grass grew here. The tree's giant trunk was gnarled with age and had a hole so big, you could curl up in it. Nettie had shown him this place. Vincent now folded himself up and curled inside the hole of the tree. Above him, on the underside of a high branch, cocoons clung to bark. One day, he knew, having seen it before, the white sacs would burst, releasing a yellow cloud of butterflies.

Vincent pictured himself in a cave, like Ali Baba. As on walls of a cave, the tree's bark was carved with ancient marks: *NW*—Nettie had played here often as a small child, she said. *BH* and *HH* and *RH*…his mother was the only one who had not carved her initials. She'd told him she'd been afraid of hurting the tree. She'd carved her initials in the house instead, on a windowpane, using the diamond of her mother's ring after she died. The ring would someday be his, she said, showing him the window in the Yellow Room: *SH*.

"But don't you dare write on windows," she warned him. "You'll break the glass!"

She needn't have told him. He'd never had done that because his writing was ugly, not her pretty hand. He'd notched his initials with a knife in the tree next to those of other Hollingworths: *VHP*.

His mother was always telling him what not to do. *Don't run on the stairs. Don't slouch at the table. Don't write with one elbow on the desk; your shoulders will slope.*

Now he heard the whine of the garden gate and uncurled from

his place in the trunk and walked to the wall of branches and peered through.

There was his mother, going into the garden, closing the gate behind her. She must have given up looking for him. She'd tied up her skirts so they wouldn't crush things in the garden, and that made her walk funny.

She was pulling on gloves and then she was on her knees in front of a white wooden trellis that Oskar had painted before he left. Its hatching was tilted. It was made to hold vines but none had grown on it yet. She touched the trellis and set it upright, as if vines were there but only she could see them.

He lost interest in watching her and stepped away from the curtain and took the folding knife from his pocket and began to play mumblety-peg, throwing the blade at the tree trunk to see how high he could make it stick.

Now he heard the gate going again. He turned and looked through the branches. Biddy was coming into the garden to join his mother, and what was she doing? Biddy's job wasn't the garden. She carried the handle of a pail over her arm, and the pail meant she was going to pick berries on the path to the lake. He wanted to go with her. He loved picking berries and she let him choose the kind of berry for the pudding she'd make. He didn't like boysenberry, but sometimes boysenberries had to be picked.

Biddy left the gate open behind her and now she was talking, calling his mother "Sarah" instead of "ma'am," which was what she called her in front of Vincent.

"Sarah, he needs you," Biddy was saying. "He needs time with his mother."

His heart leaped. Why was Biddy saying that? He had all the time with his mother he needed.

"His *mother?*" said his mother. Was her being his mother a question? After three years, was she thinking of giving him back?

273

"You ignore him. It's no good for a small child to be ignored by his mother."

Something was wrong, but he didn't know what. His mother stood so that she could look down on Biddy. She peeled off a glove and wiped her forehead with the back of her hand.

"Which of us is his mother, you make very clear to him."

"I don't," Biddy said. "He knows that you are his mother. I am his nurse. He knows the difference."

Now Vincent knew what the matter was. He loved Biddy more than he loved his mother and this was wrong of him, as it hurt Mother's feelings. He didn't blame her—she was his mother! He vowed that he would make more of an effort with her. He didn't want her to give him back!

His mother raised her voice and pointed her finger at Biddy, which was something she did when she got angry.

"His nurse whom he feels, he knows, is his mother!"

What? Biddy wasn't his mother! He wouldn't want Biddy to be his mother. That would mean he'd be poor.

"I haven't told him that, Sarah."

"You don't have to say it with words! You say it with your hovering, your hands always on him, anticipating the boy's every need. Which I—and modern experts—think is detrimental to him. Edmund and I wish to raise a manly boy, not a namby-pamby."

Vincent's fingers tightened around the handle of his knife. He was not a namby-pamby!

"What would you have me do, then," Biddy said, looking down. With the toe of her boot, she poked at leaves peeping up from the dirt.

His eyes watered and his ears grew hot.

"Do what you will," said his mother. "How am I to stop you. What would I do? Dismiss you?"

His heart leaped into his throat. If Biddy went away, who would take care of him?

"Please. Don't."

"The boy would never forgive me. I would never forgive myself."

Something hard and hot formed in his chest and he had to release it.

"*Ahhhh!*" he screamed suddenly, bursting out of the curtain and making for the garden, holding his knife above his head like a dagger. "I am the great Ali Baba," he said and the women's talk was cut short, as he'd known it would be, and Bridey's pail beat against her arm as she hurried out of the garden and toward him, but he ran around her and through the open garden gate and threw himself at his mother instead.

"A monster was after you!" he declared to her, breathless. "I slayed him."

"Thank you, darling," his mother said, taking him in her arms. "Aren't you the good boy." And both of them turned their heads toward Biddy, watching her apron strings lift and lower as she walked away, growing smaller and smaller, making her way down the hill to the thicket of berries.

Vincent

Wellington, Connecticut

1915–1923

Opa seemed to like him more than his father did. But this was, Vincent reasoned, because his father hadn't had as much time to get to know him. His father worked at a law office and was often gone before he got up, arriving home only after he was put to bed. Also, his father traveled. Sometimes to Hartford, more often to New York, his schedule depending on the comings and goings of the CNE train.

Three little windows into his father would remain vivid to Vincent for all of his life.

The first was when he was six, when his father taught him to dress like a man. On the morning of Hannah's wedding, for which Vincent was ring bearer, his father had come into Vincent's bedroom and showed him how to tuck a tie into the fold of his collar, then fasten the collar onto the shirt at the back stud, then put on the shirt and collar, close the collar with the front stud, tie the tie over and back and back over again, and when it was finished, how fine Vincent felt himself to be, looking into the pier mirror, his father behind him.

"Two typical specimens of well-dressed Wellington men," said his father, words that gave Vincent so much pleasure, he'd rolled them around in his head for days.

The next was when he was nine, after the war had been going for some time. His father had taken him to New York as a birthday present, and when they arrived in the Grand Central Terminal and emerged into the cold air of Forty-Fifth Street, confronting them on the plaza was a pyramid. It was a pyramid made of twelve thousand leather helmets, rising higher than the roof of the station. The helmets, spiked at the crown, had been collected from captured German soldiers, and by the sight of this, they knew that the war would be won.

The third was when he was ten and Vincent became bedridden with a case of the chicken pox. Days later, his father came down with it too, which surprised everyone, especially Grandmother Porter, who insisted he'd had it. But Doc Spencer declared that was impossible; if he'd had it, he couldn't get it again. Both Vincent and his father lay in torment for days, itching and being told not to scratch, getting sponged with quinine and plastered with oatmeal and delivered into and out of tubs of cold water salted with baking soda, until finally the entire business was over and his mother recorded their names and dates of affliction in the family Bible on a page headed "Illnesses." After that, Vincent found strange validation in the fact that he and his father sported in the same place on their foreheads tiny, identical, indelible scars.

Part of Vincent hoped that the war would last until he was old enough to enlist, but part of him was relieved, very relieved, that at the moment he was young enough to stay home.

The day he watched Oskar roll up bedding and strap it to a brown canvas pack on his back, he thought how uncomfortable the thin bedding would be to sleep on.

Oskar didn't mention that in his letters, however, which arrived in pale blue envelopes on pages so thin, you could almost read both sides of the letters at once. He talked about the heat in Baltimore, which was now overrun with soldiers and sailors, the fun of learning Morse code, and how he was training for an athletic contest, which was a half-mile run around the ship. This gave them an idea of how big the ship was, but he couldn't tell them the name of the ship; if he did, it would be blacked out by censors. The letters were addressed to Hollingwood and read by everyone in the house, but the one who kept them was Bridey.

One day, months after Oskar had left for the war, the brass lion knocker on the front door was banged with an insistence that identified the knocker as a bearer of a message from Western Union.

Bridey had been the one to answer the door.

Later, Opa pinned the yellow telegram to the Rand McNally map on the kitchen wall, affixing it to Gibraltar, where *Radio Operator Third Class Oscar Engel was killed in action*. Though Oskar's body never came back, a service was held for him at the church that he and Bridey had walked to on Sundays.

After that, Bridey stopped smiling. She didn't wear violets on her blouse anymore. She seemed older. The telegram and the map remained, untouched, on the wall in the kitchen for years.

It was Opa who taught Vincent to swim and to trout. Opa showed him how to catch fish even when the lake was ice. He taught him to skate on it, too, and how to know when the ice was safe for skating, and how to recognize the best ice to skate on, which was black ice.

It was Opa who helped with his application to Trowbridge. Trowbridge was a boarding school across the lake, the same one his uncle Benno had gone to, graduating in the class of 1905, its first class.

Trowbridge had been built by Mr. Trowbridge, who had known

Vincent's great-grandfather. Mr. Trowbridge had made his fortune in cigar leaves, a business that required frequent trips to Germany. He was a widower and on a train trip to Frankfurt, he had met a baroness. They married and when the new Mrs. Trowbridge came to Wellington, she was keenly disappointed. She'd expected a grand town, not a colonial backwater. To console her, her husband built a castle to remind her of childhood summers at palace estates in Bavaria. They'd had two sons who died in childhood and a daughter they bred to assume the burdens of royal duty from an early age. But the daughter resisted social climbing (such as it was in Wellington in the 1800s) and became a teacher. When she inherited the flamboyant property, she turned it into a school to provide boys of New England with the education they needed to prepare them for college. She planned a curriculum that reflected the rigor of her own education in Switzerland, which had been based on precepts held by Frederick the Great. But Trowbridge's first headmaster, who'd been lured away from Harvard College, talked her down from that ambition, pointing out that students needed preparation for lives in America, not Germany during the Prussian wars.

Vincent received his Trowbridge acceptance by telegram.

Benno counseled Vincent on what to expect, including Hell Night. He told him to prepare to be woken up and tenderized in a hot tub of water, then run with other first-formers through a gauntlet of upperclassmen swinging knotted towels.

This terrified Vincent, who was slight, with shoulders too narrow for his liking. He determined to build himself up. In preparation for entering in the fall of 1924, in addition to studying math books and grammar that summer, he pored over an old book of Benno's he found on his shelf: *The Virile Powers of Superb Manhood.* Its author, Bernarr Macfadden, was famous for his advice to boys wanting to acquire a healthy physique. He'd written many articles for issues of *Physical Culture,* which Vincent was always the first to take out of the library. The articles elucidated tactics for maximizing manliness and gaining flesh. He was vexed that his mother and Biddy wouldn't allow him to follow Macfadden's regimen for fasting, even though Vincent showed them before and after pictures that proved its positive effects. Macfadden disapproved of white bread, which he called "the staff of death," and, to please Vincent, Biddy took to mixing up crusty black bread, saying each time she pulled a loaf from the oven that it was the same bread she'd been happy to emigrate from.

He slept with a nylon stocking over his head (to keep in his strength) and lifted dumbbells (specially ordered) forty-five times a day. But at the end of the summer, when he arrived at Trowbridge with sixty other boys, he observed that most of them filled out their regulation jackets better than he did.

The first night at supper, when the scholarship boys came around to the tables, helping the maids juggle trays and plates, he recognized Osworth, the iceman's son, who he could see had developed the physique to which he himself had aspired. He guessed it was the result of having to help his father lift fifty-pound blocks of ice. Vincent tried to guess what the etiquette of addressing him was (one doesn't greet maids, but Osworth wasn't a maid, was he?), regretting that his own life of privilege, for which he was grateful, had short-shrifted him in the area of physical endowment.

Then, luckily for Vincent, just before he was to suffer it, hazing was outlawed by the masters at Trowbridge.

41

Bridey

Hollingwood

1924

Soon after Vincent left home for Trowbridge, Mr. Hollingworth went into a worrisome state of decline. He developed a cough. He lost his balance, so Bridey had to help lead him downstairs sometimes and even to navigate the flat of the hall carpets. He was sixty-seven, an old man. He hardly ever went to the factory anymore. He remained general manager of the works, but now Benno assumed responsibilities his father would never have trusted him with before. Mr. Hollingworth rose for breakfast but went back to bed in late morning and sometimes stayed there until supper, often refusing a tea tray if brought up to him.

He began to complain—a practice that he had never indulged in. He complained of mean headaches. He complained of not being able to read without the use of strange lenses. He complained of his teeth, especially the wreck of a tooth at the back of his mouth that Mr. Glover had not been able to do anything for and despite the fact that he'd gone to New York, as Glover had advised, and had all his teeth pictured.

Bridey knew something was seriously wrong when Mr. Hollingworth gave up his pipe. He didn't say he was giving it up, but the fact came to light when she found various pipes abandoned about the house—it wasn't like him to leave them around. Usually, after finishing his smoke, he was meticulous about attending to the bowl, cleaning it out with a bristle, then reaching into the pocket of his trousers or vest for a linen hankie that Bridey had washed and ironed. With a quick rub, he'd polish the little wooden bowl and the curve of the stem before setting the cleaned pipe in its place on the walnut carousel that rested at the border of the green leather blotter on his desk in the study. Sometimes he'd wander the house with the pipe unlit, which he said helped him think. Now he didn't do that anymore.

When Sarah and Edmund returned from a tour of castles in Scotland, retracing the wedding trip her parents had taken, they became worried about her father too. Doc Spencer diagnosed a case of bilious fever and agreed that Mr. Hollingworth needed a rest. He prescribed a course of tonics and patent drops from the druggist and a sleeping draft to help him at night.

And then one day, to Bridey's alarm—although Old Doc had warned of the possibility—Mr. Hollingworth succumbed to a fit of blindness.

42

Mr. Hollingworth

Hollingwood

1926

He had never been so sighted as in the days he was blind.

He had always considered himself a fearless man, but he realized that he had been brave only in the absence of fear: fear-*less*. Now, pitched into blackness, fear assaulted him, made his body perpetually cold, pervaded his pores like a terrible perfume, and he saw that courage required more from a body than its merely remaining sanguine in the absence of fear.

He feared death, which he knew was advancing upon him. More than death, he feared that his family might discover the exact nature of what he was dying from, which he'd known in his heart before Doc Spencer had closed the bedroom door and told it to him.

Syphilis! He had to silently repeat the word every now and then to himself, rolling it silently on his tongue so that his reluctant mind would take in the fact that an upstanding man from an upstanding family going to work every day in the factory built by his upstanding father's father could be a syphilitic case.

The great pox! There'd been little warning. Years before, after he'd taken Camille and her trunks to the station, his heart as heavy as one of the boxes he'd shouldered for her—after he'd written her letter after letter on pages of onionskin but never knew whether or not she'd received them (she had many addresses; she'd never written back), he'd noticed a spot. But the spot had gone away and he'd forgotten about it.

Recently, he'd made discreet inquiries in letters he wrote to relatives abroad about other matters. In this way, he discovered that Camille Brassard had died in Paris a few years before of pneumonia. Was it pneumonia?

Robbed of his sight, he was no longer a self-reliant man in his sixties; he was as helpless as a small child, needing assistance in accomplishing the smallest task.

Being blind didn't make things appear black, as he'd imagined. Instead, he saw a strange color, like a bruise. Sometimes, the bruise darkened to a purplish haze or yellowed, as a real bruise did.

Being in the dark caused him to wallow in his head for hours. His fears, he realized, had been mounting for years and now they were numerous. He feared business uncertainties, recalling profitless meetings of hardware men who agreed that soon the big fellows—American Brass and Cincinnati Works—would have the small ones crowded to the wall.

He feared that the business wouldn't be able to carry his family, as he had once believed it could do, bearing them all like a wagon entrusted with precious cargo across the vast terrain of the new century and into the next. (The Year of Our Lord 2000—he couldn't imagine it.) He feared for his family, for their unfathomable future, for the house that embraced them; would they be able to hold on to it?

He feared that he wouldn't regain his sight, that his blindness might be a condition that endured for as long as he himself did, though Doc Spencer had assured him that it would last for three days at most. The blindness was a result of a buildup of mercury, an unfortunate side effect of the bromides he was taking.

He feared developing telltale sores on his face, the sores that plagued sufferers of syphilitic cases he'd read of in books, though Doc assured him if he hadn't acquired the sores yet, he wouldn't, that the nature of the disease in his condition had already shown itself to take a different course. Still, when Bridey entered his bedroom each morning to bring him a tray, he listened for the sound of her gasp, which would disclose to him that the dreaded sores had appeared.

Being relegated to the dark felt like a form of solitary confinement, and when he was sitting alone, as he often did now, deposited by Bridey or Sarah or Edmund and urged to stay in one spot, to be safe, fears multiplied in him: the fear of injury, fear of a fall, the fear of walking outside the front door, the fear of being unaccompanied. These days, he feared being alone for long stretches of time, which was ironic, as he'd always prided himself on his independence, a trait he'd discovered, and been glad for, after his wife died.

How sensitive he was now to people's voices. Some voices of friends suddenly irritated him. Other voices were mellifluous sounds he hadn't noticed before; the gentle lilt in the words of the Irish maid Bridey particularly pleased him, though he didn't know why. Her voice was one he hadn't taken much notice of before. He could tell a presence now by smell. When Bridey approached, he knew it was her, not only by the cadence of her footfalls but by her scent, which was not unlike cinnamon.

His daughter's voice now was like milk, white and shining nourishment.

Furniture was malevolent, poking him, bruising him. "Are you all right?" his family members always asked after he'd collided with something, and why couldn't they have spoken up when they saw it was in his path?

*   *   *

His father, Phineas, who'd built Hollingwood, was a practical man, but even so, he'd been known to entertain spiritualist notions. This was evident in the shape of the turret rooms, which were octagonal, a shape seers advised Victorian architects to use to avoid corners where spirits might trap themselves.

Benjamin Hollingworth had never been a believer in the occult. He'd excused himself from rooms at parties where table tippers, women usually, in lace veils and jewelry made of large stones purported to be able to speak to the departed or hear their voices emanate from objects they had possessed in their lives. But now he discovered that inanimate objects exerted a palpable feeling, a pressure that pulled you toward them, like a magnetized force; he'd never felt this before or known it existed, though he'd heard it often enough referred to, getting places by the feel of it. It had been something (among many things) that he had distrusted. He'd discovered this when he'd woken in the middle of the night, wanting the toilet. He hadn't called anyone. He followed the feel of the walls and a force pulling him to where he wanted to go.

After three days, his sight came back to him, not washing over him in the flood he'd expected, but little by little, in layers of light that took their time turning into things he could see.

Young Doc recommended a change of treatment, from mercury bromides to a compound called 606. It was a new kind of drug, a synthetic that represented the promise of modern medicine. But Old Doc read up on it and had reservations. According to several articles, patients in later stages of the disease didn't respond well to the treatment. And making the compound was fraught with peril, as 606 powder had to be mixed with arsenic in increments so exact that even a dram's difference could result in not curing the patient, but killing him. Also, the source of the drug, where it was manufactured, mattered, as the crystalline was highly unstable in air.

Young Doc assured his father and Mr. Hollingworth that his source could be trusted. A colleague from medical college had gone into pharmacology and was promoting a reliable supply of remedies indispensable to modern men of medicine: morphine and heroin, pentobarbital, chloroform, and the general-purpose anesthetic cocaine.

But Old Doc wasn't convinced. He resumed the course of mercury treatment, adjusting the compound, and all were relieved that blindness did not recur.

43.

Bridey

Hollingwood

1923

Old Doc came to look in on Mr. Hollingworth every day, either early, before his morning rounds, or in the evening, after office hours. Whenever Bridey came into the room with a tray of beef broth or a boiled egg, she noted they weren't talking about Mr. Hollingworth's health but about other things. They recalled trouting trips they used to take with Benno in the mountains or discussed the new standard time, which was causing confusion at train stations, or the issue of the Silent Policeman, which was Wellington's talk of the day. The Silent Policeman was a painted wood cutout set up on the white line in Main Street, meant to direct drivers as to which side of the street to stay on, but many drivers were unnerved by the unexpected sight of a man in the middle of the road and swerved to avoid him, which, according to letters to the editor of the *Wellington Record,* was likely to cause more accidents than it prevented.

Bridey feared that because they were no longer speaking of Mr. Hollingworth's health, and because Doc Spencer was no longer lingering with her in the kitchen to advise on plasters or liniments or other courses of action, it meant that his illness could not be reversed.

She began to worry. Was Mr. Hollingworth's ailment something Bridey herself could catch? What would happen to her if she got sick? She was thirty-one years old. She wanted to be around for Vincent.

He was now fourteen, almost as old as Bridey had been when she'd come over. He was handsome, with thick red curls. His eyes had darkened, but they were still blue. His arms looked narrow but they contained tensile strength, just like Thom's had. He was already taller than Thom had been. She was glad Vincent would be at Trowbridge, sheltered from all that she and Thom had had to know at his age.

Mr. Hollingworth developed a cough, and the cough got better, but he began to complain of a "mean head," and the headaches became so severe that he was moved to Nettie's old room, which was the room farthest north, and Bridey ran up curtains on the sewing machine, dark velvet hangings. The slightest light hurt his eyes.

Doc Spencer was called again and prescribed a course of treatment but Mr. Hollingworth's vision remained poor.

Now his cough came back and he began to have bone pain, and Doc Spencer diagnosed a case of consumption.

Consumption! Known to be fatal and catching! It had killed her grandparents and Thom's sister too.

But Doc said the case was a light one, not serious enough to warrant removal to one of the sanatoriums.

This was said out of the hearing of Mr. Hollingworth, just outside the door, and while the words seemed to relieve Sarah, Bridey fretted.

Bridey would be the one taking care of him. What would she do if she got the consumption?

Was there a prophylactic for it? she asked. Doc said no. She'd be fine, though, he added, as long as she washed her hands before and after taking care of him. If she wore the mask and took basic precautions to protect her health (sunshine and exercise and daily doses of vitamin tonic), she needn't worry.

He showed her how to tie the green gauze mask so it could be easily taken on and off.

Doc didn't give Sarah and Edmund masks, and Bridey assumed this was because they were not with him as much as Bridey was. But when they were with him, they were careful to keep their distance. Bridey, too, kept her distance as much as possible, even wearing the mask.

"The Masked Bandit," Mr. Hollingworth called her when she first came in wearing it, bringing him a tray.

Nettie came for a visit and didn't keep her distance. She propped Mr. Hollingworth up on his pillow and pressed a wet tea cloth soaked in elderberry to his face. She did this without wearing gloves, which worried Bridey, who was glad that Nettie was past childbearing age.

Mr. Hollingworth's bone pains got worse, especially at night.

"It's like hand drills boring into my legs," he said, which made Bridey wish she could do something for him, although both Old Doc and Young Doc had assured her that there was nothing to do between doses of laudanum.

One Sunday after Mass, Bridey found herself walking in the company of the nursing nuns who lived in the gray clapboard house across the street from the church. Bridey knew they knew how to care for consumption. An ailing archbishop had stopped at the convent on his way to the cure at Saratoga, and because of the nuns' care, he didn't have to go to the sanatorium.

Bridey asked Sister Odile if she might spare a moment. Sister Odile was the kindest. She'd once told Bridey she'd felt called to the

Hawaii Territory to care for the lepers, but the bishop had refused her request. Sister Odile nodded to Bridey and told the others to walk home without her. This surprised Bridey. She hadn't expected Sister Odile to want to see Mr. Hollingworth right away; Bridey had meant only to ask for advice. But it seemed rude to refuse her.

As they neared home, Bridey worried. Shouldn't she ask permission to bring someone to Hollingwood? But no one besides Mr. Hollingworth was there. Edmund and Sarah were in Boston Corners, paying a call on an uncle.

Bridey usually entered by the back kitchen door but felt that doing so now would be a slight to the nun. She led the sister up the back way from the road to the church, then took her around the yard to the front and mounted the porch steps and wondered if she'd have to open both double doors to accommodate the width of Sister Odile's cornette. But as soon as Bridey opened one door, Sister followed her through it, twisting adroitly to achieve passage for the giant white headdress.

Bridey led Sister Odile up the stairs. Mr. Hollingworth was dozing. He had lost so much weight, he was barely there under the sheets. He woke when Sister pulled up a chair. She spoke to him kindly.

"Well, sir, you didn't expect to wake up to a Catholic nun, did you? I hope the shock of me won't set you back."

Mr. Hollingworth smiled and Bridey felt relieved.

"Get us some cool water, would you please, Bridey?" Sister held out the pitcher. Bridey wondered if she was being deliberately sent out of the room. Perhaps not. The pitcher was warm. Sister gave her his glass from the bedside, too, and Bridey was careful not to touch the rim that Mr. Hollingworth's lips had touched.

When Bridey returned, Mr. Hollingworth was asleep again, and Sister Odile walked Bridey downstairs.

"Are we alone?" the nun asked in the front hall, looking around.

Bridey said they were.

"I'll tell you," the nun said, lowering her voice and leaning as far toward Bridey as her cornette allowed. "That's not consumption."

Bridey was surprised—defying a certified doctor! "What is it, then?" she asked.

The nun, pulling on gloves, looked away, to the garlanded frames of Hollingworth ancestors gazing from the wall.

She inhaled deeply, then let out the breath.

"It's syphilis," she said. "The doctor probably thinks it best not to tell the family, so you shouldn't either."

Bridey couldn't believe it. The great pox! She'd thought only terrible gadabouts got that.

"It's years past the point of being contagious," the nun assured her. "I'm only telling you so you'll not be afraid of contagion."

And Bridey remembered Madame Brassard.

44

Vincent

Radio City Music Hall

October 1927

It was said (and Vincent believed it) that every improvement worth inventing had by now been invented. You could push an electric button and flood a room with light. There were electronics to toast your bread, warm up your blanket, even light your cigar. You could lift a small trumpet of perforated black Bakelite to your lips and talk to people halfway across the country, conversing with them as if they were in the same room. The most impressive and life-changing invention, of course, was the motorcar, which enabled you to locomote yourself to places in half the time it had taken your grandfather to get there. On hot summer days, you could get in a touring car with the roof down and cool yourself breezing down newly macadamized roads.

Vincent felt himself lucky to be born in the first generation to grow up motored. He and his friends were on the new highway now and the coachman had them zooming past towns and cornfields. Seeing the world at thirty miles an hour, watching trees and buildings go by at speed, felt natural to him in a way it never would to his father or his grandfather or even Uncle Benno.

"It's a straight eight," said HoHo (Horace Sherwin). He meant the engine, which was the new engine, somehow inherited from aeroplanes in the war. HoHo sat in the jump seat facing his companions to whom he'd left the more comfortable seating on the velvety gray bench: Vin (Vincent himself), Howdy (Harold Mingott), Dud (Derwood Wilson), and Ozzie (Osworth Hayden).

The car was a Duesenberg; it was also a limousine. HoHo's father was a merchant banker connected to a producer in Hollywood who was connected to a backer of the photoplay that everyone was talking about, though it hadn't yet opened: *The Jazz Singer.* Al Jolson would be at the premiere tonight at Radio City Music Hall. They were going to the premiere of the first talkie in New York!

Mr. Sherwin had not only gotten them tickets but persuaded Headmaster Buell to let them off campus on a Thursday on the grounds that seeing the first talkie was an educational opportunity. It would broaden the boys' musical education, he said. The boys were members of the school's Society Syncopators, who provided music for tea dances with girls from Farmington, Portia Mann, and Bennetts. HoHo played the sax, Howdy the clarinet, Dud the accordion, Ozzie the traps, and Vincent the piano, jazzing up pieces he'd learned on the ancient upright in the Hollingwood parlor. Vincent had never ridden in a Duesenberg before, the car that, everyone knew, was favored by movie stars.

"Where are we in history?" HoHo leaned in to ask.

"Rutherford Hayes," said Ozzie. "The electoral college win."

Howdy and Dud groaned. They hadn't started their papers. Ozzie, of course, had already finished his. But he was a day boy who lived at home. Vincent guessed it was easier to work at home. Plus, Oz was on scholarship. He needed to keep up his grades. Vincent was still doing research for his paper. He meant to talk to his grandfather about Hayes when he went home on Sunday.

"Jehoshaphat!" Dud exclaimed. "I can't wait till we graduate. Just seven more months. After finals, I'm taking my textbooks out to the shooting range and putting holes in them with my twenty-two." Dud was from Ohio, which made him bolder, more forward-thinking, than the others. The most progressive people in the country were pushing out to the west.

Coming to Trowbridge had vastly expanded Vincent's sense of the world.

For years, he'd been mesmerized by the sight of the Trowbridge castle in the distance, at the top of the hill, sun glinting off its ramparts, its buttresses, bastions, and keep. In quiet moments in the Trowbridge dining room, Vincent sometimes contemplated the foundress's stern countenance in the gilt-framed portrait that hung on the carved paneling. The French master had them pay frequent honor to her after classes he held in the cemetery when the weather was fine. He thought boys were better off outdoors. "Headstones make excellent backrests," he said. He ended his classes by having the boys sing the Marseillaise. Then, facing in the direction of the foundress's grave, they bowed from the waist and recited in chorus: "*Merci,* Madame Trowbridge!"

From the elocution master, he'd learned to win arguments on topics he knew almost nothing about by adopting Schopenhauer's simple stratagems for debating (appeal to authority rather than reason, admit your opponent's premises but deny his conclusions, exaggerate his opposition, et cetera). It was a method he practiced when he went home each week for Sunday dinners, causing consternation in his father and amusement in his grandfather.

He learned to appreciate Latin as much as he did music. The most remarkable achievement of the Romans was their language, claimed

Dr. Lauer, their philosophy master who also taught Latin. Quentin Lauer was famous on campus for refusing to wear an overcoat even in the cold heart of Connecticut winters. He made his way across frozen quads wearing not even a cap against the cold, only his academic robes, which billowed about him, and this habit so impressed the boys that many, including Vincent, acquired the habit of going coatless, which endured in them for the rest of their lives.

The English master taught him not to believe everything he read in books. The greatest mistake of the Donner Party, Mr. Hawkins said, was that they ignored the counsel of a mountain man whom they encountered as he passed them heading east. "There's no such cutoff," the mountain man had told them when they pointed to a map in their guidebook, *The Emigrants Guide to California.* But they didn't believe him. He hadn't written a book! Too late, they learned that the guidebook's author had never taken the route, had only worded the book to make it seem as if he had done so.

The math master took them on trips to New York to see Wagner operas.

The science master took them on a trip to the moon, illustrated with stereopticon slides.

Vincent was forever grateful for this education, which he felt was unsurpassed by even his college classes at Yale, and later he would bemoan the end of classics secondary education, the loss of which he blamed for the moral decline of youth and believed accounted, in part, for the regrettable generation gap.

The car took a sharp curve and the boys laughed to be thrown together against celluloid windows.

Such a long way he'd come from the small, frightened boy he'd been at age five, made sick by his first ride in the Model T.

HoHo checked the gold strap watch on his wrist. None of them carried pocket watches. That was the way their fathers told time.

"We can't stop home first," he said, directing his voice to the peak-capped driver whose white gloves rotated with the wheel. "It's almost seven. Take us straight to the theater, Clarence. We don't want to be late."

HoHo was a Sherwin. The Sherwins lived on Fifth Avenue, which was where Vincent would want to live if he lived in New York, though this he couldn't imagine.

One of the most surprising things he learned at Trowbridge— something that shocked him at first but that he soon came to appreciate, as it afforded him welcome relief from a burden he hadn't realized he'd been carrying—was that no one knew or cared about Hollingwood. To his surprise, the only fellows at Trowbridge who had heard of it were locals, though Hollingwood was the grandest house in town and just across the lake from the castle. But to the fellows at Trowbridge, it might have existed on the other side of the world. They rarely ventured to the other side of the lake, except for sodas or sundaes at the Jigger Shop to read magazines they didn't buy while waiting to have their rackets restrung or for a trim at the barber's, even after his father put in a boathouse and dock so that Vincent could swim over with friends in the Polar Bear Club.

Anonymity was a freedom he wasn't used to in Wellington. Growing up there, whenever he'd met someone new, he withheld the fact that he was a Hollingworth for as long as he could to delay the inevitable change that knowledge would produce in the face of a new acquaintance. Sometimes an eyebrow rose, sometimes lids fell in obsequiousness or lips upturned in censorious judgment, but whatever the reaction, there was a reaction that had nothing to do with who Vincent was.

Was he, in fact, a Hollingworth at all?

He'd been flooded with gratitude as a young boy watching the hand of his grandfather record his name on the parchment page of the family Bible, where all of the Hollingworth names had been listed. His grandfather had moved a quill across the parchment, the same quill that had been used to record the names of Hollingworths going back generations.

He sometimes let himself wonder what the name of the mother he'd been born to was. What was the name of his father? No one else listed on the parchment was Irish, and he wasn't either, thanks to an accident of occurrences that had landed him in Wellington. His vague memories of the nuns at St. Joseph's weren't fond, but he was grateful they'd placed him with real Americans, not hyphenated ones.

How glad he was that his hair wasn't the red it had been in his childhood. It had turned auburn. Before coming to Trowbridge, he'd used the new safety razor his father had given him to shave the bright red hair on his arms, hoping that would grow in auburn too, but it didn't. He'd let it grow back to cover the freckles.

Even as a young child, he'd been conscious of the need to live up to the Hollingworth name. In a book with old binding he'd found in the bookcase, he discovered that the Hollingworths had a family crest. It was a stag looking backward. And also a motto: Bear What Must Be Borne. As a teenager, he'd sent away for calling cards so inscribed, but his grandfather intercepted the package by accident in the front hall and discouraged him from using them. Just as people who lived in great homes didn't call them mansions, neither did they affix crests to their correspondence. Nothing was in worse taste, his grandfather said, than for an American to put a coat of arms on his calling card.

Vincent wondered about his grandfather's advice, thinking perhaps it was out of date.

But its wisdom was confirmed to Vincent at Trowbridge. There, he was humbled to learn that the name Hollingworth was not as luminous as he had believed. It was shadowed by names of greater consequence in the world: Dwight, Hotchkiss, Buck, Vanderpoel.

Those names, in turn, were overshadowed by others: Vanderbilt, Winthrop, Astor, Du Pont, the names of families whose offspring were not sent to Trowbridge but to Groton, where it was said that alum fathers sent a telegram to the headmaster immediately after notifying grandparents of a new son.

He also learned that New York was not the monolith it had seemed to him when he'd taken the train down from Wellington on business trips with his father or on shopping trips with his mother. Until going to Trowbridge, he'd thought of New York as a long croquet field with five times the usual number of colored balls, all set into motion, striking against each other without purpose or pattern. But now, after conversations overheard in the hallways upon curfews on Sundays, after field trips to New York and weekend visits to homes of classmates, he saw that Manhattan was more like a jigsaw puzzle, with every piece having a place and a particular meaning and the slightest irregularity in a piece being noted as a thing of import. It wasn't enough to have a Fifth or Park Avenue address; your place in the hierarchy depended on how high up on Fifth it was or if it was on the good side of Park.

"Oh, you must know the Tinsleys, they're in your building!" An exchange of addresses between mothers usually resulted in either a rush of talk or immediate leave-taking.

Mothers. His education included learning about them too. Despite how mothers were portrayed in novels, he was relieved to discover that most fellows felt the same distance from theirs as he did from his. This was to be expected, he and his friends decided. Mothers were not only of a different sex but were occupied with duties that were alien to their sons and their husbands, things with which a woman fills time: meetings and bridge clubs and volunteering and auxiliaries and managing the menus and cleaning and other duties of domestics with whom men needn't bother, even to the point of knowing their surnames.

If Vincent had a problem, he went to Biddy. Biddy was the woman in charge of him, the one who knew him better than he knew himself, who concerned herself with the habits of his digestion, who calmed his childhood fevers with teas, who doused his chicken pox with quinine, whose eyes brightened and face flushed whenever he came into her presence, who, even now, though he was eighteen (a sixth-former!) still sent him treats—scones with jellies and soft cakes and hearty slices of potato bread. She wrapped them hot from the oven in heavy cloth towels and sent them in a basket given to the milkman, whose delivery route had him stopping at Hollingwood before going to Trowbridge.

Love Biddy as he did, he tried to establish a different relationship with her. He'd refused to let her see him in the altogether since he'd turned twelve. He wouldn't let her kiss him on the mouth anymore. He stopped confiding physical intimacies, especially those that concerned his bowels and about which she still occasionally inquired. He was a man now, no longer in need of a nurse.

This, too, he discovered, was a problem common among fellows at Trowbridge—separating oneself from the woman who remembered wiping your bottom. (Though Biddy had never done this for him, as he'd arrived at five, fully capable of seeing to his own toilet, thanks very much.)

The Jazz Singer started out like other films. The credits rose to the tune of an overture. But he suddenly realized the music wasn't coming from an orchestra inside a pit; it was coming, somehow, from inside the picture.

The title cards began. He'd thought a talkie wouldn't have titles. But then Al Jolson opened his mouth to sing. The song wasn't titled—it was actually sung! And after the first few notes, Vincent found himself standing along with the rest of the crowd, clapping and whistling and shouting before sitting down so they could hear

300

the rest of the movie—hear a movie! Oh, the wonderment. Again and again, the audience burst into standing applause. When Al Jolson sang "Toot Toot Tootsie," making his hands into a bird and making bird sounds come out of his mouth, Vincent could hardly believe his ears. Who would have guessed there was so much to hear in a moving picture?

After the velvet curtains closed, Al Jolson came onstage to express his appreciation for the Vitaphone, but his words were drowned out as the crowd stood and cheered and hooted and stamped their feet. Vincent only wished his grandfather could be here. Maybe Vincent would take him when the film came to Wellington. His grandfather was sick with consumption, but the case wasn't too bad. If his coughing subsided, he could sit through it.

HoHo's father took them to the famous Café d'Arenmonville in the Hotel Knickerbocker (Caruso's favorite restaurant) where the maître d' welcomed Mr. Sherwin by name and they feasted on snail-stuffed partridge and frogs' legs and other delicacies unknown to the kitchen at Trowbridge, and then once again the Duesenberg came around and the boys piled in, taking the same places, for some reason, they'd taken when they had come. When the doors closed and the car glided north on Sixth Avenue into the park, HoHo pulled out a silver flask, a gift from his brother, unscrewed the top, tilted it into his mouth, then passed it around for the others to draw from.

"He even gave me a refill," HoHo said, and out of the large pocket of his suit jacket, he pulled a brown bottle. "It's from my parents' stash in the basement. There's so much down there, they'll never notice."

Vincent had tasted wine and beer, but he'd never taken hard liquor before. He'd heard about private stashes. Prohibition had started when he was eleven. Before that, wet families who could afford it bought inventory from distillers and owners of liquor stores and stashed it to get through the dry years that were coming.

The boys sipped and laughed and discussed the movie and whether talkies would take off or were just a fad, and one by one they nodded off, except Vincent, who finished the bottle and was sick in the car.

"Get up! Get up! Headmaster wants you!" The prefect was shaking him. It was morning.

Vincent felt as if he'd been kicked by a horse. He'd never had an alcoholic headache but now knew the gravity of the condition he'd been warned of in temperance classes at church.

The dorm room revolved about him as he painfully lifted his head from the pillow, rose from the bed, and pulled on the pants he'd draped on a chair. It was agony making his fingers work buttons and he thought of how he would explain his debauchery. Was Mr. Sherwin suing him for damages to the upholstery? He was glad that his parents were out of the country.

He hung his head as he slunk past the open door to Headmaster Buell's office. But the headmaster didn't appear to be angry. Instead, he looked sad. When Vincent entered the room, he rose from behind his massive desk, approached Vincent, and put an arm around his shoulders.

"My dear boy," he said. "Something has happened at home. A car is outside to take you there now."

"What?" asked Vincent. It was all he could do to maintain his balance. "What happened?"

"It's your grandfather," the headmaster said.

Vincent's spine went cold.

The headmaster was sorry to inform him—his grandfather had passed away in the night.

The day his grandfather died seemed to Vincent a border, and having crossed it, he knew his childhood was behind him and he'd been ushered into manhood and its responsibilities, its cares, its sobering realizations. He now saw that his grandfather's presence, his doting, his praise, his earnest discussions about what was right and wrong in the world had freed him to be a child. Vincent felt the loss of not only a grandfather, but a man who had fathered him without being his father, the way Biddy mothered him without being his mother.

He'd lost not only Opa but who he was in Opa's eyes. To Opa, he'd been a boy who could do nothing wrong.

He loved his father, and his father loved him, of course, but his father's love for him had business in it. What Vincent did, who he was and what he would become, seemed a matter of pride to his father, which it didn't to Opa—he had simply wanted him to be happy.

Perhaps now his relationship with his father would deepen, change.

But it didn't.

Vincent guessed this was because he was not his father's real son.

Once, when he was little, he overheard his mother urging his father to show more interest in him. "Take him shooting, as fathers do. Go trouting. Play ball. He's your son!"

"My adopted son," his father replied, and hearing this sent a coldness through Vincent. After that, he didn't listen at doors anymore.

His father had been most animated with him at Christmas. When he'd been small, it had become a ritual that his father helped him set up the Lionel train set he'd bought for him. The train had a wire that connected to a lamp socket and ran around the floor of Vincent's room, baggage cars and passenger cars, black engine and red caboose, a coal car filled with bits of black stone and a milk car that carried white bottles in wooden crates. The first time they set it up, his father had helped Vincent create a landscape on his bedroom floor—he'd piled up books to make mountains, filled shallow dishes with water for lakes, collected whisk brooms to use as cornfields, and stacked wooden blocks in various heights to make cities. The next year, Vincent had looked forward to making the trainscape with him again. He suggested they make it a mountainous village this time, but his father wanted to build it exactly as they'd built it before. Vincent didn't complain. He was grateful to his father for getting down on the floor and ruining the press of his trousers for the sake of playing with him.

The Christmas after Opa died, the Lionel train set was left in the attic. That was okay with Vincent. He was too old for train sets. He'd been too old for train sets for years but had engaged in the annual ritual for the sake of his father, who had given it to him.

45

Sarah

Lake Como

October 1927

On a crisp October morning, in a room gilded by Italian sun streaming in through arched windows, Edmund and Sarah sat listening to a lecture in the company of fellow travelers as excited as they were to bring home new topics of conversation. Today's after-breakfast lecture was on the history of a twelfth-century castle near Bellagio, which they would visit after luncheon. They'd have a tour of the castle, then take tea and sample from harvests of ancient olive fields and vineyards from which came the best Chiantis in the world.

The tourists were English-speaking and many were American, but some were English, some German, and Sarah and Edmund found themselves more than once on the tour having to defend their country from ridicule.

"How, in your brazen New World boasting all kinds of freedoms, can leaders get away with denying, for almost ten years now, a decent chap's right to a drink?"

The question of why Prohibition was accepted in America came up in conversation again and again. Sarah would always leave the answer to Edmund.

"The law doesn't preclude drinking," Edmund would explain, hoping to make his country sound less primitive than it was, especially in comparison to ancient seats of enlightenment. "What's prohibited is the buying or selling of alcohol." Indeed, his own firm had just settled a case defending the owner of a speakeasy who claimed to be simply sharing stockpiles in his basement. The law had, in fact, established two tiers of drinkers: law abiders who'd had the foresight and means to stock up, and lawbreakers who hadn't. Legally, Prohibition was a travesty, but the amendment had proven enriching for his firm.

The person sitting next to Sarah was a tiresome woman who sometimes wore perfume so offensive to Sarah that she found herself overcome by a sick headache. Today was such a day and when there was a break in the lecture, Sarah excused herself to go up to their room, insisting that Edmund stay behind to enjoy the lecture, as there wouldn't be many more to enjoy, since they were coming to the end of their tour.

As she was crossing the marble lobby, Sarah was accosted by a boy in a gold-buttoned service uniform that was too big for him.

"Signora Porter?" he said.

She gave a slight nod, and he handed her an envelope.

It was a cablegram. She tore it open and read it hurriedly, then looked up and asked the boy if he could help make an answer.

"*Sì, sì,*" he assured her. But when she began to speak, it became clear by the vague look in his eyes that he couldn't understand English, and she gave him a coin and then fled down a corridor. Her heels clicked loudly on marble as she passed between walls frescoed with scenes from legends, hurrying toward the hotel's receiving desk. She asked the man behind it to help her do all she needed to do at once: send a boy to call Edmund out of the lecture, compose and send an answering cable, find the tour captain and have him arrange a change of itinerary, rebook passage on a ship leaving earlier and from a port nearer Bellagio. They'd need to return home as soon as possible.

Weeks later, they finally stepped off the train at Wellington station, drawn and exhausted. Sarah breathed in the air of her hometown and felt it was altered, deprived now of the living breath of her father.

Bridey met them at the door and as she took Sarah's fur hat and gloves, Sarah found herself flooded with a curious resentment—that her father had chosen to die in Bridey's company instead of her own. But that was absurd. She was grateful to Bridey, grateful for her devoted care of her father. Before Sarah and Edmund had gone abroad in September, Young Doc had assured her that her father's condition was improving, and both he and Bridey urged her not to cancel their trip. Her father himself had urged her to go.

But now, he was gone.

Coming into the house, Sarah thought she caught a lingering scent of his pipe smoke; her eyes filled. Soon, even this trace of him would be gone.

Sarah guessed that she had cried all the tears she had for her father on the last night in their hotel room and on ensuing days and nights in the cabin on the steamer, where she would be overcome by something that reminded her of him—the sound of his voice, or veins in the hand of an old man standing next to her at the ship rail—and in its chapel where she had sought refuge in solitude. But now, as she turned toward the stairwell, when she looked into her father's study and saw his pipes at the ready, soldier-straight in their carousel, she welled up again. Edmund took her elbow and helped her upstairs.

At the post office, where Sarah was obliged to cable funds to cover the final transport of their trunk, Mrs. Cogswell the postmistress welcomed Sarah home and expressed her condolences. She remarked on the stateliness of Mr. Hollingworth's funeral service and how many had attended it—not only from the town, but from outlying districts—and she commented on who had accompanied him to the graveside despite the cold rain and who had not and what a shame that Sarah herself couldn't have been present, but what fine sights were pictured on Sarah's postal cards.

Sarah felt impaled by implied accusation but merely nodded in polite acknowledgment, setting feathers aflutter on the hat she'd purchased from a Roman milliner's window. The motion of the hat encouraged the postmistress to continue.

"I don't know that Mr. Tupper will get over it, though," she said.

"Get over what?" Sarah asked, receiving pages fed beneath brass rails. The rails had been donated long ago by her father; for years after they were installed, the postmaster had slipped her candy whenever she had come in with her mother.

"He got a scare, seeing the sign of poisoning on your father, God rest him. But Young Doc set him straight."

"What sign?"

"The telling white lines across his nails. Arsenic! But Doc said it wasn't."

And Mrs. Cogswell told her all that she knew, which was all that Mr. Tupper had told her the day they waited for the telegraph operator in the rear of the room to feed a roll of new tape into the empty transmitter.

Sarah usually stopped by Young Doc's office after a trip to the Continent to make sure nothing foreign had invaded her system. Now she went there directly.

The office was crowded—it was grippe season—but the doctor's girl ushered Sarah into his office right away.

He stood up from his desk and walked around it to greet her.

"I'm so sorry," he said, taking her gloved hand in both of his own. "Your father's passing is a loss for all of us." The gentle concern in his eyes made him look even more like Old Doc. She remembered that he'd lost his father too. Old Doc had passed away the year before from an aneurysm. A charitable fund had been set up in his name.

"I want you to tell me what happened," she said, settling into one of the hardback chairs.

He waited until she was seated before returning to his desk and taking the swivel chair. The desk had belonged to his father and she recalled, as a child, feeling alarmed by the forest of body parts he kept there, life-size anatomical models, each sectioned to show the inside of a head, a foot, a rib cage, a leg. But Young Doc kept these on a credenza behind him.

"It was a hard case," he said, stroking his beard. His head was framed by a wooden sign painted QUARANTINE saved from last year's outbreak of smallpox, which thankfully had been contained to a neighboring village. "Consumption doesn't always follow the course set down in books." He shook his head, not looking at her, and began to elaborate on the unpredictable processes of diseases which confounded prognoses.

"Perk," she interrupted, using the name she had called him when he was a child and they played games together at the beach at the Grove. She suddenly had a vision of him crossing a finish line balancing peanut shells on the back of his hand. "Could it be possible that my father...was poisoned?"

The doctor stopped talking and brought up his hands to smooth the hair at the sides of his head.

"Poisoned?" he asked. "How do you mean?"

"Mr. Tupper saw—"

"Oh, Mr. Tupper." He stopped smoothing his hair and began to pivot in half-circles in the chair. "The town's one-man party line."

She continued, "He said he saw evidence of what could be...ar-senic."

"My dear Sarah." The doctor stood, then sat. He corrected him-self. "Pardon—Mrs. Porter. Presentation of a symptom doesn't con-firm a condition. If diagnosis were so simple, I'd be out of a job. *Leukonychia striata* is evidence of several conditions, only one of which is poisoning, and that's the rarest. I said as much to Mr. Tup-per and I'd have hoped he would have relayed that to you."

"I only wondered. *Could* my father have been poisoned?"

Why in God's name was she pursuing this line of inquiry? Sarah thought. It was a preposterous notion, that her father would have been poisoned. But something in her wouldn't allow her to drop it. She felt duty-bound to press until the question raised by the post-mistress, who had surely raised it with others, was answered beyond a shadow of a doubt.

The doctor held her gaze. Neither spoke.

She had failed her father by relegating him to a lonely death. She wouldn't fail him again.

He cleared his throat as he righted a fountain pen in the brass stand on the blotter.

"Medicine isn't as certain a science as patients wish to believe," the doctor said. "I suppose poisoning is possible. But who would have administered the poison? In his last few weeks, your father had no social congress. Miss Molloy had exclusive care of him, giving him all medicines prescribed and food taken. And what could have provoked such an action in her?"

Nothing, thought Sarah, feeling ridiculous. Bridey doted on her father. She'd said he was the father she wished she had had.

"Unless you believe what they say," he added.

"What do they say?" Sarah looked up, alert.

"You know. The Irish." The doctor shrugged.

When she'd brought Bridey to Wellington, some in town had

warned against taking her in. Irish had too much heat and anger in their blood and the ones who were Catholic were not to be trusted. The Knights of Columbus were suspected by some to be stockpiling weapons in church basements, waiting for word from the pope to rise up. Sarah had dismissed these concerns, and so had her father. But now, fresh from studying Roman histories in which Celts resisted attempts to be civilized, colluding in secret brutal means of resistance . . . Sarah reconsidered.

A few minutes later, in an examining room, the doctor inquired about Sarah's travels as he looked at her throat, listened to her chest, palpated her neck, shone a light in her ears and nose and eyes, and then pronounced that nothing of a foreign nature had made its way into her.

From time to time, Sarah went into her father's room to sit, but it was months before she could make herself move anything in it.

There was so much to attend to, and she had to do it alone. Rachel had gone back to France, Hannah to Vermont.

Everything she touched opened a flood in her. The house slippers aligned in wait for him under his bed. His cuff-link jar on the top of the chiffonier. She pulled at the handles of a heavy mahogany drawer. She'd never opened it and, upon hearing Bridey approach, she shoved it back, feeling guilty as a small girl caught going through her father's things.

"Need any help, do you?" Bridey offered. Her eyes were wet. Of course, her father's passing was hard for her too. But he wasn't her father.

"Not now, thank you," Sarah said, and she turned back to the bureau. The strain between them had started when Vincent left home. What was her obligation to Bridey? To keep her employed for the rest of her life? Edmund had asked Sarah what she meant to do about Bridey now that they didn't need a full-time nurse anymore.

But surely we need a housekeeper, she'd said. And when Edmund began to speak of a day girl employed by his mother, Sarah reminded him of their frequent travel and guessed it would be asking for trouble to trust an old house like this to the care of someone who didn't live in it.

She'd need time to figure out what to do about Bridey. Sometimes she fantasized about employing a live-in who was young, a clean slate with whom she didn't share a troubling history.

But Sarah couldn't think about Bridey now. She needed to figure out what to do about all of her father's things.

In the drawers, Sarah found sheaves of old birthday cards that she and the others had penciled for him. Cuffs and collars and garters and boxes of shirt studs. The armband he wore when her mother died. Shoehorns and laces, sweaters and watch fobs and hatbands. Her father never threw out a thing. In a desk drawer were folders of correspondence, and she found a returned letter to Madame Brassard. The address on the brown tissue envelope was stamped DECEASED. Sarah was tempted to slit open the envelope and read the letter, but she decided not to and tossed it into the fire, admiring her virtue in doing so. She wasn't a Paul Pry. But as she watched flames come closer to licking the brown paper, she changed her mind and used the poker to retrieve it. Perhaps it contained something that would shed light on her father, something she ought to read—someday.

After a week, when she'd gone through the contents of all his drawers, she asked Bridey to bring up the step stool from the kitchen so she could go through the cabinet in the fireplace wall. The cubbyhole held piles of dusty account books, but in a narrow passage between them, she saw the glint of green glass. A medicine bottle. As she drew it forward by the metal collar that harnessed the cork to the neck of the bottle, she saw by the skull and crossbones on the label that it wasn't medicine—it was poison.

"'Arsenic,'" she read aloud and Bridey, who had been sweeping a hand broom against a dustpan below her, looked up.

"What is this doing in my father's room?" Sarah asked. Her voice was sharper than she had intended. She tried to make a connection between her father's books and the poison. Did arsenic have something to do with preserving books?

"Let me see," said Bridey, reaching up for the bottle. She stared at the label a long time. When she finally looked up, her face was dark, and Sarah could see tears in her eyes.

"The doctor gave it to him, I suppose," Bridey said.

"Arsenic?" Sarah said, dismounting the ladder. "The doctor gave my father arsenic for consumption?"

Bridey's face went darker. She stared at her shoes.

"Perhaps it was...a new treatment," Bridey said, not looking up.

Later, when Sarah asked Young Doc about this, he confirmed what Sarah already knew. No one with a sound medical degree would administer arsenic in the hopes of curing consumption.

But Edmund dismissed her concern. There were other bottles of arsenic about the house. In the basement, for poisoning rats. In the pantry, for mixing paint colors. He agreed that the discovery of a bottle of arsenic in a sickroom cupboard was curious, but arsenic was as common as butter. Finding a bottle of it wasn't evidence of wrongdoing. "Circumstance isn't conviction," he said. Then there was the question of motive.

"What would Bridey have hoped to gain by poisoning your father?"

When Edmund finally stopped by Young Doc's office for his own post-trip examination, he came away with a box of calming pills for Sarah, whom he'd reported to be suffering from gross excitability, a condition to be expected, Young Doc said, after the death of her father, with whom she had been close.

*   *   *

Administration of the estate of Benjamin Laverstock Hollingworth was delayed due to complications in ordering documents having to do with an old-fashioned accounting practice of entwining personal with business expenditures and with the fact of heirs living out of the country, so it wasn't until June that the will reading took place. The estate had been entrusted to Squire, Boggs, and Porter, but due to the relationship of Porter to the deceased, Phillip Boggs had been dispatched to execute it.

On the day of the reading, two discoveries were made that would greatly affect the lives of the beneficiaries. The first was that the Hollingworth fortune had suffered diminishments far beyond what any of the beneficiaries had expected.

The other was that the list of beneficiaries included Miss Brighid Molloy, who was awarded five thousand dollars due to her long and devoted service to the Hollingworth family.

Five thousand dollars! Enough to buy a motorcar and a house! And now Edmund acknowledged to Sarah that perhaps her suspicions hadn't been preposterous after all.

46

Vincent

Wellington, Connecticut

1928

After the reading of the will at his father's law office, Vincent became aware of whispers between his parents, and his mother confided to him what they were about—that Biddy had been the cause of his grandfather's death. Possibly, she'd poisoned him.

He didn't believe it. Biddy loved his grandfather. She wasn't capable of cold-hearted murder, no matter how much money she knew would be coming. Of all the people who surrounded him, Biddy seemed least concerned about money. She didn't do things for it. She lived in a small room with few furnishings and seemed content. Her most treasured possession was a crucifix! Whenever he'd visited her room, it had scared him. He'd wanted to take the nails out of the hands and feet of the figure but was afraid that doing so would cause him to fall off the wall.

If Bridey had poisoned his grandfather—which he couldn't believe—the only reason she'd do it would be out of mercy. His grandfather had been famously stoic. Perhaps he'd not told anyone his pain was unbearable. Perhaps he'd asked Bridey to help him end things. But even if that was true, Vincent doubted she would go against her God by putting out a life He saw fit to continue.

After the will reading, he found Bridey in the basement, pulling sheets through the wringer. When she saw him, her face brightened and she stopped turning the handle and took up the hem of her apron and wiped her hands.

"What are ye doing down here?" She smiled. "Cooling yourself?"

It was cooler down here. When he was small, he used to join her here on hot summer days. She'd lead him away from the tubs, across the dirt, past shelves crowded with jars of jams and pickled things. He'd hold her hand tighter as they passed the boiler, a monster that leered at him in the dark, then they'd step over a doorsill made by a log and be in one of his favorite places, a mysterious underbelly beneath the turret, a round cave that always felt cool.

"I have news," he said. "My grandfather left you a good bit of money."

She wiped her hands on her apron. "Did he, now?"

She didn't look as surprised as she ought to.

"Do you know how much?"

"Now, how would I know that?" She was bending over the wringer again. To hide her eyes, so he couldn't see them?

"Five thousand dollars."

She lifted her face and the astonishment he saw in her eyes gratified him, relieving his fears.

"You didn't make Opa die. Did you?"

"What?" Her eyebrows rose. Her eyes narrowed. A long pause. "Who says I did?"

"My mother. She says he died of arsenic poisoning. She said Mr. Tupper saw signs of it."

To his surprise, she didn't deny this.

"Vincent..."

He stared at her a moment, waiting for her to say what she surely would say—that of course she didn't poison his grandfather. His heart pounded in his ears. She gazed at the dirt floor, then looked to the wood shelf that held a year's worth of soap cakes, the stacks tied with string.

He knew that she was incapable of murdering anyone, but something was wrong. He didn't know what.

She looked up at him. She looked—guilty.

She took a step forward and reached for his cheek. "Vincent."

But he shook her away.

"I don't know you anymore," he said, through tears.

"You do, Vince, you do know me. You know me better than anyone."

Several days later, when Bridey was out, Vincent heard Sarah on the telephone. She didn't speak on the phone, she shouted into it, as if her voice had to project over miles, not wires.

He heard her say she meant to have Biddy arraigned.

"I won't fail Father in this matter," she shouted and Vincent guessed that she was talking to Aunt Hannah. Fear rose in him.

When Biddy came back, he alerted her to the imminent danger. But to his surprise, she didn't see the sense of going away.

"I won't leave you," she said.

He didn't need her. He was a grown man. He'd soon be living in New Haven, a freshman at Yale. But to her, he would always be a child in need.

"Listen," he urged, "my father is a lawyer. He is a good lawyer. If my mother wants you to, you could go to jail."

The thought of her in prison, that hard place, cut into him.

It was not until days later, when she received a telegram advising her to be ready to be deposed, that she agreed with Vincent: she must go away.

Vincent called HoHo Sherwin, who called his father, who had connections. Within a week, Vincent was saying good-bye to Biddy in a cabin on the SS *Cleveland,* bound for Ireland.

Standing on an iron stair next to her bunk in an alcove, she was the same height as Vincent. She took his face in her hands.

"Thank you," she said, her eyes shining with tears. She thumbed his bottom lip and he stepped back from her. She didn't know how to stop being his nurse.

"There's something I want to tell you," she said. "Something I shouldn't."

"Don't, then," he said. He didn't want to hear a confession. He was raw with the loss of the two people who loved him best in the world.

"You've always been a son to me, Vincent."

"I know that," he said.

She made a strange sound, a cross between a cough and a cry. Then she drew back and lifted her chin. Her eyes were wet and imploring.

"I would do anything for you, Vincent. Remember that. I'd do anything for you and for your grandfather, God rest his soul."

"I know," he said. Did he?

Now she was crying.

"Take this," she said, putting a book in his hand. It was her Catholic prayer book. How could she think he'd be helped by her prayers?

"You keep it," he said, giving it back to her. But she wouldn't take it.

"You might find comfort in its enlightenment," she said.

Did she know him so little? Anger rose—against her, against the preposterousness of her trying to convert him to her religion at this late date.

A long horn sounded.

She gently pushed at his shoulder. "Go on with ye, now. Go on, get on."

He kissed her cheek. His eyes were brimming. He guessed he'd never see her again.

He left her cabin and navigated the burnished-wood galley onto the gangplank. Battens depressed under his feet like piano keys. Once aground he walked until he was a good distance away in case she was watching him from the deck, then leaned against a lamppost, covered his face with a hand, and sobbed with an abandon that didn't matter, as he was now among strangers.

47.

Bridey

Kilconly, Eire
September 1928

Dear Adelaide,

Thank you for sending the cutting of Vincent from the paper. It lifted my heart to see the photo of him looking so handsome in his commencement cap and to read of his winning the Headmaster's Prize. I write him letters, but only in my head. I don't wish to be a burden to him. I pray the Hathaways keep good relations with the Hollingworths so that you can keep me in the know of his doings.

And you! Advanced to head housekeeper! With a sitting chamber of your own! How far you have come from that little room in the tower that was to me such a refuge. My debts to you multiply.

You wouldn't believe the changes at home. It seems all that's left of things before the Free State are fieldstones in the walls, jackdaws in the branches. Remember the McGinns' potato fields? They twitch every day with tractors and sprayers. All over the district, motorcars gun for sheep in the lanes. It's odd to see a tricolor flag flying in place of the golden harp in the blue. Even the quids are different, inked with a red so bold you can read the worth of a bill through the cloth of a man's pocket.

I reached Kilconly after weeks on the sea. Thanks to the charitableness of Vincent's connection, I went second class instead of third, and what a far sight better way to travel. Second has a deck and I spent days in a sun chair lying about like the Queen of England. Still—it was hard, doing a ten-day sail over Thom's grave, God rest him. I couldn't banish the notion of him afloat in the dark beneath.

Like you, I'd not been back home in twenty years. How could I think things on the lane would be as I'd left them, Mam at her stove and Da at the drink? But that's what I expected, as if the clocks stopped at twelve the day that I left and would remain that way until my foot touched down again on home soil.

When I reached the gate, I lifted the latch, and you'll understand me going around to the kitchen to prove that I'd not gotten above myself. But there's no bell at the door there and my knocking wasn't heard, and though it was my own home I was coming to, I didn't feel right barging into it. I went around to the front door, which Kathleen opened, and didn't it give me a start to see her face on a middle-aged matron. I guessed by the look on her she was similarly surprised at me. But she didn't fall on me crying with happiness, which was what I'd expected, as we'd once been so close. I thought perhaps her reticence was due to her not wanting to disturb the metal curlers that haloed her face. The next day was Sunday. She only turned her back to me and said in a loud voice, "Ma, Bridey's here." By which I was relieved to know our mam was still living.

Kathleen walked away and I guessed I was to follow her. I had to take my own coat and hat, but the old hooks were gone, so I laid my things on a chair and followed her into the parlor, where Mam was sitting in a stiff-back by the fire. It was then I saw how it was. Poor Mam was still with us, but her mind was gone. Like old Mrs. Quigley they tied to a chair at Quigley's candy store, remember?

I asked Kathleen how long she had been this way and Kathleen said she had written me about her and about Da, who had died, but if she did, I never received those letters. She said it was hard to keep writing into an abyss and for that I don't blame her, as I was not a diligent correspondent.

Kathleen said it was up to her to take care of Mam, as Dan was gone to a seminary in Limerick, Quinn to a factory in Tuam, Margaret to nursing school in Shannon, Nell to Dublin, where she'd married a draper, and Daisy lived with them, enrolled in a fancy secretarial course.

Kathleen was married but she had left her husband and children in Cong with his mother so she could take care of Mam.

She warned me that Mam didn't know us anymore and my heart kicked when I saw that instead of taking care of someone else's father in America, I might have been taking care of my own mother here. But Kathleen was wrong. Mam did know me. She had been dithering with a shawl on her lap, but now she looked up, and her fingers, so knotted they appeared almost braided, reached for my face.

She called me Bridey and tears came to my eyes. The hard pads of her fingers went across my cheeks and the touch of my mother called back my own girlhood, and from that moment on, it's been as if I dreamed my time in America.

Kathleen was crisp with me at first, accusing me of talking like a film star and wondering that I hadn't brought any gifts. They have gaslights now, and she followed me about, switching off keys to save on the meter. But I didn't begrudge her. I would have been the same in her place. It's only a parent who's overjoyed by the return of a prodigal.

Kathleen thawed once she realized that I meant to stay. She soon took a lorry back to her family—her real family—whom for a year she'd been able to see only when spelled.

So now here I am, the picture of daughterly devotion, taking care of my sick mother. It does me good. I read to her and sing and talk her through the roads of her past, grateful to be freed from having to recall anything that's happened since I've been gone. Mam has stopped talking, but I know she is there because when I speak of things that happened when I was little, sometimes a light comes into her eyes.

Thank you for not believing the talk. Mrs. Hollingworth Porter has her reasons for thinking the worst of me, as you are the only person besides myself to know. Someday, God willing, when you and I sit across a table again at O'Hurley's (yes, it's still here, run by the lame daughter), I'll tell you the story, omitting none of its turns.

In the meanwhile, keep well and in health and know that your family are all looking fine when I see them at church, and I often hear them blessing your name, mentioning your letters and generous enclosures, which keep your nieces in school at the convent.

Beaghmore, Eire
Christmas 1933

Dear Adelaide,

Thank you for the clipping of Vincent's graduation from college. I cried to see it. He is a man now, more handsome and fortunate than I ever imagined. I'll never forget the part you played in making that future possible for him. If you hadn't brought me to the mission those years ago, I would have ended up somewhere else and he would never have been taken in by the Hollingworths.

America's troubles splash across headlines of the newspapers here. How glad I am that despite all that is crashing there, the Hathaways hold on to the house on Fifth Avenue. Though I know it must be hard for you, with parlor maids doing the work of menservants. The world is changing and not for the best.

Please forgive my long hiatus in writing. But you'll understand when I tell you the news.

Mam passed away two years ago, God rest her soul, and at her wake I got the fright of my life. I thought I saw Thom getting up from the kneeler! What shocked me even more than the occasion of seeing a ghost was that I was seeing a Flynn attend a Molloy viewing.

Then I remembered—all that is over.

It took the war. Flynns and Molloys fought in the same trenches, and when they came back—not all of them did—the breach that divided the families was gone. The boys came back not wanting to work farms; they wanted jobs that had got going in towns.

You might recall that Denis was the reason Thom and I went to America. He'd sent us the tickets. What I didn't know was that he'd returned from Poughkeepsie. Most farmers were old, as you couldn't pay the young to take it up, but Denis was different. He was only too glad to get back to driving living cows after years in a tannery on the Hudson, breathing in smells that poisoned him as sure as poor boys were poisoned who'd swallowed gas in the war.

We got on from the start. How could we not? We had Thom in common and also America, which had let us down, in different ways. When I met Thom, I was a lovesick, blind-to-all girl. What I have with Denis has weight to it. But it is love just the same.

And so, the Molloy farm is back in the family. We have fields and meadows and an apple orchard, and I have a garden of plantings I learned to grow from Nettie.

What's more—and this is the real reason I haven't had leisure to write—we've been blessed with a child. Ailish was born a year ago, when I was forty—you can imagine how many prayers I said to Saint Anne. She has the same red hair and dark blue eyes as Vincent and what joy I take in the sight and smell of her. I feel as if I'm getting back the years of Vincent's baby-hood I missed.

How many times I long to share with Denis that he has a nephew who is the spitting image of him, a graduate of one of the best colleges in America. But I resist the devil, as Sister Jerome used to say. I raised Vincent a Hollingworth and wish him to remain one unless the Good Lord wills otherwise, and that requires a vow of silence on my part, hard as that is to observe.

I must cut this short. Ailish is awake and calling from her crib. I wish you merry holidays and much joy in the new year. May 1934 bring better times to the world.

P.S. Thanks for the magazine recipe for rice pudding but you can't get good rice here for love or money.

48

Vincent

Manhattan

1938

Vincent had believed, and his family had believed, that his future prospects lay in assuming a place at the Hollingworth Brassworks. But by the time he graduated from Yale, in 1932, the Great Depression was under way. Demand for brass wares had declined precipitously, and department-store buyers, who, for decades, could be relied on for orders, were replaced by younger men unwilling to ante up the cost of items forged by hand instead of machine. The factory had been the town's biggest employer since Vincent's great-grandfather had started it in 1846, but now it had to cut its workforce by so many that the number was reported on the front pages of papers not only in Wellington but in Hartford.

Uncle Benno had been put in charge of the factory when Vincent's grandfather left it a few years before he died, and though Vincent had been groomed for a management job there, Benno had advised him to look elsewhere. "Better take your talents out of this one-horse town," Benno had said the first Christmas Vincent was home from college.

Then came 1929. Black Tuesday.

Newspapers reported that HoHo's father, Mr. Sherwin, dressed nattily in blue serge and wearing kid gloves and spats, killed himself the next day by stepping in front of a trolley on Fifth Avenue. The trolley driver had had to be hospitalized for nervosa. At the funeral, HoHo wasn't HoHo anymore—he'd become Horace. He didn't go back to Yale.

Uncle Benno had arranged for a clerk job for Vincent with an insurance man in Hartford as soon as he graduated, but the appeal of that prospect paled considerably when a representative from an ad agency on Madison Avenue came to campus to recruit candidates for a new kind of work: market research. George Gallup (he was Dr. Gallup, a PhD, which impressed Vincent and other classmates invited to meet him) worked at Young and Rubicam, an ad agency that produced ads in magazines famous enough for Vincent to have read and made broadcast commercials on radio programs he listened to. Dr. Gallup was seeking men who wished to be on the forefront of a new frontier: helping to persuade people of the virtues of American products like Borden milk, Columbia phonographs, Fels soap, and other famous goods. While he was talking, Dr. Gallup unzipped a black case and took out a soap ad, the very one that had compelled Vincent as a boy to implore Biddy to buy bars of soap instead of making them.

Vincent had worked for Y & R for a few years, but then his old friend Osworth Hayden, who had also gone into advertising, called him about an opening at J. Walter Thompson.

"You'd be an account man, where the action is, not a guy in the outer field collecting numbers."

When Vincent made the change, his initiative was rewarded by a raise in salary, and now here he was, on the turnpike going to the New Jersey headquarters of LaBlanche Beauty Cream. Osworth was with him. He was Oz now, a first-rate copywriter.

Vincent was driving. He liked to drive. And lucky he did, because a curious but unwritten rule in the advertising business was that account men were always the ones who drove to meetings. Cars were provided as part of an account man's compensation. Vincent's car was a sweet six-cylinder Olds leased for him by the company. One of J. Walter's clients was General Motors. Vincent kept it parked in a garage at the agency, which footed the bill for garage storage too. The Graybar Building, where the agency was, had a garage, unlike the brownstone in the Sixties where Vincent lived on half of the top floor. A fifth-floor walk-up; when Benno or his parents or his aunts came to visit, Vincent met them in the vestibule and escorted them upstairs, listening to them pant, having to stop and let them catch their breath between flights as they marveled at what possessed a Hollingworth to live in such hardship. But Vincent felt lucky to have found a place in a fine neighborhood with a rent he could afford. His salary was generous, but he was afraid to overspend. Money, which had been as plentiful and unremarkable as water for years, was now a resource scarce as hen's teeth.

Oz was talking to him from the passenger seat. Oz wasn't sitting on the seat but kneeling on the floor in front of it and using the seat as a desk, penning changes to copy on the comp board again. The board wasn't really a board, it was an oversize pad of tissue paper on which an art man had drawn a girl looking in a mirror, her reflection making the mirror a sun.

"Do you like *radiant* or *luminous* to describe her complexion?" he asked Vincent, who knew enough not to weigh in. Vincent had learned early on that account men, especially junior account men, had little say in creativity in ads or commercials.

"Which do you think?" Vincent said, though it seemed to him that *radiant* was a better descriptive for the happy result of using a cream with the modern ingredient of radium in it. But maybe that was too obvious. Copywriters, for reasons obscure to him, often valued being obtuse.

"Radium is supposed to stimulate cellular vitality and assist blood circulation to brighten skin," said Oz. "Hey, maybe use *brighten*."

"That's a knockout!" Vincent agreed, putting the gearshift into first, slowing into a tollbooth. He trusted his judgment. Oz had already won statuettes, a gold for his ideas on Bromo-Seltzer. Vincent fished in his pocket for change and brought out a nickel, but seeing that it was one of the new Jeffersons, he returned it and fished again and brought out an old buffalo, which he handed to the toll taker.

Now Osworth, having penned the revision, rose and reassumed the passenger seat.

"Smoke?" he asked, pulling an Old Gold out of a pack. Vincent preferred Lucky Strikes, a client of Y & R, but now he had to be loyal to clients of the ad agency that employed him. He accepted a Gold from the cellophane pack, leaned toward the dashboard, pulled out the lighter, and touched the red eye of the coil to each of their smokes. Then he put the cylinder back into its metal socket, twisting it until it fixed itself with a little click. He pushed on a metal rectangle on the dash beside the lighter, and the ashtray tilted out. He was embarrassed to see that it hadn't been emptied of the last litter of stubs, half of which were marked by red lipstick.

"Who is she?" asked Oz, puffing rings into the windshield.

"No one," said Vincent.

"I thought the car was for client business only." Oz smiled.

"She was a client," said Vincent.

"Not Leota?" Oz said, referring to the Cutex receptionist. They both nurtured fantasies about the buxom Leota.

"No," said Vincent, guessing that Leota wouldn't have eyes for the likes of him.

He glanced at Oz flicking ash into the tray; muscles moved visibly in his enviable forearm. Oz was already married, with children. He'd married Fanny, the prettier of the dentist's twin daughters. Mr. and Mrs. Hayden lived in Brooklyn with twin boys. What was the matter with Vincent? He'd be thirty years old in a few months. But the thought of having a family sometimes scared him to the point of severe perspiration.

When he got this way, there was only one cure.

"There's a bottle in the box under the seat," he said. "Glasses in the glove compartment. Pour us a little dividend, will you?"

Bridey

Beaghmore, Ireland, and Wellington, Connecticut

September 1955

The day Bridey Molloy Flynn died in the house on the old family farm in Beaghmore, quietly, in her sleep, in a moment when Denis and Ailish were out of the room (because how could she leave them while holding their hands?), a terrible storm was brewing forty-eight hundred kilometers away. Across the wide ocean, a torrent of rain was creating the worst flood in the history of the state of Connecticut. Oaks fell, cars floated away, and hundreds of people had to be rescued by rowboats or helicopters that descended to rooftops or tree limbs where people had climbed to escape rising waters. Wellington Lake surged over stone walls, bringing up a touring car that had been submerged since 1908. Hollingwood weathered the storm without damage, but the Old Porter house on Vine lost half of its porch, which was unfortunate timing, because now that Edmund's mother had passed away, the empty house was for sale.

Vincent

Upper East Side, Manhattan

September 1955

In a doorman building on the good side of Park Avenue, Vincent knelt by the porcelain tub in the nanny's bath. It was not actually a nanny's bath. They didn't have a nanny. His mother wouldn't have thought of raising children without a nanny, but these were modern times. Benjamin Spock, whose every word his wife, Dorothy, absorbed, advised parents they didn't need experts to raise their children. They should trust their own instincts. Vincent didn't trust his own instincts. He trusted research reports.

It was Dorothy's night out, her ladies' auxiliary night, and she'd gone despite the torrential downpour. Bea, who usually cooked for them, was on vacation, visiting family in Kentucky.

It was flooding in Wellington, his mother had called earlier to tell him. The worst storm in years. She only hoped a tree wouldn't fall on the house, and Vincent wished for an invention that would allow a man to be in two places at once.

"It's just you and me tonight, kiddo," he said to the baby. Ruth was one now, squealing and happy in the tub.

Already another was on the way. They were thinking of names: Abigail, for Dorothy's grandmother; Benjamin, for his grandfather. *The names we love, we conspire to keep.* What poem was that from? Or was it some slogan? All the poets were in advertising now, copywriters who turned into bohemians after five o'clock. Sometimes he thought his classical education was a waste, given his choice of profession. But the Trowbridge pedigree impressed clients at meetings. And if he hadn't gone to Trowbridge, he wouldn't have met Oz, who'd introduced him to not only his boss, but his wife.

Vincent had everything a man could want. He lived in a beautiful apartment. He drove an Impala now, parked in a nearby garage. He'd married a Sturbridge from Massachusetts, a beautiful girl much younger than he was. (He was forty-six; she was twenty-seven.) His mother had at first worried about the age difference but then had fallen in love with Dorothy herself. They had a beautiful, perfect child, and this time next year, they'd have another.

So why was he staring at his hand shrouded in a wet washcloth? Why did he feel the need to grip the side of the tub, to steady himself against a wave of sadness?

The baby splashed again, this time so hard, she doused the cigarette he'd balanced on the shampoo shelf and it fell into the water at the other end of the tub, and as it fell, it made a little hiss. This made Ruth laugh and her laughter was infectious. He smiled as he took the soggy cigarette and flicked it into the tin wastecan Dorothy had painted with lilacs.

He took off his horn-rims and rubbed the lenses, then put them back on, pushed them against the bridge of his nose, and reached for the highball glass perched on the lid of the john. John! He'd always think of it that way. Nettie, God rest her.

51

Ruth

New York City and Wellington, Connecticut

1963–1966

Ruth, at ten, had not wanted to move from New York City to Wellington. She'd not wanted to leave her friends and teachers at the Thatcher School on Fifth Avenue and attend Wellington's small day school for girls.

"Your friends will visit, darling," her mother had promised. Her tone had been apologetic and Ruth guessed that this was because the move was her mother's fault.

Her mother was sick. Ruth had discovered this on a day that millions would remember. Ruth was in third grade, Abby in first. Thatcher had released them early because of news that the headmistress had heard on the radio: President Kennedy had been shot with a gun. He was still alive but might not live. The country went home to wait and worry.

Ruth and her sister walked home hours before their dismissal time. Mr. Kelley, the doorman, had tears in his eyes as he pulled open the glass door. Ruth and Abby ran up the back stairs (so they wouldn't have to wait for the elevator man) and swung open the service door to the kitchen, and there was their mother sitting at the Formica table, coughing. There was a bright stain on her white handkerchief, unmistakably blood.

Their mother looked up and, seeing them, brought the handkerchief quickly down from her mouth, buried it in a skirt pocket, and stood to greet them.

"What's wrong with you?" Ruth asked and her mother had said, "Nothing."

Anything having to do with blood was shameful, Ruth had learned.

Once when she was at her piano teacher's house for a lesson, she went to the bathroom and saw the teacher had left bloody underpants soaking in her bathroom sink. The sight of this alarmed Ruth and before she could close the door, there was her teacher, darting in, breathless.

"Sorry" was all she said as she wrapped the wet mess in a towel and hurried it away.

The piano lesson continued as if nothing had happened. Ruth put her all into the piece she was playing to reassure her teacher that what she had seen hadn't adversely affected her.

Not long after this, another incident confirmed Ruth's impression that blood was a cause for shame.

Her mother had hosted bridge club and after the ladies left, Ruth went to the powder room and discovered a pad soaked red in the wastebasket painted with lilacs. She'd noticed the pad while perched on the toilet, and seeing it had made her feel so anxious that she'd been unable to do what she'd come in to do. She'd pulled up her slacks and sought out her mother, who was smoking a Pall Mall at the kitchen table and talking to Bea, who was rolling pieces of silver cutlery into the felt sleeves in which they were stored.

As soon as Ruth announced her discovery, her mother stubbed

her cigarette out in the ceramic ashtray Ruth had made for her in art and hurried down the hall to the powder room. When Ruth followed her there, the pad was gone.

Soon after that, her mother gave her a pamphlet called "Becoming a Woman." She did this not by handing it to her directly, but discreetly setting it under a pillow.

"I put something on your bed for you to read," her mother had told her one day after she came in from school, adding that Ruth should feel free to ask questions if there was anything she didn't understand. Her mother warned her not to share it with her sister, who was too young to read it. Ruth had headed straight to the bedroom she shared with Abby and closed the door. There was nothing on the tufted white bedspread. She pushed aside the pillow. There was a pamphlet with a cover picture of a girl much older than she, gazing into a silver hand mirror and smoothing on a stick of red lipstick. Before opening it, Ruth returned to the door and pushed the lock in, which wasn't necessary, as her sister was at a ballet lesson and wouldn't be home for another hour or so.

Ruth lay on her stomach reading and her face grew hot as she flipped through the pages. The technical line drawings were vaguely disturbing, naming the parts of girls' bodies that were different from bodies of boys, labeled with terms she'd never encountered: *fallopian tubes* and *ovaries* and *vagina*.

The chapters had deceptively cheerful titles like "Your Wonderful Wedding Night" and "Preparing Your Body for Motherhood"—subjects Ruth felt years away from needing information about.

What troubled her was that menstruation was referred to as "your time of the month." It happened as often as once a month? A rock formed in Ruth's stomach as she thought of a future in which her body would betray her twelve times a year. She opened the bottom drawer of her bureau and hid the pamphlet between the cardboard sleeves of her coin collection where she wouldn't have to see it and be reminded of what she didn't want to think about until the time came when she couldn't avoid it.

The doctors thought her mother might get better if she stopped breathing New York City air, which was poison; you could see grime in it. The next summer, they moved up to Hollingwood for good, not just for the summer, which was what Ruth and her mother and sister usually did.

Her father lived with them only on weekends, staying at his club in the city the rest of the week because of his job with the ad agency. He was an account man, on cigarettes.

At first, Ruth's friends from New York did come, arriving at the station in the late morning and going home on the early-evening train, coming in groups of three or four, chaperoned by one of their mothers. Their visits were disorienting for Ruth. Her friends' observations made her feel as if she had immigrated to another country. Even her best friend seemed to talk to her as if she was now foreign, asking questions like "Aren't you afraid to live in a house with no doorman?" And "Wow, it's like you're a farmer now."

Their visits stopped later that summer when, after years of threats that the Wellington train station would close, it finally happened, and now the stop nearest them was Bridewell, which was a good twenty minutes away by car. The trip became too onerous for the girls and their mothers, who guessed their daughters could see Ruth when she came down for Christmas shopping and to see the windows and the tree at the Met.

Ruth's father drove her and Abby down to the city that December, but their time had been taken up with standing in line for things, now that they had to visit at peak hours, and though her best friend had said she might meet them by coat check at the Met, she didn't, although Ruth had waited for her for almost an hour before giving up and missed the ticket time of an exhibition of puppets on the third floor.

At first, the doctor's plan had worked. Ruth's mother took long walks and sat in the sun and read magazines in the gazebo, and the air of Connecticut put color back into her cheeks. This slower pace was quite a contrast to Ruth's image of her mother in New York, where she had always been hurrying out the door, pulling on her gloves, saying good-bye to Bea and herself and her sister as she left for bridge club or book club or volunteering at the hospital gift shop. But after they moved to Wellington, her mother's duties dwindled to taking a daily constitutional down the slope to the lake.

Then, even this walk became too much for her.

One of the last memories Ruth had of her mother was seeing her sitting on the chair of the telephone table in the hallway, speaking into the avocado-colored handset, then turning away from it, coughing and coughing into her hand, before turning back to continue conversation.

In Wellington, Ruth and Abby went to a girls' school that had once been a convent. Suddenly, they felt famous. Their great-great-grandfather had been governor of Connecticut for only a year but he had been known as the Governor for the rest of his life and would be remembered as the Governor for as long as his descendants lived there.

"Can the great-great-granddaughter of Governor Hollingworth have forgotten the facts of the Dred Scott case?" teased a history teacher.

For extra credit, Ruth wrote a report on how her famous ancestor had improved the lives of Wellington citizens, not only by building a house that was a landmark but by bringing train service to

Wellington and increasing the legal level of lake-fed water tables to meet the demands of neighboring farmers. She wrote the report based on a gift her father had given her the Christmas after her mother had died—a typewritten account of the history of Hollingwood. She had been vastly disappointed upon finding it rolled up in her stocking, but she was grateful for it later when it came time to write the history report.

52

Sarah

Hollingwood

1968

Sarah pulled the brass knob with one hand and jiggled the shaft of the skeleton key with the other, wiggling it back and forth in the lock plate. It took forever to open the conservatory door, which didn't need to be locked, but the knob had long ago stopped turning unless the key kept in its keyhole was properly coaxed.

The conservatory had been the library porch when Sarah was a girl. Edmund had had it done over for her for a long-ago birthday.

She couldn't believe it was almost her eightieth. She'd discouraged Vincent from planning something. Who would come? Everyone—or almost everyone—she cared about was gone. Benno, Rachel, even Hannah, the youngest of them. Edmund had passed away from his stomach cancer almost thirty years ago. She'd lived without him longer than she'd lived with him, and only now, she thought, was she finally beginning to understand him.

Wakes and funerals, funerals and wakes, that was her social life these days. Last month was a closed-casket service for Duxie, who would have been appalled that music had come not just from a church organ but from folk guitars. Her grandchildren hadn't engraved a card for the service; they'd printed a program in color, with terrible photos. And the program had a title, as if Duxie's funeral were a Broadway show. *Celebration,* it said in big, bouncy letters. It seemed to Sarah that Duxie had seen it, because after the service, she paid them back. When the hearse got to the cemetery, the driver couldn't open the liftgate. He'd locked the keys in the car. There lay Duxie in her coffin, refusing to budge, as people stood around in unseasonable heat, fanning themselves with the bright programs, waiting for the driver to come back with a duplicate key. So what they had joked about when Duxie was a girl, that she'd be late for her own funeral, came true in a sense.

Sarah herself wished to be ushered out the old-fashioned way, laid out in the parlor, with a horse to the church. She'd left Vincent instructions.

The key finally turned.

She loved the smell here—warm and heavy with fragrance. Sometimes she came here at night to just sit. To hear the croaks of frogs and ducks in the vernal pond that now stretched from the great maple in the front yard all the way out to the field. Her hearing, thank God, was still with her. Sometimes she heard even bats' wings beating the air outside and something else, too, impossible though it was: the faint murmurs of plants straining away from their roots.

She went upstairs to awaken her granddaughters. The Persephone flower bloomed only one night a year. Last spring she'd seen it, alerted by the new gardener. She'd promised herself she'd treat the girls to the show next time.

"I don't see anything," Ruth said after Sarah had led them downstairs. Ruth needed glasses but refused to wear them. She was saving up for a new thing called contact lenses. Vincent said they were the next fad, little pieces of glass that fit right onto the balls of your eyes. Sarah flinched imagining this.

"Just let me find the light," Sarah said. And when Abby observed that the lights were already on, Sarah said that those were the growing lights that stayed on around the clock, not light meant to see by. Even Mr. Tupper wouldn't have guessed that electric lights would come in so many shapes and sizes. For years, they'd carried a desk lamp from one room to another, plugging it into each room's single outlet.

Sarah flapped a hand above her head. "Here we are," she said, jerking a string.

White light flooded on, flickered off, returned, illuminating the girls in the nightgowns that Sarah had sewn for them on the old machine. They were eleven and thirteen. Sarah was the exception to the living things in this room, just coming into their beauty.

"Where is it?" asked Ruth, looking around.

Usually, the conservatory was off-limits to them.

"Come," said Sarah leading them through a gauntlet of flowering stems.

"I hope we're not too late," said Abby.

"It lasts almost an hour," Sarah assured her. "The gardener predicted eleven at the earliest..." She stopped and lifted her long pearl chain and snapped open the lid of her father's old pocket watch. "It's just ten fifty now."

Ruth yawned and Sarah restrained herself from asking her to cover her mouth. With that one, battles had to be picked. When they were little, Ruth had been the shy one, wanting to please. Abby had been more fiery. But somewhere along the line, those roles had reversed.

"Here we are!" Sarah said.

"It's just a plain cactus," said Abby, disappointed.

"You'll see," Sarah said. "The blooms are magnificent, well worth getting up for!" She hoped it was true, that the spectacle would be as stunning as last year's.

"It's got giant goose bumps," Ruth said, reaching out to touch the plant, but Sarah stayed her hand.

"You'll interfere with the blooms," she said. "Those bumps are leaves about to unfurl."

It always gave Sarah a start to see Ruth's little fingers, which were crooked in exactly the same way Bridey's had been. In certain lights, Ruth looked like Bridey—she wondered that Vincent didn't see it too. But he hadn't known Bridey when she was a girl. And now he was gone mostly, living weekdays in the city and when he was home on weekends getting distracted with calls from the office, which came even when they were at the table; the caller always insisted to Bea that the matter was urgent. Sarah felt this display of bad manners a poor example for the girls, but whenever she mentioned this in private to Vincent, he said the calls were for business and couldn't be helped, his wasn't a nine-to-five business. (Edmund's business hadn't been that either, but he'd never let the demands of the firm disturb family meals—although she didn't remind Vincent of this.)

She watched the girls bend and swerve, ballerina-like as they pointed their slippers over the roots, moving beneath vines weighted with roses, orchids, and lilies. A red hibiscus had just come in, an exotic from Hawaii: Sarah still had a hard time thinking of the leper colony as a bona fide state.

"Don't touch," she reminded them.

The girls were different as night and day. Ruth fair; Abby dark. She was already taller than Ruth, which irked Ruth no end.

Sarah had done her best for her granddaughters after Dorothy was gone. She knew what it felt like to lose a mother at their age. She'd always helped out with the fees for their extras: dancing lessons, charm school, piano, and camps. But after Dorothy went, Sarah tried to do more, to be there for them the way Aunt Gert had been there for her.

Abby had warmed to her. They'd become close, spending many enjoyable nights by a fire, Sarah teaching her crocheting or knitting or embroidering or other womanly arts that, to Sarah's dismay, were slipping from practice. Ruth always stayed in her room during these sessions, sending strains of what kids today called music down from her record player. For this, Sarah had only herself to blame. She'd bought her the record player, along with a collection of Classical Melodies for Youth, but those albums were still sealed in cellophane.

It was Ruth who she worried about. Ruth took after Bridey.

Last fall, Ruth had run away from home, which was bad enough. But she'd also stolen money to make her escape. She'd opened a pocketbook left on the bench in the front hall and ransacked Sarah's wallet. By the time Sarah discovered this, she knew Ruth was safe. A Thatcher mother had called from the city to say Ruth was with them. How had Ruth gotten to the train, a good ways away? She'd put her thumb out like a hobo! Sarah shuddered to think of what might have happened to her.

This episode had brought back to Sarah all the anger and hurt and betrayal Bridey had inflicted on her years ago. Bridey! The girl she'd taken in and trusted, with whom she'd colluded in keeping a shameful secret, to whom she'd given a life raft of respectability, letting her become close to all the people Sarah loved. Bridey, who was given not only the run of the house but the chance to see the child she'd birthed in disgrace grow up in privilege. She had even been allowed a hand in his raising—and once Vincent was grown, how had Bridey paid Sarah back? By hastening the death of Sarah's father to get at his money! That Bridey was guilty of this was beyond question, confirmed to Sarah by the fact she'd run off.

How glad Sarah was that the girls had Sturbridge in them; she only hoped it would overcome the Molloy. Sarah did her best to instill Hollingworth too. But Ruth had a knack for circumnavigating Sarah's attempts to impose discipline, and Bea was too coddling to keep her in line. Sarah was glad that Ruth would be going to boarding school next year, though the fees were appalling. All the good schools now seemed in league with one another to bankrupt the families depended upon to run things in this country.

And then, it was happening.

"Come, girls!" she said.

One by one, the bumps became leaves, slowly unfurling from the tip to the root. The edges of the leaves, which had been straight, were now scalloped, as if invisible shears had been taken to them.

"Shhh," said Abby, although no one was talking.

From the scallops, petals began to emerge.

"It's like *Fantasia*!" Ruth said. A movie Vincent had taken her to.

Now the inert green cactus was coming to life. Its buds were unfolding to reveal pale pink petals.

The air became heavy with an intoxicating scent.

"Ohhhh," they chorused.

"It's so beautiful," Ruth said.

The bloom opened into a magnificent pink flower as big as a baby's head. Then it slowly veered away on the stem.

"It's afraid of us," said Abby. (She'd become a poet, would spend the rest of her life trying to re-create the enchantment she'd felt in this moment.)

"No, that's a distinguishing mark of the specimen," Sarah said. "They sense human presence and turn away, thinking we're predators."

They watched as, one by one, the buds opened, flowered, and turned their heads. Ruth dodged around the plant, keeping the blossoms in motion until Abby begged her to stop being mean to them.

They spent a few minutes marveling at the plant in full flower. Then Sarah shooed the girls back to their beds. The next day was school.

When Sarah got up at sunrise—her usual waking time now—the petals, as expected, had dropped from the vines. Sarah collected them for a sachet she'd teach Abby to make.

53

Ruth

Hollingwood

December 1970

Ruth kept one hand on the leather-wrapped wheel of the new vinyl-roofed, aqua-colored, four-door Chevrolet, a gift from her father for her sixteenth birthday. With the other hand, she reached to the dashboard, pulled out the lighter, and lifted its red eye to the end of a Virginia Slim. It was almost Christmas, and Main Street was lined with small trees strung with colorful bulbs that lit up at night, installed by the town decoration committee, an annual expense underwritten by obliging store owners. Many townspeople were out shopping, ringing the bell in the door of the hardware store or the grocer's or taking in sun on a wood bench by the old stone trough filled and refilled by the endless fountain or chatting on the sidewalk outside the white-spired church where Ruth's grandmother Sarah would be buried tomorrow.

Ruth offered a cigarette to Connie in the passenger seat, but Connie waved it away, as Ruth had known she would. Connie didn't smoke anything, not even cigarettes. She said she didn't like the burn in her throat, but Ruth wondered if Connie was more afraid—

had reason to be more afraid—of being caught. The cigarette dangled between Ruth's lips, which she'd frosted the last time they'd stopped for a light, smoothing on a new pale lipstick while looking into the rearview.

From the dashboard radio, Jimi Hendrix became Janis Joplin—Casey Kasem played their songs regularly now because they had just died. Everyone was dying these days. A classmate's brother had been killed last month in Vietnam. A Dionne quintuplet had died. And now, her grandmother.

Connie reached over and turned up the volume. *Good,* Ruth thought. *We like the same music.*

"It's like Bedford Falls from *It's a Wonderful Life,*" remarked Connie.

Most visitors to Wellington were taken in by the town's picture-perfect setting. What Ruth resented was that it wasn't perfect below the surface.

"Unlike George Bailey, I escaped," Ruth said.

Ruth and Connie were juniors at the Portia Mann School. (Since 1875, its students had joked about a school for girls having the word *Man* in it.) They had away passes to attend the funeral of Ruth's grandmother, who had died from a heart attack.

"I need someone with me on the drive," Ruth explained to Miss Beacon. She wanted company, and the company of Connie in particular. Ruth and her best friend, Pottsy, weren't speaking again. Ruth wanted to hurt Pottsy by pretending she was now best friends with the new girl.

It was a two-hour drive downstate to Wellington, Ruth reminded her, and she'd never driven it before. "I need someone to help me follow the maps."

Miss Beacon had given them passes, releasing them both from a French exam.

Ruth was a lifer at Portia Mann, but Connie had transferred

there recently from a school in Chicago. All the best boarding schools were now taking students like Connie. Ruth and her friends were in vocal support of it. It was only fair that Negroes, who'd been brought to this country against their will, should finally be given the chance to receive fine educations.

The class had formally welcomed Connie with a special tea but the first time Ruth actually spoke to her was at a meeting of the record club, where Connie had shown them a new kind of dance called the grind. She'd taken off her sweater and demonstrated a way to move your hips that made Ruth understand what dance was *for*, unlike the cotillion dances she'd learned in New York at the Knickerbocker Club, the box step, the Charleston, the Lindy, the rumba, and other dances that no one did anymore.

Most grandmothers had nicknames, but Ruth's father's mother had always been Grandmother Sarah.

She'd been a stern grandmother, sterner than Nana, their mother's mother, who had died when Ruth and her sister were little. The nice grandma and the mean one, she and her sister had called them.

At Hollingwood, there were many rooms they'd not been allowed to play in, many things they'd not been allowed to touch. Ruth and Abby speculated that their grandfather Edmund, whom they'd never met, had been driven to an early death by his unyielding wife.

But Grandmother Sarah wasn't always stern. Sometimes, just when you expected she'd give you the stink-eye for some minor infraction like not wearing a slip or forgetting to write a thank-you note, she'd break into a smile and her old eyes would become soft and she'd say how much she loved you and what a lucky grandmother she was.

And she gave the best presents. It was uncanny how she'd hear you talking in July about something you wanted and there it was under the Christmas tree. Ruth would never forget the thrill of seeing a Brownie camera box, its cellophane reflecting colored lights.

Ruth wondered if anyone recognized her car. Probably not. The car was too new for most people to know it was hers. At the crosswalk, old Philomena Spencer peered pointedly through the passenger window.

Good! Ruth wanted neighbors to take notice of the fact that Connie was colored. It was 1970, about time the town got a taste of integration, which was happening all over the country, except in towns like Wellington. The world was changing; things were happening that would have been unthinkable before—college kids killed by National Guards, the Beatles breaking up because of Yoko, sit-ins and marches taking over the streets—but Wellington was the same as it always was. But now that the voting age was eighteen instead of twenty-one, more people who thought like Ruth would be having a say.

Now Connie was taking white gloves out of the purse on her lap and putting them on.

"You don't have to wear them yet," Ruth protested. "The service isn't until tomorrow."

"Okay," Connie said, and she took off the gloves, finger by finger, pulling at seams that topped each of her digits.

Ruth guessed Connie was nervous and she felt sorry for this. She realized that, for Connie, this trip must feel like a journey to a strange land, just as going to Connie's house would have been for Ruth. Ruth hadn't asked Connie specifics about her neighborhood in Chicago, hadn't wanted to embarrass her by making her describe where she guessed Connie's family lived. Ruth imagined burned-out tenements, broken windows, the sound of gunfire. She half hoped Connie might invite her to a ghetto someday.

Her grandmother's passing felt distant to Ruth, like something that had happened on Pluto. Not like her mother's death a few years ago, which had definitely been something that had happened to her.

The fact of her mother being gone, totally gone from the earth, still undid Ruth at random moments. Last week she'd had to leave the common room during an old movie on television when Lana Turner pulled out a handkerchief—people had stopped using handkerchiefs, but her mother had persisted in this old-fashioned habit. Ruth's last glimpse of her mother was of her tucking a handkerchief into the sleeve of the monogrammed bed jacket Ruth and Abby had bought her for Christmas. Her sister had it now.

"I didn't realize Trowbridge was so close to you," Connie said, gazing across the lake they were circling. Ruth knew that she was thinking of Roy, the boy she had been matched up with at the electronic computer dance a few weeks before.

Trowbridge was a boys' school, but even if it had admitted girls, Ruth wouldn't have gone there. Not only because it would have kept her in a town she felt desperate to escape but because her father had gone there and that was enough to turn her against it.

Ruth's father, Vincent, stood for everything Ruth hated: starched white collars, knotted ties, the hypocrisy of churchgoing-ness by someone whose living was made off lying to people. He despised the new music, the new ways of dressing and speaking and eating. He hated even yogurt, the benign new health food from Switzerland, where people lived to be a hundred and three. She'd tricked him into tasting it by spooning it onto his strawberries one morning. He'd thought it was whipped cream. "Shepherd's fare," he'd called it, pushing away the bowl, pointing out that shepherds had to eat it but he need not. He'd lowered his foot on the floor bell under the dining-room carpet and Bea had swung through the door from the kitchen and taken it away.

When they'd moved up to Wellington, Bea had come with them. This solved the problem of finding good help for the house, which Ruth's grandmother said you couldn't get in 1964. The past few years the Hollingwood kitchen had seen a parade of locals who had either quit or been fired. Lilah, who had lived in for years, had gone back to Virginia to spend the rest of her days with her husband, who refused to move north.

Her grandmother liked Bea. Bea knew how to keep house; she made good, plain food and she wasn't Irish—her grandmother would never hire another Irish.

"What's your sister's name again?" Connie asked.

"Abigail, but we call her Abby," Ruth said. Abby was two years younger than they were. She would be graduating from eighth grade and joining them at Portia Mann next year unless Ruth could manage to talk her into going to Emma Willard or Foxcroft or one of the other places. Ruth felt proprietary about Portia Mann. It was where she felt free to explore hidden aspects of herself in order to achieve her true personality; she didn't relish the thought of having to search for herself with her sister looking on.

She sometimes wished that she and her sister were friends. But how could they be friends? They were as different as chalk and cheese, as everyone said. Ruth was interested in all that was going on in the wide world, while Abby would rather keep her nose in a book than have a conversation with someone.

Here was one thing Ruth hadn't worked out—Bea was colored, like Connie, and she wondered if she ought to prepare Connie for this. She'd rehearsed various phrases behind the wheel, trying them out silently in her mind, but of all the things she came up with during the drive, none sounded exactly right. As they reached the property, pulling past stone gateposts and through wrought-iron gates standing open for them, Ruth decided to say nothing to Connie, hoping her silence would lead Connie to believe that her race had escaped Ruth's broad-minded notice.

Ruth dropped her leather valise on the doorstep and fell into Bea's arms and hugged her tightly. In Ruth's mind, Bea had become her mother after her own mother died. She'd loved Bea since babyhood; sometimes she worried that she loved her more than her own mother. Bea understood Ruth and knew how things worked in the world with boys, with girls, with teachers and camp counselors. She'd advised her on topics that even her own mother wouldn't discuss, and most of the time, Bea's advice had proven to be accurate.

It felt good to be in Bea's warm embrace again, but for the first time in Ruth's memory, Bea stopped hugging first. Why? Was Bea upset by the death of her grandmother? But Ruth knew their relationship had never been easy. Maybe Bea cared more about her grandmother than Ruth knew. The ways of adults were sometimes unfathomable.

Ruth stepped back from Bea and gestured to Connie standing behind her.

"Bea, this is Connie, my friend from school," she said. "Connie, this is Bea." Usually when she introduced Bea, she added "our maid," but something prevented Ruth from saying that now.

Connie reached out her hand to be shaken and Bea surprised Ruth by not reaching to meet it; she just waved her hands vaguely and insisted that they "come in, don't catch your death." She used both hands to pull shut the carved mahogany door behind them, though two hands weren't necessary.

Bea didn't do what she usually did when guests came, which was to offer to take their coats for them, removing felt covered hangers from the front hall closet. So Ruth asked Connie for her coat herself, but Connie didn't give it to her, shaking her head and pulling the plaid wool tighter around her.

The elaborate cast-iron register in the hallway started its nightly banging.

Connie flinched.

"The furnace in the basement," Ruth explained. "It's been in our family since the Civil War." Ruth sidled up to one of the registers as a new blast of heat came through, standing as close to the decorative steam pipes as she dared to without burning her thighs. Her wool coat was a mini. Anyone who cared to look closely would see goose bumps through the holes of her fishnet stockings.

"Abby went with your father to the train to pick up the cousins," Bea said, speaking to Ruth. Then she turned her broad back and headed down the hall toward the kitchen, calling over her shoulder, "Your grandmother, God rest her, is in the front parlor."

Was Ruth expected to pay respects to her dead grandmother right off the bat? Ruth guessed that she was.

"You don't have to come with me," Ruth said to Connie, wanting to spare her. "You can wait here." Ruth pointed to a roll-armed bench in the hallway, upholstered in striped silk, set under a fresco. Whole walls had been frescoed to imitate marble when the house had been built, but only a patch of the original remained, looking like a pop-art canvas.

"That's okay," said Connie. She followed Ruth down the hallway.

Ruth braced herself to see her grandmother dead. It was late afternoon and the setting sun reddened the walls of the parlor and the faded carpets as Ruth and Connie approached the casket.

Then, there she was. Grandmother Sarah, wearing her navy suit, pinned with the diamond comet she always wore on special occasions. She'd promised it would be Ruth's one day, and now Ruth wondered if it was going to be buried with her. In front of the casket was a kneeler with a red velvet cushion. Ruth knelt on it while Connie stood behind her.

The woman lying in the casket looked like her grandmother but also didn't. Death had drained her grandmother's face of the power she'd wielded. She'd been the only one who could tell her father what to do. Her pancake makeup was heavier than usual. The eyes behind her gold-rimmed glasses were closed. The lips were a shade of purple lipstick that Ruth had never seen her grandmother wear. Her hair lay in an odd arrangement of white puffs around her face. Her waxy hands were folded and in them lay a stem of an orchid, which reminded Ruth of forays with her grandmother into the conservatory. Flowers, not people, were her grandmother's passion.

Now Ruth tried to think loving thoughts of her grandmother, crowding out memories of "You must rise above your nature" and "How you walk affects your very character."

Ruth recalled the time her grandmother had brought her and Abby up to the attic and showed them the box of dolls she had played with as a girl. They weren't baby dolls, they were *lady* dolls, their faces china, their dresses long stiff gowns. They wore slippers that buttoned and had real hair. The dolls had been a gift from Grandmother Sarah's own mother—an ancestry so ancient as to be unimaginable.

"Good-bye," she whispered and rose from the kneeler, and to her surprise, Connie took her place there. Connie bowed her head and rested her forehead on folded hands and her lips moved and she looked so sad that Ruth was ashamed—it was as if Connie's grandmother had died instead of her own.

"You're home!" It was Abby, running into the parlor to greet her. Seeing Connie, she stopped. The cushion sighed as Connie rose from the kneeler.

"Connie, this is my sister, Abby," said Ruth, turning away from the casket. She felt strange carrying on a conversation in front of their dead grandmother.

"Abby, this is Connie, a friend from school."

Abby's eyes were wide. Inexplicably, she curtsied, something she hadn't done since they were required to do it every morning when greeting the headmistress at Thatcher's.

Now here came her father—you could smell the bourbon a mile away. He welcomed Connie with a warm handshake, then introduced her to his cousins from Philadelphia. They, too, welcomed Connie.

Ruth was surprised to find herself disappointed by the fact that neither her father nor his cousins appeared to be shocked or even surprised by Connie's skin color, though Ruth knew they were prejudiced. The last time they visited, they had quoted from what they said was a scientific study stating that Negroes were genetically less intelligent than white people.

Bea served dinner for six in the candlelit dining room and it felt odd to see shy cousin Verne sitting in Grandmother Sarah's chair opposite her father, but her father had insisted that Verne should take it. Most of the talk was about arrangements for the funeral; the casket would be closed and hoisted onto an old-fashioned carriage drawn by a horse and they'd walk in solemn procession behind it from the church to the cemetery.

At the end of the first course, cousin Mildred glanced over at Connie, who was spooning the last of the soup from her bowl the right way, by pushing the spoon away from, not toward, herself.

"What good manners you have," cousin Mildred remarked to Connie, indulging her with a smile.

"Thank you, ma'am," Connie said, looking down at her bowl. "What good manners you have too."

In this moment, Ruth hoped that Connie would be Pottsy's permanent replacement as her best friend.

Later, Connie startled them by saying her family owned a boat on a lake, too. A cabin cruiser named *Comeuppance* docked on Lake Michigan. It hadn't occurred to Ruth that Connie might have come from a home that wasn't impoverished. Discovering that Connie came from a background as privileged as hers disappointed Ruth— and this disappointment was monstrous of her.

After dinner, Ruth gave Connie a tour of the house, which was what any new visitor to it seemed to desire.

The house had many rooms, but the one Ruth most relished showing Connie was the room in which her great-grandfather had been murdered. It was a guest room now.

"You're not making me sleep here, are you?" asked Connie, cowering in the doorway. The room was the White Room. Everything in it was white, even the floors. "How did he die?" Connie asked, and Ruth told her the story that Grandmother Sarah had told her many times, about the Irish maid who slipped arsenic into his toddy to get the fortune promised to her in his will.

Connie glanced around the room as if afraid of finding the murderess still there.

After the tour, they went back to Ruth's bedroom and sat on the beds. Ruth needed a cigarette. But when she flicked her lighter, it didn't light.

Searching for a matchbook, Ruth opened the drawers of a bureau that had been moved in here after she'd left for school.

She pulled open the top drawer, but it was so full, it took a while to open and close it again. It had everything but matches in it: old stamps and fountain pens and inkwells gone dry and a jeweled letter opener in the shape of a sword, its blade engraved with old-fashioned lettering, most of which had been rubbed away. The letters that remained spelled THOR.

"Hey, you could use this as a prop in that Greek play you're doing in drama," Ruth said.

She threw it to Connie. But Connie threw it back. The drama mistress said props had to be big enough to be seen from the back row.

The next drawer Ruth opened was crammed with old letters.

"Here's a matchbook," said Connie, pulling it out of a night-stand and tossing it to her.

Ruth lit up and they spent the rest of the evening reading old letters out loud to each other. Many were love letters from her grandfather Edmund, sweet and heartfelt letters that made Ruth wonder how he could have fallen for someone so stern. She was sorry she never knew this warm, funny man.

Greater love no man can display than to write a love letter on his new-fangled mechanical typewriter.

Beneath the pile of letters were instruction manuals for outdated appliances like an electric cigar lighter and an electric cream separator. Equally fascinating was a booklet tied in ribbon: *What the Marrying Maiden Needs to Know.* Ruth untied the ribbon and began reading pages of precepts that were hilarious in light of how liberated women were in the 1970s.

Marriage is universally anticipated in the feminine mind with the highest expectations and hopes...

When a man does something wrong, we must look to the woman behind him...

At the bottom of the drawer, caught in a crevice, was an envelope addressed to someone in France. There was a burn mark at a corner. The envelope had never been opened. *Madame* was written on it in penmanship so beautiful, it looked like something that might be made in calligraphy class. Across it was a rubber-stamped DECEASED.

"Maybe we shouldn't read that one," Connie said, but Ruth was already using the sword opener to slit the top of the envelope.

It was hard to read the old-fashioned cursive, but Ruth began, aloud, "'My darling Camille.'"

She stopped. Her eyes grew wide.

"I can't believe it!" Ruth said, looking up from the letter. She tossed it to Connie. "My murdered great-grandfather had syphilis!"

"Oh my God!" said Connie, throwing the letter back to Ruth as if she were afraid of being contaminated by it. "How awful!"

But Ruth didn't think it was awful. She thought it was great. The next time her father went on about her need to uphold Hollingworth decency and decorum, she had something to knock him right off his high horse. She only wished the secret was about a relative who lived now instead of so long ago, he might as well be a character in a novel.

Ruth folded the letter and tucked it into a back pocket of her velvet hot pants.

She wondered if the maid had been his mistress; perhaps she'd killed him for catting around.

54

Emma

Manhattan

2001–2002

By October, it was all over the news. They'd given up looking for people alive. Even rescue dogs with cameras strapped to their necks were said to be suffering from depression due to the fact they weren't able to find anyone.

But Emma couldn't make herself give up hope that her father might be still alive, hovering in an air pocket in the tangle of molten steel, calling out to rescuers, waiting to be heard. Workers were still digging carefully, it was reported, so as not to disturb the pile (they called it "the pile" now), moving slowly, patiently, avoiding any disturbance that might cause part of the pile to collapse. The last man rescued, three weeks ago, had been found by a policeman digging with only a pair of his handcuffs.

If anybody could survive a disaster, her father could. He was stronger than anyone! He ate food hotter than anyone else could. He'd run marathons and could hold his breath underwater longer than anyone else on the lake. Her father would make it down flights of stairs first.

By November, her mother was still putting up signs on walls already covered with signs for the missing; storefronts and pillars, bus-stop shelters and subway stations were papered with faces and messages pleading with passersby.

Have you seen this man? Peter Connelly, 86th floor.

Rosella Maria Hernandez, 98th floor. Brown hair, brown eyes, 29, birthmark on left knee.

Nelson Herbert, 100th floor. Window washer. Red hair. Brown eyes. We miss you! We love you!

There were signs on tables set up by the sidewalk, little shrines made of tiny candles and icons of saints, roses.

Emma and her mother hadn't given up hope. Because her mother was Ruth Porter, a commercial photographer who knew art directors, her father's sign stood out from the rest.

HAVE YOU SEEN THIS MAN? The type was bold and in font big enough that you didn't have to get close. JACK DUFFY, AGE 47. LAST SEEN MORGAN STANLEY, 46TH FLOOR. NORTH TOWER 2. The phone number was her mother's studio extension. It was just seven numbers—this was before 212 had to be added to local numbers. The photo of him had been taken by her mother last summer at a family reunion at Hollingwood. He wore his new red glasses. He was smiling his big, goofy smile that could light up a room. Emma had been next to him in the picture, but her mother had cut her out except for her shoulder, which gave Emma a pang each time she looked at the picture.

Her mother took flyers with her when she left for work every morning, along with thumbtacks and Scotch tape. Emma did too. You never knew. Last week they'd heard that someone related to someone who worked for someone they knew had turned up in a hospital, not remembering anything. One of the nurses had recognized the patient's face on a poster. This story gave them hope for a while.

Her father was a survivor. He'd been a Boy Scout. He'd learned survival skills. He'd taught Emma how to fish, how to light a fire, how to tie a knot. When it came time for her to go to summer camp, he'd wanted to send her out west, but her mother insisted on the girls' camp in Massachusetts where she and Emma's aunt Abby had learned tennis and sailing and archery. Life skills of the gentry, her father had said.

They didn't give up until December, when her father's watch was found. Morgan Stanley had given him a titanium watch. They deduced from the watch, for reasons they explained but she didn't follow, that her father had died quickly, had not been subjected to lingering pain.

Once her father was gone—really gone—she gave in to her mother's pleas and agreed to apply to the Trowbridge School for next year. It was where her grandfather had gone. If they moved up to Hollingwood, Emma could be a dayhop there; that was her mother's plan. Emma wasn't so sure.

She'd always been a good student, but now her grades dropped. It seemed pointless to plan for a future if the world could fall apart at any moment.

Her new best friend became Isabelle, the girl who'd left Thatcher last year to go to Stuyvesant. It was a public school downtown, next to the Towers. You had to take a special test to get in. Isabelle had gotten in, saving her parents thousands of dollars, but after that Tuesday, the school had closed for a while and her parents had sent her back to Thatcher. They were worried that the air downtown was toxic, even though authorities were saying it wasn't. Isabelle was allowed to return despite Thatcher's no-readmittance policy.

She wasn't Isabelle anymore. She was Izzi. "I feel like a palindrome now," she said.

Emma hadn't been close to Izzi before, though she was one of the few other classmates at Thatcher who lived downtown. A couple of days after it happened, when people who lived south of Houston were allowed to go home to retrieve things, Emma told her mother she was going down after school to get Ari. Ari was Ariel, a now-nine-year-old Balinese cat her father had given Emma for her fifth birthday. Emma had named her for the character in *The Little Mermaid.* "That's the first movie I saw in a theater, too" said Izzi, with whom Emma found herself on the Number 6. Emma was glad for her company, especially when they came up at Spring Street and it was like they were walking into a war zone. Dust made their eyes itch. The air smelled like an electrical fire. They had to show their IDs at checkpoints to soldiers in camouflage uniforms with machine guns slung over their shoulders. Streets usually clogged with traffic were eerily empty. Mercer Street was so deserted, a man was teaching his daughter how to ride a bicycle there. Emma remembered how happy she'd been the day her father had taught her to ride in Washington Square Park, how surprised she'd been to realize she could keep going after he'd let go.

When Emma reached home, everything, even her poor, starving cat, was covered with white dust. Emma couldn't get out of her mind that some of it might be her father's ashes.

For a month, Emma and her mother and the cat lived with her mother's friend Connie on the Upper West Side. Connie's two kids, Ty and Whitney, were in boarding schools, so there was room.

After the checkpoints lifted and downtowners were allowed to move back, Emma and Izzi started riding the subway to school together. It was good to have someone with you, because every time you got on the train, you had to hear people talk about the day you most wanted to forget.

The freshman trip to Washington, D.C., was canceled that spring. Instead, they went downtown on a field trip to the Tenement

Museum to see an apartment where real immigrants had lived. The apartment was only three rooms and one window. It didn't have a bathroom. You used a toilet in the hallway or an outhouse in the yard. The yard was where you did your laundry, too, in a tub you filled with a pump. There was no running water in the apartment. You pumped it into a pail and carried it upstairs.

"Do you know how much a pail of water weighs?" the guide asked. Nobody did, so he told them. Ten pounds. Which was as heavy as two bags of Ari's litter. Emma couldn't imagine having to carry that up five flights of stairs every time she wanted to wash her hair.

There had once been a fire in the apartment, he said. You could tell by black marks on the walls. A few artifacts original to the apartment were displayed: a pipe, a tea strainer, a stuffed teddy bear, a special cross to protect against fire and famine.

One night in March, an artist installed searchlights where the Towers used to be and two beams shot for miles straight into the sky. It was like they were probing for everyone who'd been lost in the attacks. There was an opening ceremony for the installation and she and her mother received invitations, but they didn't go. They were weary of tributes by then. Emma could see the columns of lights from her bedroom window. That night, in bed, she cried remembering a birthday gift she'd given her father, a special certificate she'd sent away for, commemorating a star that had been named after him.

Later that week, Emma came home to a thick ivory-colored envelope her mother had left on the kitchen counter. It was unopened, addressed to Emma. She knew immediately that it was an acceptance from Trowbridge. She hoped that the stretch of months before summer would cause her mother to change her mind about leaving New York—but it didn't.

"Daddy's going to be ninety-three this year. He needs me," her mother said.

Hearing her mother say "Daddy" never failed to make Emma swallow back tears.

For a while, Emma had imagined she might persuade her mother that she could live with Izzi and come up on weekends. Izzi's mother had called her mother to say it was okay—but Emma's mother wouldn't hear of it.

They moved after school let out in June.

55

Emma

Trowbridge School

September 2002

From the street, Hollingwood looked a lot bigger than it was. This was because of the way it was built, long and shallow like a ship. It was designed like that to let in the light, her grandfather said. From the outside, the house seemed to go on and on. But once you were inside, you saw that the rooms were small and the house wasn't deep, which was the way most homes in the country were built. Still, it was big. Bigger than the country houses of most of her friends at Thatcher, who had way more money than her family did. But their houses were by the ocean, where land values were higher.

Only four people lived at Hollingwood now: her mother, her grandfather, Arlette, and herself. So why did it feel as if people were always on top of her?

She guessed she would board.

It was her fifth night at Trowbridge and she was spending it in a graveyard. She'd come here every day so far. To sit with the dead people. To remember her father. She'd already forgotten the exact sound of his voice.

Sometimes she imagined her father still alive, wandering a mall in New Jersey, wearing the suit he'd worn that day, the shoes her mother hated but that he liked to wear because the soles were rubber and they were good for walking and he liked walking to work.

She hadn't gotten to say good-bye to him. He'd come home late the night before and when he tapped at her door, she'd pretended she was already sleeping. If she'd opened the door, his talk would have been endless, she'd thought then. She'd been instant-messaging with friends on her computer. She'd turned down the volume knob so he wouldn't hear. She'd been too tired to talk to him. She'd had a Latin quiz the next day. When she'd woken the next morning, the front door was clicking shut.

I'm sorry, Daddy, she said to the moon.

She watched dark squares become yellow in the west wing of the castle. Her school was a castle, though no one here called it that. But that's what locals at the swimming grove called them, *the rich kids in the castle.* But they weren't all rich kids. Her roommate was on scholarship. She herself wasn't rich, or at least not as rich as most kids here seemed to be.

It was Friday night. Students were crossing the quad, going back to their dorms. She'd heard there would be partying later, but she knew she wouldn't be invited. Her real friends were at Thatcher.

Her mother had e-mailed to ask if Emma wanted to come home for the weekend. But Hollingwood wasn't home. No home would be home without her father in it. Her home was still Greene Street, where she'd lived all her life and where she had a sunny bedroom on the fifth floor of a loft building where the elevator was a cage and pillars held up a tin sky full of stars—a place that would be someone else's home when the market came back.

"You like hanging in graveyards too?" She turned. A boy she recognized. Rhodes, who had gone to Hasbrook, a boys' school in the city, around the corner from Thatcher. He was one of the cool kids there. At the coffee shop where everyone went at free periods, he was usually surrounded by others. She didn't think he'd noticed her, but maybe he had.

He sat next to her without being asked. She wouldn't have thought to ask him, but now that he was beside her on the stone bench, she filed that away for next time: *It is okay to ask a boy to sit next to you.*

"It's the only place I can come to think my own thoughts," he said. "And—to talk to my mom."

"Cell phones work here?" She was surprised. People in Wellington prided themselves on having no cell service. Lack of cell service was touted in the literature for Trowbridge.

"No," he said, grinning. He had a good smile. His eyes were dark and his hair was blond, an unusual combination, in Emma's experience. "My mom passed away a few years ago. I talk to her here."

"I'm sorry," said Emma. Was he a Trowbridge? The stones were ancient, most of the dates worn away. It was a cemetery for only the foundress and her family, they'd said on a tour. "Your mom's buried here?"

"Uh—no. My mom's in a box on the mantel in our place on Park. But I come here sometimes to remember her, you know?"

A window flung open inside her. He, too, had lost a parent. How long had it taken him to get over it?

"You're the girl whose dad was in the Towers, aren't you?" His directness was a balm. Everyone here knew, but no one said anything.

She nodded. She was afraid if she spoke, she would cry. She took her hands from the cold granite bench, brought them together, inserted them between her thighs, and moved her palms back and forth, as if that friction would generate warmth. The sun was down. It was getting cold.

"I saw you in chapel," he said. She'd seen him too.

Chapel had been the first anniversary. There was a general prayer and her father's name had been mentioned. She couldn't believe it had been a year.

"I'm Rhodes," he said. "My mom died three years ago. Cancer." As he spoke, his right hand fished for something in the back pocket of his jeans.

"I'm sorry," she said. But she thought he was lucky. If she'd known her father was going to die, she would have had time to be nicer to him.

He brought out a joint. "You smoke?" he said and when she said yes, he produced a lighter and lit the joint behind a hand curled to hide the flame. She guessed he did this in case a prefect was looking out a window.

"Good stuff," she said after he handed it to her, although she wasn't sure if it was.

"Supply's always superior after summer break," he said. "Rizal brings souvenirs from Dubai. Don't know what we'll do when he graduates next year."

"What year are you?" she asked, handing back the joint. She was glad he wasn't a senior. Or a sixther, as seniors were called here.

"Fifth," he said. "Year of fear and college applications."

Emma sighed in empathy. And gratitude. She was already high. She liked getting high, which, whenever she smoked, she thought she should do more often. It freed her from having to think about things.

"Admissions guy from Yale told my dad the best thing he could do to get me in was to move to North Dakota. It's the least represented demographic in the Ivy pool. You're from the city, right? Hate to break it to you, but same goes for you."

"Trust me, my mom's not moving to North Dakota. She lives just over there," Emma said, pointing. "It's where she grew up."

"Your mom lives in a boathouse?"

Once Emma got high, she started to giggle, and that usually progressed to uncontrollable belly laughing. The thought of her mother, with her good shoes and good furniture, moving into the boathouse without electricity or even a bathroom was hilarious.

"Whoa, don't fall off," Rhodes said, gently pulling on the collar of her father's plaid button-down. She wore his clothes now. The thought of her father made her steady again.

"No, she lives in a house you can't see, on a hill behind it." The house was famous in town, profiled in local magazines and borrowed for benefit galas. One of the surprises of coming to Trowbridge was discovering that most of the students here hadn't heard of it.

They didn't speak for a while, smoking down the joint. Crickets chirped. A guitar strummed in the distance.

"What was your dad like?" he asked, which was the nicest thing he could have said, because talking about him made her dad come alive for a minute.

"He taught me things, like how to read stars. When he wasn't at work, he liked to goof around. He told the best scary stories. He quit smoking because of me when I was one day old. He just threw the pack away. He said it was easy to do when he thought of my new little pink lungs."

She couldn't say more because then she would cry.

"He sounds like a great dad," Rhodes said. "I wish my mom had done that for me. She didn't even stop smoking after she got sick. Watching her light up was like having to watch her hang herself in slow motion."

Emma didn't know what to say. She put her head on his shoulder. He smelled good, like coconuts.

They sat, not talking, for a while. Then he leaned down to kiss her. His mouth tasted sweet. He moved his tongue in exactly the right way.

Should she let him do more?

She was just stoned enough to have sex with him. She was pretty sure she was the only girl in her dorm who hadn't had sex. Most of her Thatcher friends hadn't done it yet. But they went to a girls' school. At Trowbridge, she didn't have that excuse. She didn't want to be the only virgin on campus.

His hand moved under her shirt, to her bra.

She hoped he wouldn't be disappointed to discover how little of her there was without padding.

He didn't seem disappointed. He began stroking, flicking her nipples, and darts were zinging all over her body.

The world could fall apart again at any moment. What was she waiting for?

Rhodes stood up and pulled off his sweatshirt and spread it on the soft ground, making a bed for them on the grass. His white T-shirt was luminous against the black sky. Lights were going on in the castle. A salmon-colored moon rose behind one of the turrets.

She took his hand and lay down with him.

She wouldn't tell him it was her first time. She didn't want to spook him. She didn't want him to know this was sex she'd remember for the rest of her life.

Ever so slowly, he unzipped her jeans, and she was being kissed where she'd never been kissed before, which felt so good it made her toes curl.

She didn't know guys could do that to girls.

But after a minute, she made him stop, worried that virginity was something he might be able to sniff.

Then he was sitting up and she was afraid he'd figured it out and decided not to go through with it. She'd heard guys had rules against doing it with virgins.

"This just feels so right," he said. "Does it feel right to you?"

"Yes," she said. And out of nowhere, he produced a condom.

She worried that her inexperience would betray her. But apparently, she'd seen enough screen sex to know how to act. *I am having sex with a boy at boarding school,* she thought as he moved above her, his shoulder obscuring, then revealing the moon.

It didn't hurt like Izzi had warned her it would. It felt nice. Just—nice. Nothing more. The best part was seeing the urgency of his need. He almost looked as if he were having a seizure. Then it was over.

He rolled off her, onto his back, and threw an arm over his face as if to shield his eyes from the brightness of the moon. They lay in silence for a few minutes.

She felt as if she ought to say something.

He turned to her and kissed her cheek. "Was it good for you?"

"Yes!" she said brightly. Should she say more?

He blew air out of his mouth, the meaning of which she could not discern.

They were both wet and sticky. Was it rude to dry herself off? Should she try to dry him off too? But with what? She couldn't defile her father's shirt.

Sex required so many decisions. Why weren't these mentioned in conversations about sex that people her age were always having?

And then he was standing, pulling on boxers. Where was the condom? Had it fallen off?

"Want to go to a party in Hamlin?" he asked.

Was he leaving her? She'd imagined they'd sit and talk until curfew.

"I think I'll just stay here for a while," she said, raising her hips to pull up her jeans. She'd just had sex for the first time. With him! But of course, he didn't know that.

She watched him move away from her. Then—what was he doing? Throwing his weight against a gravestone! The stone rocked back and forth. Why was he desecrating a grave? The back of her neck went cold. Was he having some sort of an episode? He pushed the stone back and forth until it loosened like a tooth. He rested the stone against another behind it. Then he got down on his hands and knees and reached into the cavity. He pulled out a bottle.

"Party time!" He held the bottle over his head in both hands, like a trophy.

So that's what he'd come for. She watched him jump the gate and go back to the castle.

"You almost missed curfew!" Bekkah said, carrying her shower caddie over her wrist like a purse.

Emma followed her to the lavatory.

Do I look different? There were several showers going and she rubbed a clearing in the steamed glass.

The only difference was that the whites of her eyes were bright red. She hoped Bekkah didn't notice. Weed was a disciplinary offense.

The next day was Saturday, and here was a bad thing about boarding school—there were classes on Saturday. Every pore in her was alert for the appearance of Rhodes in the hallways, but he, being a fifther, was on a different schedule.

After classes, Emma had Ultimate Frisbee. You had to choose a sport, and this was the only one she thought she might be decent at—her father had taught her to throw a Frisbee in Washington Square Park.

She skipped lunch so she'd have time to get her look right; instead, she stopped by the feed bar, poured herself a bowlful of Lucky Charms, then added milk, which turned satisfyingly pink.

She took the bowl to her room and stood in front of the full-length mirror, trying things on and taking them off.

When she got to the field, only boys were playing. A lot of the girls were lying at the edge of the field, soaking up sun. The boys, wearing board shorts and T-shirts and baseball caps on backward, were jumping and retrieving. They reminded Emma of dogs in a park.

Emma walked over to join the girls. Some lay directly on the grass, some on their sweatshirts. All had rolled down the waistbands of their shorts and pulled up their shirts to their bra lines to tan their flat stomachs. Emma was glad about what she'd decided to wear, which was what they were wearing.

"You here for Ultimate?" said a girl, not opening her eyes.

"Uh-huh," Emma said, lying down on the grass beside her.

"Coach is late. He had to take his kid to day care."

This was another difference between Thatcher and boarding school. Here, teachers had lives. They lived in houses you could see and they had spouses and children they had to attend to. At Thatcher, it was like teachers didn't exist outside the classroom.

Emma turned her head to say, "Okay," and saw from her vantage point in the grass that one of the boys on the field was Rhodes. Her heart started pumping so loud, she was afraid it was setting off vibrations that could be felt in the ground.

But the other girls didn't notice.

"Did you get a haircut?" said one to another. "It looks all even now."

"My mom finally took me to Luigi's before we drove up. Getting an appointment took forever."

Emma had never been to Luigi's, though plenty of her Thatcher classmates went there. Emma got her hair trimmed at Astor Place for ten dollars. For the first time, she wondered how Luigi would make it look different.

Now Rhodes was jumping to catch a thrown disk. Was it Rhodes? She couldn't be sure. She was staring into the sun. A silhouette that resembled him was stretching and catching, then returning to the ground with a little bounce of his knees.

She felt a shadow fall over her.

"Did anyone order from Sushi Garden?"

A paunchy middle-aged man was holding up a white paper bag.

The girl lying beside Emma pulled down her shirt and rose to a sitting position. She cupped her hands around her mouth.

"Sushi Garden! Did anyone order?"

The boy who had just caught the Frisbee tossed it behind him and started toward them. As he got closer, Emma saw it was definitely Rhodes. Muscles moved in his calves as he walked. She wanted him to notice her—and wanted him not to. What if he didn't like how she looked in daylight?

"Thanks," he said to the man. He gave Rhodes a pen and handed him a receipt on a clipboard.

At Trowbridge, money seemed not to exist. Everything was paid for by signing pieces of paper.

Rhodes exchanged his signature for the bag and tried to stuff the bag in his shorts pocket, but it wouldn't fit, even though the pocket extended from his hip to his knee. He shrugged and looked Emma's way and his smile grew broader. He began to move in her direction. Emma panicked and flushed in anticipation—of what? A kiss? Should she sit up or not? She didn't want to seem eager. But he stopped before he reached Emma. He bent toward the girl next to her, and Emma saw by his proprietary touch to the back of her neck, they were more than just friends. They kissed, unhurried.

"Get a room, you two," a girl said with a groan.

"You offering yours?" Rhodes laughed. Then he was walking away from them, onto the field. He tossed the white bag onto a pile of clothing by the water Igloo.

Carefully, slowly, Emma got to her feet.

"Don't go, here comes Coach," someone said, but Emma was already moving away, walking as fast as she dared, rounding the last pillar of a stone porch to where she couldn't be seen from the field. She cooled her head against a wall and vomited pink against the gray limestone.

Then a guy was beside her, holding out a bunch of paper napkins. She took them, grateful.

"Are you okay?" he asked. He was in her lab class. His eyes were kind.

"Yeah," she said. When she straightened, she felt dizzy.

"I'm Liam," he said.

"I'm Emma."

"I know."

56

Emma

Hollingwood

October 2002

Emma sat on the outskirts of conversation as if she were a small, sparsely populated country adjacent to nations of greater consequence on a map that had never been drawn but that existed in her mind and in the minds of the others around her.

She sat with the day students even though she was a boarder.

Across an ocean of parquetry, on the north side of a room that had been designed for the receiving of guests when the receiving of guests required a room, boys in ties and dark jackets stood talking in front of a fireplace so big, it looked like the mouth of a tunnel.

Emma pretended to be reading to make it seem as if she were an island by choice. She stared at the pages of *Snow Falling on Cedars,* required reading for English, a story about an outsider accused of killing a member of a close-knit community.

Late, she read, and the word rose within her. She was at least a week late, maybe more. She couldn't be sure. She never marked down dates, never before having had the need to.

Late. The word swelled around her; the conversations of others.

You're late for the van.

Don't be late for chorus.

Instant-message her we'll be late.

The word pulsed, orbs of sepulchral sound—*late, late, late, late, late*—five chimes as the great clock in the corner struck the hour. On other days at this hour, the clock presided mutely, its chimes absorbed by the din. But today was Saturday. Dinner was late.

"Sorry I'm late, hon," said her mother as Emma got into the car. "I had to pick up Daddy's medicine."

Hearing "Daddy" tugged at something beneath Emma's breastbone.

"You didn't want to bring a friend home for dinner?" asked her mother, who thought of her time at boarding school as the best days of her life.

I don't want to go to Trowbridge anymore, Emma didn't say, grateful that talking was made impossible as her mother navigated the car over the drawbridge, suspension chains shrieking, uneven wood planks groaning under the tires of the SUV.

Emma had to think of a way to cushion the words so that her mother would receive them, as windows at Hollingwood had to be opened after winter with a hammer wrapped in toweling to temper blows to the casing.

"Welcome home, pumpkin," said Arlette. "I made you chicken and mashed." Arlette would always think of Emma as five, something for which Emma felt grateful.

Dinner was a mostly silent affair. The clink of cutlery, the attempts at conversation by her mother.

"Did you get your walk in today, Daddy?" her mother asked, speaking loudly. Her mother still had a father.

Emma's sixteenth birthday was only weeks away. It was on a Monday this year. Emma dreaded spending it with kids who didn't know her, didn't care about her. By that day—she'd know if she was pregnant.

Her grandfather didn't look up. He was intent on spearing a cherry tomato with his salad fork. He was ninety-three but the only thing wrong with him besides needing a cane was that he couldn't hear without hearing aids. He often turned the volume low or turned them off completely.

"We got there," confirmed Arlette, swinging through the door with a basket of bread that she set on the table. "He did good."

"Thank you," her mother murmured, her eyes full of gratitude. Her mother and grandfather had never gotten along. She guessed her mother would have had a more relaxed time sitting in the kitchen talking with Arlette. But then, so would Emma. Why didn't they ask Arlette to join them, to sit in her father's empty chair to Emma's right? But this would never happen at Hollingwood, where things were done as they always had been and no one invited the help to sit down.

Now her grandfather was turning his attention to the slices of chicken already cut on his plate. He ate in the British way, taking up meat with his knife, which Emma's mother used to forbid her to do.

Now her mother was aiming conversation at her.

How is . . .

When does . . .

Emma nodded obligingly, chewing slowly, slowly, glad it was not polite to talk with your mouth full.

The clock on the mantel chimed, its music mingling with gongs from the clock on the stair landing. But the loudest sound was one only Emma could hear: the siren calling from the box in her backpack upstairs. She'd read the instructions. Results weren't reliable unless you took the test in the morning.

"Have you given more thought to your birthday?" her mother

asked, spearing a brussels sprout, acting as if she'd not asked this several times before.

"I don't want a party, Mom."

"I was thinking of taking you out to a restaurant, you and your friends."

"I don't have any friends."

"It's three weeks away," said her mother. "You'll have friends by then. Or it could be just you and your roommate Becky."

"Bekkah, Mom. And she's not my friend."

Her mother's fork paused in the air. "Oh, Emma. She seems lovely. Don't not give her a chance just because she's from Iowa."

"Ohio." And now Emma heard herself blurting out what she'd meant to broach with her mother in private.

"I don't want to go to Trowbridge anymore! I want to switch schools." She wanted to go back to Thatcher. She could live on Greene Street; the loft hadn't yet sold. But she'd wait to suggest this. It was better to chip away at her mother's defenses little by little rather than trying to batter them down all at once.

She pictured her father, against all odds, walking in the front door. *Here I am,* he'd say, dropping his leather briefcase by the door. *I'm home.*

Her mother murmured so that only Emma could hear. "Honey, see how you feel next semester. If you're still unhappy—"

"I will be," said Emma, using her fork to build up the remaining rampart of mashed potatoes. "I hate it there. I want to go to normal school."

Her grandfather looked up from his plate.

"So how is my fellow Trowbridger doing?" he said to Emma.

Her mother cut her a look of warning. For the first time, Emma wondered if her grandfather's deafness was a ruse.

"A centenarian, no less." He dabbed his still-folded cloth napkin at his lips. Her grandfather was class of 1928. His yearbooks were stacked behind glass in the bookcase. Rows of boys who looked like men, with short, slicked hair, some parted in the middle, all wearing shirts and ties, some with pants cuffed at the knees and striped socks descending into shoes laced from toe to ankle, like ice skates. She guessed that most of them were already dead.

If Emma stayed at Trowbridge, she'd be in the hundredth class to graduate. WELCOME TO THE CENTENARIAN CLASS OF 2005 said a banner still hanging above the portcullis. Emma hadn't known what a portcullis was then and found out too late to be included in the class photo taken there on the first day. Perhaps her absence was portentous.

"Fine, Opa," she said, using her old nickname for him. If she had a baby, he'd be its great-grandfather.

"I remember my first weeks across the lake. Weeks of longing and sadness and sickness for home."

Tears welled in Emma's eyes.

"My nurse made the best scones. Light but heavy with butter. We got good butter before Beaumont Dairy sold out. I missed those scones at Trowbridge severely, along with everything else. She'd sneak a basket of them to the milkman, who would sneak them to the kitchen staff, who would sneak them to me. It helped immensely. Food can be a great reliever of ills."

As if reminded of the restorative value of bread, he took a slice from the basket, lifted the silver lid of the butter dish, and knifed out a pat. That was the difference between her mother and Arlette. Her mother kept butter in the refrigerator so when it came to the table it was hard as a rock. Arlette left butter out to soften all day, which was more considerate of people.

"Food's pretty good over there now, Dad," said her mother.

This was true. There was a pasta station, one for paninis, a salad bar, all kinds of burgers, Thai night and Indian and French and Italian. But food was no reason to stay at a school.

He continued. "Your great-great-grandfather who built this house was sent to boarding school when he was just eight. Did you know that?"

She shook her head. This was one she'd not heard.

"The school was in Ellsworth, eleven miles away. He ran away the first week, walking all the way home. They sent him back with only a reprimand."

"Oh, Daddy, that was a million years ago," her mother said. "And it's awful they sent him back. At eight!"

Emma wonders if this was a story told to her grandfather to keep him at Trowbridge. Had he, too, wanted to run away? He'd have had to walk far less than eleven miles to get home. He'd have had to circle only half the lake.

"Well, they didn't make him walk," said her grandfather, painting the remains of his roll with more butter. "They sent him back in a gig."

"A gig?" asked Emma.

"Horse and carriage," he said and Emma pictured the carriage house not as the garage it was now but filled with the horse-drawn vehicles it was built to shelter.

She wished she'd lived in that easier time.

After dinner, Emma went down to the dock for a smoke, putting on a hoodie, hiding the pack in a pocket. As she descended the hill, nearing the water, she could hear partying at Trowbridge. Laughter carried. She strained to hear conversation. Were Rhodes and Meredith there? She listened for the sound of his voice. They hadn't talked since that night. While walking down the hall last week, they passed each other, and his arm had brushed hers, and he'd hastened his step, hurrying away from her, saying something to the boy he was walking with.

She couldn't stay at that school. She didn't trust herself. Surely, she'd make another mistake. Not with a boy, maybe, but with something else. There were so many rules that she didn't know. How did you learn them? They weren't written down. Going to Trowbridge was like walking the field next to Hollingwood. From afar it looked easy, but once you were in it, you were constantly tripping over roots and rocks that were hidden.

If she was pregnant, the closest place was the city. Her mother would bring her, though this would require Emma submitting to hours of tearful talk and a painful lecture. She wondered if getting an abortion would hurt. How long would it take? Boarding school was so scheduled. Prelims were coming up. She didn't have time!

She took the cigarettes out of her pocket and flicked the lighter. She wondered if the light could be seen from across the lake.

Dark had descended; the castle stood illuminated on the crest of the hill. All those windows in various shapes—crosses and slits and squares and domes—lit from within. Laughter carried again, sent to her like foreign currency she couldn't spend on this shore.

The next morning, the cat woke her, stepping across her face.

This was the day she'd find out.

Her best friends at Trowbridge so far were guys, Liam and Zach. ("Zach and Liam," Zach always corrected.)

She couldn't share this with them.

She extracted the box from her backpack.

Suddenly the door swung open. There was her grandfather!

That was the problem with doors at Hollingwood. None of them locked. All of them took skeleton keys that were either lost or jumbled in a drawer in the breakfast room.

"Pardon me, Ruthie," he said, pulling the door shut abruptly. This used to be her mother's room when she was a girl.

It was like her grandfather was living in the past, present, and future simultaneously.

Emma unhooked a robe from the back of the door, pocketed the test strip and page of instructions, went to the bathroom and peed in the cup, then took the cup upstairs to the attic.

Dead flies and dead mice and old trunks and brittle leather skates and old wooden skis. She placed the cup on the ledge of a window and seated herself beside it on a trunk covered with old-fashioned travel stickers. She reread the directions. She must wait fifteen minutes. She pushed the button of her G-Shock watch.

She needed a cigarette. From her perch on the trunk, she flipped up the sheet covering the table. This was where she often came to smoke. She opened a drawer in the table and felt around for the pack she'd left there. Her hands closed around it. But when she drew it out, she saw that it wasn't the pack, it was a soft-covered book so small, it fit into her palm.

She reached again into the drawer and felt around. There it was. Good. She'd tucked a matchbook into the cellophane. She lit up and hastened the cigarette to her lips and took a long drag.

She opened the window and ashed out to the world.

The book was an old prayer book covered in leather so old it was peeling away. The first page was blank. A name was written in old-fashioned ink: Brighid Molloy. Emma thumbed pages thin as tissue: *Feasts and Fasts. Litany of the Saints. Prayers for Deliverance.*

She checked her wrist: three minutes and sixteen seconds to go. The plastic cup glowed white on the sill, a crystal ball.

She turned back to the book. There was a faded brown ribbon, marking a page: *Prayer During Time of Desperation.*

She'd say the prayer. What could it hurt?

"'I beg your intercession to help me now in my urgent need and grant my earnest petition'—"

Her watch buzzed. Time.

The strip was blue! The prayer had worked!

*　　*　　*

"You're up early," her mother said, looking up from the Style section.

"Boarding school imbues one with the habit of keeping regular hours," said her grandfather, his eyes on the obituaries.

Emma took a mug from a row of mugs set upside down on the green-painted shelf. The paint was an odd green, almost blue, a color once believed to keep mosquitoes away. As mosquitoes were rarely encountered in the kitchen, Emma guessed it might work.

She set the cup on a depression in the slate counter and poured coffee from the carafe, then took her cup to the table and slid into one of the straight-backed chairs that had needed to be recaned since she was little.

She took the *New York Times Magazine* from the pile of papers. The cover said, "The Way We Live Now."

"Get me a scissors, will you, my dear?" said her grandfather, by which Emma knew he was talking to her. Ruth was rarely, if ever, *my dear.*

"Christopher Gray did a profile of our old building on Park. I want to send it on to your aunt Abby."

Her grandpa was always cutting things out and mailing them, sometimes without an accompanying note. Once, at camp, an envelope addressed to her in his spindly handwriting contained nothing but a mystifying article on rock formations.

Emma crossed the room and opened the junk drawer that, for as long as she could remember, contained every household item that could be wanted: string and tape and matches and candles and—here they were—scissors. It also held items that hadn't been wanted for years: stamp booklets, cassette tapes, film canisters, speaker wire.

There were keys, hundreds of them, some threaded with little handwritten tags. Someday, Emma meant to find the key for her room.

She brought the scissors to her grandfather. They were long sewing scissors in the shape of a bird. The beak of the bird was the blades. She handed them to him by the ears of the implement, as Arlette had long ago taught her to do.

"Don't cut it out before I read it, Dad!" cried her mother.

He ignored her, snipping away at the newsprint. Her mother pushed herself up from her chair and took her coffee cup out of the room. Whenever Grandpa did or said something that upset her, her mother had learned to give herself a time-out. Emma heard her footsteps going down to the basement, where she had a darkroom set up in a closet built to enclose an old laundry sink.

Her grandfather's hands shook. The beak of the bird trembled as it opened and shut across the page.

"Who was Brighid Molloy?" Emma asked him.

"What?" The beak stopped moving as he looked up. "Who told you about her?"

"No one," said Emma. She pulled the little book out of the pocket of her robe, opened it to the page where the name was written.

"Where did you get that?" asked her grandfather.

"In the attic. I was looking for something...for a school project."

He reached for the book and she handed it to him. He stared at the signature. "Brighid Molloy. They called her Bridey. She was my nurse when I was a boy. She was the one..." He hesitated.

"I remember," said Emma. It was an old family story. Her mother told her. The Irish maid poisoned someone with arsenic. No one ever wanted to stay in that room.

"She didn't do it," said her grandfather. "She got a bad rap." Emma looked up, surprised by his vernacular. *Rap* was something her mother would say. "Nothing was proved," he continued. "But in some eyes, people are guilty until proven innocent."

Emma knew her mother disagreed with him about this.

"But what happened to her baby?"

Her grandfather's eyes narrowed. "She didn't have a baby. She never married."

Emma took the book from him, flipped to a page, and pulled out a folded piece of paper. "It's a receipt dated April 1909 for 'an infant boy.'"

"Let me see that," he said.

"Emma!" Ruth called from the kitchen. "Come help me empty wastebaskets. It's Sunday and the dump closes at one."

57.

Vincent

Hollingwood

2002

Vincent had twice thrown the little book away.

The first time was just after he'd said good-bye to her on the boat. After walking the galley and down the gangplank, he'd passed a trash heap and tossed the book onto it, thinking to rid himself of evidence—she hadn't known him at all.

But a few minutes later, his shoulder had been tapped from behind. A felt-hatted man held out the book to him.

"You dropped this," he said. Vincent had taken the book from the man's hand, and the hand had held open for a coin. Vincent hadn't given him one.

Once home, he'd tossed the book into a waste bin.

He smoothed the receipt. She'd had a son. Born the same year he himself had been born. Was that why she felt so connected to him?

Carefully, because the book was falling apart, he turned to the flyleaf. There was her signature, in ink gone brown. He ran the pad of his forefinger over her name, as if rubbing her name could conjure her person.

He flipped through its pages. *Septuagesima. Quinquagesima.* Latin was such a beautiful language. Dr. Lauer had been buried in winter; almost all of his former Latin class had attended, and though it had been a cold day, most strode from parking to the chapel not wearing coats.

She'd underlined something: *We see now through a glass in a dark manner; but then face to face.*

The passage was starred. In the margin: *See pg. 193.* He thumbed through pages. They were browned, gilt edges faded.

But the book seemed to end at page 191. Then he saw that the last few pages were stuck together, and with his nail (Ruth had forgotten to trim his nails), he separated them. They were meant to be blank, but she'd written on one. The ink was still blue.

Dear God who relinquished His only Son to the loving arms of Mary and Joseph, guide my son on his journey. Make me ever grateful for his home of abundance and for the sheltering presence of Sarah and Edmund. Amen

A long-ago talk in a garden: *Which of us is his mother, you make very clear to him.*

Biddy wasn't only his nurse. Biddy was his mother.

What strength of love it must have taken her to keep the secret from the world, from him.

Sarah was Mother. She would always be Mother. But he was raised by the woman who had given him birth.

He felt a surge of tenderness for Mother then. He ached to recall how many times he'd shunned her for Biddy.

But what did it matter? It was all so long ago. He stood and walked to the black plastic bag meant to go to the dump. He willed his hands to be steady. He untwisted a wire, opened the bag, dropped in the book, and retwisted the wire in a knot Opa had taught him, a locking twist that couldn't be undone.

58.

Ruth

Hollingwood

2005

She'd renovated the house so her father could stay in it. Her father was ninety-six years old. There was a lovely nursing home in town, with a long waiting list, but Ruth never put her father's name on it. She wanted to keep him at home for as long as she could. She wanted to give him what he needed, something she'd not done for him for most of her life.

She'd had no idea what taking care of a man at the end of his days would entail—and yet, she was doing it. It was a healing.

She'd turned his bedroom closet into a bath and one of the maid's rooms into a laundry room, for which she'd had to rewire the western side of the house. She'd grown weary of having to do multiple loads in the basement. She'd been shocked by how much laundry a man at the end of his life could require. It had taken four men to maneuver the machines upstairs, and once they were moved, she'd expanded the darkroom. It was amazing how much people would pay for old-process prints of photos of their historic homes.

There were only the two of them living in the house now, but many people came and went: housekeepers, visiting nurses, hospice workers, the pastor of the Congregational church, who, to Vincent's recurring dismay, was a woman.

It was late afternoon. Vincent was dozing. Ruth was sitting in the old rocker next to him, reading.

She was glad he was finally getting some rest. He'd told her this morning that he'd had a bad night. The night nurse had confirmed it, saying he'd read to him from old children's books he'd requested from the glassed case in the library. He'd not been in pain, but he'd not slept at all.

For breakfast, she'd given him a pill smashed into powder and put in a juice. She added another powder to thicken the juice. Soon, she'd been told, he wouldn't be able to swallow at all. She ached to think of him missing Emma's graduation from Trowbridge—he'd have loved seeing his granddaughter in her velvet robes and the centennial pomp. But the part of him that would have seen it was already gone.

The doorbell sounded its long tinny buzz and she put down the magazine and crossed the room on tiptoe, avoiding the spot on the floor where the wood creaked so as not to wake him.

She descended the spiral stairs and, once downstairs, crossed the hallway to the front vestibule so she was not there to see her father's clenched hand fall open, nor to hear a soft thud, nor to watch the marble roll across faded floral designs and onto sloped wood, where it followed a crevice between planks of hemlock, disappeared under a rise in the baseboard, accelerated down a slope between lathes, dropped behind plaster, skirted a nail head, fell into a dusty channel between studs, clinked against an old bottle tilted at precisely the right angle to receive it, and stopped.

"Hello," said Ruth to a new visiting nurse, and as she stepped in, a sound so faint as to be almost imperceptible clinked in the wall, and both turned toward the sound, then turned away, and one woman led the other down a long corridor and up the winding stairs of the old house.

59

Ruth

Wellington, Connecticut

2012

The envelope had been forwarded from their former address on Greene Street by the couple who'd bought the loft from Ruth. It was an official letter from the New York City medical examiner requesting a DNA sample from Emma.

Emma had been living in Vermont since her graduation from Middlebury. Ruth explained the request to her over the phone. "They want to confirm that the remains are..." She faltered.

"Daddy," Emma said.

There were several options for providing a sample. The easiest was a mail-in service, and Ruth arranged to have a sample kit mailed to her.

In the weeks it took to receive the results, Ruth listened to Jack's voice again and again. She'd memorized the words, but that didn't matter. Hearing his voice brought him back to her. She'd saved the recordings he'd left on the machine in a folder on her hard drive, labeled "Target Heart Rates" so Emma wouldn't happen upon them when fixing something on Ruth's computer. Maybe someday she'd share the recordings with Emma, but Ruth feared that hearing Jack's voice might be too much for her still.

First came the time stamp in the impersonal voice of a female robot:

Message received September eleven at eight fifty-nine a.m.

And now there was *his* voice, sounding calm and unafraid. *Hi, Ruthie, it's Jack. In case you get this message, there's been an explosion. In Trade One. That's the other building. I'm okay, so don't worry.*

And then came the next message, the last time he'd talked to her.

Hi, babe. Jack again. Looks like we'll be stuck here in Two for a while. I'm okay. Don't worry. Tell Emma not to worry either.

It had been the worst day of her life, but she'd stayed up all night, not wanting it to end, not wanting her last day with Jack in it to be over.

A social worker from the victim compensation fund called with the news. The match was positive. Jack's remains had been found.

And now they had to do what felt almost cruel.

To comply with Jack's wishes, they had to cremate his remains.

60

Ruth

Hollingwood

2016

Ruth rose from the muslin seat cushion of the rented party chair and turned, along with two hundred and ten others, to see the bride walk down the aisle.

It wasn't a church aisle but a grassy corridor between two sections of chairs set out on the Hollingwood lawn. The grass was laid with white silk that had been unrolled after the bridesmaids and flower girl had proceeded to the gazebo.

How lucky they were with the weather today. Despite predictions of rain, it was a glorious June afternoon, the sky cloudless, the lake shimmering below the field like a necklace of diamonds.

She wished that Jack were here. One thing about people who die—they stay their age. If Jack came back to walk Emma up the aisle, he'd be a man fifteen years younger than Ruth.

How much simpler their own wedding had been. They'd married with forty in attendance in a rented town house in Murray Hill. Even though the rental fee had been modest, her father had considered it a waste. Why marry in a town house when they could have had Hollingwood for free? But that was in the early eighties, when people raised in the sixties were still in rebellion against shows of excess.

Emma was doing what her father wished Ruth had done—marrying at Hollingwood. We strive hardest to please our parents after they've gone. What was that poem by Billy Collins? About speeding past a cemetery where your father lay, seeing him rise up and give you a knowing look of disapproval. She'd spent years professing not to care about that look. But in the end, she showed her father—and herself—she did care.

Zach's mother, Sylvia, glanced at Ruth from across the aisle. They gazed moist-eyed at each other. Emma was lucky in her in-laws. Sylvia and Saul had made multiple drives from Bethesda to help plan this day. They'd hosted a party last night at the Black Hart Inn. So many parents from Trowbridge were there, it felt like a Trowbridge parents' weekend. Except now their kids weren't teenagers, they were thirty. Well, Emma wasn't quite thirty. She'd be thirty in October. "Just under the wire," one of the parents remarked and other parents had smiled, but their kids looked blank. Getting married before thirty had been important to Ruth's generation. Now kids didn't seem to care about it anymore. You could freeze your eggs and have babies until fifty. She hoped Emma wouldn't do that. Ruth liked to imagine herself someday soon sitting under a sunbrella, watching grandchildren net fish from the dock.

How handsome Zach looked, framed by the freshly painted gazebo, its slats festooned with boughs of pink-and-lemon-colored roses her grandmother had cultivated—the suffrage rose.

Ruth had never seen Zach in a suit before. Whenever he and Emma had come down from Vermont, they wore muck boots and work clothes and always smelled faintly of the apples they grew. They'd restored an old orchard of heritage apples to start a business making heirloom cider. When Ruth had graduated from college, kids sent out résumés. Now, it seemed, they sent out proposals for funding.

Emma's bridesmaids stood in a row, their unmatched long floral dresses blowing in the breeze. Their casual clothes were in stark contrast to the severe black robes worn by the presiding minister. Emma and Zach had agreed to the minister as long as the ceremony wasn't too religious.

"I specialize in spiritual but nondenominational," Pastor Barbara had assured them.

The violinist started in as the harp player plucked the first notes of Lohengrin's wedding march, and now here was Emma coming up the aisle. She was beautiful; her dress was ivory silk, its sheer back made of vintage handmade lace found in a trunk in the attic.

"I've never seen such fine stitching," the seamstress had said. She'd also attended to the old family veil. Now the veil lifted and lowered, floating about Emma's radiant face as she walked arm in arm with Nick, the man with whom Ruth had stood in the chantry of the church last year, repeating the vows Pastor Barbara said.

Ruth's eyes filled as she touched the diamond brooch her grandmother had treasured. As her daughter and husband neared, Nick's eyes locked on hers and they exchanged wordless volumes. Ruth could see Emma's eyes through the veil. They were bright and brimming. Emma and Nick moved toward Zach and toward a future that no one could know. Yet—joyfully, they advanced.

After the ceremony, guests were directed to make their way to the reception in a tent so big, it stretched from the west lawn into the field.

The wedding planner had received glowing recommendations from mothers of other brides in the area. Thanks to Twyla Flaws, the tables looked beautiful, white-linen rounds decorated by jars and bottles that Ruth, at the planner's urging, had been collecting for months. Twyla had been right. Filling those jars and bottles with local roses and peonies and wildflowers added a lovely country touch. Too bad her grandmother's conservatory garden of heritage blooms had long ago been turned into her office.

Ruth started her rounds of guests at the tables, hoping she'd remember everyone's name. She was suddenly grateful to the calligrapher for scripting names on the cards in boldface.

"What a beautiful bottle," said a young woman at table five. Ruth congratulated herself for remembering—Jennifer! She'd come to Trowbridge in Emma's senior year, an exchange student from Korea. Now she was a buyer of Americana for Sotheby's.

Ruth had seated Jennifer next to Connie's daughter, Whitney, but that chair was empty, and she berated herself for having forgotten to reassign the seat after Connie called her last week.

"She'll be in Hawaii, stumping for Hillary," Connie had said. "The reward, I guess, for campaign workers who spent time in Utah." Ruth had been sorry that Whitney couldn't come but was glad that she'd probably be getting time on the beach, because how hard would volunteers have to work when their candidate was guaranteed to be president?

"Where did you get this bottle?" continued Jennifer. "This shade of blue glass is quite rare."

"Really?" Ruth said. "The contractor found it in a wall when we rewired." She kept moving. A few seats over sat Connie, who stood and gave Ruth a hug. Ruth felt sorry for Connie having to make two cross-country trips in a month. It was a busy time of year for her at the Getty, where Connie worked in development. They'd roomed together a few weeks ago when she'd come back for their fortieth at Portia Mann.

"It's a poison bottle," said Jennifer, tipping it carefully to examine its base. "Some of them are worth hundreds of dollars."

"Hey, there's something in the bottom," said a little boy sitting across from her. Ruth didn't recognize him. He must be the Cohen side.

"Poison?" Connie said. "Honestly? Are you trying to do away with us, Ruthie?"

"What kind of poison?" asked the man next to Jennifer.

"Arsenic and old lace—it's an old Hollingwood tradition," Ruth said, laughing.

Jennifer asked for the Wi-Fi code, looking down at her phone.

"Sorry," said Ruth. "No cell towers here. But there's a woman at the next table who'd love you to sign her petition to put one in the Catholic church steeple."

The boy rose from his seat.

"I can get you on," he said, coming around to Jennifer's chair.

A moment later, Jennifer said, "It's 606! You can tell by the raised numbers on the side of the glass!"

"Is that like an advancement over Formula 409?" Connie asked. "I've just discovered that's the best way to get rid of Japanese beetles." Her house on a hill had beautiful gardens.

"The compound was mixed with arsenic and used to treat syphilis before they had penicillin." This was Zach's uncle, a gynecologist. The pattern in his tie was bottles of Absolut made to look like sperm, a tie he wore wryly to weddings, joking that he meant to remind new couples of their biologic imperative.

Jennifer laughed. "Syphilis! Who in this house had syphilis? Surely not a Hollingworth?"

Ruth and Connie looked at each other. Suddenly, they were teenagers again, fishing in drawers for matches for cigarettes. The letter that Ruth found in the Rose Room long ago had disintegrated in the pocket of her hot pants sent to the laundry. She'd never gotten to show it to her father after all.

But if arsenic was mixed with 606 to cure syphilis—Ruth tightened her grip on the back of a chair—perhaps her father had been right all along. Perhaps the maid had been innocent.

"What's syphilis?" asked the boy. He'd gone back to his seat. But now the ceviche was coming, brought by servers in black who were balancing plates on the length of their arms, and Ruth moved to take her place at the head table.

At the end of the meal, after Bekkah had led a rousing rendition of the old school song, Izzi had played a song on her guitar, and Abby had cried a heartfelt poem into the mike, after the last toast was made to the health and long happiness of the new Porter-Cohens, guests were urged to walk down the hill to see fireworks over the lake.

The boy shifted in his chair and knelt to make himself higher in it. He leaned and reached toward the center of the table. Carefully, with both hands, he maneuvered the bottle across the cloth. He pulled out the flowers and tossed them onto the grass. Then he tilted the bottle over his open palm. Water streamed out and, along with it, a glass marble. The boy held the marble up to the light. Then he slipped it into his pants pocket and followed the wedding party down to the lake.

Bridey

Hollingwood

1928

She hurried down to the lake where she sometimes swam before house duties began. This morning, she'd swim to help clear her head, to help her decide what she would do. She was horrified by the prospect of being blamed for a murder. But accusing Young Doc of making a mistake in the medicine would likely expose the nature of Mr. Hollingworth's ailment, which would ruin the family's good name. And ruining the family's good name would risk ruining her son's future.

She waded into the water, stepping gingerly on rocks until the water reached the skirt of her bathing dress. The surface was calm and glassy. Not even boats were out yet.

A full moon lingered, outshone by the sun, valiant in its persistence to keep a place for itself.

Above, to the east, a pink five-fingered cloud moved across the sun, as if a divine hand were reaching to pluck it from the sky. But Bridey knew the sun would remain.

Vincent himself had sent the telegram advising Bridey that she was going to be questioned. The postmistress had told her, thinking he'd played a prank. Vincent wanted her gone, and who could blame him? Her staying would only bring trouble.

But how could she go? How could she leave him?

Bridey took a deep breath and plunged, feeling in turmoil, forcing herself out to the water's dark center.

She turned back to shore, filled with resolve. The light cut her eyes. She couldn't see land but moved toward where she knew the land was. She stroked the water, propelling herself toward what she could not see, her hands pushing away from and then circling back to her breast, helping the water carry her as Mr. Hollingworth had taught her to do, moving steadily toward what was waiting for her.

Epilogue

2018

From: Brigid Flynn <brflynn@msn.com>
Sent: Monday, March 5, 2018 7:24 PM
To: emmaporter1986@gmail.com
Subject: from a relative

Dear Emma,

I am writing to you on behalf of the Flynns from County Galway, Ireland. We just saw your match to our haplogroup and a match to me of 36/37. Were you adopted? Are you interested in seeing how you're related to our Flynn clan?

My name is Brigid Flynn. According to our DNA, we share the same great-great-grandmother, Brighid Molloy Flynn.

I'm the granddaughter of Ailish, her daughter. Ailish was raised in Beaghmore, near the Mayo border. She met my grand-father when American filmmakers went over to shoot *The Quiet*

Man. They married and she moved back with him to LA, which is where I am from.

I'm an only child and so was my grandmother.

That's why our genetic connection to you was so shocking to us.

We hadn't the least idea that Brighid Flynn had a son.

Acknowledgments

This book would not have been written if John "Jay" Holley Rudd hadn't sold us the house built by his great-great-great-grandfather. Thanks to him and to members of the Holley/Rudd family, especially Louise "Weezie" Hannegan, Charles Keil, and Theodore O'Neill, for sharing photos and memories of Holleywood, the historic house that serves as the architectural template for Hollingwood.

I am indebted to Richard McGuire, author of the graphic novel *Here,* which inspired me to attempt in narrative form what he achieves in visuals, shattering the space-time continuum for readers by rendering simultaneous occurrences of past, present, and future events.

I'd like to acknowledge the late Edward Callaghan, whose letters to my mother from 1980 to 1996 portray vivid descriptions of everyday life in early twentieth-century America. His passages contributed to several scenes in this book. I gave Vincent his birthday.

I am grateful to my late uncle Ray Whelan, who, thanks to the miracle of technology, can still be heard recounting riveting details of life in the previous century. A nod of gratitude to my Browne relatives in Kilconly, Ireland, a town I have fictionalized in drawing Bridey's birthplace.

Acknowledgments

I was greatly aided in my research by Katherine Chilcoat, former town historian of Salisbury, Connecticut, who shared her extensive knowledge of turn-of-the-century New England and provided archival source materials that were critical to making this story come to life.

Heartfelt thanks to my agent Kate Johnson for uniting me with my editor Judy Clain. I am grateful to Judy for her excellent guidance and for taking a chance. Thanks to Judy and her assistant Alexandra Hoopes and to the whole team at Little, Brown for their enthusiastic support of this book and for the care they put into preparing it, especially Jayne Yaffe Kemp, who shepherded production.

Thanks to copyeditor Tracy Roe, who made me look better on almost every page and whose day job as a physician made her input on passages containing medical matters indispensable.

Thanks to the readers of prototype versions of this manuscript: Claire Held, Judith McGuire, Jane Otto, Carol Paik, Katherine Ross, and Abigail Thomas. Special thanks to my sister, Margaret Klein Abruzese, for multiple reads, critiques, and suggestions that helped shape this book throughout many stages of its writing. Without their input, this wouldn't be the book that it is.

Thanks to Karen Braziller, without whom this novel wouldn't have been completed until next century. I am grateful to her for editorial insights and for the readers she gathered to make critical contributions to this novel during various stages of its development: Daphne Beal, Nina Collins, Elizabeth Ehrlich, Kira von Eichel, Madge McKeithen, and Lucinda Treat. And to Mark and Suzanne Winkelman for providing us with a conducive space.

For invaluable advice and guidance on this manuscript in its nascent form, thanks to members of the Salon, especially Will Blythe, Chip Brown, Claudia Burbank, Lynne Guillot-Marquet, Jeanne McCulloch, Dawn Raffel, Danya Reich, Kate Walbert, and Catherine Woodard.

Acknowledgments

Special thanks to generous friends and family who shared information and insights that contributed to the rendering of events and settings in the story: Maurice Beer, Margaret Garvey, Berel Held, Jack and Beth Isler, Mary Lanier, Ellen Mahoney, Raymond and Judith McGuire, Jane Otto, Maxine Paetro, Liz Pryor, Kathleen Voldstad, Marge Klein, David Langdon, Mary Skinner, Margie Thomson, and Hanne Vorkapitch.

To Darren Winston for introduction to Mrs. C. S. Peel.

To Sandra Hunter, for seeing that a scene in my first chapter needed sound, and to her and the rest of the Hawthornden Castle Class of February and March 2018 for their support and encouragement. I am grateful to Hamish Robinson and the late Drue Heinz and the board of directors of the Hawthornden Castle International Retreat for Writers for providing me with the time and silence I needed to finish this book.

Deepest thanks to my family for their support and forbearance.

And, honestly, I couldn't have written a book like this without Scrivener.

Historical Notes

I was surprised to discover how much research was required to write a work of fiction set in the past. I found that I was unacquainted with many things that were part of the fabric of everyday life for my parents and grandparents. Here are a few notes from my research. Forgive any errors—I'm a novelist with no illusions about qualifying as a historian.

606, chapters 42, 60: In the early part of the twentieth century, when syphilis was exacting a toll on public health similar to that of HIV in recent times, a newly discovered arsenic-based cure named Salvarsan, also known as 606, was marketed as "a magic bullet." Such careful handling of it was required that its developer Paul Ehrlich warned that "the step from the laboratory to the patient's bedside...is extraordinarily arduous and fraught with danger." The cure was a powder that had to be mixed with water and administered intravenously, but to spare my readers, I've taken the liberty of leaving it in powder form.

Collins, Billy, poem, chapter 60: The poem referred to is "No Time."

Comstock Act, chapter 19: Named for Anthony Comstock, special agent of the U.S. Post Office, this federal statute passed in

1873 provided for the fine and imprisonment of anyone mailing or receiving "obscene," "lewd," or "lascivious" publications, including literature on contraception. It wasn't until 1971 that Congress removed language that made it a crime to send information on contraception through the U.S. mail.

Early maternity wear, chapters 20, 21: Lane Bryant built her business on the first clothing line designed for women who were pregnant. (Her company should have been Lena Bryant, but a bank officer writing a business loan incorrectly recorded her name on a form.) In 1904, the only maternity wear was the maternity corset, and at that time, Lane Bryant's new designs couldn't be advertised because pregnancy was considered a condition not fit for public discussion. Lane Bryant's first ad ran in 1911 with the headline "Maternity Wardrobes that Do Not Attract Attention." Inventory sold out the day after the ad appeared in the *New York Herald.*

Flood of August 1955, chapter 49: One of the worst in Connecticut's history. Two back-to-back hurricanes caused eighty-seven deaths and so much damage that state safety measures, river monitoring, and zoning laws were changed.

Heat wave of 1911, chapter 25: On July 4, 1911, the northeastern United States reported record temperatures. An eleven-day heat wave set in, causing the deaths of 380 people. By July 13, New York had reported 211 people dead from the excessive heat.

Ladies' Mile, chapters 7, 17: This was the finest shopping district in New York City at the end of the nineteenth century, crowded with high-end retailers serving the well-to-do. It was an area along Fifth Avenue of about twenty-eight blocks, going from Fifteenth Street to Twenty-Fourth Street and stretching east to Park Avenue and west to Sixth Avenue. It was the only part of New York then considered safe enough for women to shop without male companions. In 1906, B. Altman's became the first big department store to move away from the Ladies' Mile, heading uptown to Fifth Avenue and Thirty-Fourth Street. Soon, other department stores followed.

Lauer, Quentin, chapters 44, 57: Dr. Lauer is based on a philosophy professor of the same name who taught at Fordham College (1954–1990). Like the character in this novel, he eschewed wearing a coat and is remembered with fondness by former students, some of whom adopted the habit.

Lying-in hospitals, chapters 24, 26, 27: In 1900, only 5 percent of women in the United States gave birth in hospitals. Most babies were delivered by midwives. Obstetrics was a fairly new specialty, and doctors were eager to take business from midwives, whose competency they maligned. The doctors built maternity hospitals called lying-ins where they could administer anesthesia and spare themselves the trouble of going from house to house to attend their patients. Business skyrocketed. Demand exceeded the supply of trained doctors, and ads were placed in newspapers throughout the country inviting medical students who wanted experience to come to New York and pay ten dollars each for the opportunity to work for two weeks straight delivering babies. (For more on this, see Randi Epstein's book *Get Me Out,* cited in the bibliography.) While thousands of babies were successfully delivered, malpractice and childbed-fever epidemics cost many lives.

Macfadden, Bernarr, chapter 40: Predecessor of Charles Atlas and Jack LaLanne, he was a prolific author and publisher and a proponent of unorthodox ideas on how to increase the strength and health of young men. He founded *Physical Culture* magazine in 1899 and edited it until 1912, and he established "healthatoriums" throughout the East and Midwest.

Mission of Our Lady of the Rosary for the Protection of Irish Immigrant Girls, chapters 5, 7, 11: In 1883, a priest whose

parents had emigrated from Cork founded a Catholic boardinghouse to provide temporary housing and employment to
arriving immigrant girls. He hired Mrs. Boyle to be its first
matron. Women of all nationalities were welcomed. The shelter was located at 7 State Street in Lower Manhattan, and during its first twenty-five years, the mission served over 100,000
of the 307,823 Irish girls who arrived in the Port of New
York.

Mother's Day, chapter 15: This holiday was conceived in the United
States by Anna May Jarvis, a feminist and temperance activist.
The first one was celebrated on May 10, 1908, in Grafton, West
Virginia, and in Philadelphia. Her idea spread and the next year
the holiday was celebrated in New York City and elsewhere in
the Northeast. Eventually, the second Sunday in May was hailed
from pulpits all over the country as a day on which to honor
mothers, and, to the delight of florists, white carnations became
the popular symbol. Mother's Day was proclaimed a national
holiday by President Woodrow Wilson in 1914.

Mumblety-peg, chapter 39: A once-popular outdoor game using
pocketknives, when every boy carried one.

Nevo, chapters 16, 24: An early cooling device for the home, this
"cold air stove" was the precursor to the air conditioner. The
Nevo (*oven* spelled backward) weighed two hundred pounds
and cost the equivalent of eleven thousand dollars today. It
didn't catch on.

Paper knife, chapters 8, 19: Books used to be printed on large
sheets of paper that were then folded and bound. The folding
created sealed edges that had to be sliced open before the book
could be read. Paper knives, often sold as souvenirs at tourist
sites, were flat blades made usually of bone or wood and just
sharp enough to cut through paper.

Persephone flower, chapter 52: This invention is based on the night-blooming cereus, the common name that refers to several kinds of flowering cacti that bloom, dramatically, one night a year.

Prohibition, chapters 44, 45: The Eighteenth Amendment, which prohibited the production, transport, sale, and purchase of alcohol, took effect on January 17, 1920, and continued until its repeal on December 5, 1933. Prohibition caused crime to spike across the country, especially organized crime, which received a major boost from a new opportunity for enterprise. Strong liquor surged in popularity because potency made smuggling liquor more profitable. Because the Eighteenth Amendment prohibited selling alcohol but not drinking it, "wet" families of means prepared for the coming dry years by stacking boxes of bottles in basements, attics, and storage rooms before the amendment officially took effect.

Pry, Paul, chapter 45: Refers to a nosy person, taken from the name of a too-inquisitive character made popular by an American song written in 1820.

Quincy, chapter 19: American euphemism for toilet, used in the Victorian Age, probably in reference to John Quincy Adams, who was the first to have one installed at the White House.

Radiated beauty products, chapter 48: As soon as radium was discovered in 1898, manufacturers sought commercial uses for it. Believing that radium vitalized all living tissue, they sold it as an ingredient in cosmetics. Several companies in England and France developed popular lines that included radium-fortified cream, rouge, compact powders, hair tonics, soaps, and rejuvenating pads that could be strapped to the face. The products didn't catch on in the United States, not because consumers worried about the danger of radiation, but because they were skeptical that an ingredient as costly as radium would be added in enough quantity to effect change.

September 11, 1905, chapter 7: In New York on this date, an elevated train crashed at Ninth Avenue and Fifty-Third Street, a notorious curve where the Sixth and Ninth Avenue Els diverged. Twelve people died, some falling from train windows to the street below.

Sigel, Elsie, chapter 12: This nineteen-year-old granddaughter of a Civil War hero commuted from Riverdale to work as a missionary at the Chinatown Rescue Settlement in Manhattan, where, in 1909, her decaying body was found in a trunk. The case, still unsolved 109 years later, was told as a cautionary tale to girls doing mission work in New York City.

Silent Policeman, chapter 43: In the early part of the twentieth century, when more and more cars were taking to the roads, towns that couldn't afford to dedicate a policeman to direct traffic during "rush hours" erected wooden signs at intersections instead. The practice was discontinued after drivers complained that it caused more accidents than it prevented.

Suffrage movement, chapter 35: The first national demonstration for women's suffrage took place in Washington, D.C., on March 3, 1913, the day before Woodrow Wilson's presidential inauguration. Eight thousand women marched down Pennsylvania Avenue in support of women's right to vote. Mrs. Emmeline Pankhurst was a British suffragist who toured the United States on behalf of women's rights, and she made a speech in Hartford, Connecticut. The Nineteenth Amendment granting women the right to vote was enacted on August 26, 1920.

Talkies, chapter 44: The first talking films were made possible by the Vitaphone, an invention owned by Warner Brothers that allowed sound to be synchronized with film reels. To show *The Jazz Singer* in 1927, a projectionist had to manually sync each of fifteen film reels to its own phonograph record containing dialogue and music. The first talkies still used title cards and minimized dialogue. Studio heads were slow to embrace the new technology, skeptical that audiences would want to hear movies as well as see them. For several years, films were produced in two versions: silent and sound.

Triangle Shirtwaist Factory fire, chapters 21, 22: On March 25, 1911, a fire broke out in a factory and resulted in the deadliest industrial disaster in the history of New York and one of the deadliest in U.S. history. That day, 146 garment workers, mostly young women ages sixteen to twenty-three, died in a fire that they couldn't escape due to a then-common practice of locking doors to stairwells and exits in order to prevent workers from taking unauthorized breaks. The fire led to legislation requiring improved safety standards in factories and spurred the growth of the International Ladies' Garment Workers' Union (ILGWU).

Victory Way pyramid, chapter 40: In 1918, a pedestrian walk named Victory Way was created on Park Avenue north of Grand Central Station, between Forty-Fifth and Fiftieth Streets. At the end of it, captured German war equipment was displayed, including a pyramid made of twelve thousand German helmets, most still with spikes.

Selected Bibliography

This novel owes debts of details to the authors, editors, and publishers of the following:

Books

Fiction

Atwood, Margaret. *Alias Grace.* New York: Doubleday, 1996.

Donoghue, Emma. *The Wonder.* Boston: Little, Brown, 2016.

Finney, Jack. *From Time to Time.* New York: Scribner, 1996.

————. *Time and Again.* New York: Simon and Schuster, 1970.

Fitzgerald, F. Scott. *This Side of Paradise.* 1920. Reprint, New York: Dover, 1996.

Lewis, Sinclair. *Babbitt.* 1922. Reprint, New York: Penguin, 1996.

Manning, Kate. *My Notorious Life.* New York: Scribner, 2013.

Marquand, John P. *The Late George Apley.* Boston: Little, Brown, 1936.

Maxwell, William. *So Long, See You Tomorrow.* New York: Alfred A. Knopf, 1980.

McDermott, Alice. *The Ninth Hour.* New York: Farrar, Straus and Giroux, 2017.

McGuire, Richard. *Here.* New York: Pantheon, 2014.

O'Brien, Edna. *The Light of Evening.* Boston: Houghton Mifflin, 2006.

————. *Saints and Sinners.* Boston: Little, Brown, 2011.

Santmyer, Helen Hooven. *"...And Ladies of the Club."* New York: Penguin Putnam, 1984.

Simonson, Helen. *The Summer Before the War.* New York: Random House, 2016.

Sittenfeld, Curtis. *Prep.* New York: Random House, 2005.

Slimani, Leila. *The Perfect Nanny.* Trans. Sam Taylor. New York: Penguin, 2018.

Smith, Betty. *A Tree Grows in Brooklyn.* 1943. Reprint, New York: Harper, 2001.

Tanabe, Karin. *The Gilded Years.* New York: Washington Square Press, 2016.

Tóibín, Colm. *Brooklyn.* New York: Scribner, 2009.

———. *Nora Webster.* New York: Scribner, 2014.

Wharton, Edith. *The Age of Innocence.* New York: D. Appleton, 1920.

———. *The Custom of the Country.* 1913. Reprint, New York: Penguin Classics, 2006.

———. *The House of Mirth.* New York: Charles Scribner and Sons, 1905.

———. *Old New York.* New York: D. Appleton, 1924.

Whitehead, Colson. *The Underground Railroad.* New York: Doubleday, 2016.

Nonfiction

Amelinckx, Andrew K. *Hudson Valley Murder and Mayhem.* Charleston, SC: History Press, 2017.

Anonymous. *Don'ts for Mothers.* 1878. Reprint, London: A and C Black, 2011.

———. *To Roslin from the Far West with Local Descriptions.* Edinburgh: Johnstone, Hunter, 1872.

Baker, Russell. *Growing Up.* New York: Congdon and Weed, 1982.

Beeton, Isabella. *Mrs. Beeton's Book of Household Management.* Originally published in twenty-four installments by S. O. Beeton from 1859 to 1861. Reprint, Hertfordshire, UK: Wordsworth Editions, 2006.

Benin, Leigh, et al. *The New York City Triangle Factory Fire.* Charleston, SC: Arcadia, 2011.

Blum, Deborah. *The Poisoner's Handbook.* New York: Penguin, 2011.

Bryson, Bill. *One Summer.* New York: Doubleday, 2013.

The Butterick Book of Recipes and Household Helps. New York: Butterick Publishing, 1927.

Carpenter, Teresa, ed. *New York Diaries 1609–2009.* New York: Modern Library, 2012.

Cassidy, Frederic G. *Dictionary of American Regional English.* Cambridge, MA: Harvard University Press, 1985–2012.

Codman, Ogden, and Edith Wharton. *The Decoration of Houses.* New York: Charles Scribner's Sons, 1914.

Epstein, Randi Hutter. *Get Me Out: A History of Childbirth from the Garden of Eden to the Sperm Bank.* New York: W. W. Norton, 2010.

Fielding, William. *What Every Married Woman Should Know.* Girard, KS: Haldeman-Julius, 1924.

Goddard, Gloria. *Confidential Chats with Wives.* Girard, KS: Haldeman-Julius, 1927.

Gross, Leslie. *Housewives' Guide to Antiques.* New York: Cornerstone Library, 1963.

Hayes-McCoy, Felicity. *The House on an Irish Hillside.* London: Hodder and Stoughton, 2012.

Hecht, Elaine, ed. *Salisbury Historic Impressions.* Dalton, MA: Studley, 2002.

Helberg, Kristin. *The Victorian House Coloring Book.* New York: Dover, 1980.

Hempel, Sandra. *The Inheritor's Powder.* New York: W. W. Norton, 2014.

Hewins, Caroline M. *A Mid-Century Child and Her Books.* New York: Macmillan, 1926.

Jefferson, Margo. *Negroland.* New York: Pantheon, 2015.

Jewett, Frances Gulick. *Good Health.* Boston: Ginn, 1906.

Kisseloff, Jeff. *You Must Remember This: An Oral History of Manhattan from the 1890s to World War II.* New York: Schocken Books, 1989.

Kolowrat, Ernest. *Hotchkiss: A Chronicle of an American School.* New York: New Amsterdam, 1992.

Loudon, Mrs. (Jane). *The Ladies' Flower-Garden of Ornamental Greenhouse Plants.* London: William Smith, 1848.

Lyons, Rosemary, ed. *Our Town, Our Voices 1905–2003.* Coxsackie, NY: N.P., 2006.

Mansfield, Katherine. *Journal of Katherine Mansfield.* New York: Alfred A. Knopf, 1927.

McCabe, James D., Jr. *New York by Gaslight.* 1882. Reprint, New York: Arlington House, 1984.

McCourt, Frank. *Angela's Ashes.* New York: Scribner, 1996.

———. *'Tis.* New York: Scribner, 1999.

McMillen, Jean, ed. *Sarum Samplings 1.* Salisbury, CT: Salisbury Association, 2014.

———. *Sarum Samplings 2.* Salisbury, CT: Salisbury Association, 2016.

———. *Sarum Samplings 3.* Salisbury, CT: Salisbury Association, 2016.

Milner, John. *Key of Heaven; or, A Manual of Prayer.* Winterberg, NY: John Baptist Steinbrener, 1900.

Moreno, Barry. *Ellis Island.* Charleston, SC: Arcadia, 2003.

Morrison, Sarah Koester. *Memoirs of the Charles F. Koester House, an Intimate Portrait.* Marysville, KS: Sarah Koester Morrison, 2017.

O'Neill, Therese. *Unmentionable: The Victorian Lady's Guide to Sex, Marriage and Manners.* Boston: Little, Brown, 2016.

Opel, Frank. *Tales of Bygone New England.* Secaucus, NJ: Castle, 1988.

Peel, C. S., Mrs. *How to Keep House.* London: Constable, 1915.

Rand, Christopher. *The Changing Landscape.* New York: Oxford University Press, 1968.

Raverat, Gwen. *Period Piece.* London: Faber and Faber, 1971.

Revi, Albert Christian, ed. *Collectible Iron, Tin, Copper and Brass.* Secaucus, NJ: Castle, 1974.

Roiphe, Anne. *1185 Park Avenue.* New York: Free Press, 1999.

Roman, James. *Chronicles of Old New York.* New York: Museyon, 2010.

Rosslyn, Helen, and Angelo Maggi. *Rosslyn, Country of Painter and Poet.* Edinburgh: National Gallery of Scotland, 2002.

Schlereth, Thomas J. *Victorian America.* New York: Harper Collins, 1991.

Shapiro, Laurie Gwen. *The Stowaway.* New York: Simon and Schuster, 2018.

Spaeth, Louis A. *Coming Motherhood, Practical Suggestions Relating to Maternity and the Care of Infants and Children.* Philadelphia: Peter Reilly, 1907.

Taggart, Caroline. *Guide to Running One's Home.* London: National Trust Books, 2012.

Trollope, Frances Milton. *Domestic Manners of the Americans.* New York: Alfred A. Knopf, 1949.

Vermilyea, Peter C. *Hidden History of Litchfield County.* Charleston, SC: History Press, 2014.

Wharton, Edith. *French Ways and Their Meanings.* London: Macmillan, 1919.

Williams, Henry Lionel, and Ottalie K. Williams. *How to Furnish Old American Houses.* New York: Pellegrini and Cudahy, 1949.

Wilson, Edmund. *The Twenties.* New York: Farrar, Straus and Giroux, 1975.

Periodicals

Chatterbox (1894, 1903).

"The Woman's Club Movement." *Journal of Education* (March 3, 1930).

Epicure (December 1907 to November 1908).

Laundry Manual (1902).

Physical Culture (1920).

Ladies' Home Journal (Christmas 1890).

Sites of Research

9/11 Memorial and Museum, New York City
Allen Room at the New York Public Library, New York City
Barnes Museum, Philadelphia, PA
Charleston Museum, Charleston, SC
Connecticut Historical Museum, Hartford, CT
Edsel Ford Memorial Library, Hotchkiss School, Lakeville, CT
Ellis Island Museum, New York City
Hawthornden Castle Library, Lasswade, Scotland
Historical Society of New York
Lyndhurst, Tarrytown, New York
Morgan Library, New York City
Museum of the City of New York, New York City
National Library of Scotland, Edinburgh
Salisbury Association Historical Society, Salisbury, CT
Scoville Memorial Library, Salisbury, CT
Tenement Museum, New York City

About the Author

Helen Klein Ross is the author of two novels, *What Was Mine* and *Making It: A Novel of Madison Avenue,* and creator of *The Traveler's Vade Mecum,* a crowdsourced poetry anthology of new poems with titles from old telegrams. Her poetry, essays, and fiction have appeared in *The New Yorker,* the *New York Times,* and literary journals and anthologies. Ross spent decades as a copywriter and creative director at global ad agencies on both coasts. She graduated from Cornell University and received an MFA from the New School. She lives with her husband in New York City and Lakeville, Connecticut.